PENGUIN INTERNATIONAL POETS

THE POETRY OF SURVIVAL

Daniel Weissbort was born in London in 1935 and educated at St Paul's School, Cambridge University and the London School of Economics. He is currently director of the translation workshop at the University of Iowa. With Ted Hughes he was co-founder of *Modern Poetry in Translation* (1965–83), now *Poetry World*. In addition to three volumes of his own poetry, he has published numerous prose and poetry translations and has edited three anthologies, including the Penguin *Post-War Russian Poetry* and *Russian Poetry: The Modern Period*.

THE POETRY OF SURVIVAL

POST-WAR POETS OF CENTRAL
AND EASTERN EUROPE

EDITED AND INTRODUCED BY
DANIEL WEISSBORT

PENGUIN BOOKS

To the memory of
Vasko Popa
1922–1991

PENGUIN BOOKS

Published by the Penguin Group
Penguin Books Ltd, 27 Wrights Lane, London W8 5TZ, England
Penguin Books USA Inc., 375 Hudson Street, New York, New York 10014, USA
Penguin Books Australia Ltd, Ringwood, Victoria, Australia
Penguin Books Canada Ltd, 10 Alcorn Avenue, Toronto, Ontario, Canada M4V 3B2
Penguin Books (NZ) Ltd, 182–190 Wairau Road, Auckland 10, New Zealand

Penguin Books Ltd, Registered Offices: Harmondsworth, Middlesex, England

First published by Anvil Press Poetry Ltd 1991
Published in Penguin Books 1993
1 3 5 7 9 10 8 6 4 2

Copyright © Daniel Weissbort, 1991
All rights reserved

The moral right of the author has been asserted

Printed in England by Clays Ltd, St Ives plc

CONTENTS

Part Two

MIROSLAV HOLUB (1923–)

TYMOTEUSZ KARPOWICZ (1921–)

PREFACE

THE INTRODUCTION to this anthology was written in 1985–6, with a paragraph on 'perestroika' inserted in early 1989. As I read and listen to reports on the pluralistic transformations occurring in Central Europe, I feel constrained to take one last look at the collection before it goes to press. There is no need to comment at length on the astonishing end to a decade that was largely dominated, in the West at least, by alleged *realpolitik*, and notions of style or image rather than substance. Yet I cannot escape the feeling that we are witnessing, dramatically highlighted, not merely the substitution of one set of ruling groups for another, but a transfer of trust between the generations of the concerned. Furthermore, as apparently radical as have been the consequences of this surge of energy, of this will-to-change, activists today seem, at least on first sight, to be less encumbered with the ideological baggage of earlier revolutions of the modern era – which, however, is not to say that the inevitable resurgence of nationalism should not be closely monitored.

The writings not only of a Havel ('The Power of the Powerless') but of a Herbert too ('The Power of Taste') look more prophetic now than they did – or, perhaps, more *truly* realistic? – one reason maybe why the Czechs and Slovaks, at this moment, have leant towards Havel rather than Dubček as President of the Republic. What appeared to be optimism, or at best speculative forays, rather like playing chess, now seems more like sober analysis. The writers who, through the difficult and often tragic times, continued to keep distinctions alive, to insist on individual values in the face of collectivist pressures, to expose the unscrupulousness, the hypocrisies, and finally sheer incompetence of rulers, surely played an essential part (as they have periodically done throughout the troubled history of Central Europe) in educating, inspiring, and finally empowering the reformers.

Where does this leave their writing? Well, of course, it leaves it where it was before, and yet it is also bound to change the way we receive it. Poets such as Herbert, Holub, Pilinszky, Różewicz, Amichai, by the insistent clarity and subtlety of their writing in the dark times demonstrated, in a quite elemental, unambiguous form, the resilience of the human spirit, its ability to resist concerted efforts to confuse it, the better to control it. The lucidity achieved remains a standard, the texts themselves constituting a kind of testament for today. The force of their example is being validated at this moment. They have proved equal, that is, to a challenge that seemed bent on the ultimate subversion of all the civilized proprieties. They were, in truth, the survivors, and their survival was more immediately crucial than we had ever imagined. That for so long it has not looked as if their hopes would begin to be fulfilled in their own lifetimes – who would, in the oppressively stagnant Brezhnev years, have predicted the arrival of a Gorbachev? – makes their survival (although, of those mentioned above, János Pilinszky, alas, is no longer living) doubly poignant. Their sense and experience of history, their continued alertness, lead one to believe that they will exert a positive influence on the political and social restructuring that now seems to be under way.

DANIEL WEISSBORT
London, December 1989

INTRODUCTION

'I CANNOT UNDERSTAND that poetry should survive when the men who created that poetry are dead. One of the premises and incentives for my poetry is a disgust with poetry. What I revolted against was that it had survived the end of the world, as though nothing had happened' (Tadeusz Różewicz, quoted by Michael Hamburger in *The Truth of Poetry*). That 'end' is described, with a kind of entomological fury, by another Polish writer, Tadeusz Borowski, in *This Way to the Gas, Ladies and Gentlemen*; the Hungarian-born Élie Wiesel has written extensively on the Holocaust, but see especially his first, autobiographical, novel *Night*; a particularly grotesque account may be found in the emigré Polish writer Jerzy Kosinski's novel *The Painted Bird*. This is to name only three of the better known narrations. Anybody wishing to discover not only the facts, but to draw closer to the actual experience, is likely to be overwhelmed or oppressed by the volume of documentary evidence assembled, the multiplicity of attempts artistically to represent something so unprecedentedly horrible that it bedevils every effort to do so, the very idea of artistry having become problematical. A central theme of Élie Wiesel's work, as it is of that of George Steiner (see his *Language and Silence*, for instance), is the impulse to keep silent, if only for fear of traducing or reducing the experience, denying or aestheticizing it, betraying the 'millions of the mouthless dead', to borrow a particularly appropriate image from a First World War poem. Hence the oft-quoted remark by the philosopher T. W. Adorno that after Auschwitz to write a poem is barbaric ('Nach Auschwitz ein Gedicht zu schreiben, ist barbarisch').

A contrary impulse, however, also exists: to bear witness, to ensure that the silence which engulfed those millions does not consume also the survivors. This is, perhaps, what it means to survive. To say nothing may, in effect, be to collude with the forces of destruction. To speak out, on the other hand, is not only proof in itself, evidence of a kind of survival, but also a vindication of it. While it is not without moral danger to continue working in a medium that has been so grossly abused by the purveyors of a corrupt and vicious philosophy, and while those who choose or are obliged to remain silent command our respect, to speak out, to return (as Ted Hughes writes in his Introduction to Vasko Popa's *Collected Poems*), 'to the simple animal courage of accepting the odds', is the indispensable guarantee of what might, in these circumstances, be called an afterlife. We feel for, and with, those who imperil their souls by letting the necessary words come. To quote Różewicz again: 'I regard my own poems with acute mistrust. I have fashioned them out of a remnant of words, salvaged words, out of uninteresting words, words from the great rubbish dump, the great cemetery.'

This, then, is an anthology that centres on the work of the first post-war generation of poets, who one way or another took the risk of addressing, of trying to express, what many regarded as inexpressible, incommunicable, whose early adult years coincided with the era of global conflict, and who were subsequently caught up in the Stalinist, Soviet-backed or -imported totalitarian revolutions which after the war transformed Central and Eastern Europe socially and politically. If these revolutions, representing a clean sweep, were welcomed by many at a time when the traditional solutions or compromises held little attraction, when there was literally nothing to build on except ruins, it became clear that a tyranny had been imposed, as ideologically and physically oppressive as that which it had replaced, and less murderous only insofar as man's destructive energies had for the time been exhausted and the new balance of power in Europe permitted only a cold war. So, those foolhardy enough to try to communicate their essential humanness assumed a double, if connected, burden. It is hard even to imagine what this entailed. To quote Ted Hughes again: 'They must be reckoned among the purest and most wide awake of living poets.'

It is, indeed, this clairvoyant quality, leaving little room for the customary decorations of art, that perhaps best typifies their work. The urgency of the content tended to eliminate all but the most unambiguous prosodic conventions. Inner exploration that characterizes so much of Western art was checked in Eastern Europe as a luxury that could neither be tolerated by artists, nor was tolerated, it must be said, by the utilitarian cultural establishment which transmitted the behests of its political masters and, during the heyday of Stalinism and even after, demanded *partiinost*, or explicit support for party objectives whatever they might be and to whatever extent they might fluctuate. Paradoxically, then, it was the official ideology which, in a sense, defined the rules of artistic conduct for all. Inwardness, under these circumstances, became a form of protest too (with the exception of the endless anodyne nature lyrics sanctioned by the literary bureaucrats). But this option was available only to a very few. The challenge posed by present conditions and recent history could not, as a matter of course, be evaded, except insofar as a more or less alert censorship obliged writers to adopt Aesopian strategies or devices which to some extent stimulated resourcefulness and creativity, though they also risked compromising the entire enterprise.

All of this, however, is discussed at length by numerous commentators and observers, as well as by those directly involved, such as Czesław Miłosz, in *The Captive Mind*, a kind of inner history of the crucial, immediate post-war period in Poland, as it affected artists and intellectuals. A thoughtful general introduction is provided by A. Alvarez in his 1965 Penguin volume *Under Pressure*, based on a series of feature broadcasts on the BBC Third Programme between 1961 and 1964, in which a number of East European intellectuals were interviewed. This, together with the *Penguin Modern European Poets* series edited by Alvarez, which first made the works of significant East European poets available to us in book form, represented a pioneering effort, just as the more recent American Penguin series *Writers from the Other Europe* edited by Philip Roth, focuses exclusively, for the first time, on fiction writers from the region. Edwin Morgan, a notable translator of Russian and Hungarian poetry, in his Open University course *East European Poets* (The Open University, Unit 32, 1976), supplies a sensible and succinct account of the work of Zbigniew Herbert, Miroslav Holub and Vasko Popa. With the limited easing of the so-called Thaw that followed Stalin's death in 1953, cultural exchange between Eastern Europe and the West increased, permitting contacts between writers on both sides. Among other manifestations of this trend in England was the establishment in 1967 of Poetry International, a series of annual readings under the auspices of the Poetry Book Society, which gave the public its first opportunity to hear some of these remarkable poets in person. The dialogue continues. In recent years, the growing number of emigrés has made us increasingly aware of an evolving reality of which, only a short while ago, we were more or less ignorant. The spate of articles and essays by such writers as the Czech novelist Milan Kundera (see, for instance, his 'The Tragedy of Central Europe', *New York Review of Books*, 26 April 1984), Vaclav Havel ('The Power of the Powerless') and by many others, emigrés and non-emigrés, in such journals as the University of Michigan's *Cross Currents* (an annual collection of writings from and about Eastern and Central Europe) renders any remarks that I might make here largely superfluous and even presumptuous.

Nevertheless, I have included brief observations on aspects of the poets whose work follows, thus confirming or serving notice that the present selection of poems is a personal one and should not be regarded as an attempt to represent the region or even the particular poets as a whole. And perhaps a few words are not entirely out of place, since it seems to me we may have come to a parting of the ways between awareness and indifference, a common enough (though deadly) phenomenon in an age of news saturation. At the risk of appearing perverse, one has to admit that increased sophistication is not proof against this. It is as if a kind of complacency has substituted itself for our earlier ignorance. We understand, therefore we may now forget, if not forgive. In a remarkable self-interview, the late Primo Levi (author of *Survival in Auschwitz* and *The Reawakening*) draws our attention precisely to this danger. It is worth quoting him at length. In answer to the question, 'How do you explain the Nazis' fanatical hatred of the Jews?' he writes:

> Perhaps one cannot, what is more one must not, understand, because to understand is almost to justify. Let me explain: 'understanding' a proposal or human behaviour means ... to 'contain' it, contain its author, put oneself in his place, identify with him. Now no normal man can ever identify with Hitler, Himmler, Goebbels, Eichmann, and endless others. This dismays us, and at the same time gives us a sense of relief, because perhaps it is desirable that their words (and also, unfortunately, their deeds) cannot be comprehensible to us. They are non-human words and deeds, really anti-human, without historical precedents, with difficulty comparable to the cruellest events of the biological struggle for existence. The war can be related to this struggle but Auschwitz has nothing to do with the war. War is a terrible fact, to be deprecated, but it is in us, it has its rationality, we 'understand' it.
>
> But there is no rationality in the Nazi hatred: it is a hate that is not in us, it is outside man ... We cannot understand it, but we can and must understand where it springs from, and we must be on our guard. If understanding is impossible, knowing is imperative, because what happened can happen again.*

The distinction between understanding and knowing is crucial. It is their 'knowledge' which these poets share with us.

For nearly twenty years I have been trying to assemble a collection based on the work of a few major figures of the first post-war Central European generation (I would have called it 'East European' earlier, but the term, as Kundera has shown, is dismissive, as well as being

* Translated by Ruth Feldman, *Shema: Collected Poems of Primo Levi*, Menard Press, 1976.

historically and even geographically inaccurate). I encountered their work in the mid-sixties, when Ted Hughes and I started the magazine *Modern Poetry in Translation*, mainly in order to provide a platform for it; Ted Hughes also urged the establishment of the annual Poetry International readings referred to earlier. During my association with the Carcanet Press – largely in order to help promote a series dedicated to poetry in translation – plans for an anthology of East European poetry were discussed with James Atlas (who edited the Carcanet selection of Attila József), and when I joined the University of Iowa in the mid-seventies to direct the Translation Workshop, I discovered that Paul Engle, who with his wife had founded the International Writing Program, had been collecting similar material for an anthology in the series published by the University of Iowa Press. But in spite of these promising initiatives and Iowa City's oddly advantageous position, we did not succeed, either jointly or separately, in getting a book out at the time. More recently yet another enterprise, under the aegis of Joseph Brodsky (with whom, too, I had discussed the idea of an anthology), resulted in a hefty volume edited by Emery George and published by Ardis: *Contemporary East European Poetry* (1983). I might have been tempted to withdraw at this point, except that the Ardis anthology, which aimed to represent all nations from the Baltic to the Black Sea, as well as the whole spectrum of post-war poetry in that region, was also very different from the one I had in mind. Furthermore, the Ardis translations were in general newly commissioned, while I hoped to draw retrospectively on the many collections of translated poetry, as well as the issues of *Modern Poetry in Translation*, which first brought these poets to the notice of an English-language audience and which conveyed the excitement of discovery. In other words, the need for an unashamedly exclusive anthology forefronting, at least once, certain members of a generation which now seemed in danger of a kind of historical-literary entombment was, if anything, even more urgent.

Obviously had I not believed that the work of these poets belonged together, I should not have bothered to compile this anthology. Even if it springs from distinct cultural traditions, history has joined it generationally in a way that transcends language or national boundaries. (It reminds one, in some ways, of the work of the First World War poets, whose linguistic resources may have been inadequate, but who nevertheless also struggled to express a new reality.) The work has a newness which obviously derives from the unprecedentedly grievous circumstances of its composition, even though, of course, it was not entirely new, since nothing ever is. It was timely rather than timeless, but that is what it had to be, and it is that dedicated timeliness, that provisional quality, which paradoxically makes it likely to endure.

But need anything be added to the above, in this era of *perestroika* when so many 'new' nations – non-aligned Third World as well as Central European – are finding a place for themselves between the two major forces and are speaking out that much more autonomously, with confidence and conviction, given that the great power dialogue or confrontation has shown itself to be remarkably sterile or insensitive to their concerns and interests? It seems to me that while the changing situation perhaps alters or broadens our historical perspective, it does not reduce the significance of the work under consideration. Is art, in general, measured by its practical effects? To some extent doubtless it is. But these effects are themselves a matter for speculation: there is rarely a direct observable causal relationship. What seems to be happening internationally may be a measure of the success of writers such as Popa, Różewicz, Holub, Pilinszky, Herbert and Amichai, or it may not. We cannot tell. But whatever the case, the timeliness, as I put it, but also the timelessness of their message and their art is undiminished. In fact, more and more they come to look like the exemplary guardians of those values for which they stood. It is surely far too soon for us to be lulled once more by apparently propitious developments. That is, these should be welcomed and encouraged, but circumspectly, taking into account complexities and subtleties that we cannot afford to disregard but which so often escape the notice of our rhetoric-prone political leaders. The political and emotional maturity, the discriminating sensibility of writers such as those represented in the anthology is as needed as ever, even if much of their work will seem to have acquired more of a historical patina with the changing of the old guard in the Soviet Union, if not, so far, in the USA.

To sum up, my purpose has been simply to showcase relatively few poets, along with a brief sampling of the work of some of their outstanding predecessors. It is arguable that I might have left the latter out, but the fair-minded *littérateur* in me got the better of the purist. Nor did I wish to give the impression that there was an absolute demarcation between the pre- and post-war generations. At first, in the same spirit, I also included some more recent poets born in the forties, such as the Hungarian György Petri, or the Poles Stanisław Barańczak and Adam Zagajewski. But here I came to feel that the perspective offered was distracting and even potentially misleading. (In other words, this is a highly tendentious anthology!) While assembling my notes for the biographies and bibliographies of the poets, and for my introduction, as well as for a course on the poetry of Eastern Europe which I taught at the University of Iowa, I came across a number of interviews, articles or essays by the poets themselves. It seemed useful to append a selection of these since they are of a piece with the poetry, and certainly convey the concerns of their authors with greater immediacy than I can muster. Since there was room only for a very few, I decided to limit the selection to interviews or talks (both, in the cases of Herbert and Różewicz) by the poets who had first claimed and continued to engage my attention.

Many readers will be struck by the absence from this collection of a number of distinguished, indeed household names such as that of the late Sándor Weöres. This has partly to do with the problems of translation, and also with the perhaps related question of content. Much of the poetry I have included embodies with particular clarity experiences associated with total war and the totalitarian political solutions that were imposed after the war. In any case, the historico-political and the personal have fused to such an extent that to call this poetry simply political is misleading, even if the political reality manifests itself throughout. It represents a more capacious and resonant, more fully realized type of political poetry, just as politics in our time has come to affect people's lives so much more pervasively. Much of it thus addresses another traditional theme of poetry, one generally thought of as being at the other end of the spectrum from politics, namely love. One thinks of Yehuda Amichai, or Wisława Szymborska, but particularly Anna Swir, a late addition to the collection. Why love or erotic poetry should find a place here is not hard to understand – the most intimate or private expression of human emotion balancing, and in a sense challenging, the most public. There are other fine writers, though, like the Yugoslav Vesna Parun, also a member of the first post-war generation, whose love poetry seems to me to belong to a less local strain, more pure, more resistant to – one might even say, less corrupted by – historical actuality.

A *sine qua non* for inclusion was authenticity, as it struck me, in English translation. This would seem to go without saying, yet it is not so obvious. That 'the translation should read like a poem in English' does not quite define what I was after. It should, but it need not be *instantly* recognizable as such. The result with the present anthology has been a peculiar coherency, though I am fairly certain this is not due simply to my personal tastes being reflected. I should not go so far as to claim that translatability is a sufficient measure of a work's success. Nevertheless, a remarkable fact about the writing of the first post-war generation of

Central European poets represented here *is* precisely its translatability, whereas poetry, as we all know, is the least translatable of literary forms. It is worth noting that some of the most successful translations have been accomplished by translators whose native language is not English (for example Czesław Miłosz, George Theiner, Adam Czerniawski), who are mediating in a literal sense, since they themselves are able to occupy a middle ground between languages. This interesting phenomenon, which contradicts the well-known axiom that you can translate, particularly in the case of poetry, only into your native tongue, seems to support my contention that the poetry in question is indeed peculiarly translatable. By this I do not mean that it is *easy* to translate, though to claim that it translates itself, as it were, is not entirely nonsense, since it embodies, as I have already suggested, so much of our political and social reality that it has transformed our notion of poetry, shaping it to itself, generating an unprecedentedly universal or meta-lingual code. Insofar as poetry represents a particularly intense effort of assimilation and projection, it might be said that the work of these poets has quite simply transformed what we understand. It has created a fund of poetic resources, less bound than most to the linguistic conventions or traditions of the host culture.

This comprehensiveness, doubtless itself a result of circumstances and pressures, this concentration on issues that are no respecter of frontiers, has naturally facilitated translation. But what is particularly encouraging about a literary phenomenon which some are inclined to view in terms of loss of cultural identity, or as faceless cosmopolitanism, is that when men and women speak purposefully or urgently enough, it appears they may after all be heard by other men and women. A potential danger is that poets will start writing with the translation of their work (particularly into English, the *lingua franca* of the twentieth century) in view. This is, to some extent, inevitable, and not necessarily an entirely negative development, even though it challenges the notion of cultural integrity.

One can speculate about the reasons for the universality (to use a problematic term), or the translatability (to use a scarcely less problematic term) of this poetry. The main one has already been suggested, namely the prolonged crisis affecting Western culture as a whole, as reflected in two hugely destructive world wars and the totalitarian subversion of Central Europe, central psychically as well as geographically. But there is more to it even than this, or we would have a whole galaxy of poets, whereas in fact there are comparatively few. Certain general characteristics are shared by many, but finally only a handful continue to persuade: perhaps more than are represented in this anthology but not, I think, so many more.

What then is it, to try to be a little more specific, that seems to make this work so eminently translatable? Edwin Morgan talks about the 'clear-eyed' quality in the work of East European poets, while in a recent review ('Noble Poet', *New York Review of Books*, 18 July 1985), A. Alvarez writes of Herbert: 'He has been marvellously served by his translators but perhaps his persistent lucidity has made their task a little easier.' Ted Hughes, as we have seen, refers to these poets as among the most 'wide awake'. Subtle as it often is, this writing is also particularly direct; it is visionary, while remaining securely attached to actual situations. It makes great demands on its translator yet at the same time firmly guides him or her, so that the range of possible choices (while remaining formidable enough) is also quite precisely circumscribed; translating this work may be, more than usually, like participating in a single process that began with its creation, joining forces with the author, as it were, rather than seeking objectively to transfer meanings and effects that already exist. It seems to be *de rigueur* not to paraphrase or transcribe into a more familiar idiom. Hence my earlier remark that the English translation need not be *instantly* recognizable as a 'poem in English'.

Be that as it may, am I making excessive claims on behalf of a small number of poets (one cannot call them a group, still less a school) which I insist on defining only obliquely, that is in terms of translatability? I think not. Nor do I intend to denigrate writers whose work might not translate so readily; indeed, its very recalcitrance may be a token of its excellence. I have, for instance, included only a little of what might be regarded as marginal work by Vladimír Holan, while remaining acutely aware that it does not fairly represent his œuvre. But then, even the core figures in this collection are not represented in all phases of their work. As I have said, I believe that the translatability of their poetry, particularly of the fifties and sixties, is due at least in part to their engagement on so many levels with their times and ours. It seems to me that, whatever its subsequent virtues, it achieved a degree of relatedness then that deserves special notice. Their work, or much of it, itself having stood the test of time, in a way set standards by which the work of others may be measured, even though, of course, it never asked or aspired to do that.

Translatability, then, has been my guide. In fact, what in the first place drew me personally to translation was, I now see, precisely this quality in poets such as Amichai, Herbert, Holub, Pilinszky, Popa and Różewicz.

Translatability has confirmed for me their status and has also permitted me to add others, or some parts of the works of others, to this collection. It has remained a reliable yardstick, even if obscured of late by a plethora of uninspired or utilitarian poetry translations. It is an aura that embraces their work. A kind of fellowship, not so much of individuals as of consciences, has come into being, and it is this which I celebrate in the present collection. I realize only too well that this Introduction poses more questions than it answers. But to have attempted to answer them would not have done, when what follows is the poetry, an immeasurably more appropriate response. In a sense, I am writing this, while at the same time trying to hold my tongue. But maybe my obliquities and evasions will help locate the anthology in a time and a place. And that, at least, is in the spirit of a poetry that concerns itself with such particularities.

Finally, then, I am presenting here the survivors, not just in the general sense, but those whose work too has survived a test, translation, which it never asked to take but which was more urgently part of its destiny than was realized at first – on account of which all of us have reason to be grateful.

DANIEL WEISSBORT
London – Iowa City

Part One

Part One

Bertolt Brecht

BERTOLT BRECHT (1891–1956) was born in Augsburg, Bavaria, and studied medicine and natural science in Munich. His first plays date from the period immediately after World War One, and include *The Three-Penny Opera*, as well as a collection of poems and songs, *Die Hauspostille* (Domestic Breviary, 1927). This somewhat nihilistic, pre-Marxist period was succeeded by a didactic phase, extending from the late twenties until the mid-thirties, and ended with his conversion to Communism. Brecht's greatest plays and poetry belong to the late thirties and the forties, when he produced, among others, *Mother Courage and Her Children* (1939). *Swensborger Gedichte* (Swendborg Poems) also appeared in 1939. Brecht fled Nazi Germany in 1933, spent some time in Denmark and Finland, and eventually took refuge in the United States, in Hollywood. He was obliged to appear before the Un-American Activities Committee in 1947, after which he returned to Germany and founded the Berliner Ensemble in East Berlin in 1949. During the final phase of his career, he accomplished much of his innovative work as a stage director and theatrical writer, forming his theory of 'epic theatre', which held that the theatre's primary function is to awaken the audience politically and to convince it of the need to embrace a Marxist programme. But in spite of his devotion to the Communist cause, his experimental methods, not surprisingly, were stigmatized as decadent, even if he himself continued to enjoy a kind of privileged status.

As his note 'On Rhymeless Verse with Irregular Rhythm' (1939) suggests, Brecht was looking for a way to embody in his poetry the rhythms, the expressiveness, of the spoken rather than the literary language. The technique he developed, springing from his theatrical experience, he called 'gestic', and to illustrate it he turned to Martin Luther's translation of the Bible: 'The Bible's sentence "pluck out the eye that offends thee" is based on a gest – that of commanding – but it is not entirely gestically expressed, as "that offends thee" has a further gest which remains unexpressed, namely that of explanation. Purely gestically expressed, the sentence runs "if thine eye offends thee, pluck it out" (and this is how it was put by Luther, who "watched the people's mouth")' (*Brecht on Theatre*, edited by John Willett, New York, 1964). Brecht characterizes his 'German Satires', which were written for German Freedom Radio, thus: 'It was a matter of projecting single sentences to a distant, artificially scattered audience. They had to be cut down to the most concise possible form and to be reasonably invulnerable to interruptions (by jamming). Rhyme seemed to me to be unsuitable, as it easily makes a poem seem self-contained, lets it slide past the ear. Regular rhythms with their even cadence fail in the same way to cut deep enough, and they impose circumlocutions, a lot of everyday expressions won't fit them: what was needed was the tone of direct and spontaneous speech. I thought rhymeless verse with irregular rhythms seemed suitable' (*op. cit.*).

Brecht described his early collection, *Domestic Breviary*, as 'intended for the practical use of friends'. This already suggests a revolt against the traditional view of poetry as something apart from, or above, the generality of human concerns, rather than organically part of it. On the other hand, it might be regarded also as opening the door to a propagandistic or pedagogical utilitarianism, not so far removed in principle from the official cultural ideology, later, of socialist realism. In practice, Brecht by and large managed to remain objective, rather than simply following the party line, protected, it is true, by his great international prestige. Though, in a sense, his is a public poetry, it is relatively free of the hectoring quality of much so-called politically committed verse. Brecht's long-term concern with demystifying poetic language enabled him to resist the most stultifying effects of dogma. Clearsightedness never deserted him, even if he retained to the end a certain optimism about the prospects of socialism in Eastern Europe, which earned him an ambivalent reputation in that part of the world, as well as in the West, particularly in the Cold War atmosphere of the forties and early fifties. It is this lucidity which is, perhaps, his most useful legacy to his post-war successors.

THE BURNING OF THE BOOKS

When the Regime commanded that books with harmful knowledge
Should be publicly burned and on all sides
Oxen were forced to drag cartloads of books
To the bonfires, a banished
Writer, one of the best, scanning the list of the
Burned, was shocked to find that his
Books had been passed over. He rushed to his desk

On wings of wrath, and wrote a letter to those in power
Burn me! he wrote with flying pen, burn me! Haven't my books
Always reported the truth? And here you are
Treating me like a liar! I command you:
Burn me!

John Willett

BAD TIME FOR POETRY

Yes, I know: only the happy man
Is liked. His voice
Is good to hear. His face is handsome.

The crippled tree in the yard
Shows that the soil is poor, yet
The passers-by abuse it for being crippled
And rightly so.

The green boats and the dancing sails on the Sound
Go unseen. Of it all
I see only the torn nets of the fishermen.
Why do I only record
That a village woman aged forty walks with a stoop?
The girls' breasts
Are as warm as ever.

In my poetry a rhyme
Would seem to me almost insolent.

Inside me contend
Delight at the apple tree in blossom
And horror at the house-painter's speeches.
But only the second
Drives me to my desk.

John Willett and Ralph Manheim

THE FISHING-TACKLE

In my room, on the whitewashed wall
Hangs a short bamboo stick bound with cord
With an iron hook designed
To snag fishing-nets from the water. The stick
Came from a second-hand store downtown. My son
Gave it to me for my birthday. It is worn.
In salt water the hook's rust has eaten through the binding.
These traces of use and of work
Lend great dignity to the stick. I
Like to think that this fishing-tackle
Was left behind by those Japanese fishermen
Whom they have now driven from the West Coast into camps
As suspect aliens; that it came into my hands
To keep me in mind of so many
Unsolved but not insoluble
Questions of humanity.

Lee Baxendall

I, THE SURVIVOR

I know of course: it's simply luck
That I've survived so many friends. But last night in a dream
I heard those friends say of me: 'Survival of the fittest'
And I hated myself.

John Willett

WAR HAS BEEN GIVEN A BAD NAME

I am told that the best people have begun saying
How, from a moral point of view, the Second World War
Fell below the standard of the First. The Wehrmacht
Allegedly deplores the methods by which the SS effected
The extermination of certain peoples. The Ruhr industrialists
Are said to regret the bloody manhunts

Which filled their mines and factories with slave workers. The
    intellectuals
So I heard, condemn industry's demand for slave workers
Likewise their unfair treatment. Even the bishops
Dissociate themselves from this way of waging war; in short the
    feeling
Prevails in every quarter that the Nazis did the Fatherland
A lamentably bad turn, and that war
While in itself natural and necessary, has, thanks to the
Unduly uninhibited and positively inhuman
Way in which it was conducted on this occasion, been
Discredited for some time to come.

John Willett

CHANGING THE WHEEL

I sit by the roadside
The driver changes the wheel.
I do not like the place I have come from.
I do not like the place I am going to.
Why with impatience do I
Watch him changing the wheel?

Michael Hamburger

THE SOLUTION

After the uprising of the 17th June
The Secretary of the Writers' Union
Had leaflets distributed in the Stalinallee
Stating that the people
Had forfeited the confidence of the government
And could win it back only
By redoubled efforts. Would it not be easier
In that case for the government

To dissolve the people
And elect another?

Derek Bowman

THE ONE-ARMED MAN IN THE UNDERGROWTH

Dripping with sweat he bends down
To gather brushwood. The mosquitoes
He fends off with shakes of the head. Between his knees
He laboriously bundles his firewood. Groaning
He straightens himself, holds up his hand to feel
If it's raining. Hand upraised
The dreaded SS man.

Derek Bowman

THIS SUMMER'S SKY

High above the lake a bomber flies.
From the rowing boats
Children look up, women, an old man. From a distance
They appear like young starlings, their beaks
Wide open for food.

Michael Hamburger

THE MASK OF EVIL

On my wall hangs a Japanese carving
The mask of an evil demon, decorated with gold lacquer.
Sympathetically I observe
The swollen veins of the forehead, indicating
What a strain it is to be evil.

H. R. Hayes

THE FRIENDS

The war separated
Me, the writer of plays, from my friend the stage designer.
The cities where we worked are no longer there.
When I walk through the cities that still are
At times I say: that blue piece of washing
My friend would have placed it better.

Michael Hamburger

LETTER TO THE ACTOR CHARLES LAUGHTON
CONCERNING THE WORK ON THE PLAY
THE LIFE OF GALILEO

Still your people and mine were tearing each other to pieces when
   we
Pored over those tattered exercise books, looking
Up words in dictionaries, and time after time
Crossed out our texts and then
Under the crossings-out excavated
The original turns of phrase. Bit by bit –
While the housefronts crashed down in our capitals –
The façades of language gave way. Between us
We began following what characters and actions dictated:
New text.

Again and again I turned actor, demonstrating
A character's gestures and tone of voice, and you
Turned writer. Yet neither I nor you
Stepped outside his profession.

Michael Hamburger

Vladimír Holan   CZECHOSLOVAKIA

VLADIMÍR HOLAN (1905–1980) was born in Prague. Early collections of his poetry include *Triumf smrti* (The Triumph of Death, 1930), *Vanuti* (Breezes, 1932) and *Oblouk* (The Arc, 1934). These poems are richly metaphorical, with a strong metaphysical content. The rise of fascism and World War Two led to the politicization of Holan's work, but hardly surprisingly he fell into official disfavour with the repressive, post-1948 Stalinist régime in Czechoslovakia, turning to translation (Rilke, Baudelaire, Ronsard, Lermontov and others) and writing children's books. With the liberalization of the sixties Holan published such collections as *Na postupu* (Advancing, 1964) and *Bolest* (Pain, 1965). His long meditative poem *Noc s Hamletem* (A Night with Hamlet, 1964) won him many admirers among the young. His later poetry is stylistically simpler and more informal than his pre-war verse.

Holan's formulations, whether aphoristic or discursive, are extremely discriminating and precise, carefully distinguishing between objects or ideas that seem to overlap. He sees the ominous, even sinister, in the ordinary, his focus subtly changing to embrace future as well as past. His is a poetry of metamorphoses, in which language implicitly acknowledges its own limitations. There is no stridency, no pontification, the poetry being, rather, apocalyptical, but unfolding in a single discrete movement that makes scarcely a ripple in the psychic atmosphere. Yet, as the critic Zdeněk Kožmín remarked, his 'works are suffused with the atmosphere of the world, *after* the war, *after* the revelations of ... the tragedy of the personality cult' (*Plamen*, September 1965). The brevity and clarity of the pieces chosen below are so immediately a consequence of life experience that the writing appears paradoxically to have shed all traces of subjectivism. Holan is an exemplary writer, who keeps his nerve when those about him are losing theirs. One can readily understand that his verse should have become a rallying point and an inspiration for younger poets in the sixties.

MOTHER

Have you ever watched your old mother
making up the bed for you,
how she pulls, straightens, tucks in and smoothes the sheet
so you won't feel a single wrinkle?
Her breathing, the motion of her hands and palms
are so loving
that in the past they are putting out that fire in Persepolis
and now calming some future storm
off the China coast or in unknown seas.

Ian and Jarmila Milner

HOW?

How to live? How be simple and literal?
I was always looking for a word
that had been spoken only once,
or a word that had not been spoken at all.
I should have looked for ordinary words.

Nothing can be added
even to unconsecrated wine.

Ian and Jarmila Milner

THE CHICKEN

The doors open by themselves
before an angel. At other times a chicken
comes from the yard into the kitchen
and looks round at the company with so critical an eye
that they do not wait to see how it will end
but quickly cross themselves in self-defence.

Ian and Jarmila Milner

GLIMPSED

Glimpsed from the train, which takes shadow for truth.
But she was truly beautiful
and bareheaded,
bareheaded as if an angel
had left his head there
and gone off with the hat.

Ian and Jarmila Milner

BETWEEN

Between the idea and the word
there is more than we can understand.
There are ideas for which no words can be found.

The thought lost in the eyes of a unicorn
appears again in a dog's laugh.

Ian and Jarmila Milner

YOU'RE THINKING OF CHILDREN

You're thinking of children, of their
here and now, everything now,
without a thought of when
or where.... What's the good of looking at
yourself in a mirror,
they ask, simply because
they haven't yet been in love.... Yes,
only children don't need a double.

Ian and Jarmila Milner

EPOCH

By the images of things
we are still in time.

But today, before the sower has taken a step,
the reaper is already there.

It seems
there will be neither dead nor living ...

Ian and Jarmila Milner

BUT

The god of song and laughter long ago
shut the doors of eternity behind him.
Since then only at times
a dying memory echoes in us.
And since then only the pain
is never life size,
it is always larger than man
and yet must lodge within his heart.

Ian and Jarmila Milner

THE OLD PRIEST

We met on Charles Bridge, it was snowing.
I had not seen him for almost twenty years.
Did I complain? I suppose so, since he comforted me,
and when I spoke of sin, said gently:
'Yes, how else should we know you
at the Last Judgement!'
And when that did not help, he said all of a sudden:
'My son, it seems to me that in your verses
you now reject abstraction ... Your desire for simplicity
would be praiseworthy if only it were subtle ...

But it is as if you, with a part of your spirit,
the most adventurous part,
did not wish to partake of the divine power.
Do you mean to say that you don't like to drink wine?'

George Theiner

RESURRECTION

Is it true that after this life of ours we shall one day be awakened
by a terrifying clamour of trumpets?
Forgive me, God, but I console myself
that the beginning and resurrection of all of us dead
will simply be announced by the crowing of the cock.

After that we'll remain lying down a while ...
The first to get up
will be Mother ... We'll hear her
quietly laying the fire,
quietly putting the kettle on the stove
and cosily taking the teapot out of the cupboard.
We'll be home once more.

George Theiner

REMINISCENCE

After wandering for so many hours up and down
in vain looking for the pimpernel, we came out of the woods
and at high noon found ourselves on the moors.
The rarefied air was like tin. We gazed
at the hillside opposite, thickly grown
with shrubs and trees. They were still, like us.
I was just about to ask something
when, in that unmoving, quiescent, chillingly
enchanted mass a single tree,
in one single spot,
suddenly began to quiver

like a quarter-tone, but without sound.
You would have thought it was exulting for joy,
out of a sheer love of adventure.
But then that tree began to rustle,
the way silver rustles when it turns black.
But then that tree began to tremble,
like the skirt of a woman who touches
a man's clothes while reading a book in a madhouse.
But then that tree began to shake and sway,
as if it were being shaken and swayed by someone
who was looking into the black-eyed pit of love –
and I felt as if I were to die this minute . . .

'Don't be frightened,' said my father, 'it's only an aspen!'
But to this day I remember how pale he turned
when later we reached that spot
and underneath the aspen found an empty chair . . .

George Theiner

Peter Huchel   GERMANY

PETER HUCHEL (1903–1981) was born in Berlin and studied literature and philosophy there, as well as in Freiburg and Vienna. From 1925 until 1940 he worked as a freelance writer and translator. He served in the East during the war, and then for three years was an editor and producer of radio plays for East Berlin Radio, eventually becoming its artistic director. From 1949 to 1962 he was editor-in-chief of *Sinn und Form* (Sense and Form), a leading literary journal, but was unable to adapt himself to Party requirements. This eventually led to his dismissal and to eight years of imposed provincial isolation. In 1971, Huchel received permission to move to the West, living first in West Germany and then in Italy. Although he began publishing poetry in 1924, he did not win acclaim until he published his post-war collections: *Gedichte* (Poems, 1948), *Chausseen Chausseen* (Highways, Highways, 1963), *Gezählte Tage* (Counted Days, 1972) and *Die neunte Stunde* (The Ninth Hour, 1979).

Huchel's poetry is one of cold, comfortless landscapes. Unredeemed, indifferent, Man seems almost to have been absorbed into these landscapes. Or only his traces remain, as though he were already extinct, obsolete. Or, again, only the sound of him is heard, as a ghostlike presence, whose suffering exists, infiltrating and infusing that desolate natural world. The solitary, individual figures that do appear have been abandoned: they simply go through the motions dictated by their terminal destinies. It is, also, as if one were listening to one's *own* breathing, the nightmare grown unendurably real and close.

LANDSCAPE BEYOND WARSAW

March with its sharp pick
splits the ice of the sky.
From the cracks light pours
billowing down
on the telegraph wires and bare main roads.
At noon white it roosts in the reeds,
a great bird.
When it spreads its claws, brightly
the webs gleam out of thin mist.

Nightfall is brief.
Then more shallow than a dog's palate
the sky arches.
A hill smokes
as though still the huntsmen
were sitting there by the damp winter fire.
Where have they gone?
The hare's tracks in the snow
once told us where.

Michael Hamburger

ROADS

Choked sunset glow
of crashing time.
Roads. Roads.
Intersections of flight.
Cart tracks across the ploughed field
that with the eyes
of killed horses
saw the sky in flames.

Nights with lungs full of smoke,
with the hard breath of the fleeing
when shots
struck the dusk.
Out of a broken gate
ash and wind came without a sound,
a fire
that sullenly chewed the darkness.

Corpses,
flung over the rail tracks,
their stifled cry
like a stone on the palate.
A black

humming cloth of flies
closed over wounds.

Michael Hamburger

WINTER BILLET

I sit by the shed,
oiling my rifle.

A foraging hen
with her foot imprints
lightly on snow
a script as old as the world,
a sign as old as the world,
lightly on snow
the tree of life.

I know the butcher
and his way of killing.
I know the axe.
I know the chopping-block.

Across the shed
you will flutter,
stump with no head,
yet still a bird
that presses a twitching wing
Down on the split wood.

I know the butcher.
I sit by the shed,
oiling my rifle.

Michael Hamburger

KING LEAR

At the quarry's edge
he comes walking up,
the iodine rag
wrapped round his right hand.

In poor villages
he cut knotty wood
for his lentil soup.

Now in the dry shadow
of torn clouds
he returns
to his crown
in the glen.

Michael Hamburger

IN THE RUSH ODOUR of Danish meadows
still Hamlet lies
staring into his white face
that gleams in the water ditch.

The last word
remains unspoken,
it swam off on the backs of beavers.
Nobody knows the secret.

Michael Hamburger

Edvard Kocbek YUGOSLAVIA (Slovene)

EDVARD KOCBEK (1904–1981) was born in Slovenia. He studied Romance languages and literature in Paris. Between the two World Wars he worked as a teacher, and also edited the Catholic literary magazine *Driz* (Action). Kocbek belonged to the pre-war circle of young Catholic socialist intellectuals who later rebelled against the dogmatism of the Church hierarchy. During the war, in which he served as a partisan, he was a member of the Executive Committee of the Liberation Front, and after the war he became, for a while, the Vice-President of the People's Republic of Slovenia. Besides three collections of poetry – *Zemlja* (Earth, 1934), *Groza* (Terror, 1963) and *Pričevanja* (Report, 1969), he published two volumes of partisan memoirs in 1947 and 1951. A collection of short stories, *Fear and Courage*, was attacked by Party critics for its existentialist, personalist views. To date there is no collection of Edvard Kocbek's poetry available in English, but one has recently been completed by Michael Scammell and the Slovene poet Veno Taufer.

Kocbek's vision is both concrete and symbolic. There is a close identification with historical processes, or more immediately with the catastrophes of the era, especially with war, and the way it transforms and transposes, shrinking distances, rendering distinctions unintelligible. Here is a more personal engagement, but also a toughness of spirit that prevents his being overwhelmed. Perhaps Kocbek's practical involvement in active resistance enabled him to keep despair at bay. A secure grasp of circumstances, his own material existence, has the effect of disencumbering his imagination, permitting him to make forays that add a further dimension to a poetry already filled with the details of daily life and the overspillings of history.

HANDS

I have lived between my two hands
as between two brigands,
neither of them knew
what the other was doing.

The left hand was foolish because of its heart,
the right hand was clever because of its skill,
one took, the other lost,
they hid from each other
and only half-finished everything.

Today as I ran from death
and fell and rose and fell
and crawled among thorns and rocks
my hands were equally bloody.
I spread them like the cruciform branches
of the great temple candlestick,
that bear witness with equal ardour.
Faith and unfaith burned with a single flame,
ascending hotly on high.

Michael Scammell and Veno Taufer

THE GAME

I hold a chipped bowl in my hands
and wait in the camp kitchen queue.
And when I glance forward and back
I am shocked by a marvellous insight –
only now do we see ourselves right.
Someone has changed and revealed us,
as though shuffling a pack of cards,
cheekily, naughtily, rarely,
but above all, as in all games,
the odds are mysteriously even
and he has summoned our secret truth.

He that burrowed now walks upon air,
he that declaimed speeches now stammers in his dreams,
he who slept upon straw now commands the brigade
and the quiet woodcutter is full of questions;
he that quoted Homer is building bunkers
and he that ate in Paris is shaping a spoon;
the drinker licks the dew, the singer harkens to the silence,

the sexton sows mines, the miser collects wounds,
the farmhand is a stargazer, the coward a commando,
the poet a mule driver, the dreamer a telegraphist
and the local Casanova a trusty guide.

I hold a chipped bowl in my hands
and I look to my front and look back
and I can't stop looking at images,
a procession of ghosts, spirits on pilgrimage,
the winking of truths, the revelation of fates.
Someone has changed and defined us,
as though shuffling a pack of cards,
cheekily, naughtily, rarely.
And then I see myself at last
and reel under the weight of dreams –
all are within me, as in a young mother.

Michael Scammell and Veno Taufer

A LONGING FOR JAIL

I was too late for the most important
spiritual exercises of my life,
I am left without proof
of my true value.
Each jail is a treasury,
a secret drawer, a jealous
torture chamber, the most important stage
of a butcher's martyrdom before he is
corrupted by a naked woman holding a knife.
I missed the delight of that love,
I would die easier if I had counted out
the squares on the floor of my solitary cell
and completed in my thoughts the transparent frescoes
on the dusty pane
and gazed through the walls
at the frontier posts of mankind.
Now you have collapsed, my cell,
disintegrated to openness,

the world no longer consists of redeeming cruelty,
it is but a sabbath courtyard.
You can test me no more,
I am no longer a figure for the Christmas crib,
for a puppet show or display of robots.
I am preparing myself for a different game –
look, I am turning into a little grey mouse,
my hiding places are all around,
tonight I shall sleep in the sleeve of a child
with no right hand, tomorrow I shall dream
in the echo of a shadow that sleeps after its voyage
through a fairytale that has no end.

Michael Scammell and Veno Taufer

DIALECTICS

The builder demolishes houses,
the doctor advances death
and the chief of the fire brigade
is the arsonists' secret leader,
clever dialectics say so
and the bible says something similar:
he who is highest shall be lowest
and he who is last shall be first.

There's a loaded rifle at the neighbour's,
a microphone under the bed
and the daughter is an informer.
The neighbour goes down with a stroke,
the microphone's current fails,
and the daughter goes to confession.
Everyone clings to a ram's belly
when sneaking from the cyclops' cave.

I hear in the night discordant music
coming from the circus tent,
sleepwalkers walk the highwire,
wobbling with uncertain arms,

and their friends yell underneath
to rouse them from sleep,
for whoever is up must come down
and whoever's asleep let him sleep more soundly.

Michael Scammell and Veno Taufer

Czesław Miłosz

CZESŁAW MIŁOSZ (1911–) was born in Szetejnie, Lithuania. He received a law degree from the University of Vilnius, where he was associated with the left-wing literary group 'Żagary', whose members were known as 'catastrophists'. Milosz's first book of poems, *Poemat o czasie zastygłym* (A Poem of Time Frozen), was published in Vilnius in 1933. During the war, Miłosz worked with the Warsaw underground in occupied Poland, editing a clandestine anthology of anti-Nazi poetry. In the post-war period he served as cultural attaché in Washington and Paris, but by 1951 increasing cultural regimentation persuaded him to settle in France. His collection of essays *The Captive Mind* (1953) was probably the first work from Central Europe to come to terms with the psychological and moral dilemmas facing intellectuals under totalitarianism. In 1960 Miłosz moved to the United States and settled in California, where he became Professor (now Emeritus) of Slavic Literature at the University of California at Berkeley.

After the war Miłosz published both poetry and translations. His own work includes *Światło dzienne* (Daylight, 1953) and *Traktat poetycki* (A Treatise on Poetry, 1957). Translations include the first Polish version of T. S. Eliot's 'The Waste Land' (1946), as well as work by Simone Weil, Zbigniew Herbert and Walt Whitman, and the anthology *Post-War Polish Poetry* (1965). His *History of Polish Literature* (1969) is still the most comprehensive work on the subject, while several volumes of essays have also appeared, among them *Native Realm: A Search for Self-Definition* (1968) and *Emperor of the Earth: Modes of Eccentric Vision* (1977). Czesław Miłosz was awarded the Nobel Prize for Literature in 1980.

Thematically and stylistically, Miłosz's range is quite extensive, from highly personal dream narrative, remembrance of things past, to apocalyptic vision and meditation on the crisis of modern culture. This makes it hard to place his poetry and has perhaps stood in the way of its wider appreciation, much of it, however brilliantly executed, appearing almost parodistic; he is, to some extent, the victim of his own versatility. Even though in his later years honours have been lavished upon him as a poet, one wonders whether this is due rather to somewhat superficial changes in the media's orientation than to an increased understanding of his work. Miłosz is best regarded as a non-specialist man of letters, in an older, continuing, European tradition. His writings as social and literary critic, novelist, poet and anthologist-translator – his highly selective *Post-War Polish Poetry* was a revelation for many English-language readers – are part of a single, if not particularly unified, process. He has assembled a kind of discontinuous, metaphysical-psychological chronicle. Miłosz appears at times to be without preconceptions; but then, in order to be able to survey, to review, he must suspend judgement, even if judgements press continually upon him and, through him, upon his readers. One senses in him a reluctance to accept a position that historical and personal circumstances have thrust upon him.

A POOR CHRISTIAN LOOKS AT THE GHETTO

Bees build around red liver,
Ants build around black bone.
It has begun: the tearing, the trampling on silks,
It has begun: the breaking of glass, wood, copper, nickel, silver,
   foam
Of gypsum, iron sheets, violin strings, trumpets, leaves, balls,
   crystals.
Poof! Phosphorescent fire from yellow walls
Engulfs animal and human hair.

Bees build around the honeycomb of lungs,
Ants build around white bone.
Torn is paper, rubber, linen, leather, flax,
Fiber, fabrics, cellulose, snakeskin, wire.
The roof and the wall collapse in flame and heat seizes the
   foundations.
Now there is only the earth, sandy, trodden down,
With one leafless tree.

Slowly, boring a tunnel, a guardian mole makes his way,
With a small red lamp fastened to his forehead.
He touches buried bodies, counts them, pushes on,
He distinguishes human ashes by their luminous vapor,
The ashes of each man by a different part of the spectrum.
Bees build around a red trace.
Ants build around the place left by my body.

I am afraid, so afraid of the guardian mole.
He has swollen eyelids, like a Patriarch
Who has sat much in the light of candles
Reading the great book of the species.
What will I tell him, I, a Jew of the New Testament,
Waiting two thousand years for the second coming of Jesus?
My broken body will deliver me to his sight
And he will count me among the helpers of death:
The uncircumcised.

Czesław Miłosz   *Warsaw, 1943*

CAFÉ

Of that table in the café
where on winter noons a garden of frost glittered on window panes
I survived alone.
I could go in there if I wanted to
and drumming my fingers in a chilly void
convoke shadows.

With disbelief I touch the cold marble,
with disbelief I touch my own hand.
It – is, and I – am in ever novel becoming,
while they are locked forever and ever
in their last word, their last glance,
and as remote as Emperor Valentinian
or the chiefs of the Massagetes, about whom I know nothing,
though hardly one year has passed, or two or three.

I may still cut trees in the woods of the far North,
I may speak from a platform or shoot a film
using techniques they never heard of.
I may learn the taste of fruits from ocean islands
and be photographed in an attire from the second half of the
    century.
But they are forever like busts in frock coats and jabots
in some monstrous encyclopedia.

Sometimes when the evening aurora paints the roofs in a poor
   street
and I contemplate the sky, I see in the white clouds
a table wobbling. The waiter whirls with his tray
and they look at me with a burst of laughter
for I still don't know what it is to die at the hand of man,
they know – they know it well.

Czesław Miłosz   *Warsaw, 1944*

ON THE OTHER SIDE

> '*Some hells present an appearance like the ruins of houses and
> cities after conflagrations, in which infernal spirits dwell and
> hide themselves. In the milder hells there is an appearance of
> rude huts, in some cases contiguous in the form of a city with
> lanes and streets.*' – EMANUEL SWEDENBORG

Falling, I caught the curtain,
Its velvet was the last thing I could feel on earth
As I slid to the floor, howling: aah! aaah!

To the very end I could not believe that I too must ...
Like everyone.

Then I trod in wheel-ruts
On an ill-paved road. Wooden shacks,
A lame tenement house in a field of weeds.
Potato-patches fenced in with barbed wire.
They played as-if-cards, I smelled as-if-cabbage,
There was as-if-vodka, as-if-dirt, as-if-time.
I said: 'See here ...', but they shrugged their shoulders,
Or averted their eyes. This land knew nothing of surprise.
Nor of flowers. Dry geraniums in tin cans,
A deception of greenery coated with sticky dust.
Nor of the future. Gramophones played,
Repeating endlessly things which had never been.
Conversations repeated things which had never been.
So that no one should guess where he was, or why.

I saw hungry dogs lengthening and shortening their muzzles,
And changing from mongrels, to greyhounds, then dachshunds,
As if to signify they were perhaps not quite dogs.
Huge flocks of crows, freezing in mid-air,
Exploded under the clouds ...

Jan Darowski

A FELICITOUS LIFE

His old age fell on years of abundant harvest.
There were no earthquakes, droughts or floods.
It seemed as if the turning of the seasons gained in constancy,
Stars waxed strong and the sun increased its might.
Even in remote provinces no war was waged.
Generations grew up friendly to fellow men.
The rational nature of man was not a subject of derision.

It was bitter to say farewell to the earth so renewed.
He was envious and ashamed of his doubt,
Content that his lacerated memory would vanish with him.

Two days after his death a hurricane razed the coasts.
Smoke came from volcanoes inactive for a hundred years.
Lava sprawled over forests, vineyards and towns.
And war began with a battle on the islands.

Czesław Miłosz and Lillian Vallee

Nelly Sachs GERMANY

NELLY SACHS (1891–1970) was born in Berlin into a wealthy and cultured Jewish home. She was privately educated and never attended university. In 1940 she emigrated to Sweden with her mother, aided by her friend, the Swedish writer Selma Lagerlöf. In Sweden she supported herself by translating Swedish poetry into German. At the same time she began to read deeply in Hasidic and Biblical literature. Her first collection of verse had appeared in Germany in 1921. *In den Wohnungen des Todes* (In the Habitations of Death, 1946) and *Sternverdunkelung* (Eclipse of a Star, 1949) were published in Germany and the Netherlands respectively. Subsequent collections include *Und niemand weiß weiter* (And No One Knows How To Go On, 1957) and *Flucht und Verwandlung* (Flight and Metamorphosis, 1959). With the publication of the mystery play *Eli* in 1962, Sachs' reputation began to spread beyond West Germany, and in 1966, jointly with S. Y. Agnon, she was awarded the Nobel Prize for Literature. She died in Stockholm.

The primary reality in Sachs' almost Biblical poetry of lamentation is the sheer physical pain of loss. She cannot separate herself from the sufferer, she cannot turn away. Later she came to see the suffering of the Jewish victims in a wider context of death and renewal. But it is in her war-time poetry, written in exile yet not far from the scene of slaughter and destruction, and in her immediate post-war poetry, that she identifies most fully and most movingly with the tortured and condemned. Her later work, in contrast to that of Paul Celan's, for instance, appears, at least in translation, tentative, almost arbitrary at times, as if whatever spiritual resolution she achieved never quite found its correlative. It is, indeed, as if she had exhausted herself, in some essential sense, with the magnificent earlier lyrical impulse which drew on traditional Jewish sources to convey her sorrow and lend the silent victims her voice.

ALREADY EMBRACED BY THE ARM OF HEAVENLY SOLACE

Already embraced by the arm of heavenly solace
The insane mother stands
With the tatters of her torn mind

With the charred tinders of her burnt mind
Burying her dead child,
Burying her lost light,
Twisting her hands into urns,
Filling them with the body of her child from the air,
Filling them with his eyes, his hair from the air,
And with his fluttering heart –

Then she kisses the air-born being
And dies!

Michael Roloff

A DEAD CHILD SPEAKS

My mother held me by my hand.
Then someone raised the knife of parting:
So that it should not strike me,
My mother loosed her hand from mine.
But she lightly touched my thighs once more
And her hand was bleeding –

After that the knife of parting
Cut in two each bite I swallowed –
It rose before me with the sun at dawn
And began to sharpen itself in my eyes –
Wind and water ground in my ear
And every voice of comfort pierced my heart –

As I was led to death
I still felt in the last moment
The unsheathing of the great knife of parting.

Ruth and Matthew Mead

WHAT SECRET CRAVINGS OF THE BLOOD

What secret cravings of the blood,
Dreams of madness and earth
A thousand times murdered,
Brought into being the terrible puppeteer

Him who with foaming mouth
Dreadfully swept away
The round, the circling stage of his deed
With the ash-grey, receding horizon of fear?

O the hills of dust, which as though drawn by an evil moon
The murderers enacted:

Arms up and down,
Legs up and down
And the setting sun of Sinai's people
A red carpet under their feet.

Arms up and down,
Legs up and down
And on the ash-grey receding horizon of fear
Gigantic the constellation of death
That loomed like the clock face of ages.

Michael Hamburger

IF I ONLY KNEW

If I only knew
On what your last look rested.
Was it a stone that had drunk
So many last looks that they fell
Blindly upon its blindness?

Or was it earth,
Enough to fill a shoe,
And black already

With so much parting
And with so much killing?

Or was it your last road
That brought you a farewell from all the roads
You had walked?

A puddle, a bit of shining metal,
Perhaps the buckle of your enemy's belt,
Or some other small augury
Of heaven?

Or did this earth,
Which lets no one depart unloved,
Send you a bird-sign through the air,
Reminding your soul that it quivered
In the torment of its burnt body?

Ruth and Matthew Mead

CHORUS OF THE RESCUED

We, the rescued,
From whose hollow bones death had begun to whittle his flutes,
And on whose sinews he had already stroked his bow –
Our bodies continue to lament
With their mutilated music.
We, the rescued,
The nooses wound for our necks still dangle
before us in the blue air –
Hourglasses still fill with our dripping blood.
We, the rescued,
The worms of fear still feed on us.
Our constellation is buried in dust.
We, the rescued,
Beg you:
Show us your sun, but gradually.
Lead us from star to star, step by step.
Be gentle when you teach us to live again.

Lest the song of a bird,
Or a pail being filled at the well,
Let our badly sealed pain burst forth again
and carry us away —
We beg you:
Do not show us an angry dog, not yet —
It could be, it could be
That we will dissolve into dust —
Dissolve into dust before your eyes.
For what binds our fabric together?
We whose breath vacated us,
Whose soul fled to Him out of that midnight
Long before our bodies were rescued
Into the ark of the moment.
We, the rescued,
We press your hand
We look into your eye —
But all that binds us together now is leave-taking,
The leave-taking in the dust
Binds us together with you.

Michael Roloff

Leopold Staff   POLAND

LEOPOLD STAFF (1878–1957) was born in Lwów and studied law, philosophy and Romance languages at the university there. His first published poem appeared in 1900 in a student magazine, his first volume of poetry, *Sny o potędze* (Dreams of Power), in 1901. It was followed by sixteen other volumes, the last, *Dziewięć Muz* (Nine Muses) appearing a year after his death. Having run the gamut of poetic forms, after World War II Staff developed a laconic, epigrammatic, paradoxical style that aligned him closely with poets far younger than himself: Tadeusz Różewicz, for instance, greatly admired his work and influenced him, as well as being influenced by him. He was also a prolific translator, his translations including works by Heraclitus, Michelangelo, Ronsard, Spinoza, Goethe, Nietzsche, Strindberg and Thomas Mann.

   Staff's quietness and gentle humanity in the final phase of his work is such that one must listen hard to catch the tremors of the age. And yet it is this very quietness that is so potent – which constitutes the particular virtue of a poetry that has been clarified, cleared of all impurities and excrescences. The irony is there, but so mild as almost to contradict itself – a wryly regretful smile, almost private. Staff's long career links the post- and pre-Holocaust eras.

SPEECH

You don't have to understand a nightingale's song
To admire it.
You don't have to understand the croaking of frogs
To find it intoxicating.
I understand human speech
With its duplicity and lies.
If I didn't understand it
I would be the greatest poet.

Adam Czerniawski

FOUNDATIONS

When I built upon sand
The house fell down.
When I built upon a rock
The house fell down.
This time I shall start
With chimney smoke.

Adam Czerniawski

DUCKWEED

For Jan Parandowski

In an ancient overgrown park
I stood near a pond
Thick with a coat of weeds.
Thinking
That the water must once have been clear
And that it should be so again
I picked up a dry branch
And skimmed the green patina
Guiding it to the weir.

A sober wise man
His brow scored with thought
Surprised me at this task
Saying with a gentle smile
Of condescending rebuke:
'Don't you begrudge the time?
Each moment is a drop of eternity,
Life a twinkling of its eye.
There are so many deserving causes.'

I walked away shamed
And throughout the day
Meditated on life and death,
On Socrates
And the immortal soul,

On the pyramids and Egyptian corn,
I considered the Roman Forum and the moon,
The dinosaur and the Eiffel Tower ...
But it all came to nothing.

When I returned the following day
To the same spot
By the green-coated pond
I saw
The wise man, his brow smooth,
Quietly
Skimming the weedy surface
With the branch I had thrown away,
Guiding the green to the weir.

Birds sang in the branches
Trees rustled softly.

Adam Czerniawski

KINGDOM

My kingdom for a horse!
We cry only
When the kingdom's already lost.

Adam Czerniawski

PORTRAIT

He was always the same
Though his face was always different
And his name always new.
The sequence of his years
Conflicted with time.
No master could render his likeness
In a single stone,
So they passed his form

From hand to hand
Like torchbearers.

An ancient master
Presented him as a powerful nude athlete
Who from his thrusting stance
Is to hurl a discus into the future;
But his gaze was fixed upon such distant goal
That for two thousand years
The discus has not left his hand
Which froze in a futile
Unfulfilled intention.

Then Donatello carved him
As the knight of Or San Michele
Where, not naked but dressed in armour,
He leans upon a shield
Marked with a cross.
But the spear, the flame of its blade upturned,
Took root in his palm
When Evil with a dragon jaw
Writhed at his feet.

Finally Michelangelo scored
Crushing with a hammer
A marble lump of dead flesh
Which the sorrowing mother
Supports by the arms
When her son can no longer bear
His own inhuman saintliness.

Adam Czerniawski

Anna Świrszczyńska   POLAND

ANNA ŚWIRSZCZYŃSKA [Swir] (1909–1984) was born and grew up in Warsaw, where she attended university. She also spent much time in the Polish countryside with her father, an artist. In Warsaw during the war she worked as a waitress and joined the literary underground. After the war she moved to Kraków and wrote poems, plays and stories for children, under the name of Anna Swir. Before her death she had published nine volumes of poetry, as well as a great number of plays and stories.

The sketches from Swir's collection *Building the Barricade*, represented by the first three poems printed below, have a telegrammic quality. There is no stepping aside from them, no getting out of the way – they come at you too fast. Cruelty, dehumanization, the fracturing effects of extreme suffering, the disintegration of values, are recorded. There is a breathlessness about this writing, as if she gave herself no time to sum up (or judge), beyond the summing up that the eye does in a flash. Very occasionally there is a trace of something like sentimentality, but usually Swir has disengaged from her material before this can happen. Other poems address with utter frankness her situation as a woman, aging but still in need of sensual contact, of erotic fulfilment, the horror of her wartime experiences being neither magnified nor reduced but given a fuller human dimension and context by this work. Swir's poetry is beyond irony, generally even beyond bitterness, except insofar as the truth has a bitter taste. It springs from an unshrinking recognition of the objective facts; there is, thus, little if anything superfluous about it. With an utter lack of affectation she sets side by side her personal experiences and the dreadful afflictions and sufferings that have affected people in general. There is no self-aggrandisement in this. A benignly rigorous pragmatism informs all her mature work.

THE GOOD LORD SAVED HER

A woman lay dying on a pallet in a gateway,
in the pallet were dollars.
Another woman was sitting beside her,
waiting for her to die.

Then she ran through the streets with the dollars,
bombs were falling.
She prayed: oh good Lord, save me.

And the good Lord saved her.

Magnus J. Krynski and Robert A. Maguire

THEY LAY DYING SIDE BY SIDE

'Your husband's lying here in the next bed.'
'Your wife's lying here next to you.'
They lay dying side by side,
each muffled up in his own suffering,
not looking at the other.

They grappled with death,
sweat pouring, teeth gnashing.

At dawn
the husband looked toward the window.
'Will I live to see the day?' he asked.

They died side by side,
without so much as a glance at each other.

Magnus J. Krynski and Robert A. Maguire

HE WAS LUCKY

To Prof. Władysław Tatarkiewicz

The old man
leaves his house, carries books.
A German soldier snatches the books
flings them in the mud.

The old man picks them up,
the soldier hits him in the face.

The old man falls,
the soldier kicks him and walks away.

The old man
lies in mud and blood.
Under him he feels
the books.

Magnus J. Krynski and Robert A. Maguire

A VISIT

In a home for incurables
I visited a woman who was about to die.
She embraced me,
I felt through her gray shirt
the tiny bones of her brittle body
which would no longer arouse lust or tenderness.

'I don't want this, take me away.'
Near us, a retarded woman was vomiting.

Czesław Miłosz and Leonard Nathan

TERMINALLY ILL

Every morning he is astounded again,
always for the first time,
every time more violently than before.

He is astounded relentlessly,
with impressive energy,
passionately, fiercely, vehemently,
till he is out of breath.

He pants with astonishment,
he chokes,
he gluts himself on astonishment,

he drowns like a puppy thrown into deep water,
he shivers, trembles, cries with astonishment.

That the affliction came to him
against which there is no help.

Czesław Miłosz and Leonard Nathan

THE GREATEST LOVE

She is sixty. She lives
the greatest love of her life.

She walks arm-in-arm with her dear one,
her hair streams in the wind.
Her dear one says:
'You have hair like pearls.'

Her children say:
'Old fool.'

Czesław Miłosz and Leonard Nathan

HE IS GONE

The finger of death touched me,
the world tumbled down
on me.

I am lying under the rubble,
hands broken,
legs broken,
backbone mangled.

People are passing
at a distance.
I call. They do not hear,
They have passed. I am dying.

The dearest man arrives.
He looks for a moment. Does not understand anything.
Leaves.

He is tenderhearted,
he is gone to comfort others.

Czesław Miłosz and Leonard Nathan

A VERY SAD CONVERSATION AT NIGHT

'You should have many lovers.'
'I know, dear.'
'I had many women.'
'I had men, dear.'
'I am finished.'
'Yes, dear.'
'Don't trust me.'
'I don't trust you, dear.'
'I am afraid of death.'
'Me too, dear.'
'You won't leave me.'
'No, dear.'
'I am alone.'
'So am I, dear.'
'Hug me.'
'Good night, dear.'

Czesław Miłosz and Leonard Nathan

WE ARE GOING TO SHOOT AT THE HEART

We will kill our love.

We will strangle it
as one strangles a baby.
We will kick it
as one kicks a faithful dog.

We will tear out
its live wings
as one does it
to a bird.

We will shoot it in the heart
as one shoots
oneself.

Czesław Miłosz and Leonard Nathan

Part Two

Yehuda Amichai ISRAEL

YEHUDA AMICHAI (1924–) was born in Würzberg, Germany. In 1936, at
the age of twelve, he emigrated with his parents to Israel. During World
War Two he served with the Jewish Brigade. He saw active service both
in the Israeli War of Independence and later on in the Sinai campaign.
Amichai worked as a schoolteacher for many years. He has given many
readings abroad, especially in the United States, and his work has been
particularly widely translated, including his novel *Not of This Place, Not of
This Time* (1981) and several volumes of poetry. His *Selected Poems* in
translation was published by Penguin Books in 1988.

Amichai's use of imagery, drawing on Biblical and historical Jewish
sources is tender rather than ironic. His strength seems to come from the
recognition of weakness. The flow of his imagination is guided and
controlled by an unaffected judiciousness, an ingenuous self-awareness.
Amichai is a man *in* the world, rather than of the world. The wryness
about himself does not partake of that self-hating, self-castigating qual-
ity for which Jews are so famous. He is the enemy of exaggeration, the
exponent of level-headedness, though he is well known too for his
elaborate use of metaphor. Indeed, the closest Amichai perhaps comes
to a certain kind of formalism is in his metaphors (sometimes clusters of
them), which are almost like conceits; he regards the metaphor as one of
the greatest inventions of man (see Appendix 1). Drawing on such a wide
range of material, the whole of history being eternally present, Amichai's
poems are particularly rich and entertaining. What unifies them is a tone
of voice, compounded of human considerateness and sheer good sense.

So, celebrating his likeness with other men, though in an unassertive
manner, since to be assertive would be to lift himself above them,
Amichai does not try to make more of historical or personal circum-
stances than may be; that is, he does not dramatize, because the drama is
within and all about him and need not be added. But sometimes his
memory, his situation as a kind of focal point or meeting place for
memories, becomes a burden. He is not so much overwhelmed or
overawed by the multiplicity, the multi-dimensionality, the historic
density of things, as he is simply tired by it, weary almost unto death, yet
even then, not quite – because this tiredness too is part of the human
condition, just as the burden itself is inescapable. His is a poetry that has
moved beyond irony, because what he has to say is both too urgent and
too ancient for that.

SUMMER OR ITS ENDING

It was summer
or its ending.
That afternoon you were
dressed for the first time
in your shroud,
and never noticed,
because of the printed
flowers on its cloth.

Dennis Silk

LUXURY

My uncle is buried at Sheik Bad'r.
The other one is scattered in the Carpathian mountains.

My father is buried at Sanhedria,
My grandmother on the Mount of Olives.
And all their forefathers
Are buried in the ruined Jewish cemeteries in the villages of Lower
    Franconia,
Near rivers and forests which are not Jerusalem.

My father's father kept heavy-eyed
Jewish cows in their sheds below the kitchen –

And rose at four in the morning.
I inherited his early rising,
My mouth bitter with nightmares
I attend to my bad dreams.

Grandfather, Grandfather,
Chief Rabbi of my life,
As you sold unleavened bread on the Passover Eve,
Sell my pains –
So they stay in me, even ache – but not mine,
Not my property.

So many tombstones are scattered behind me –
Names, engraved like the names of long-abandoned railway
     stations.

How shall I cover all these distances,
How can I keep them connected?
I can't afford such an intricate network.
It's a luxury.

Assia Gutmann

From TRAVELS OF A LATTER-DAY BENJAMIN OF TUDELA

I am a solitary man, not a democracy.
The executive, the amatory and the judicial arms in one body.
The hating power and the hurting power
the blind power and the dumb power.
I wasn't elected. I am a demonstration. I raise
my face like a placard. Everything is written there. Everything.
Please, there's no need to use tear gas,
I'm weeping already. There's no need to disperse me.
I'm dispersed.
The dead are also a demonstration.
When I visit my father's grave, I see
the tombstones raised by the dust below:
They're a large demonstration.

Ruth Nevo

KING SAUL AND I

I

They gave him a finger, but he took the whole hand
They gave me the whole hand: I didn't even take the little finger.
While my heart
Was weightlifting its first feelings
He rehearsed the tearing of oxen.

My pulse-beats were like
Drips from a tap
His pulse-beats
Pounded like hammers on a new building.

He was my big brother
I got his used clothes.

2

His head, like a compass, will always bring him
To the sure north of his future.

His heart is set, like an alarm clock
For the hour of his reign.
When everyone's asleep, he will cry out
Until all the quarries are hoarse.
Nobody will stop him!

Only the asses bare their yellow teeth
At the end.

3

Dead prophets turned time-wheels
When he went out searching for asses
Which I, now, have found.
But I don't know how to handle them.
They kick me.

I was raised with the straw,
I fell with heavy seeds.
But he breathed the winds of his histories.
He was anointed with the royal oil
As with wrestler's grease.
He battled with olive-trees
Forcing them to kneel.

Roots bulged on the earth's forehead
With the strain.
The prophets escaped from the arena;
Only God remained, counting:

Seven ... eight ... nine ... ten ...
The people, from his shoulders downwards, rejoiced.
Not a man stood up.
He had won.

    4
I am tired,
My bed is my kingdom.

My sleep is just
My dream is my verdict

I hung my clothes on a chair
For tomorrow.

He hung his kingdom
In a frame of golden wrath
On the sky's wall.

My arms are short, like string too short
To tie a parcel.

His arms are like the chains in a harbour
For cargo to be carried across time.

He is a dead king.
I am a tired man.

Assia Gutmann

MAYOR

It's sad
To be the Mayor of Jerusalem.
It is terrible.
How can any man be the mayor of a city like that?

What can he do with her?
He will build, and build, and build.

And at night
The stones of the hills round about
Will crawl down
Towards the stone houses,
Like wolves coming
To howl at the dogs
Who have become men's slaves.

Assia Gutmann

JEWS IN THE LAND OF ISRAEL

We forget where we came from. Our Jewish
Names from the exile reveal us,
Bring up the memory of flower and fruit, medieval cities,
Metals, knights that became stone, roses mostly,
Spices whose smells dispersed, precious stones, much red,
Trades gone from the world.
(The hands, gone too.)

The circumcision does it to us,
Like in the Bible story of Shechem and the sons of Jacob,
With pain all our life.

What are we doing here on our return with this pain.
The Longings dried up with the swampland,
The desert flowers for us and our children are lovely.
Even fragments of ships, that sunk on the way,
Reached this shore,
Even winds reached. Not all the sails.

What are we doing
In this dark land that casts
Yellow shadows, cutting at the eyes,
(Sometimes, one says even after forty
Years or fifty: 'The sun is killing me.')

What are we doing with souls of mist, with the names,
With forest eyes, with our lovely children, with swift blood?

Spilt blood isn't roots of trees,
But it's the closest to them
That man has.

Harold Schimmel

INSTRUCTIONS FOR A WAITRESS

Don't remove the glasses and plates
from the table. Don't rub
the stain from the cloth. It's good to know:
people were here before me.

I buy shoes which were on another man's feet.
(My friend has thoughts of his own.)
My love is another man's wife.
My night is 'used' with dreams.
On my window raindrops are painted,
in the margins of my books are notes by others.
On the plan of the house in which I want to live
the architect has drawn strangers near the entrance.
On my bed is a pillow, with
a hollow of a head now gone.

Harold Schimmel

ALL THE GENERATIONS BEFORE ME

All the generations before me
donated me, bit by bit, so that I'd be
erected all at once
here in Jerusalem, like a house of prayer
or charitable institution.
It binds. My name's
my donors' name.
It binds.

I'm approaching the age
of my father's death. My last
will's patched with many patches.
I have to change my life and death
daily to fulfill all the prophecies
prophesied for me. So they're not lies.
It binds.

I've passed forty.
There are jobs I cannot get
because of this. Were I in Auschwitz
they would not have sent me out to work,
but gassed me straightaway.
It binds.

Harold Schimmel

From SEVEN LAMENTS FOR THE WAR-DEAD

6

Is all of this
sorrow? I don't know.
I stood in the cemetery dressed in
the camouflage clothes of a living man: brown pants
and a shirt yellow as the sun.

Cemeteries are cheap; they don't ask for much.
Even the wastebaskets are small, made for holding
tissue paper
that wrapped flowers from the store.
Cemeteries are a polite and disciplined thing.
'I shall never forget you,' in French
on a little ceramic plaque.
I don't know who it is that won't ever forget:
he's more anonymous than the one who died.

Is all of this sorrow? I guess so.
'May ye find consolation in the building
of the homeland.' But how long

can you go on building the homeland
and not fall behind in the terrible
three-sided race
between consolation and building and death?

Yes, all of this is sorrow. But leave
a little love burning always
like the small bulb in the room of a sleeping baby
that gives him a bit of security and quiet love
though he doesn't know what the light is
or where it comes from.

Chana Bloch

From PATRIOTIC SONGS

2

The war broke out in autumn at the empty border
between sweet grapes and oranges.

The sky is blue, like veins in a woman's tormented thighs.

The desert is a mirror for those looking at it.

Sad males carry the memory of their families
in carriers and pouches and hunchback-knapsacks
and soul-bags and heavy eye-bladders.

The blood froze in its veins. That's why it can't be spilled,
but only broken into pieces.

4

I have nothing to say about the war,
nothing to add. I'm ashamed.

All the knowledge I have absorbed in my life
I give up, like a desert
which has given up all water.
Names I never thought I would forget

I'm forgetting.

And because of the war I say again,
for the sake of a last and simple sweetness:
The sun is circling round the earth. Yes.
The earth is flat, like a lost, floating board. Yes.
God is in Heaven. Yes.

11

The town I was born in was destroyed by shells.
The ship in which I sailed to the land of Israel was drowned later in
    the war.

The barn at Hammadia where I had loved was burned out.
The sweet shop at Ein-Gedi was blown up by the enemy.
The bridge at Ismailia, which I crossed to and fro on
the eve of my loves,
has been torn to pieces.

Thus my life is wiped out behind me according to an exact map:
How much longer can my memories hold out?

The girl from my childhood was killed and my father is dead.

That's why you should never choose me
to be a lover or a son, or a bridge-crosser
or a citizen or a tenant.

15

Even my loves are measured by wars:
I am saying this happened after the Second
World War. We met a day before the
Six-Day war. I'll never say
before the peace '45–'48 or during
the peace '56–'67.

But knowledge of peace
passes from country to country,
like children's games,
which are so much alike, everywhere.

34

Let the memorial hill remember, instead of me,
that's his job. Let the park in memory remember
let the street names remember
let the famous building remember
let the house of worship in the name of God remember
let the rolling scrolls of the law remember
let memorial services remember, let the flags remember
those multicoloured shrouds of history (the
corpses they wrapped have anyhow turned to dust),
let dust remember, let dung remember
at the gate, let afterbirth remember.

Let the wild beasts and the sky's birds eat and remember.
Let all of them remember, so that I can rest.

Yehuda Amichai and Ted Hughes

THE DIAMETER OF THE BOMB

The diameter of the bomb was thirty centimetres
and the diameter of its effective
range – about seven metres.
And in it four dead and eleven wounded.
And around them in a greater circle
of pain and time are scattered
two hospitals and one cemetery.
But the young woman who was
buried where she came from
over a hundred kilometres away
enlarges the circle greatly.
And the lone man who weeps over her death
in a far corner of a distant country
includes the whole world in the circle.
And I won't speak at all about the crying of orphans
that reaches to the seat of God
and from there onward, making
the circle without end and without God.

Yehuda Amichai

AN APPENDIX TO THE VISION OF PEACE

Don't stop after beating the swords
into ploughshares, don't stop! Go on beating
and make musical instruments out of them.

Whoever wants to make war again
will have to turn them into ploughshares first.

Glenda Abramson and Tudor Parfitt

TOURISTS

Visits of condolence is all we get from them.
They squat at the Holocaust Memorial,
They put on grave faces at the Wailing Wall
And they laugh behind heavy curtains
In their hotels.
They have their pictures taken
Together with our famous dead
At Rachel's Tomb and Herzl's Tomb
And on the top of Ammunition Hill.
They weep over our sweet boys
And lust over our tough girls
And hang up their underwear
To dry quickly
In cool, blue bathrooms.

Once I sat on the steps by a gate at David's Tower, I placed my two
heavy baskets at my side. A group of tourists was standing around
their guide and for a moment I became their reference point. 'You
see that man with the baskets? Just right of his head there's an arch
from the Roman period. Just right of his head.' 'But he's moving, he's
moving!' I said to myself: redemption will come only if their guide
tells them, 'You see that arch from the Roman period? It's not
important: but next to it, left and down a bit, there sits a man who's
bought fruit and vegetables for his family.'

Glenda Abramson and Tudor Parfitt

A SONG OF LIES ON SABBATH EVE

On a Sabbath eve, at dusk on a summer day
when I was a child,
when the odours of food and prayer drifted up from all the houses
and the wings of the Sabbath angels rustled in the air,
I began to lie to my father:
'I went to another synagogue.'

I don't know if he believed me or not
but the lie was very sweet in my mouth.
And in all the houses at night
hymns and lies drifted up together,
O taste and see.
and in all the houses at night
Sabbath angels died like flies in the lamp,
and lovers put mouth to mouth
and inflated one another till they floated in the air
or burst.

Since then, lying has tasted very sweet to me,
and since then I've always gone to another synagogue.
And my father returned the lie when he died:
'I've gone to another life.'

Chana Bloch

Ingeborg Bachmann   AUSTRIA

INGEBORG BACHMANN (1926–1973) was born in Klagenfurt. She stu-
died jurisprudence and philosophy at Innsbruck, Graz and Vienna and
received her doctorate in 1950 for a dissertation on the critical reception
of Martin Heidegger's existentialist philosophy. Her first book of poems,
Die gestundete Zeit (Time Deferred), appeared in 1953 and won the
literary prize of the Gruppe '47. In 1959 she became the first person to
hold the chair of poetics at the University of Frankfurt. In the same year
she was awarded the Prize of the War Blind for *Der gute Gott von
Manhattan* (The Good Lord of Manhattan), a radio play. For her
collection of stories *Das dreißigste Jahr* (1961, English translation *The
Thirtieth Year*, 1964), she was awarded the Berlin Critics Prize. She was
inducted into the West Berlin Academy of Arts that same year. She also
received the Georg Büchner Prize (1965), and the Austrian National
Medal (1968). After nearly two decades of writing poetry and short
prose, her first novel *Malina* appeared in 1971. She had stopped writing
poetry years before this publication and was often asked in interviews
what prompted her to move entirely to fiction. Her entire output of
poetry was two slim volumes. In 1973 she died as a result of a fire in her
Rome apartment. In 1978 a complete edition of her work was published
in Germany.

The metaphorical richness of much of Bachmann's earlier verse,
represented here in the utopian vision of 'Safe-Conduct', contrasts
quite sharply with some of her later poetry. There, the syntax seems to
break down, as though the very language were reformulating itself – the
relationship between Celan's work and Bachmann's is worth exploring
in this and other respects. Born close to the border between Carinthia
and Slovenia, Bachmann felt herself also to be on the border of language,
exploring, like Ludwig Wittgenstein, whose influence she acknowledges,
the limits of linguistic expression. And yet even if she is preoccupied with
propelling the language of poetry as far as she or it can go, her poetic
œuvre is an attempt to bring back together the poles of European life, her
North and her South, her German lands and her Italy. From this
attempt, she resurrects a perennial message of harmony – political,
cultural and ecological.

But while Bachmann's last poems must lead into silence, the poet
herself was not silenced. Her non-poetical writings continued in the

more accessible vein that social and political commitment required. After all, in 1963, ten years before her untimely death, she had said in an interview (quoted by Mark Anderson, one of her translators): 'I am not overly fond of poetry and don't read it willingly. In my reading, poems take up a very small place.' We note a similar, if more caustic, distancing from poetry in Tadeusz Różewicz (see Appendix 8); it is as if poetry, in the post-Auschwitz world, had been set a task which in the nature of things could not be accomplished. Poetry measures us by not measuring up. The limitations of the enterprise are severe, yet in spite of what Bachmann has intimated, the attempt has to be made. Whatever can be done, must be done, and in the end there is much healing energy in Bachmann's anguished *œuvre*.

EVERY DAY

War is no longer declared,
but simply continued. The unheard of
has become the everyday. The hero
keeps clear of battles. The weak
are pushed to the front-lines.
The uniform of the day is patience,
the decoration the paltry star
of hope above the heart.

It's awarded
when nothing more happens,
when drum-fire ceases,
when the enemy becomes invisible
and the shadow of eternal armament
covers the sky.

It's awarded
for desertion of flags,
for courage in the face of the friend,
for betraying unworthy secrets
and disregard
of every command.

Daniel Huws

SETTLEMENT

I came into the pasture-ground
after night had fallen
and could smell the earth in the meadows
and the wind, before it stirred.
Love no longer grazed,
the bells had died away,
the grass-tufts languished.

A horn stood out of the ground,
stuck fast by the leader of the herd,
rammed down in the dark.

I pulled it out of the earth,
I raised it to the sky
with all my strength.

To cram this land with sound
I blew the horn,
intending
in the coming wind
and among the swaying grass-stems
to live out every origin.

Daniel Huws

SAFE-CONDUCT

With sleep-drunken birds
and trees shot through by wind
the day gets up and the sea
empties on it a foaming mug.

The rivers flow to the great water,
and the land puts love-promises
in the mouth of the pure air
with fresh flowers.

The earth wants to bear no mushroom clouds,
nor to spew any creature before the sky,
but with anger lightning and rain to abolish
the outrageous voices of destruction.

It wants to see the gaudy brothers
and the grey sisters wake up with us,
the king fish, the royal nightingale
and the fire-prince salamander.

For us it plants coral in the sea.
Woods it commands to be silent,
marble to swell the beautiful vein,
dew to pass over the ash once more.

The earth wants a daily safe-conduct
into the universe out of night,
so that still for all our tomorrows the beauty
of young grace will spring from the old.

Daniel Huws

EXILE

A dead person, I wander
no longer registered anywhere
unknown in the realm of the prefect
supernumerary in the golden cities
and the young-leaved countryside

already long disposed of
and provided with nothing

Only with wind with time and with sound

I who can't live among people

I with the German language
this cloud about me

that I take as a house
float through all languages

Oh how the cloud grows black
dark sounds rain sounds
only a few fall

Then it carries the dead one up into brighter regions.

Daniel Huws

GO, MY THOUGHT

Go, my thought, as long as a word clear enough for flight
is your wing, lifts you and goes
where the light metals sway,
where the air is sharp
in a new understanding,
where weapons speak
of a single kind.
Defend us there!

The wave bore a piece of driftwood high and sinks.
Fever pulled you to its breast, lets you fall.
Faith has moved only a mountain.

Let stand what stands, go, my thought!

Filled with nothing other than our suffering.
Conform to us wholly!

Mark Anderson

YOU WORDS

For Nelly Sachs, poet and friend

You words, come, after me!
And though we've gone a long way,
too long, we must go
on, we'll never reach the end.

The sky isn't getting light.

The word
can only
pull other words behind it,
one sentence another.
So world would like,
finally,
to obtrude itself,
already be said.
Don't say it.

Words, after me,
so that this hunger for words,
statement and counterstatement
– does not become final.

For a while let
none of the senses speak,
let the muscle heart
exercise differently.

Let be, I say, let be.

Not into exalted ears,
nothing, I say, whispered,
no thoughts about death,
let be, and after me, not mild
nor bitterly,
not comforting
without consolation

not designating,
thus not without signs –

And above all not this: the image
in the web of dust, hollow roll
of syllables, last words.

No dying word,
you words!

Mark Anderson

NO DELICACIES

Nothing pleases me anymore.

Should I
dress a metaphor
with an almond blossom?
crucify syntax
on a trick of light?
Who will beat his brains
over such superfluities –

I have learned to be considerate
with the words
that exist
(for the lowest class)

hunger
      disgrace
            tears
and
                  darkness

with unclean sobbing,
with despair
(and I despair even of despair)
of the enormous misery,

the bedridden, the cost of living –
I will get by.

I don't neglect the word
but myself.
The others know
godknows
how to help themselves with words.
I am not my assistant.

Should I
take a thought captive,
lead it into an illuminated sentence cell?
Feed eye and ear
with first-class word tidbits?
Investigate the libido of a vowel,
ascertain the lover's value of our consonants?

Must I,
with this hail-battered head,
with writing cramps in this hand,
under the pressure of three hundred nights,
rip this paper apart,
sweep away the plotted word operas,
destroying thus: I you and he she it

we you?

(Still should. The others should.)

My share, it should be dispersed.

Mark Anderson

TRULY

     For Anna Akhmatova

Whoever has not choked on a word,
and I say unto you,

whoever knows merely how to help himself,
and with words –

there's no helping him.
Not in the short run
and not in the long one.

To make a single sentence tenable,
to endure it in the ding-dong of words.

No one writes this sentence
who doesn't under-write.

Mark Anderson

Johannes Bobrowski GERMANY

JOHANNES BOBROWSKI (1917–1965) was born in Tilsit. His studies in art history in Berlin were interrupted by the war, in which he served on the Eastern front. It was there he began to write poetry. He was a prisoner-of-war in Russia until 1949, when he returned to Germany, living in East Berlin and working as an editor for a publishing house until his sudden death in 1965.

Michael Hamburger has reported that Bobrowski told him he wrote every poem as though it were to be his last (see Hamburger's useful introduction to *Shadow Lands*, 1984). As Hamburger remarks, Bobrowski's poems seemed anomalous. East German poetry was expected to be either 'progressive', or dry and ironical, whereas Bobrowski's was deeply elegiacal, Huchel being the only East German poet whose work in any way resembles his. He became known in West Germany only in 1960, with the appearance of some poems in an anthology devoted to East German poetry. His first book, *Sarmatische Zeit* (Sarmatian Time), appeared in 1960. In 1961 he was awarded the West German Gruppe '47 Prize, the first of a number of such prizes. Between then and his death he wrote two novels and three collections of short prose. *Schatten-land Ströme* (Shadowland Rivers), his second collection of poems, was published in 1962. *Wetterzeichen* (Weathersigns) appeared posthumously, in 1966. Thanks to the dedication of Donald Carroll, who founded a publishing company largely in order to publish Bobrowski in English translation, a collection appeared, also posthumously, in 1966.

Bobrowski seems to test, to invoke shadowy forces from deep within the historical context, in an effort to reintegrate a world that has come apart, to rediscover that which will bind it. Perhaps the dislocation, disjunction, disengagement, is inevitable, an integral component of the poetic language that he deploys with such undoubted lyrical force.

THE LATVIAN AUTUMN

The thicket of deadly nightshade
is open, he steps
into the clearing, the dance

of the hens round the birch-stumps is forgotten, he walks
past the tree round which the herons flew, he has sung
in the meadows.

Oh that the swath of hay,
where he lay in the bright night,
might fly scattered by winds
on the banks –

when the river is no longer awake,
the cloulds above it, voices
of birds, calls:
We shall come no more.

Then I light you your light,
which I cannot see, I placed
my hands above it, close
round the flame, it stood still,
reddish in nothing but night
(like the castle which fell
in ruins over the slope,
like the little winged snake
of light through the river, like the hair
of the Jewish child)
and did not burn me.

Ruth and Matthew Mead

THE VOLGA TOWNS

The stretch of wall.
Towers. The slope of the bank. Once
the wooden bridge broke. Tartar fires moved
through the plains. Night came talking,
a wandering friar with a straggly
beard. The mornings
leapt up, the cisterns
stood full of blood.

Walk about on the stone.
Here in the glassy noon
Minin raised his hand
to shade his eyes. Then shouts
flew up, towards the water, Stenka's
arrival – the Siberians walk
on the bank, up to their waists
in the undergrowth, their
forests follow them.

There
I heard
a human mouth calling:
Come into your house
through the bricked-up door,
fling open the windows
against the sea of light.

Ruth and Matthew Mead

WHEN THE ROOMS

When the rooms are deserted
in which answers are given, when
the walls, and narrow passes fall, shadows
fly out of the trees, when the grass
beneath the feet is abandoned,
white soles tread the wind –

the bush of thorn flames,
I hear its voice,
where no question was, the waters
move, but I do not thirst.

Ruth and Matthew Mead

PLACE OF FIRE

We saw that sky. Blackness
moved on the river, the fires
beat, darkness with trembling
lights stepped forward in front
of the wood on the bank, in animal hide.
We heard
the mouths in the foliage.

That sky stood
unmoved. And was made
of storms and tore us forward,
screaming we saw the earth
ascending with fields and rivers,
forest, the flying fires
benumbed.

The river remained deep. The pungence
of damp grass
rose. The voice of the cricket
lifted behind us, there was
a tree behind us,
the black alder.

We saw the sky that
perished in the darkness, sky
of fields and flying ancient
groves. Steps came
across the marsh, they
stamped out the fires.

Ruth and Matthew Mead

Nina Cassian ROMANIA

NINA CASSIAN (1924–) is a composer as well as a prolific writer of fiction and poetry. She has also translated widely, including works by Shakespeare, Mayakovsky, Brecht, Ritsos, Morgenstern, Celan and Benn, and has herself been translated into many European languages. She has worked as a journalist and editor, and has illustrated her own books for children. In 1982 Nina Cassian won the Bucharest Writers Association award for *De îndurare* (For Mercy), and the following year received an award for *Numărătoarea inversă* (Count Down). Other well-known collections are *Ambitus* (Ambit, 1969), *Cronofagie* (Time Devouring, 1970), *Requiem* (1971) and *O sută de poeme* (One Hundred Poems, 1975). In 1985 she was a visiting professor at New York University, teaching creative writing, and gave readings of her work in New York City. She was a special guest at the PEN Congress of 1986, and the same year was awarded a Yaddo Fellowship and a Fulbright Fellowship to continue her literary projects. She also attended the International Writing Program at the University of Iowa. She is currently living and working in New York.

Nina Cassian is essentially a poet of the everyday, but *her* everyday is so highly charged as to have a mythic, or at least surrealistic, dimension. The surrealism comes with the territory, as well as springing from the Romanian modernist tradition to which she belongs. While not appearing to confront larger social or political issues, as do many of the other poets in the present collection, she nevertheless comes to occupy contiguous ground simply by focusing on her own experience. Her poetry is the purest expression of an existence on the border between literature and experience, too immediate to be reflective in the ordinary sense of the word, yet entirely true to its own intuitions. Cassian's ongoing poetic account of her life has the authenticity of a journal (she has also integrated an actual diary into a large prose chronicle, *Diary of a Diary*, as yet unpublished). Lacking distance, perhaps, this experiential, existential verse, as a totality, possesses an hallucinatory force, projecting the nightmarish outlines of the age. Cassian's strength is that of vulnerability. The endurance needed to survive such emotional openness is of a type fomented by the part of Europe from which she comes and the times through which she has passed. There is humour, passion, spontaneity, imaginative extravagance, but principally – and this sums it all up – there is courage.

GHOST

A rug of dead butterflies at my feet,
dead and limp
(they don't experience rigor mortis).
I, on the other hand, am quite healthy:
I've extracted my liver,
plucked out my lungs,
wrenched out my heart,
and nothing hurts any more.

To become a ghost
is a solution
I weakly recommend.

Christopher Hewitt

I LEFT THOSE WALLS

I left those walls
smeared with my blood –
it was an atrocious massacre.
Now I'm flying over the city
not like a Chagall bride
beside her bridegroom, the violinist,
but like a winged nightmare
with an entire biography of dirty feathers.

I should have left a long time ago,
before being exterminated by solitude,
by the random hatchets of the lumberjacks
who cut down men,
of the cannibals who feast on brains,
I should have –
but who knows the limits of endurance?
We wait, we keep on waiting,
and the days pass, life passes by;
the black worms dig their corridors
in our bones; in our eyes

light's milk gets sour;
our tongue inflates like a scolding mollusc.

But, see, I left that house of massacre,
I am a nightmare-bird now;
everyone hears the beating of my wings,
nobody recognizes me.

Nina Cassian and Naomi Lazard

THE OTHER LIFE

About all these I write freely
but they terrorize me.
I name a seagull
and its shadow covers me,
the shadow of its beak drills through my skull,
a blood shadow trickles down my cheek.
I say 'hunger' or 'good bye',
and 'hunger' drowns my eyes in their sockets,
'hunger' melts my chest and belly,
and as for 'good bye' it tears my love apart,
it opens up my arms,
so that everything falls out.

In writing them, I wanted to free them
but they know only how to seize and devour,
they feel free only when they kill.
They do not believe in the other life of the Poem.

Cristian Andrei and Daniel Weissbort

ORBITS

The orbit I describe in my environment,
cautiously, so as not to strike birds with my forehead,
tables, or the elegant plants, merciless
on their steel armatures;

                    the way I pass, hissing
over the compact waters whose interior maw
is ready to suck me in, near dangerous statues
whose kaleidoscopic eyes are moving
in their empty sockets at certain hours;
the orbit my body follows
through deformed objects which I manage to avoid
despite their unpredictable contours,
my arm in danger every moment
of being ripped from shoulder to the tip of forefinger,
                    the extremity that precedes me,
                    the part that indicates distances;
any moment my hip can be severed;
my orbit continues, that whirligig
whose meaning I used to know, forgot
                    and from time to time remember
when I pass very close to a primordial event –
then I thrill like a carnivorous flower
                    shaken out of indifference
                    when an object touches its petals;
at which time the notions of *beginning, end, right, left,*
forward, backward become perfectly clear to me
for that moment alone;
then my orbit possesses me once more:
my only care is to avoid striking the vertebrae
of the giant saurians who are constantly being exhumed
in vaster and vaster numbers, not to be impaled
on the blue spire of a skyscraper, not to be swallowed
by the wave-functions that crisscross
                    the matrix of the universe:
however, who can tell? – it is possible
that I am immobile and surrounded by orbits,
that the wind which ruffles my hair
is caused by the rapid passage of a flying table,
a statue rushing by – or it is possible
that we are all turning in our orbits
trying to avoid a collision course,
the crash occurring just when an object
loses the instinct of its own nature,
the plant that of a plant,

the wave that of a wave,
the bird that of a bird,
and me – of mine.

Naomi Lazard

THE RABBIT

The rabbit
   who invented that shriek
   to elicit the hunter's compassion
   though neither hunter nor dog
   was ever deterred from
   snatching up his body
   like a fur glove
   warm from recent wearing
The rabbit
   who could only invent that shriek
   (far bolder than his own anatomy)
   to confront Death
The rabbit
   whose excruciating ludicrous shriek
   is his only notion of solemnity

Christopher Hewitt

PART OF A BIRD

Even now my breast bone's aching
when I remember how I was running
because the smell of petunias invaded everything.
Ah, God, how warm it was around
my legs, bare, long and free
and evening fell over the sea,
over a crowd, gathered there, and over
the strange deserted pavilion
where we played and I
didn't even think about my ugly head

and other children hadn't noticed it either
because we were all running too fast instead
so the transparent eagle of evening wouldn't get us
and the hum of adults from the street
and the sea, the sea, which threatened (protected?)
that *fine del primo tempo.*

It was forever summer, a light summer
a summer of water and sandals, immune
to that alcohol, soon to be called Love,
– and in the deserted pavilion (in vain you'd look for it,
it's either been removed with two fingers
from its ring of earth by War, or by some
useful work, or else forgotten)
we were playing childhood, but, in fact,
I can't remember anyone, I don't think
there was another child apart from me,
because, see, I can only remember
a lonely flight into mystery
staged by the gestures of the sea, I remember
only the happiness, oh God, of leaning
with bare arms and legs on warm stones,
of sloping ground, with grass,
of the innocent air of evening.

Flowers smelt dizzily in that place
where, a little above men and women,
who definitely smelt of tobacco,
hot barbecue and beer, I
was running, unaware of my ugly head,
breaking, in fact, the soft head from the flower
and kissing it on the lips
while the sea also smelt more strongly
than now, it was wilder, its seaweed
darker, and cursed the rocks
even more in the way it whipped them.
It wasn't far from home
to that place, I could run there
and back and no one would miss me,
in four steps and eight jumps I was there,

but, first, I stole from fences
feathers of peacocks left between slats,
most beautiful feathers, I've not seen since
with the immense blue green eye
and with golden eyelashes so long
that I was holding a whole bird in my hands
not part of one
and I was tearing at feathers
stuck between slats
tearing at something from the mystery
of those fiendish courtyards
and then I was running toward that deserted pavilion
from the edge of the sea
and I was running round it and through it
through derelict rooms
where mad martins battered themselves against walls,
with the ceiling bursting outside and in, as if within me.

I wore a short sleeveless dress
the colour of sand when sun runs out of strength
and in the autumn I should have gone to school,
and the performance of the sea kept breaking my rib cage
to make me more roomy, that's why
my heart was beating and even now the cage in my chest hurts
at the memory of that beat of the sea
while attempting to enter me
especially at evening when flowers fade
without losing their colour completely,
staying pink with tea, violet with milk,
losing only their stems in the darkness,
floating, beheaded, at a certain height
above the grass which had also vanished.
This is a tremendous memory,
absolutely unforgettable,
the feeling of a light, unchained body,
invulnerable, perfect, my head
just a natural extension of it,
supervising only its speed and orientation.
Yet I never hurt myself,
I can't remember ever having fallen that summer.

I was light, extremely healthy,
inspired, and if I wasn't flying
it was only because I preferred to run on earth
and not for any other reason.

And after that ...
What was I saying? Ah, yes, I had long bare legs
and bare slender arms
and in the deserted pavilion there was this strange coolness
as if an invisible sea had breezed through it ...

And after that ...
– Where was I? Ah, yes, the flowers full of night ...
like sacred smoke
and my lonely flight
through gentle and benevolent mysteries ...

And after that?

Andrea Deletant and Brenda Walker

SAND

My hands creep forward on the hot sand
to unknown destinations;
perhaps to the shoreline,
perhaps to the arms from which they were severed
and which lie on the beach
like two decapitated eels.

Nina Cassian and Naomi Lazard

MORNING EXERCISES

I wake up and say: I'm through.
It's my first thought at dawn.
What a nice way to start the day
with such a murderous thought.

God, take pity on me
– is the second thought, and then
I get out of bed
and live as if
nothing had been said.

Andrea Deletant and Brenda Walker

US TWO

My God, what a dream I had:
the two of us, more passionate than ever,
making love like the first couple on earth …
– and we were so beautiful, naked and wild,
and both dead.

Nina Cassian

CAPITAL PUNISHMENT

I scraped off your smile with nails.
Licked away your eyes. And now
you're nothing but a blank oval, where if I feel like it
I can paint a massacre
or draw a simple flower.
I could even unscrew it – with care –
and leave it lying about close by.

From now on – that's where you start – at the knot in your tie.

Nina Cassian

LIKE ANA*

Once I entered
a house of love with you
and left it fleeing
from misunderstanding,
hating the long street
and starless sky.
Then the first stone fell
on my heart.
Now the building's finished.
No more breathing inside.

Nina Cassian

* Ana was the wife of a master builder in the Romanian legend Mesterul Manole, in which her sacrifice was required to ensure the durability of his building.

Paul Celan

PAUL CELAN (1920–1970), whose given name was Paul Antschel, was born in Czernowitz, Bukovina. His parents were deported by the Nazis in 1942 and did not return. Celan himself barely managed to escape. In 1947 he moved to Vienna, and in 1948 settled permanently in Paris. During the fifties Celan worked as a lecturer at the École Normale Supérieure. His first collection of poems, *Der Sand aus den Urnen* (The Sand from the Urns), was published in 1948. Many of Celan's earlier poems were incorporated into his second collection, *Mohn und Gedächtnis* (Poppy and Memory, 1952). In 1955 he published *Von Schwelle zu Schwelle* (From Threshold to Threshold). He received the prize of the Kulturkreis in Bundesverband der deutschen Industrie in 1957, and a year later the literary prize of the city of Bremen. His fourth collection of poems, *Sprachgitter* (Speech-Grille), appeared in 1959. A piece of prose fiction, *Gespräch in Gebirge* (Conversation in the Mountains), for which he received the Georg Büchner Prize, followed the next year and was to remain his only publication of fiction. In 1961 he published a major essay on poetry and poetics entitled *Der Meridian* (see *The Chicago Review*, No. 2, Winter 1978, for a translation and commentary), this being his Büchner Prize acceptance speech. Many collections followed, including *Die Niemandsrose* (The No-Man's Rose, 1963), *Atemkristall* (Breath-Crystal, 1965), *Atemwende* (Breath-Turn, 1967). In 1968 *Fadensonnen* was published. In 1970, the year Celan committed suicide by drowning, *Lichtzwang* appeared, followed by the posthumous *Schneepart* the next year. Celan was also a notable translator, especially of the Russian poet Osip Mandelstam, for whose work he felt a special affinity.

Celan's is an extraordinarily condensed poetry, much of which, especially the late work, seems hardly to transcend the boundaries of a private code. Yet, so coherent is this code, so cogently constructed, that as one stays with it, so one learns to read it – which is to say, one is transformed, changed, by it. Within the framework not just of a given language, but of German, the language of the murderers, he succeeds, by radically disrupting normal syntactical and lexical practice, in creating a mode of speech consistent with the purposes he had in mind, yet not so specialized as to be utterly inaccessible to the uninitiated, a *tour de force* without precedent in post-war writing. It is difficult to say whether what Celan does with German is regenerative or redemptive – is it proper even to speak of redemption or guilt in this connection? – or whether, in fact, by taking the words, with their inevitably sinister echoes and deploying them like counters in his own desperate game, he is not, through a supreme effort of will, turning his back on the legacy of German, not ignoring it, or hiding from it, but in effect dominating and ultimately nullifying it. Thus, if his work is redemptive, it is redemptive of humanity as a whole. On the other hand, its relationship to the language in which it is written is particularly involved and intimate. To translate it out of that language is to orphan it, even if its parentage is already profoundly ambiguous, even more radically than is usually the case in translation. The demands made on the readers of these translations are inevitably that much greater. Or perhaps Celan's is only the start of a still larger and more complex enterprise, which was beyond his powers – as it would be beyond the powers of any single individual – to complete.

A number of articles are listed in the bibliography. Particular attention is drawn to John Felstiner's several articles on translating him, which examine the peculiar recalcitrance of his poetry, leading in the case of 'Death Fugue', for instance, to the translation of the poem, at certain crucial points, *back* into German, in an almost sacramental completion of the translational circle.

DEATHFUGUE

Black milk of daybreak we drink it at evening
we drink it at midday and morning we drink it at night
we drink and we drink
we shovel a grave in the air there you won't feel too cramped
A man lives in the house he plays with his vipers he writes
he writes when it grows dark to Deutschland your golden hair
    Marguerite
he writes it and steps out of doors and the stars are all sparkling he
    whistles his hounds to come close
he whistles his Jews into rows has them shovel a grave in the
    ground
he orders us strike up and play for the dance

Black milk of daybreak we drink you at night
we drink you at morning and midday we drink you at evening
we drink and we drink
A man lives in the house he plays with his vipers he writes
he writes when it grows dark to Deutschland your golden hair
    Marguerite
your ashen hair Shulamith we shovel a grave in the sky there you
    won't feel too cramped
He shouts jab the earth deeper you there you others sing up and
    play
he grabs for the rod in his belt he swings it his eyes are blue
jab your spades deeper you there you others play on for the dance

Black milk of daybreak we drink you at night
we drink you at midday and morning we drink you at evening
we drink and we drink
a man lives in the house your goldenes Haar Marguerite
your aschenes Haar Shulamith he plays with his vipers
He shouts play death more sweetly Death is a master from
    Deutschland
he shouts scrape your strings darker you'll rise then in smoke to the
    sky
you'll have a grave then in the clouds there you won't feel too
    cramped

Black milk of daybreak we drink you at night
we drink you at midday Death is a master aus Deutschland
we drink you at evening and morning we drink and we drink
Death is ein Meister aus Deutschland his eye is blue
he shoots you with shot made of lead shoots you level and true
a man lives in the house your goldenes Haar Margarete
he looses his hounds on us grants us a grave in the air
he plays with his vipers and daydreams der Tod ist ein Meister aus
    Deutschland

dein goldenes Haar Margarete
dein aschenes Haar Sulamith

John Felstiner

ASPEN TREE, your leaves glance white into the dark.
My mother's hair was never white.

Dandelion, so green is the Ukraine.
My yellow-haired mother did not come home.

Rain cloud, above the well do you hover?
My quiet mother weeps for everyone.

Round star, you wind the golden loop.
My mother's heart was ripped by lead.

Oaken door, who lifted you off your hinges?
My gentle mother cannot return.

Michael Hamburger

CORONA

Autumn eats its leaf out of my hand: we are friends.
From the nuts we shell time and we teach it to walk:
then time returns to the shell.

In the mirror it's Sunday,
in dream there is room for sleeping,
our mouths speak the truth.

My eye moves down to the sex of my loved one:
we look at each other,
we exchange dark words,
we love each other like poppy and recollection,
we sleep like wine in the conches,
like the sea in the moon's blood ray.

We stand by the window embracing, and people look up from the
    street:
it is time they knew!
It is time the stone made an effort to flower,

time unrest had a beating heart.
It is time it were time.

It is time.

Michael Hamburger

TENEBRAE

We are near, Lord,
near and at hand.

Handled already, Lord,
clawed and clawing as though
the body of each of us were
your body, Lord.

Pray, Lord,
pray to us,
we are near.

Wind-awry we went there,
went there to bend
over hollow and ditch.

To be watered we went there, Lord.

It was blood, it was
what you shed, Lord.

It gleamed.

It cast your image into our eyes, Lord.
Our eyes and our mouths are so open and empty, Lord.
We have drunk, Lord.
The blood and the image that was in the blood, Lord.

Pray, Lord.
We are near.

Michael Hamburger

THERE WAS EARTH INSIDE THEM, and
they dug.

They dug and they dug, so their day
went by for them, their night. And they did not praise God,
who, so they heard, wanted all this,
who, so they heard, knew all this.

They dug and heard nothing more;
they did not grow wise, invented no song,
thought up for themselves no language.
They dug.

There came a stillness, and there came a storm,
and all the oceans came.
I dig, you dig, and the worm digs too,
and that singing out there says: They dig.

O one, o none, o no one, o you:
Where did the way lead when it led nowhere?
O you dig and I dig, and I dig towards you,
and on our finger the ring awakes.

Michael Hamburger

PSALM

No one kneads us again out of earth and clay,
no one conjures our dust.
No One.

Blessed art thou, No One.
In thy sight would

we bloom.
In thy
spite.

A nothing
we were, are now, and ever
shall be, blooming:
the nothing-, the
No-One's-Rose.

With
our pistil soul-bright,
our stamen heaven-waste,
our corona red
from the purpleword we sang
over, oh over
the thorn.

John Felstiner

MANDORLA

In the almond – what dwells in the almond?
Nothing.
What dwells in the almond is Nothing.
There it dwells and dwells.

In Nothing – what dwells there? The King.
There the King dwells, the King.
There he dwells and dwells.

     Jew's curl, you'll not turn grey.

And your eye – on what does your eye dwell?
On the almond your eye dwells.
Your eye, on Nothing it dwells.
Dwells on the King, to him remains loyal, true.
So it dwells and dwells.

Human curl, you'll not turn grey.
Empty almond, royal-blue.

Michael Hamburger

I HEAR THAT THE AXE HAS FLOWERED,
I hear that the place can't be named,

I hear that the bread which looks at him
heals the hanged man,
the bread baked for him by his wife,

I hear that they call life
our only refuge.

Michael Hamburger

LARGO

You of the same mind, moor-wandering near one:

more-than-
death-
sized we lie
together, autumn
crocus, the timeless, teems
under our breathing eyelids,

the pair of blackbirds hangs
beside us, under
our whitely drifting
companions up there, our

meta-
stases.

Michael Hamburger

A LEAF, treeless
for Bertolt Brecht:

What times are these
when a conversation
is almost a crime
because it includes
so much made explicit?

Michael Hamburger

NOTHINGNESS, for the
sake of our names
– they gather us in –,
sets its seal,

the end believes us
the beginning,

in front of
masters going
mute around us,
all things unsundered, in witness
comes a clammy
brightness.

John Felstiner

Hans Magnus Enzensberger   GERMANY

HANS MAGNUS ENZENSBERGER (1929–) was born in Kaufbeuren. He studied languages, literature and philosophy at three German universities and at the Sorbonne, and was active in student theatre. After receiving his doctorate, he worked in radio for several years. Since then he has lived both in Germany and abroad, in Europe, the United States, Mexico and Cuba, but has spent much of his time in Frankfurt and Munich. In 1965 Enzensberger founded the journal *Kursbuch*, which became an important political and literary forum for critical and artistic debates. As one of the most influential political and social essayists of post-war Germany, he remained its editor until 1975. Enzensberger has received several prizes, among them the prize of the German Critics Guild (1962) and the Georg Büchner Prize (1963), and has long been a member of the Gruppe '47. He is fluent in several European languages and has also translated widely, including works by William Carlos Williams, César Vallejo and Pablo Neruda.

Enzensberger (rather like Harold Pinter) makes effective use of contemporary jargon, advertising slogans, and political rhetoric. His tone tends often to be angry, slangy and satirical. It is our disposable world, disabused, illusionless, that is targeted. The trappings, rewards, honours offered by post-war society are subjected to a taunting, mocking attack. It is not that we do not understand or *know*, it is just that somehow we lack the volition to challenge injustice or oppression. Instead, a narrow, purely personal will to survive (possibly a legacy from the camps?) prevails – every man for himself. We use language, quite self-consciously, to convince ourselves that there is nothing we can do to change things. We seek consolation, soothe our consciences, by asserting that we are realists (each his own *real*politican), that the traditional virtues are no longer any concern of ours. This seems, if anything, the greater delusion, the greater dishonesty, and it is Enzensberger's principal subject. His contempt for consumerism, for a mass culture that caters to the lowest common denominator, uniting us only in a primitively opportunistic manner, so that like Gadarene swine we join in a mad, self-annihilating rush, is expressed in biting terms. A radical who is sceptical of the radical tradition, Enzensberger has lived too close to the centre of political events to be taken in. Yet he remains committed to change, even if sometimes (as in the conclusion to 'The Sinking of the Titanic') he appears to despair and to question the very point of his own survival.

FOR A SENIOR COLLEGE TEXTBOOK

don't read odes, boy, timetables
are more exact. unroll the sea-charts
before it is too late. be on your guard. don't sing.
the day will come when they paste upon the door
new blacklists and brand their mark on those who answer no.
learn to pass unrecognized, to change quarters,
identity and face: you'll need to more than i did.
become adept at minor treason,
the sordid daily escape. the encyclicals
will do to make a fire, manifestos
to wrap up butter and salt
for the defenceless. anger and endurance
are necessary to blow into the lungs of power
the deadly powder, ground fine
by such as you, who have learnt much
and are fastidious in their ways.

Eva Hesse

LAST WILL AND TESTAMENT

get your flag out of my face, it tickles!
bury my cat inside, bury her over there,
where my chromatic garden used to be!

and get that tinny wreath off my chest, it's rattling too much;
toss it over with the statues on the garbage heap,
and give the ribbon to some biddies to doll themselves up with.

say your prayers over the telephone, but first cut the wires,
or wrap them up in a handkerchief full of bread crumbs
for the stupid fish in the puddles.

let the bishop stay at home and get plastered
give him a barrel of rum,
he's going to be dry from the sermon.

and get off my back with your tombstones and stovepipe hats!
use the fancy marble to pave an alley where nobody lives,
an alley for pigeons.

my suitcase is full of scribbled pieces of paper for my little cousin,
who can fold them into airplanes, fancy ones for sailing off the
    bridge
so they drown in the river.

anything that's left (a pair of drawers a lighter a fancy birthstone
and an alarm clock) i want you to give to callisthenes the junk man
and toss in a fat tip.

as for the resurrection of the flesh however and life everlasting
i will, if it's all the same to you, take care of that on my own;
it's my affair, after all. live and be well!

there's a couple of butts left on the dresser.

Jerome Rothenberg

SONG FOR THOSE WHO KNOW

something must be done right away
that much we know
but of course it's too soon to act
but of course it's too late in the day
oh we know

we know that we're really rather well off
and that we'll go on like this
and that it's not much use anyway
oh we know

we know that we are to blame
and that it's not our fault if we are to blame
and that we're to blame for the fact that it's not our fault
and that we're fed up with it
oh we know

and that maybe it would be a good idea to keep our mouths shut
and that we won't keep our mouths shut all the same
oh we know oh we know

and we also know that we can't help anybody really
and that nobody really can help us
and that we're extremely gifted and brilliant
and free to choose between nothing and naught
and that we must analyse this problem very carefully
and that we take two lumps of sugar in our tea
oh we know

we know all about oppression
and that we are very much against it
and that cigarettes have gone up again
oh we know

we know very well that the nation is heading for real trouble
and that our forecasts have usually been dead right
and that they are not of any use
and that all this is just talk
oh we know

that it's just not good enough to live things down
and that we are going to live them down all the same
oh we know oh we know

that there is nothing new in all this
and that life is wonderful
and that's all there is to it
oh we know all this perfectly well

and that we know all this perfectly well
oh we know that too
oh we know it
oh we know

Hans Magnus Enzensberger

PORTRAIT OF A HOUSE DETECTIVE

he lolls in the supermarket
under the plastic sun,
the white patches on his face
are rage, not consumption,
a hundred packets of crispy crackers
(*because they're so nourishing*)
he sets ablaze with his eyes,
a piece of margarine
(the same brand as mine:
goldlux, because it's so delicious)
he picks up with his moist hand
and squeezes it till it drips.

he's twenty-nine,
idealistic,
sleeps badly and alone
with pamphlets and blackheads,
hates the boss and the supermarket,
communists, women,
landlords, himself
and his bitten fingernails
full of margarine (*because
it's so delicious*), under
his arty hairstyle mutters
to himself like a pensioner.

that one
will never get anywhere.
wittler, i think, he's called,
wittler, hittler, or something like that.

Michael Hamburger

POEM ABOUT THE FUTURE

two men appear on a tractor
(chou en lai is in moscow)
two men in stone-grey overalls
(nobel prize winners in evening dress)
two men with slender sticks
(gold medals from tokyo)
at the wayside amid yellow leaves
(the dead guerillas of vietnam)

among the clay-yellow leaves
two men in grey overalls
put up slender sticks at the wayside
one left one right every fifty paces
dark sticks in bright november
(chou en lai is in moscow)

two men in grey overalls
scent in the shallow november light
the snow that will cover
leaves and men

till no way is to be seen
only at every fiftieth pace
a slender stick on the left
a slender stick on the right
so that the snow-plough
will find a way
where no way is to be seen

Michael Hamburger

VENDING MACHINE

he puts four dimes into the slot
he gets himself some cigarettes

he gets cancer
he gets apartheid
he gets the king of greece
federal tax state tax sales tax and excise
he gets machine guns and surplus value
free enterprise and positivism
he gets a big lift big business big girls
the big stick the great society the big bang
the big puke
king size extra size super size

he gets more and more
for his four dimes
but for a moment all the things he is getting himself
disappear

even the cigarettes

he looks at the vending machine
but he doesn't see it
he sees himself
for a fleeting moment
and he almost looks like a man

then very soon he is gone again
with a little click
there are his cigarettes

he has disappeared
it was just a fleeting moment
some kind of sudden bliss

he has disappeared
he is gone
buried under all the stuff he has gotten
for his four dimes

Hans Magnus Enzensberger

From *The Sinking of the Titanic*

THE REPRIEVE

Watching the famous eruption of a volcano on Heimaey, Iceland,
which was broadcast live by any number of TV teams,
I saw an elderly man in braces showered by sulfur and brimstone,
ignoring the storm, the heat, the video cables, the ash
and the spectators (including myself, crouching on my carpet
in front of the livid screen), who held a garden hose,
slender but clearly visible, aimed at the roaring lava,
until neighbors joined him, soldiers, children, firemen,
pointing more and more hoses at the advancing fiery lava
and turning it into a towering wall, higher and higher,
of lava, hard, cold and wet, the color of ash, and thus postponing,
not forever perhaps, but for the time being at least,
the Decline of Western Civilization, which is why
the people of Heimaey, unless they have died since,
continue to dwell unmolested by cameras
in their dapper white wooden houses,
calmly watering in the afternoon
the lettuce in their gardens, which, thanks to the blackened soil,
has grown simply enormous, and for the time being at least,
fails to show any signs of impending disaster.

SIXTEENTH CANTO

The sinking of the *Titanic* proceeds according to plan.
It is copyrighted.
It is 100% tax-deductible.
It is a lucky bag for poets.
It is further proof that the teachings of Vladimir I. Lenin are
    correct.
It will run next Sunday on Channel One as a spectator sport.
It is priceless.
It is inevitable.
It is better than nothing.
It closes down in July for holidays.
It is ecologically sound.

It shows the way to a better future.
It is Art.
It creates new jobs.
It is beginning to get on our nerves.
It has a solid working-class basis.
It arrives in the nick of time.
It works.
It is a breathtaking spectacle.
It ought to remind those in charge of their responsibility.
It isn't anymore what it used to be.

TWENTY-NINTH CANTO

What were we talking about? Ah yes, the end!
There was a time when we still believed in it
(What do you mean by 'we'?), as if anything
ever were to founder for good, to vanish
without a shadow,
to be abolished once and for all,
without leaving the usual traces,
the famous Relics from the Past –

a curious kind of confidence!
We believed in some sort of end then
(What do you mean by 'then'? 1912? 1917? '45? '68?)
and hence in some sort of beginning.
By now we have come to realize
that the dinner is going on.

Roast Turkey, Cranberry Sauce
Boiled Rice
Prime Roast Beef
Baked Potatoes with Cream
Watercress Salad
Champagne Jelly   Coconut Sandwich
Viennese Ice Cake
Assorted Nuts   Fresh Fruit
Cheese   Biscuits
Coffee

Not even the eight hundred crates of shelled walnuts,
the five grand pianos, the thirty cases
of rackets and gold clubs for Mr Spaulding,
last seen at 42 degrees 3 minutes North
and 49 degrees 9 minutes West,
have been lost for all times:
here, before our eyes, they are bobbing up again
(What do you mean by 'here'?), 65 years after the fact –

Bottled messages, and no end to the end!
All our love, scribbled down
on a cardboard box before drowning,
menus fished from the high seas,
picture postcards, the paper soaked,
the ink blurred with wine, with tears, with brine,
signs of life, hard to decipher, hard to get rid of –

Not to mention the Final Reports
of the competent Courts of Inquiry,
the expert opinions, pamphlets and memoirs,
and the Transactions of the Royal Commission,
twenty-five thousand pages
read by no one –

Relics, souvenirs for the disaster freaks,
food for collectors lurking at auctions
and sniffing out attics.
That April night's menu
has been reprinted in full facsimile,
and every month there is a new issue
of the *Titanic Commutator*, Official Organ
of the Society for the Investigation of Catastrophe –

Plans to lift the wreck by means of divers,
by gas balloons or by submarines,
The Original *Titanic* Model Set,
· plastic, washable, one yard long,
copyright Entex Industries, Inc.,
$29.80 postpaid, a money order,

from Edward Kamuda, 285 Oak Street, Indian Orchard, Mass.
Full return privileges guaranteed!

True, the reproduction of a lifeboat
does not save anybody, the difference
between a life jacket and the word *life jacket*
makes the difference between survival and death –

But the dinner is going on regardless,
the text is going on, the sea gulls
follow the ship to the very end.
Let us stop counting on the end! After all,
we take no account of the fact
that our days are counted.

Something always remains –
bottles, planks, deck chairs, crutches,
splintered mastheads–
debris left behind,
a vortex of words,
cantos, lies, relics –
breakage, all of it,
dancing and tumbling
after us on the water.

THIRTY-THIRD CANTO

Soaked to the skin I peer through the drizzle, and I perceive
my fellow beings clutching wet trunks, leaning against the wind.
Dimly I see their livid faces, blurred by the slanting rain.
I don't think it is Second Sight. It must be the weather.
They are right on the brink. I warn them. I cry, for instance, Watch
    out!
There's the brink! You are treading slippery ground, ladies and
    gentlemen!
But they just give me a feeble smile, and gallantly they retort: Same
    to you!
I ask myself, is it just a matter of a few dozen passengers,

or do I watch the whole human race over there, haphazardly
hanging on to some run-down cruise liner, fit for the scrapyard
and headed for self-destruction? I cannot be sure. I am dripping
    wet
and I listen. It is hard to say who the seafarers over there
may be, each of them clutching a suitcase,
a leek-green talisman, a dinosaur, or a laurel wreath.

I hear their feeble laughs, and I shout at them unintelligible words.
The unknown man covering his head with sodden newspapers
is presumably K., an itinerant biscuit salesman;
I've no idea who the man with the beard is; the one with the
    maulstick
is a painter called Salomon P.; the lady who sneezes incessantly
must be Marilyn Monroe, while the gentleman clad in white,
holding a manuscript wrapped in black oilcloth, is undoubtedly
    Dante.
These people are filled to the brim with hope and with criminal
    energy.
In the downpour they keep their dinosaurs on the leash,
they open their suitcases and lock them again,
chanting in unison: 'The world will end on May thirteen /
We die / and that is awfully mean.' Hard to say
who is laughing here, who pays attention to me and who doesn't
in this steam bath around me, and how close we are to the brink.

I can see my fellow beings going down very gradually, and I call out
to them and explain: I can see you going down very gradually.
There is no reply. On distant charter cruises there are orchestras
playing feebly but gallantly. I deplore all this very much, I do not
    like
the way they all die, soaked to the skin, in the drizzle, it is
a pity, I am severely tempted to wail. 'The Doomsday year,' I wail,
'is not yet clear / so let's have / so let's have / another beer.'

But where have the dinosaurs gone? And where do all these sodden
    trunks
come from, thousands and thousands of them drifting by,
utterly empty and abandoned to the waves? I wail and I swim.

Business, I wail, as usual, everything lurching, everything
under control, everything O.K., my fellow beings probably
    drowned
in the drizzle, a pity, never mind, I bewail them, so what?
Dimly, hard to say why, I continue to wail, and to swim.

Hans Magnus Enzensberger

Jerzy Ficowski POLAND

JERZY FICOWSKI (1924–) served in the Polish army at the outset of World War Two. He wrote and translated poetry, but frequently found his work banned in Poland during and after the Stalin years. Ficowski has translated Spanish poetry, Jewish popular writings, and is also an expert on gypsy folklore (the fate, for instance, of the gypsies of Czechoslovakia during the war has been a preoccupation of his), and an ethnographer. He has edited the works of the Jewish–Polish novelist Bruno Schultz, murdered in a wartime ghetto.

Ficowski writes a barer poetry, with a narrower range, than that of his contemporary and friend Zbigniew Herbert. He remains stubbornly concerned with the victims of World War Two, with rendering the extremity of their situation. Herbert puts it well and succinctly in his foreword to the slim collection of Ficowski's work, *A Reading of Ashes*, which appeared in England in 1981: 'It seems to me that Ficowski's muse is Mnemosyne, or, expressed more simply, memory. We are bitterly aware that no writing, however moving and noble, can save the world, or even a single human being. From that drawback one should arrive at a positive conclusion, that no power, no tribunal can absolve us from condemning a crime and speaking on behalf of the victims.' Paradoxically, as Herbert suggests, strength seems to be drawn from the acknowledgement of impotence. Through remembering, and not just remembering but also finding, the approximate means of embodying that memory, Ficowski tries to satisfy his 'sense of responsibility for the collective duty, and assume a duty of bearing witness to truth' (Herbert's words again). In 'Cogito Ergo', printed below, a complex compliment to Zbigniew Herbert, it is as though the silence itself is learning to speak.

I DID NOT MANAGE TO SAVE …

I did not manage to save
a single life

I did not know how to stop
a single bullet

and I wander round cemeteries
which are not there
I look for words
which are not there
I run

to help where no one called
to rescue after the event

I want to be on time
even if I am too late

Keith Bosley and Krystyna Wandycz

THE SEVEN WORDS

> *'Mummy! But I've been good! It's dark!' – words of a child*
> *being shut in a gas chamber at Bełżec in 1942, according to the*
> *statement of the only surviving prisoner; quoted in Rudolf*
> *Reder*, Bełżec (1946)

Everything was put to use
everyone perished but nothing was lost
a mound of hair fallen from heads
for a hamburg mattress factory
gold teeth pulled out
under the anaesthetic of death

Everything was put to use
a use was found even for that voice
smuggled this far in the bottom of another's memory
like lime unslaked with tears

and bełżec opens sometimes right to the bone
and everlasting darkness bursts from it
how to contain it

and the protest of a child who was who was
though memory pales
not from horror
this is how it has paled for thirty years

And silences by the million are silent
transformed into a seven-figure sign
And one vacant place is calling calling

Who are not afraid of me
for I am small and not here at all
do not deny me
give me back the memory of me
these post-Jewish words
these post-human words
just these seven words

Keith Bosley and Krystyna Wandycz

BOTH YOUR MOTHERS

For Bieta

Under a futile Torah
under an imprisoned star
your mother gave birth to you

you have proof of her
beyond doubt and death
the scar of the navel
the sign of parting for ever
which had no time to hurt you

this you know

Later you slept in a bundle
carried out of the ghetto
someone said in a chest
knocked together somewhere in Nowolipie Street
with a hole to let in air
but not fear
hidden in a cartload of bricks

You slipped out in this little coffin
redeemed by stealth

from that world to this world
all the way to the Aryan side
and fire took over
the corner you left vacant

So you did not cry
crying could have meant death
luminal hummed you
its lullaby
And you nearly were not
so that you could be

But the mother
who was saved in you
could now step into crowded death
happily incomplete
could instead of memory give you
for a parting gift
her own likeness
and a date and a name

so much

And at once a chance
someone hastily
bustled about your sleep
and then stayed for a long always
and washed you of orphanhood
and swaddled you in love
and became the answer
to your first word

That was how
both your mothers taught you
not to be surprised at all
when you say
I am

Keith Bosley and Krystyna Wandycz

OVID TWICE EXILED

so he was exiled from rome
and long in the barbarous lands of tomis
shackled to the horizon
he knew how to keep up the pace
wandering along any paths of necessity
and didn't stumble over a blade of grass
on his way to a meeting with the yoke

then he repented on a level road
became a two-time exile
eo modo drove out
of himself
ovid

he also sang of a fish which
is voluntarily silent
and envied the cricket
who is audible
ever further and further
from the house at sulmo
for the more accurately he made his way to it
the more unerringly
he went in the opposite direction

thus twice exiled
wherever he found himself
he could no longer find himself

Frank J. Corliss Jr and Grazyna Sandel

COGITO ERGO*

I think therefore I am not
in the forum   My address

* Besides the obvious reference to Descartes, a more immediate reference is to
the cycle of poetry, *Pan Cogito* (1974), by Zbigniew Herbert. Pan Cogito is a
humorously befuddled Everyman who is nevertheless called upon by the exigen-
cies of our times to live up to his heroic past and be true to his calling as a man.

has been confiscated   I say
yes that's me still me   I recognize
What do you hear? Same old story
the silence is heard ever more quietly
under the direction of transistors
and very happy carnivals
Silence has high blood pressure
each drop in it bleeds
it has the right to speak for me
it measures me
this is my *res* because public
I'm learning to sound it out
this mute Polish
an arsenal succinctly silent
for me for you
for the time

Frank J. Corliss Jr and Grazyna Sandel

PAWIAK 1943

It was exactly eleven
steps from wall to wall
in the Pawiak Prison*
from to from to
wall wall wall wall
and eleven and back again

I walked this

till today
for so many cramped years
if I set out
then I begin
with the twelfth step

Frank J. Corliss Jr and Grazyna Sandel

* Pawiak was the Nazi prison in Warsaw, now a war memorial and museum.

Zbigniew Herbert   POLAND

ZBIGNIEW HERBERT (1924–) was born in Lwów. He studied law and philosophy in Warsaw, Cracow and Toruń. Although some of his earlier poems appeared in magazines, his first collection, *Struna światła* (A Chord of Light), could not be published until after Stalin's death, in 1956. In 1957 he published a second volume, *Hermes, pies i gwiazda* (Hermes, Dog and Star). *Studium przedmiotu* (A Study of the Object) was published in 1961. In 1974 a new book of poems, *Pan Cogito* (Mr Cogito) appeared. Herbert is also a notable essayist on art-historical themes and has written plays for radio. His poetry has been translated into many languages, and he has given readings and lived in various parts of Europe and in the United States.

It is tempting to compare the poetry of Zbigniew Herbert and Tadeusz Różewicz, invidious as such comparisons generally are. But since it was Różewicz who was among the very first East European poets to make a significant impact in the West after the war (partly, no doubt, on account of his singleminded concentration on the fundamental dilemma of survival), some observers, including the present writer, were a little dubious about Herbert, with his larger variety and thematic range. There was an odd reluctance to acknowledge the versatility, the universality, of his achievement, even if one was also repeatedly being won over by his lucidity and the power of his vision.

The foundations that Herbert laid in the fifties and sixties have permitted him to continue developing into the seventies and eighties (which, it seems, has not been possible, at least in poetry, for Różewicz). Herbert, thus, is as relevant now as he was earlier on, indeed even more so, since his work now has depth, in terms of his own achievement as a writer, as well as because he has continued to draw, however idiosyncratically or ambivalently, on the Western cultural heritage. The balance between personal involvement and commitment to humanistic values (individual dignity, freedom), between the determination or need to bear witness and a larger historical-cultural vision, have been preserved. But I think it is too facile to explain this in terms of detachment, or even irony, though irony, of course, enters into it. On the contrary, I believe it to be a measure of Herbert's toughness, that he has been able to remain *un*detached for so long. There is also the precision, objectivity, concreteness of his work (not the kind of object-centredness sought by the New

Novelists of post-war France), which runs the whole gamut from description of things to evocation of distant epochs. He does not – as he himself intimates in the interview printed here (see Appendix 3) – try to escape into history, into the past, or into some theoretical construct. History for him (as for Amichai, for instance, though Amichai's historical vision is more personal or intimate) is eternally present. One is put in mind of Eliot too (and of Pound); but the integration of this material into Herbert's work – the historical circumstances, of course, being different – is more complete or structural, since the crisis he faced was so much more acute. Whereas the Western poets, as A. Alvarez puts it in his introduction to the *Selected Poems of Zbigniew Herbert* (1968), 'create worlds which are autonomous, internalized, completely in their own heads, Herbert's is continually exposed to the impersonal, external pressures of politics and history'. Though Alvarez was here contrasting Herbert's type of poetry with that of, say, a Robert Lowell, 'deliberately exploring the realm of breakdown and madness', there is a sense in which, paradoxically, Eliot's cultural-historical preoccupations too were drawn from his own head. The idea of an objective correlative implies a conscious, almost deliberate, or arbitrary, effort to reach outside oneself for what with Herbert was already pressing on, invading, his inner space. To exchange one rather crude metaphor for another, it is as if the historical experience to which Herbert has been exposed has simultaneously shed light on the entire Western historical tradition, revealing, as never before, its fatal singleness and consistency. Herbert simply describes – in striking detail – what is presented to him. For these and other reasons, it has been exceptionally difficult to keep this selection of his poetry within the necessary bounds.

THE LONGOBARDS

An immense coldness from the Longobards
They sit tightly in the saddle of a pass as in abrupt chairs
In their left hand they hold auroras
In their right hand a whip and they lash glaciers beasts of burden
The crackling of fire the ash of stars the swing of a stirrup
Under their nails under eyelids
Nubs of alien blood are black and hard like flint
The burning of firs the barking of a horse the ash

On the crags they hang a snake beside a shield
Upright they march from the north sleepless
Nearly blind the women near the fires are rocking red children

An immense coldness from the Longobards
Their shadow sears the grass when they descend into the valley
Shouting their protracted nothing nothing nothing

Czesław Miłosz

From *Reconstruction of a Poet*
(A RADIO PLAY)

HOMER: Poetry is a shout. Do you know what remains of a poem when you remove the clamour?
ELPENOR: No.
HOMER: Nothing.

*   *   *

PROFESSOR: Beside Anonyn of Miletus, Anonym of Milo is a dwarf beside a giant
   water drips from a tap
... unimportant and common topics. Anonym does not shrink from devoting a poem to a tamarisk, a common plant, prolific and useless.

HOMER: I told of battles
          towers and ships
          butchered heroes
          and butchering heroes
          but I forgot one thing.
          I told of a sea storm
          collapse of walls
          corn on fire
          and hills overturned
          but I forgot the tamarisk

       when he lies
       pierced with a spear

the mouth of his wound
closes up
he sees not
the sea
the city
nor friend
he sees
near to his face
a tamarisk

he ascends
to the uppermost
dry twig of the tamarisk
and avoiding
brown and green leaves
tries to
soar into the sky

without wings
without blood
without thought
without –

PROFESSOR: The insignificance of theme goes hand in hand with degeneration of form.

*　　　*　　　*

HOMER: . . . In darkness and in silence my body was ripening. It was like the earth in the spring, full of unforeseeable possibilities. A new tactile covering was growing over my skin. I began to discover myself, to investigate and to describe.

To begin with I shall describe myself
starting from my head
or better still from my leg
to be exact from my left leg

or from my hand
from the little finger of my left hand

my little finger
is warm
slightly bent towards the middle
ending in a nail

It consists of three sections
it grows directly from the palm
if it were separated from it
it would be quite a large worm

it is a special finger
the only left-hand little finger in the world
given to me directly
other left-hand little fingers
are cold abstractions

with mine
we have a common date of birth
a common date of death
and a common loneliness

only my blood
beating out dark tautologies
fastens the distant shores
with the thread of existence.

Very carefully, I began to investigate the world. Everything which I had known about it until then was useless. Like scenery from a different play. I had to perceive everything anew, beginning not with Troy, not with Achilles, but with a sandal, with a buckle of the sandal, with a stone kicked carelessly on a path.

A stone is a creature
of perfection
equal to itself
observing its limits
filled accurately
with stony meaning

with a smell unlike anything else
scares nothing awakens no desires

its zeal and coolness
are right and full of dignity

I feel a great reproach
when I hold it in my hand
and to its noble body
penetrates a false warmth

Stones cannot be tamed
they will look at us till the end
with a brilliant steady eye.

I shall never go back to Miletus. That's where my shout has stayed. It could catch me in some dark alley and kill me.

between the shout of birth
and the shout of death
look intensely at your nails
at a sunset
at a fish tail
and what you will see
do not take to market
do not sell at reduced prices
do not shout

the gods like lovers
like enormous silence

between the clamour of the beginning
and the clamour of the end
be like an untouched lyre
which has no voice
yet has all

This is only the beginning. The beginning is always ridiculous. I am sitting on the lowest step of the Temple of Zeus the Miraculous and I praise a little finger, a tamarisk, stones.

I have neither disciples nor listeners. Everybody is still overawed by the great fire of the epic. But it is dying. Soon there will be nothing but charred remains which will be overwhelmed by grass. I am the grass.

Sometimes I think I may be able with new poems to inspire new people, who will not add metal to metal, shout to shout, fear to fear. But instead, grain to grain, leaf to leaf, feeling to feeling. And word to silence.

Magdalena Czajkowska

AT THE GATE OF THE VALLEY

After the rain of stars
on the meadow of ashes
they all have gathered under the guard of angels

from a hill that survived
the eye embraces
the whole lowing two-legged herd

in truth they are not many
counting even those who will come
from chronicles fables and the lives of the saints

but enough of these remarks
let us lift our eyes
to the throat of the valley
from which comes a shout

after a loud whisper of explosion
after a loud whisper of silence
this voice resounds like a spring of living water
it is we are told
a cry of mothers from whom children are taken
since as it turns out
we shall be saved each one alone

the guardian angels are unmoved
and let us grant they have a hard job

she begs
– hide me in your eye
in the palm of your hand in your arms
we have always been together
you can't abandon me
now when I am dead and need tenderness

a higher ranking angel
with a smile explains the misunderstanding

an old woman carries
the corpse of a canary
(all the animals died a little earlier)
he was so nice – she says weeping
he understood everything
and when I said to him –
her voice is lost in the general noise

even a lumberjack
whom one would never suspect of such things
an old bowed fellow
catches to his breast an axe
– all my life she was mine
she will be mine here too
she nourished me there
she will nourish me here
nobody has the right
– he says –
I won't give her up

those who as it seems
have obeyed the orders without pain
go lowering their heads as a sign of consent
but in their clenched fists they hide
fragments of letters ribbons clippings of hair
and photographs
which they naïvely think
won't be taken from them

so they appear
a moment before
the final division
of those gnashing their teeth
from those singing psalms

Czesław Miłosz

I WOULD LIKE TO DESCRIBE

I would like to describe the simplest emotion
joy or sadness
but not as others do
reaching for shafts of rain or sun

I would like to describe a light
which is being born in me
but I know it does not resemble
any star
for it is not so bright
not so pure
and is uncertain

I would like to describe courage
without dragging behind me a dusty lion
and also anxiety
without shaking a glass full of water

to put it another way
I would give all metaphors
in return for one word
drawn out of my breast like a rib
for one word
contained within the boundaries
of my skin

but apparently this is not possible

and just to say – I love
I run around like mad
picking up handfuls of birds
and my tenderness
which after all is not made of water
asks the water for a face

and anger
different from fire
borrows from it
a loquacious tongue

so is blurred
so is blurred
in me
what white-haired gentlemen
separated once and for all
and said
this is the subject
and this is the object

we fall asleep
with one hand under our head
and with the other in a mound of planets

our feet abandon us
and taste the earth
with their tiny roots
which next morning
we tear out painfully

Czesław Miłosz

VOICE

I walk on the sea-shore
to catch that voice
between the breaking of one wave
and another

but there is no voice
only the senile garrulity of water
salty nothing
a white bird's wing
stuck dry to a stone

I walk to the forest
where persists the continuous
hum of an immense hour-glass
sifting leaves into humus
humus into leaves
powerful jaws of insects
consume the silence of the earth

I walk into the fields
green and yellow sheets
fastened with pins of insect beings
sing at every touch of the wind

where is that voice
it should speak up
when for a moment there is a pause
in the unrelenting monologue of the earth

nothing but whispers
clappings explosions
I come home
and my experience takes on
the shape of an alternative
either the world is dumb
or I am deaf

but perhaps
we are both
doomed to our afflictions

therefore we must
arm in arm
go blindly on
towards new horizons

towards contracted throats
from which rises
an unintelligible gurgle

Czesław Miłosz

A KNOCKER

There are those who grow
gardens in their heads
paths lead from their hair
to sunny and white cities

it's easy for them to write
they close their eyes
immediately schools of images
stream down from their foreheads

my imagination
is a piece of board
my sole instrument
is a wooden stick

I strike the board
it answers me
yes – yes
no – no

for others the green bell of a tree
the blue bell of water
I have a knocker
from unprotected gardens

I thump on the board
and it prompts me
with the moralist's dry poem
yes – yes
no – no

Czesław Miłosz

FIVE MEN

1

They take them out in the morning
to the stone courtyard
and put them against the wall

five men
two of them very young
the others middle-aged

nothing more
can be said about them

2

when the platoon
level their guns
everything suddenly appears
in the garish light
of obviousness

the yellow wall
the cold blue
the black wire on the wall
instead of a horizon

that is the moment
when the five senses rebel
they would gladly escape
like rats from a sinking ship

before the bullet reaches its destination
the eye will perceive the flight of the projectile
the ear record a steely rustle
the nostrils will be filled with biting smoke
a petal of blood will brush the palate
the touch will shrink and then slacken

now they lie on the ground
covered up to their eyes with shadow

the platoon walks away
their buttons straps
and steel helmets
are more alive
than those lying beside the wall

3
I did not learn this today
I knew it before yesterday

so why have I been writing
unimportant poems on flowers

what did the five talk of
the night before the execution

of prophetic dreams
of an escapade in a brothel
of automobile parts
of a sea voyage
of how when he had spades
he ought not to have opened
of how vodka is best
after wine you get a headache
of girls
of fruit
of life

thus one can use in poetry
names of Greek shepherds
one can attempt to catch the colour of morning sky
write of love
and also
once again
in dead earnest
offer to the betrayed world
a rose

Czesław Miłosz

OUR FEAR

Our fear
does not wear a night shirt
does not have owl's eyes
does not lift a casket lid
does not extinguish a candle

does not have a dead man's face either

our fear
is a scrap of paper
found in a pocket
'warn Wójcik
the place on Długa Street is hot'

our fear
does not rise on the wings of the tempest
does not sit on a church tower
it is down-to-earth

it has the shape
of a bundle made in haste
with warm clothing
provisions
and arms

our fear
does not have the face of a dead man
the dead are gentle to us
we carry them on our shoulders
sleep under the same blanket

close their eyes
adjust their lips
pick a dry spot
and bury them

not too deep
not too shallow

Czesław Miłosz

THE RETURN OF THE PROCONSUL

I've decided to return to the emperor's court
once more I shall see if it's possible to live there
I could stay here in this remote province
under the full sweet leaves of the sycamore
and the gentle rule of sickly nepotists

when I return I don't intend to commend myself
I shall applaud in measured portions
smile in ounces frown discreetly
for that they will not give me a golden chain
this iron one will suffice

I've decided to return tomorrow or the day after
I cannot live among vineyards nothing here is mine
trees have no roots houses no foundations the rain is glassy flowers
     smell of wax
a dry cloud rattles against the empty sky
so I shall return tomorrow or the day after in any case I shall return

I must come to terms with my face again
with my lower lip so it knows how to curb its scorn
with my eyes so they remain ideally empty
and with that miserable chin the hare of my face
which trembles when the chief of guards walks in

of one thing I am sure I will not drink wine with him
when he brings his goblet nearer I will lower my eyes
and pretend I'm picking bits of food from between my teeth
besides the emperor likes courage of convictions
to a certain extent to a certain reasonable extent
he is after all a man like everyone else

and already tired by all those tricks with poison
he cannot drink his fill incessant chess
this left cup is for Drusus from the right one pretend to sip
then drink only water never lose sight of Tacitus
go out into the garden and come back when they've taken away the
   corpse

I've decided to return to the emperor's court
yes I hope that things will work out somehow

Czesław Miłosz

ELEGY OF FORTINBRAS

     For C.M.

Now that we're alone we can talk prince man to man
though you lie on the stairs and see no more than a dead ant
nothing but black sun with broken rays
I could never think of your hands without smiling
and now that they lie on the stone like fallen nests
they are as defenceless as before The end is exactly this
The hands lie apart The sword lies apart The head apart
   and the knight's feet in soft slippers

You will have a soldier's funeral without having been a soldier
the only ritual I am acquainted with a little
There will be no candles no singing only cannon-fuses and bursts
crepe dragged on the pavement helmets boots artillery horses
   drums drums I know nothing exquisite
those will be my manoeuvres before I start to rule
one has to take the city by the neck and shake it a bit

Anyhow you had to perish Hamlet you were not for life
you believed in crystal notions not in human clay
always twitching as if asleep you hunted chimeras
wolfishly you crunched the air only to vomit
you knew no human thing you did not know even how to breathe

Now you have peace Hamlet you accomplished what you had to
and you have peace The rest is not silence but belongs to me
you chose the easier part an elegant thrust
but what is heroic death compared with eternal watching
with a cold apple in one's hand on a narrow chair
with a view of the ant-hill and the clock's dial

Adieu prince I have tasks a sewer project
and a decree on prostitutes and beggars
I must also elaborate a better system of prisons
since as you justly said Denmark is a prison
I go to my affairs This night is born
a star named Hamlet We shall never meet
what I shall leave will not be worth a tragedy

It is not for us to greet each other or bid farewell we live on
    archipelagos
and that water these words what can they do what can they do
    prince

Czesław Miłosz

FROM MYTHOLOGY

First there was a god of night and tempest, a black idol without eyes, before whom they leaped, naked and smeared with blood. Later on, in the times of the republic, there were many gods with wives, children, creaking beds, and harmlessly exploding thunderbolts. At the end only superstitious neurotics carried in their pockets little statues of salt, representing the god of irony. There was no greater god at that time.

Then came the barbarians. They too valued highly the little god of irony. They would crush it under their heels and add it to their dishes.

Czesław Miłosz

APOLLO AND MARSYAS

The real duel of Apollo
with Marsyas
(perfect ear
versus immense range)
is held at dusk
when as we already know
the judges
have awarded victory to the god

tightly bound to a tree
meticulously flayed of his skin
Marsyas
shouts
before the shout reaches
his tall ears
he rests in the shadow of that shout

shuddering with disgust
Apollo is cleaning his instrument

only apparently
is the voice of Marsyas
monotonous
and composed of a single vowel
A

in reality
Marsyas
tells
of the inexhaustible wealth
of his body

bald mountains of liver
white ravines of aliment
rustling forests of lung
sweet hills of muscle
joints bile blood and shudders

the wintry wind of bone
over the salt of memory

shuddering with disgust
Apollo is cleaning his instrument

now to the chorus
is joined the backbone of Marsyas
in principle the same A
only deeper with the addition of rust

this is beyond the endurance
of the god with nerves of plastic

> along a gravel path
> hedged with box-trees
> the victor departs
> wondering
> whether out of Marsyas' howling
> will not one day arise
> a new kind
> of art – let us say – concrete

suddenly
at his feet falls
a petrified nightingale

he turns his head
and sees
that the tree to which Marsyas was tied
is white

completely

John and Bogdana Carpenter

BIOLOGY TEACHER

I can't remember
his face

he stood high above me
on long spread legs
I saw
the little gold chain
the ash-grey frock coat
and the thin neck
on which was pinned
a dead necktie

he was the first to show us
the leg of a dead frog
which touched by a needle
violently contracts

he led us
through a golden microscope
to the intimate life
of our great-grandfather
the slipper animalcule

he brought
a dark kernel
and said: claviceps

encouraged by him
I became a father
at the age of ten
when after tense anticipation
a yellow sprout appeared
from a chestnut submerged in water
and everything broke into song
all around

in the second year of the war
the rascals of history
killed the teacher of biology

if he reached heaven –

perhaps he is walking now
on the long rays
dressed in grey stockings
with a huge net
and a green box
gaily swinging on his back

but if he didn't go up there –

when on a forest path
I meet a beetle scrambling
up a hill of sand
I come close to him
click my heels
and say:
– Good morning professor
would you let me help you

I lift him over carefully
and for a long time look after him
until he disappears
in the dark faculty room
at the end of the corridor of leaves

John and Bogdana Carpenter

DAMASTES (ALSO KNOWN AS PROCRUSTES) SPEAKS

My movable empire between Athens and Megara
where I ruled alone over forests ravines precipices
without a sceptre with a simple club without the advice of old men
dressed only in the shadow of a wolf

nor did I have subjects
if I had subjects they did not live as long as dawn

experts on mythology are mistaken who call me a bandit

in reality I was a scholar and social reformer
my real passion was anthropometry

I constructed a bed with the measurements of a perfect man
I compared the travellers I caught with this bed
I couldn't avoid – I admit – stretching limbs cutting legs

the patients died but the more there were who perished
the more I was certain my research was right
since what kind of progress is without victims

I longed to abolish the difference between the high and the low
I wanted to give to disgustingly varied humanity a single form
I did everything to make people equal

my head was cut off by Theseus the murderer of the innocent
    Minotaur
the one who used a woman's ball of yarn to escape from the
    labyrinth
a clever one without principles or vision of the future

I have a well-grounded hope that others will continue my labour
and bring the task so wonderfully begun to its end

John and Bogdana Carpenter

PAN COGITO ON VIRTUE

1

It's not surprising
she is not the bride
of real men

generals
strongmen
despots

they are followed down the ages
by that weepy old maid

in a terrible Salvation Army bonnet
who nags

she fetches a portrait of Socrates
from an old lumber-room
a cross kneaded in bread
old words

— while all around in a splendid life roars
pink like an abattoir at dawn

one could almost bury her
in a silver casket
of innocent souvenirs

she shrinks
like hair in the throat
like a buzz in the ear

2

My God
if only she were a little younger
and prettier

marched with the spirit of the times
swung her hips
to the beat of fashionable music

perhaps real men would then
fall in love with her
generals strongmen despots

if only she took more care
looked human
like Liz Taylor
or the Goddess of Victory

but she stinks of
mothballs
her lips are sealed
she reiterates the great No

insufferably stubborn
comic like a scarecrow
like an anarchist's dream
like the lives of saints

Adam Czerniawski

THE ABANDONED

1
I missed
the last transport

stayed in a city
which is not a city

without morning papers
without evening news

there are no
prisons
clocks
water

I enjoy
great vacations
vacated from time

I take long strolls
down avenues of burned houses
sugar
broken glass
rice

I could write a treatise
on the sudden change
of life into archaeology

2
there is a great silence

the artillery in the suburbs
has choked on its valour

but sometimes
one hears
the toll of falling walls

and the muted thunder
of sheet metal swaying in the air

there is a great silence
before the night of the predators

sometimes
an absurd aeroplane
appears in the sky

dropping leaflets
calling for surrender

I would surrender gladly
if I knew to whom

3
now I live
at the best hotel

a dead porter
presides in the lounge

from a hill of rubble
I walk straight to
the second floor
into the suite
of a former lover
of the former chief of police

I sleep on sheets of newspapers
cover myself with a poster
proclaiming the final victory

the bar still holds
medicines for loneliness

bottles of yellow liquid
with a symbolic label
– Johnnie
  tipping his top hat
  departs briskly to the West

I hold no grudge against anyone
for being abandoned

I forfeited
luck
and my right hand

on the ceiling
a lightbulb
like an inverted skull

I wait for the victors

drink to the fallen
drink to the deserters

I rid myself
of evil thoughts

abandoned by even
the premonition of death

Michael March and Jarosław Anders

THE POWER OF TASTE

For Professor Izydora Dąmbska

It didn't require great character at all
our refusal disagreement and resistance
we had a shred of necessary courage

but fundamentally it was a matter of taste
                              Yes taste
in which there are fibres of soul the cartilage of conscience

Who knows if we had been better and more attractively tempted
sent rose—skinned women thin as a wafer
or fantastic creatures from the paintings of Hieronymus Bosch
but what kind of hell was there at this time
a wet pit the murderers' alley the barrack
called a palace of justice
a home—brewed Mephisto in a Lenin jacket
sent Aurora's grandchildren out into the field
boys with potato faces
very ugly girls with red hands

Verily their rhetoric was made of cheap sacking
(Marcus Tullius kept turning in his grave)
chains of tautologies a couple of concepts like flails
the dialectics of slaughterers no distinctions in reasoning
syntax deprived of beauty of the subjunctive

So aesthetics can be helpful in life
one should not neglect the study of beauty

Before we declare our consent we must carefully examine
the shape of the architecture the rhythm of the drums and pipes
official colours the despicable ritual of funerals

          Our eyes and ears refused obedience
          the princes of our senses proudly chose exile

It did not require great character at all
we had a shred of necessary courage
but fundamentally it was a matter of taste
                              Yes taste
that commands us to get out to make a wry face draw out a sneer
even if for this the precious capital of the body the head
                                                  must fall

John and Bogdana Carpenter

Miroslav Holub   CZECHOSLOVAKIA

MIROSLAV HOLUB (1923–) was born in Pilsen. He studied medicine at Charles University, Prague, and went on to earn a doctorate in immunology from the Czechoslovak Academy of Sciences. He has worked as an immunologist and researcher in Prague for most of his life. Besides several collections of articles, Holub has published many volumes of poetry, among them *Denni sluzba* (Day Duty, 1958), *Achilles a zelva* (Achilles and the Tortoise, 1960), *Tak zvane srdce* (The So-Called Heart, 1963), *Beton* (Concrete, 1970) and *Naopak* (On the Contrary, 1982). He has travelled widely and read his work in many countries. He has also lived and taught creative writing for periods in the United States.

As a professional scientist, Holub is diffident about his 'position' in the literary world, in the literary tradition of his country. He indicated as much in a reply (in English) to a letter I sent him, posing a number of loaded questions:

> Growing up with our poets of the Nezval–Holan–Seifert tradition and having an almost religious admiration for the French surrealists, I had an immanent feeling that poetry was something transcendental – something which I could never achieve, only imitate at best. After World War Two, Prévert was translated by Adolf Kroupa and this was the first encounter which suggested to me that I might be not that far…. My first book appeared, after many years and editorial hesitations, when Jan Grossman became my editor and assured me that the Prévert-derived design was good for me. This was a year after I went to Warsaw and got books by the poets of the Herbert–Drozdowski–Bialoszewski–Grochoviak generation and by Różewicz, and discovered that it might not only be poetry that I was writing, but that it might even be the poetry of the time. I even learned a little Polish and collaborated on the first book of Herbert in Czech. Then more reassuring correspondences occurred – with the SF [San Francisco] poets, with Kunert, Popa and Enzensberger…. And, of course, about the time when my first book appeared, a compact group, the 'Poetry-of-Everyday-Life' group, was formed in Prague and through them I became a member of the literary community, an outside member who would never presume to label himself a poet, only a writer writing in the line of development from the old avant garde to a

new one, less academic and more concerned with the general
life-experience.

In another part of his answer, responding to a somewhat inchoate
invitation to comment on a certain 'universality', a non-exclusive quality,
about the poetry of his generation, Holub continues:

> If there was some quality, it may have been related to the fact that it
> was not poetry in the traditional Czech sense at all. The essential trait
> was not to be emotional in words; if inevitable, so only behind the
> words. Poetry did not need words; or it needed them only as the
> simplest way of revealing the images and the message. It was a naked
> poetry stripped of words. This type of poetry may be very national in
> the deeper sense, but is not that much language-related. Besides
> (never having formally studied English), all my life (as a scientist) I
> needed it, on an almost daily basis, and my syntax became even in
> Czech sort of English-related. Later I sometimes had in mind that
> this or that poem might first appear in translation and had the
> translatability and transfer, I mean geographical transfer, in mind.

Holub's poetry, particularly that of the fifties and sixties, is exception-
ally free and clearsighted. It owes something, perhaps, to the American
objectivists and to W. C. Williams, in particular, but as with Herbert,
history's shaping force is quite evident too. Holub's scientist's eye
enables him also to see life as a continuum of living forms, rather than
from a narrowly anthropocentric point of view. But this does not mean
that he is cold or indifferent to the fate of humanity, or to the suffering of
individual human beings. Indeed, the casual, almost light-hearted (non-
professional) quality of much of his poetry, spare though it be, allows him
to take on a wide range of often very painful human emotions and
feelings, without being overwhelmed by them. His compassion acquires
a new, rather eerie perspective. Where a Herbert might view the present
through the lens of history, Holub views it through the lens of a lens! If
sometimes this does not protect his poetry from what looks rather like
sentimentality, it certainly does not neutralize his human sympathies
either. An occasionally gentle and witty, occasionally quite fierce, sur-
realism constitutes one of the means whereby he puts out 'tips into the
world of scooters, skyscrapers and streptomycin ...' (from an interview
on Prague Radio, quoted by A. Alvarez in his introduction to *Selected
Poems*, 1967). His explorations or experiments, though, are generally
guided by a concern for the suffering of ordinary folk, whose nobility and

heroic powers of endurance are among his principal themes. He is committed both to scientific truth in itself, and to the search for what is dynamic and constantly evolving, that search being another of the essential human attributes that must be defended against dogma and absolutism.

THE FLY

She sat on a willow trunk
watching
part of the battle of Crécy,
the shouts,
the gasps,
the groans,
the tramping and the tumbling.

During the fourteenth charge
of the French cavalry
she mated
with a brown-eyed male fly
from Vadincourt.

She rubbed her legs together
as she sat on a disembowelled horse
meditating
on the immortality of flies.

With relief she alighted
on the blue tongue
of the Duke of Clervaux.

When silence settled
and only the whisper of decay
softly circled the bodies

and only
a few arms and legs
still twitched jerkily under the trees,

she began to lay her eggs
on the single eye
of Johann Uhr,
the Royal Armourer.

And thus it was
that she was eaten by a swift
fleeing
from the fires of Estrées.

George Theiner

DEATH IN THE EVENING

High, high.

Her last words wandered across the ceiling
like clouds.
The sideboard wept.
The apron shivered
as if covering an abyss.

The end. The young ones had gone to bed.

But towards midnight
the dead woman got up
put out the candles (a pity to waste them),
quickly mended the last stocking,
found her fifty nickels
in the cinnamon tin
and put them on the table,
found the scissors fallen behind the cupboard,
found a glove
they had lost a year ago,
tried all the door knobs,
tightened the tap,
finished her coffee,
and fell back again.

In the morning they took her away.
She was cremated.
The ashes were coarse
as coal.

George Theiner

A HELPING HAND

We gave a helping hand to grass –
                    and it turned into corn.
We gave a helping hand to fire –
                    and it turned into a rocket.
Hesitatingly
cautiously
we give a helping hand
to people
to some people –

George Theiner

ŽITO THE MAGICIAN

To amuse His Royal Majesty he will change water into wine.
Frogs into footmen. Beetles into bailiffs. And make a Minister
out of a rat. He bows, and daisies grow from his finger-tips.
And a talking bird sits on his shoulder.

There.

Think up something else, demands His Royal Majesty.
Think up a black star. So he thinks up a black star.
Think up dry water. So he thinks up dry water.
Think up a river bound with straw-bands. So he does.

There.

Then along comes a student and asks: Think up sine alpha
greater than one.

And Žito grows pale and sad: Terribly sorry. Sine is
between plus one and minus one. Nothing you can do about that.
And he leaves the great royal empire, quietly weaves his way
through the throng of courtiers, to his home in a nutshell.

George Theiner

NAPOLEON

Children, when was
Napoleon Bonaparte
born? asks the teacher

A thousand years ago, say the children.
A hundred years ago, say the children.
Nobody knows.

Children, what did
Napoleon Bonaparte
do? asks the teacher.

He won a war, say the children.
He lost a war, say the children.
Nobody knows.

Our butcher used to have a dog,
says Frankie,
and his name was Napoleon,
and the butcher used to beat him,
and the dog died
of hunger
a year ago.

And now all the children feel sorry
for Napoleon.

Káča Poláčková

WINGS

> *There is*
> *the*
> *microscopic*
> *anatomy*
>
> *of*
> *the whale*
> *this is*
> *reassuring*

— WILLIAM CARLOS WILLIAMS

I

We have
a map of the universe
for microbes,
we have
a map of a microbe
for the universe.

We have
a Grand Master of chess
made of electronic circuits.

But above all
we have
the ability
to sort peas,
to cup water in our hands,
to seek
the right screw
under the sofa
for hours

This
gives us
wings.

George Theiner

IN THE MICROSCOPE

Here too are dreaming landscapes,
lunar, derelict.
Here too are the masses
tillers of the soil.
And cells, fighters
who lay down their lives
for a song.

here too are cemeteries,
fame and snow.
And I hear murmuring,
the revolt of immense estates.

Ian and Jarmila Milner

SUFFERING

Ugly creatures, ugly grunting creatures,
Completely concealed under the point of the needle,
    behind the curve of the Research Task Graph,
Disgusting creatures with foam at the mouth,
    with bristles on their bottoms,
One after the other
They close their pink mouths
They open their pink mouths
They grow pale
Flutter their legs
    as if they were running a very
    long distance,

They close ugly blue eyes,
They open ugly blue eyes
    and
    they're
    dead.

But I ask no questions,
no one asks any questions.

And after their death we let the ugly creatures
  run in pieces along the white expanse
  of the paper electrophore
We let them graze in the greenish-blue pool
  of the chromatogram
And in pieces we drive them for a dip
  in alcohol
  and xylol
And the immense eye of the ugly animal god
  watches their every move
  through the tube of the microscope

And the bits of animals are satisfied
like flowers in a flower-pot
  like kittens at the bottom of a pond
  like cells before conception.
But I ask no questions,
  no one asks any questions,
Naturally no one asks
Whether these creatures wouldn't have preferred
  to live all in one piece,
  their disgusting life
  in bogs
  and canals,
Whether they wouldn't have preferred to eat
  one another alive,
Whether they wouldn't have preferred to make love
  in between horror and hunger,
Whether they wouldn't have preferred to use
  all their eyes and pores to perceive
  their muddy stinking little world
Incredibly terrified,
Incredibly happy
In the way of matter which can do no more.

But I ask no questions,
  no one asks any questions,
Because it's all quite useless,
Experiments succeed and experiments fail,
Like everything else in this world,

in which the truth advances
like some splendid silver bulldozer
in the tumbling darkness.

Like everything else in this world,
    in which I met a lonely girl
    inside a shop selling bridal veils,

In which I met a general covered
    with oak leaves,
In which I met ambulance men who could find no wounded,
In which I met a man who had lost
    his name,
In which I met a glorious and famous, bronze,
    incredibly terrified rat,
In which I met people who wanted to lay down
    their lives and people who wanted to lay down
    their heads in sorrow,
In which, come to think of it, I keep meeting my
    own self at every step.

George Theiner

THE FOREST

Among the primary rocks
where the bird spirits
crack the granite seeds
and the tree statues
with their black arms
threaten the clouds,

suddenly
there comes a rumble,
as if history
were being uprooted,

the grass bristles,
boulders tremble,
the earth's surface cracks

and there grows

a mushroom,

immense as life itself,
filled with billions of cells
immense as life itself,
eternal,
watery,

appearing in this world for the first

and last time.

George Theiner

SILENCE

Garlands of fatted words are strung through the city
    from mouth to mouth,
Since spring the voices have blared from pillar to post
    and now pitch on the shoulders of autumn,
The youths babble their birdshit in the official ear,
    nothing venture nothing win,
And eight Hail Marys have coaxed a calf
    out of a barren cow.

The ton-heavy drone of voices climbs
    to the first heaven.
But despite the cock-a-doodle-do, despite
    the bogeymen of the woods and lip-smacking devourers
    of dried butterflies,
In the beginning and the end silence
    endures like a knife,
The silence drawn from the sheath at the moment
    when we have our backs
    to the last wall,
When we lean upon
    nothing but the green breath of the sea,

When we lean upon
   the sheer weight of the earth,
When we lean upon
   ourselves alone,
Screened by our sweat from words.

It is the silence we learn
   the whole of a lifetime,
The silence in which you hear
   a small boy
   ask deep within,
What do you think, mum?

Ian and Jarmila Milner

A HISTORY LESSON

Kings
like golden gleams
made with a mirror on the wall.

A non-alcoholic pope,
knights without arms,
arms without knights.

The dead like so many strained noodles,
a pound of those fallen in battle,
two ounces of those who were executed,

several heads
like so many potatoes
shaken into a cap –

Geniuses conceived
by the mating of dates
are soaked up by the ceiling into infinity

to the sound of tinny thunder,
the rumble of bellies,
shouts of hurrah,

empires rise and fall
at a wave of the pointer,
the blood is blotted out –

And only one small boy,
who was not paying the least attention,
will ask
between two victorious wars:

And did it hurt in those days too?

George Theiner

INVENTIONS

Wise men in long white togas come forward during the
Festivities, rendering account of their labours,
and King Belos listens.

O, mighty King, says the first, I've made a pair of wings
for your throne. You shall rule from the air. –
Then applause and cheering follow, the man is
richly rewarded.

O, mighty King, says the second, I've made a self-acting
dragon which will automatically defeat your foes. –
Then applause and cheering follow, the man is
richly rewarded.

O, mighty King, says the third, I've made a destroyer
of bad dreams. Now nothing shall disturb your royal sleep. –
Then applause and cheering follow, the man is
richly rewarded.

But the fourth man only says: Constant failure has dogged
my steps this year. Nothing went right. I bungled everything
I touched. – Horrified silence follows and
the wise King Belos is silent too.

It was ascertained later that the fourth man was
Archimedes.

George Theiner

THE LESSON

A tree enters and says with a bow:
   I am a tree.
A black tear falls from the sky and says:
   I am a bird.

Down a spider's web
   something like love
     comes near
      and says:
    I am silence.

But by the blackboard sprawls
   a national democratic
   horse in his waistcoat
   and repeats,
   pricking his ears on every side,
   repeats and repeats
    I am the engine of history
    and
    we all
    love
    progress
    and
    courage
    and
    the fighters' wrath.

Under the classroom door
trickles
a thin stream of blood.

For here begins
the massacre
of the innocents.

Ian and Jarmila Milner

THE CORPORAL WHO KILLED ARCHIMEDES

With one bold stroke
he killed the circle, tangent
and point of intersection
in infinity.

On penalty
of quartering
he banned numbers
from three up.

Now in Syracuse
he heads a school of philosophers,
squats on his halberd
for another thousand years
and writes:

one two
one two
one two
one two

Ian and Jarmila Milner

BRIEF THOUGHTS ON CATS GROWING ON TREES

In the days when moles still held their general meetings
    and were able to see better, it happened
    that they wished to know what existed
    above.
And they elected a commission to investigate.

The commission delegated a sharp-sighted, quick-footed
    mole. Leaving his bit of mother earth
    he sighted a tree and a bird sitting on it.

And so a theory was formulated that up there
    birds grew on trees. But
    some moles thought it
    too simple. And they selected another mole
    to find out whether birds did grow on trees.

It was the evening hour and cats
    miaowed in the trees. Miaowing cats
    grow on trees, reported the second mole.
And so originated an alternative theory about cats.

The conflicting theories disturbed the sleep
    of a neurotic old member of the commission. He crept out
    to have a look himself.
    It was night and pitch dark.

Both wrong, announced the venerable mole.
    Birds and cats are optical illusions caused
    by the refraction of light. In reality, above
    is the same as below, only the earth is thinner and
    the upper roots of a tree whisper something,
    but only a little.

And there the matter rested.

Since then moles have remained underground,
    do not appoint commissions nor
    assume the existence of cats,

and if they do, then only a little.

Ian and Jarmila Milner

BRIEF THOUGHTS ON CRACKS

Something cracks every moment because
    everything cracks one day, an egg,
    armour, a book's spine.

The human spine may be
    the only exception, though
    much depends on pressure, time and place.
    Such cases are therefore rare.
    Hardly any. Because
    there are so many pressures, places and times
    around.

Cracks are normally stuck together. It is not on record
    that anyone would want to go about cracked,
    not even the whip-crackers.

Cracks are mended with wax, paraffin,
    soldered, bandaged. Or talked out of existence. This most of all.

But a mended egg is no longer an egg,
    soldered armour is no longer armour,
    a bandaged heel is an Achilles heel and
    a man talked out of existence is not the man he was,
    rather the Achilles heel of others.

Worst of all is when hundreds of mended eggs
    pass themselves off as best eggs and hundreds
    of suits of soldered armour as true armour,
    thousands of cracked people as monoliths.

Then it's all one huge crack.

All we can do in the world of cracks is
    now and then to call out, Mr Director, mind your step on the
        stairs,
    you have a crack, if I may say so.

That's all. Afterwards there's only more cracking.

Ian and Jarmila Milner

BRIEF THOUGHTS ON FLOODS

We were brought up to believe
      a flood occurs when
      water rises above all limits,
      covers woods and dales, mounds and mountains,
      places of temporary and permanent residence,

so that
      men, women, honoured greybeards,
      babes and sucklings, beasts of the field and forest,
      lemmings and leprechauns
      huddle together on the last rocks
      sinking in the steely waves.

And only some kind of ark ... and only
      some kind of Ararat ... Who knows?
      Reports on the causes of floods strangely
      vary. History is a science
      founded on bad memory.

Floods of this nature should be taken lightly.

A real flood
      looks more like a puddle.
      Like a nearby swamp.
      Like a soaked wash-tub.
      Like silence.
      Like nothing.

A real flood is when bubbles
      flow from our mouth
      and we think they are
      words.

Ian and Jarmila Milner

ACHILLES AND THE TORTOISE

'Achilles will never catch the tortoise' – ZENO OF ELLEA

In the satin shade of an olive tree
Zeno shakes his head.

> For Achilles sinks in exhaustion
> like a dog chasing its tail,
> and the tortoise moves on
> to its burial in the sand,
> to hatch eggs,
> to drop dead,
> to be born,
> to swim over the Hellespont,
> to chew a primrose.

Zeno shakes his head.

> For Achilles will hardly run a thousand metres
> and the tortoise
> crawls
> forever.

In the satin shade of an olive tree,
shaking his head,
Zeno dies.

> Achilles
> in his golden shin-guards,
> splendid and celebrated,
> gets up and readies himself
> for the last battle.

> But
> what is the name
> of the tortoise?

Stuart Friebert and Dana Hábová

THE JEWISH CEMETERY AT OLSANY, KAFKA'S GRAVE, APRIL, SUNNY WEATHER

Lurking under the maple trees
a few forlorn stones
like scattered words.
Loneliness so close
it has to be made of stone.

The old man at the gate,
a Gregor Samsa
who didn't metamorphose,
squinting
in the naked light,
answering every question:

Sorry, I don't know.
I'm not from Prague.

David Young and Dana Hábová

Tymoteusz Karpowicz POLAND

TYMOTEUSZ KARPOWICZ (1921–) was born in Zielona. He studied Polish philology at Wrocław University, where he received his doctorate and later joined the faculty. Karpowicz has published poetry, short fiction, plays and literary criticism. In 1974, after attending the University of Iowa's International Writing Program, he became Professor of Polish literature at the University of Illinois, at Chicago Circle. Karpowicz's first publication was a collection of short stories, *Legendy pomorskie* (Pomeranian Legends), which appeared in 1948. That same year he also published his first volume of poetry, *Żywe wymiary* (Living Dimensions), which was followed ten years later by another volume of poetry, *Kamienna muzyka* (Stone Music, 1958). Four more collections of poems appeared in the next few years: *Znak równania* (Equation Sign, 1960), *W imię znaczenia* (In the Name of Meaning, 1962), *Trudny las* (Difficult Forest, 1964) and *Odwrócone światło* (Reversed Light, 1972). So far none of his work has appeared in book form in English translation.

Karpowicz's more recent poetry, which has been called 'linguistic', is not represented in the present selection, but rather the more Aesopian work of his middle period. His principal field of investigation appears to have been the possibility or impossibility of self-expression, the agony of silence. His poem 'A Lesson of Silence' succinctly and with a subtly controlled irony conveyed the atmosphere of an entire age, which, with dire consequences, had imposed the most rigorous artificial restraints. On second thoughts, though, perhaps it is misleading to characterize Karpowicz's technique here as Aesopian, his purpose being too urgent to admit of the kind of disjunction suggested by that term. Rather, the 'trees rising mute above the fields' *are* 'the hair of the horror-stricken'. In these poems Karpowicz identifies with the natural world, with the creatures and objects that surround us. This is an intent, listening poetry, meditative and alert. Both the strength and fragility of a sort of composure are represented, as is the strain of a suffocating muteness and the traumatic impact of its disruption.

THE PENCIL'S SLEEP

when the pencil undresses for sleep
he firmly resolves
to sleep stiff and black

the innate inflexibility
of all the piths of the world
helps him
the spinal cord of the pencil
will break rather than bend

he never dreams of waves or hair
only of soldiers
standing to attention
or coffins

what stretches out in him
is straight
what stretches beyond
is crooked
Goodnight

Andrzej Busza and Bogdan Czaykowski

THE DOG WHICH BARKED ITSELF OUT

The dog barked itself
to its kennel
from head
to tail
it would have barked on
but came to an end
measuring four paws
across

now it's screening
in the moon

not a dog
but a case
with the barking
taken out

the chain
next to it
has a ring
of irony

Andrzej Busza and Bogdan Czaykowski

A LESSON OF SILENCE

whenever a butterfly
happened to fold
too violently its wings
there was a call silence please

as soon as one feather
of a startled bird
jostled against a ray
there was a call silence please

in that way were taught
how to walk without noise
the elephant on his drum
man on his earth

the trees were rising
mute above the fields
as rises the hair
of the horror-stricken

Czeslaw Milosz

HUNTING

I lurk on the floor of silence
to escape the jostling sounds
I want to flower with silence
prefigure birds
with intimations of their forms
as the clear air prefigures
a tall mountain

is it a betrayal of thing love hope
the gates of your house and mine

a good hunter blends subtly with the forest
becomes part of its green throng
grows in it like a beech tree fern guelder-rose
then the big game comes to the green hand
and dies of its greenness

consider silence it is like a forest
break a twig there it explodes like a gun

Jan Darowski

SILENCE

silence is sucking the earth dry
in the disembowelled drum of a valley
echo-roots wither
too weak to raise
even one breath

in terror
I clutch at hands
for god's sake let us breathe
let us breathe even if not with our own strength
let us live even if not with our own hearts

when stones arise and sail
the sky in place of birds
let us beat even if not with our own arms
if only to make the air round us tremble

Jan Darowski

THE RIFLE

I speak directly
from the heart
to the brain

if I jam I smash
teeth by order

I've got a head
for knowing the hand

my sight is to the rear
yet I can see ahead

Jan Darowski

Artur Miedzyrzecki   POLAND

ARTUR MIEDZYRZECKI (1922–) was born in Warsaw. He has written ten books of poetry, four volumes of criticism and five collections of fiction. He has also published translations of Racine, Molière, Rimbaud, Emily Dickinson, Apollinaire, Osip Mandelstam, W. C. Williams, René Char, Yves Bonnefoy and others. His own poems and prose writings have been translated in France, Germany and other countries. His first collection of poetry was published during World War Two, when he was a junior artillery officer in the Polish division of the British Eighth Army, fighting in the Italian campaign. After the war he studied history and literature in Bologna and Paris. He was vice-president of the Polish Writers' Union during the 1960s and he is now vice-president of Polish PEN, which was temporarily suspended under martial law. He has edited literary magazines and has lectured at many European and American universities, including Harvard. From 1970 until 1972 he was a member of the International Writing Program at the University of Iowa. He won the PEN Club Literary Prize in Warsaw in 1971, the French Prix Annuel de Traduction in 1977, and the Polish Society of Authors ZAIKS literary prize in 1981.

In his introduction to *14 Poems* (1972), Artur Miedzyrzecki states that: 'The major subject of poetry today is not the problem of poetics but the situation of man and his spirit. ...' He aligns himself unequivocally with those of his generation whose work may be seen as responding to this challenge: 'I think creative poetry should be the opposite now to what might be called the versification game. And I am in natural sympathy with the poets who try today to join the objective description of essential things and the civic passions, the sphere of dream and the sense of history – a vital quality for a poetry which is anxious to be open, veracious, in constant repudiation of each form becoming conventional with time.' Like Herbert (and unlike Różewicz), Miedzyrzecki does not begin by rejecting the past wholesale; instead, he sees the human struggle as a perennial one, the present, with all its unexampled horrors, echoing that past. 'Modern dilemmas and unprecedented conflicts are accompanied by the universal hope of humanization, absolutely new in its problems and very close in its essence to the heroic confidence of the old European humanism.'

In his more recent poetry (translated here by the Polish poet, Stanisław Barańczak), Miedzyrzecki has achieved a far greater simplicity, eschewing the sometimes quite elaborate and learnedly allusive historical allegories he favoured earlier, as though the detachment and irony achieved through such devices were no longer necessary for him. The contrast between these two stages of his work is stark, but it is suggestive of what one takes to be, perhaps, an essential if scarcely comforting development in the poetic consciousness of Central Europe. It is as if a despair that was voiceless before is only now learning to speak. Whether this is a terminal skill, as it were, or representative of a new phase in the history of survival remains to be seen.

PENGUINS

The protective instinct among the Emperor penguins
(Adolf Remane, *Das soziale Leben der Tiere*)
Attains monstrous dimensions:
It reaches a point where one nestling
Is looked after by dozens of parents

The drive to hatch the eggs
And to warm and feed the nestlings
(Observed and described by Adolf Portmann and Sapin-Jaloustre)
Is all-powerful for the Emperor penguins
The impulse for possession and care of the nestling
Is so strong among these birds
That the natural historian Wilson calls it most pathetic:

*...As soon as the nestling leaves the brood-fold on
the abdomen of the adult bird or is abandoned by it,
a compact throng of excited penguins appears ...
These are birds without progeny who want to
appropriate the nestling ... Converging on the
nestling, and furiously pecking away at each other,
each adult bird attempts to set it on its feet, to keep it
from being exposed on the ice ...*

Their love is touching
And relentless
During this violent adoption
The young are wounded
Some of them fall
Others try to escape
They squeeze into cracks in the ice
And prefer to freeze or starve to death
Rather than suffer that terrible affection
That murderous excess of care

The ornithologist Schüz once overhead a young penguin crying out
    in despair:
Why wasn't I born a stork?
Mother would eat me by mistake
And I could have some peace

Artur Miedzyrzecki and John Batki

AT WORK

Gentle Locke sits down to write his famous treatise
He sees tiny titmice alighting outside his window
Each day he hangs a piece of suet for them
Each day two scarlet cardinals appear
And each day they fly away at his first movement
Though he'd never chase them away they are so beautiful

When they return a moment later Locke holds his breath
In front of him extends the landscape of England
He looks at the snow cheerfully sparkling on the hills
He hears from behind the reassuring crackle of flames in the
    fireplace
He feels a blissful peace circulating inside

Suddenly his features harden and fury shoots from his eyes
He remembers the Stuarts

Artur Miedzyrzecki and John Batki

END OF THE GAME

Instead of becoming the empress of joined kingdoms
As suggested by her father's counsellors
Instead of renouncing her vain delusions
In favour of the great four-poster of history where in full view of
    the world
Foetuses of dynasties are conceived
And even the earliest embryo can be assured of the profoundest
    happiness
Which his reign will secure for his future subjects

Instead of living up to these basic obligations of sovereigns
Which time and again were called to her mind by her father the
    king
Princess Wanda rejects the marriage offer of a mighty duke
And plunges into the Vistula

The game is therefore interrupted
The dark century begins
And there isn't even a chronicler to record with care
The dialogue of Polish Creon and Polish Antigone

We all come from her
On this land of suicidal leaps
Where so often there was no other way out
And there are always so many gaps in documents

Artur Miedzyrzecki and John Batki

29–77–02

Realistic dreams with a whiff of terror
I've got to call the number 29 77 02
I call with no luck from God knows what cities
I want to talk to the beautiful S. M.
We were friends ages ago
But she's either dead or she's forgotten
The phone booths are dark and dusty

The dials are falling off or don't work
We're sitting with Julia at a table covered in white
It's a party thrown by our classmates' parents
We don't know anyone there
We feel depressed and sad and I wake up
It's the night from March seventh to the eighth in Normandy
I turn on the lamp I write down the phone number
Tugboats call each other in the fog

Stanisław Barańczak and Clare Cavanagh

WHAT DOES THE POLITICAL SCIENTIST KNOW?

What does the political scientist know?
The political scientist knows the latest trends
The current states of affairs
The history of doctrines

What does the political scientist not know?
The political scientist doesn't know about desperation
He doesn't know the game that consists
Of renouncing the game

It doesn't occur to him
That no one knows when
Irrevocable changes may appear
Like an ice-floe's sudden cracks

And that the natural resources
Include the knowledge of the venerated laws
Ability to wonder
And sense of humour

Stanisław Barańczak and Clare Cavanagh

CAN YOU IMAGINE

Absence
Can you imagine
Absence
Not as the opposite
Of something that is and breathes
Or a gap in the universal presence of things
Or a catchword that calls for symbol's mediation
Or for dialectic quibbles
But as infinite transparence
Where no images take root
A colourless invisible monochromy
Absence
Something that's not there
That's not there anywhere

Stanisław Barańczak and Clare Cavanagh

THE GOLDEN AGE

So what if clowns and gnomes
Run the show at the royal court
Calabacillas, called the idiot from Coria
Barberousse the coxcomb
Pablo de Valladolid the nitwit reciter

The Golden Age is the Golden Age
Philip the Fourth's favourites have nothing to do with it
Only the scribblers from outside the palace walls count
Gongora Calderon Lope de Vega Tirso de Molina

And who cares after all whom Velazquez paints so beautifully
The grand duke on horseback or the jester Hodson with his dog

Stanisław Barańczak and Clare Cavanagh

AT THE CAVE

You can come to terms with anyone
Even a troglodyte
You only have to keep your head
To be patient
To offer him a lamb a herd of oxen a few sheep
To figure out his reasons right after he yells
To guess them from his gestures and his glance
When his eyes get blood-shot, then he's mad
Call the soldiers and make them take back what they brought
When he thumps his chest, then he's happy
Order the same thing once again
He drinks sugar water
Alcohol apparently isn't advisable

You have to understand him that's all
Don't meddle with his tastes
Demand the impossible
He's cruel by our standards
But he's got his own logic
This is a different configuration from a different culture
We must make him feel that we can respect it
Show kindness and sympathy
Not provoke him

Stanisław Barańczak and Clare Cavanagh

Slavko Mihalić YUGOSLAVIA (Serbo-Croat)

SLAVKO MIHALIĆ (1928–) was born in Croatia. He worked for many years as a journalist, and as editor in a publishing house. The author of fourteen collections of poetry, Mihalić has received critical acclaim and numerous awards. His poetry has been translated into a number of European languages.

There is an ethnographic density about Mihalić's work. He picks his way among mythologized forces which incorporate landscapes or cityscapes, as well as among disembodied screams and other manifestations of extreme distress. His are deeply pessimistic poems, telling of voyages whose destination will never be reached, of confusion of identity and place, of invisible, virtually unpresent witnessing. He is surrounded by an almost impenetrable uproar and gloom, a kind of chaos, a teeming deadness, out of which no order proceeds. It is as if his body, the body in which he finds himself, is also part of a larger one surrounding it. An enveloping vision of hell, Dantesque, is generated by his work. Only in 'Second-Class Citizen' is there a glimmer of hope, evoking a saviour who may at least precipitate out of the moribund, yet seemingly indestructible, forces of negativity a kind of resolution.

SECOND-CLASS CITIZEN

He made peace with eternity,
and that's why his name, perhaps,
has been crossed out from the list
of those equal before the law.

At night with burning eyes
he speaks of ancestries and origins
on the other side of the cosmic ocean,
and that's why, perhaps,
there's no room for him at the feast table of the world-wise.

Always before locked doors,
bit by bit he forgets human speech.

What could he say to those
who substituted power for sense,
violence for love?

The birds and flowers of the fields
are happy, greeting him
just the way the stars do.
That's where his home is:
nowhere and everywhere.

And perhaps, truly,
one day he'll be the guide
to the dead rulers of the world.
Restrained and smiling,
he'll show them their places
in the well-earned oblivion.

Charles Simic

THE EXILE'S RETURN

He's now the ruler of the country which once exiled him,
He's not a king or the king's minister, he just does what he wants,
watching from the window the crowds of the deluded roam the
    streets,
himself wise and handsome since he's free of purpose.

Yes, now he's like a child and also like a tomb.
At times, it seems to him, that beside two hands he has wings.
But he won't fly. He knows it's enough to feel that, like the sea
which feels almighty and still doesn't go about rearranging the
    continents.

The greatest adventure is a flower in a glass of water.
With extraordinary energy he has concentrated all his faith into it.
Now, deeply just, he leans over, waiting to wither,
serenely, the way ashes fall from a cigarette.

Peter Kastmiler and Charles Simic

I CANNOT SAY THE NAME OF THE CITY

I cannot say the name of the city
Perhaps tomorrow I'll be killed at the hands of a friend
Perhaps drunk I'll betray his secret ways
Perhaps on all sides the spies lie in wait for me
Perhaps I will plant the firebomb in the main street
Perhaps the foundations beneath us are cracking

Perhaps heroes lose their courage in a decisive moment
Perhaps we have all forgotten why we started

The drunken wheel of fate turns
Blacksmiths forge shackles all night
Whores chase children away in the dark
The restless dead peer out of graves
And soon even the mad dogs will leave

Perhaps in their hurry they'll condemn me innocently
Perhaps I really did do something
Perhaps tonight I along with others will hang someone
Without a word someone who just happens along

I don't dare I can't I am not allowed
To say the name of the city

Peter Kastmiler

LARGE GRIEVING WOMEN

We are encircled by large grieving women.
In nights of solitude they grow even bigger,
at times, dividing secretly into two-three,
at times, joining again toward daybreak,

now already much too large, intended for some other world where
    passions are more generous.
Silently they gaze with their opaque eyes,
unable to fight back,

still one hears within them a pain, somewhat like the sound of
   stones rolling.

When they reach the unknown limit, they turn into mountains,
lie down at their own feet and become plains.
Whoever today walks over the earth forever gently brushes against
   women.

They flood over the heavens, too, a bit.
They are also the woods that stand on the horizon.
Everywhere their sedentary, already weary hugeness.

Charles Simic

DRINKING SPREE BENEATH THE OPEN SKY

How drunk I got tonight
That was some binge beneath the open sky
On the banks of the river where the fearful dare not go

The darkness swarmed with magicians
Like comets they hurled their fluttering cloaks through me
For a long while so that I was already choking

The river teemed with upturned fish and drowned fishermen

Absolutely no one bothered with me
While the meteors were falling into that posterior world
I must have been very small I must have been well-behaved

With my bottle of brandy and my short pants
With my skinny arms and my trimmed hair
With my large eyes that needed nothing

Peter Kastmiler

ELEGY

From the old settlements only the writings
remain. A large piece of yellow paper
stretches from south to north. It too
is beginning to rot. At midnight, the dirge
which only the stone-hearted one understands,
rustles into the dream. Senseless horror.
Meat falling off the bones.
Weeping that will never reach its own cheek.

Wretched paper, parsimonious its explanation
of the end. Why even save anything
when from all the luxury only a clumsy drawing
remains? No one to take it in hand.
Even the bodies are no longer real.
They float on the edge of appearances.
A whole world deprived of its rights
dims within them. Next to it,
the one that conquered lasts a bit longer.
His purpose: to deny the existence of that
which in any case is no more.

Charles Simic

SCREAMS IN THE DARK

A scream that climbs a candle.
Great hollow scream above the feverish city.
The heavens now can be ripped open too.
Every moment we expect to hear the news:

nothing exists – except our troubles.
The stain of the scream on the shimmering table of midnight.
Useless the effort to move my fat fingers;
I'm choking – there's a scream around my neck.

The scream of the flower on the balcony
has already torn out its roots.

Soon even flowers won't know how to grow.
They'll run with us around the room.

The drunken scream of a man who in the dark
centre of the world, (inside-out), discards parts
of whose existence he didn't know till now.
On the bottom he finds another homuncular self.

The scream of the window that no longer sees.
The scream of the clock that runs on screams.
Only yesterday we believed in the firm existence of
some other solution: that it doesn't matter

what we do, that someone else
will redeem our madness and then we'll
twist his neck. However, we found ourselves
utterly alone with our nakedness.

With the small hope in love.
With the even smaller hope in justice.
The scream of a lit cigarette in the night.
The scream of screams and the pale flame of a cry.

Charles Simic

ATLANTIS

In heavy drink and in love,
especially under the effect of some old illness,
truly we see them hung from the sky:
three ships like three fairy godmothers.

We hear them distinctly, when the wind's howl
and the wildness of buxom waves –
at night, with the windows dimmed,
and the lewd whispers, in the hour of prayer,

when they're identical with our curses –
we hear them, discern them, but they never arrive

although they're always out there
just over the line of the horizon.

It's not for the sake of more space that they're coming to discover
    us.
Still, somehow they never reach our seas:
The armoured bow, the stern, the fluttering sails –
as if we were invisible, as if we didn't exist.

Fate seemingly unable to make up its mind.
Here History stops before our famous unreality;
alone we cannot break out of the magic circle,
held back as we are by our excessive gift of prophecy.

Never, never will we be discovered!
Never, never will we begin to exist!
Not even Columbus, not even a single Columbus will escape the
    curse.
The world will perish powerless before Atlantis.

Charles Simic

THE MORNING ROAR OF THE CITY

Every morning you return from a long
voyage. Return out of some kind of death
and metamorphosis, where silently
the branches of your childhood sway,
and those others, even more hushed, that wait
beyond all existence. You leave behind
wisdom, the pure music of your body,
perhaps love, perhaps oblivion, perhaps
the bliss of tears. You leave your true self
which remains empty without worrying
that you won't be back again, since
it's the only one who knows for sure
whether you're there or here, where you sit
by the window and watch how in the sun's fire
the day itself returns with all its platoons.

The morning roar of the city grows,
at first terrifying, as if the murderer is
coming with his dogs and helpers –
then more and more bearable to your ears –
until you yourself, or someone else
awaken within you, and identical,
doesn't begin himself to roar.

Charles Simic

UNDER THE MICROSCOPE

You live under the microscope.
You go into a tavern, break glasses,
ashtrays, and the one above
darkly hunched over the lens,
grits his teeth. You phone a friend,
but there's somebody else on the line;
his heavy breathing gives him away.
He's sick of your long walks in the rain
nights by the open window, barefoot races
with the daybreak over the dew.

You play the comb and tissue paper and feel
he doesn't like it, doesn't know
how to interpret it. Perhaps
the song has a wicked intention?
Where's the key to the secret
whose doors were walled in? He's restless
on his chair, sweat drips off
his forehead onto the glass, his nerves
are strained, he's really gotten thin
the last few years and won't see a doctor.
Tightly he grips the microscope in hope

you'll fall first. And you blossom!
Transformed by the knowledge that you're dragging
someone else down to hell, someone so wise
that he knows you better than you know yourself

as a member of that species meant for gratuitous
extinction. You carouse. You go around
with whores. Gather nasty diseases.
And still you glow. How to tell him that in all that there's much
sense. It can be seen reflected

in his feverish eye, in the trembling
of his hand and that cough. The mouthing
                    of your words.

Charles Simic

ON THE CARPET, STARING AT MYSELF

Some celebration.
One by one they all left me.
The last ones found it the hardest.
They suffered so much on account of themselves.

Then, my lightbulb left me,
And an assortment of other things.
Finally, even memory.

A beaten world rose up foolish with freedom,
And I, inordinately exalted to be its ruler,
Curl-up on the carpet and stare at myself.

Peter Kastmiler

Ágnes Nemes Nagy   HUNGARY

ÁGNES NEMES NAGY (1922–) was born in Budapest, and studied Hungarian, Latin and art history at the University of Budapest. She taught secondary school for years before devoting herself entirely to writing. She has also worked as an editor. Her first collection of poems, *Kettös világban* (In a Double World) was published in 1946, winning her the Baumgarten Prize. Her 1969 volume, *A lovak és az angyalok: Válogatott versek* (The Horses and the Angels: Selected Poems), brings together three additional collections of her poetry. In 1981 her collected poems came out under the title *Között* (Between). She has also published essays on poetry and has translated plays by Corneille, Racine, Molière and Brecht, and poetry by Rilke, St John Perse and many others. She was a member of the International Writing Program at the University of Iowa.

Nagy's translator Bruce Berlind comments on the peculiar concreteness of her language (a quality shared with other poets in this collection), and Nagy herself, in a preface she wrote especially for the English translation of her poetry (1980), memorably discusses the naming that takes place in her work. What she has to say, however, is of more general relevance too, and is worth quoting at length:

> The poet is the specialist of emotion. In practising my craft, it has been my experience that the so-called emotions have at least two layers. The first layer carries the known and acknowledged emotions.... The second layer is the no man's land of the nameless.... I think it is the duty of the poet to obtain citizenship for an increasing horde of Nameless emotions....
>
> Our century, this painfully complicated century, has taught us, among other things, that many of the crucial things in our lives happen in domains beyond the senses, among atoms and solar eruptions, nucleic acids, and ozone shields. The significance of what we are incapable of seeing through, in the usual meaning of the term, of what on the anthropomorphic level of our lives we do not know, has greatly increased, and this is as true of scientific knowledge as of the knowledge of self which may be (also) acquired through art. The two of them jointly – knowledge of the world and knowledge of self – delegate poetry on its difficult twentieth-century voyage of discovery into the land of nameless ones....

This unknown is communicated to me mainly by objects; that is why I try to relay objects to the reader: a geyser, a branch, the fragment of a statue, a streetcar, which may bring with them memories of war (war: the fundamental experience of my generation), or the experience of nature (living with nature: one of the threatened nostalgias of modern man), perhaps the myth of an Egyptian pharaoh (the modern myth: a model of our awareness of life). It would therefore be easy enough for me to say that I'm what is called an objective lyric poet, in the sense that objects attract me and also in the sense that the objectivity of the lyric tone attracts me. At the same time I could also say that I'm attracted by the intense tension which is generated by these objects at the moment when they rise above the general feeling of endangerment, as expressions or perhaps counterpoints of that endangerment. Because, when all's told, I love objects. . . .

Ágnes Nemes Nagy's poetry gives the impression of great concentration, of a simultaneous feeling-and-thinking through. She is able to identify and trace the passage of forces that affect her, almost as though everything were taking place in slow motion. It is rather like a stately, and at the same time sinister or ominous, dance or procession, paradoxically both spontaneous and premeditated. One senses that she is primarily an intellectual who, through almost trancelike identification with the natural world, has situated herself within the objects of that world, drawing vitality from an ambience from which most of us have virtually excluded ourselves. There is, thus, about Nagy's landscapes, a nightmarish, post-apocalyptic finality in which the speaker is so penetrated by her vision that she has virtually ceased to exist as a separate entity, but has become part of what she describes. A strenuous enterprise of reintegration is underway, in the realization that the very survival of what is being reintegrated is still much in doubt.

LAZARUS

He sat up slowly, and around his left side
all his long life's muscles ached.
His death was torn from him like caked
gauze. Rising was as hard as having died.

Frederic Will

SIMILE

The one who has pulled his oar in a start of storm
stretching his biceps absurdly
while he pushed at the rockhard footpiece;
and whose right arm has felt to him
suddenly weightless, unused, with
the oar tumbling back from the broken loom;
whose whole body has, then,
trembled and jerked off balance –
that one knows what I know.

Frederic Will

TREES

What must be studied. The winter trees.
How they're shrouded with frost to the footpads.
Immovable curtains.

What must be learned is that streak,
where the crystal is already steaming,
and the tree swims into mist,
like a body in the memory drifting.

And the river behind the trees,
the wild duck's muted wings,
and the blind-white blue night
where hooded objects loom,
what must be learned in this place
are the trees' inexpressible acts.

Bruce Berlind

I CARRIED STATUES

I carried statues on the ship,
their enormous anonymous faces.

I carried statues on the ship
to the island, to take their places.
Between the ear and the nose
was an angle of ninety degrees,
for the rest their faces were blank.
I carried statues on the ship,
and in that way I sank.

Bruce Berlind

THE GEYSER

It started. First the salts.
A new crystal forms when it breaks down.
It started. The frozen heel of
the whole globe stomped it into the ground.
Then the concavities. It strained
under weights out of all proportion,
slowly with its slender body it squeezed
into agony between crumpled rocks,
and without warning a chasm, a
cavern-sized reverberation, and next
once more the black snailshell
of the gigantic stony brain, it
ground itself down to gaps and clods,
the screw-thread, already smoking,
got hotter and hotter, till finally –

It gushed upward. And stayed there.
A lanky perpendicular moment
pinned to the steaming icefields.
The leap itself was bodiless,
a watery muscle of pure silver,
stretched-out, preposterous –
                                        Then it fell down.
The jet withdrew in the body,
in the briny belly of the smoking earth.
And now and again the hollow mine-shaft

jerked, as rattling, retreating,
its receding bestial heart beat back once more.

Bruce Berlind

PINETREE

Large, yellow sky. A mountain ridge
weighs on the level field.
On the magnet-earth motionless
dark iron-filings of grass.

A stray pinetree.
Something humming. Cold.
Something humming: in the bark-shredded,
scaly-rooted pinepost's
immense trunk now travels
a paleolithic telegram.

Above a bird, a nameless
bird in the sky – knitted
eyebrows, faceless –
behind it now the light fades,
falling eyelids, blind window –
only humming, only the night buzzing
invisible, from black foliage,
charred wrinkled treetops
whose black heart crackles to a purr.

Bruce Berlind

THE GHOST

This was the table. Its surface, its legs.
This was the cord. This was the lamp.
And a tumbler was beside it. Here it is.
This was the water. And I drank from this.

And I looked out the window.
And I saw: the mist falling slantwise,
a large heavenly willow trailing its boughs
in the dark lake of the evening meadow,
and I looked out the window,
and I had eyes. And I had arms.

I live among chair-legs now.
I'm knee-high to everything.
Back then I shouldered into the place.
And how many birds there were. How much space.
As the petals of a wind-blown wreath
of flame, shredded and streaming,
were soaring, sputtering in swarms,
and with one boom burst asunder,
as a heart would crack asunder
into bird-fragments, would fly apart –
this was the fire. This was the sky.

I'm leaving. I would touch the tiles of the floor
over and over with my fingers, if I could.
I'm a low draft on the road,
drifting. I don't exist any more.

Bruce Berlind

DIALOGUE

– Unhand me, flagpole! Why do you keep me from the wind?
– Alone, you'd be tatters. As it is, a streamer, streamer.

Bruce Berlind

BIRD

There's a bird perched on my shoulder,
twin-bird, bird born with me.
It's grown so large, grown so heavy,
each step I take is torture.

Dead weight, dead weight, dead weight on me.
I'd shove it off – it's tenacious,
it claws into my shoulder
like the roots of an oaktree.

An inch from my ear: the sound
of its horrible bird-heart throbbing.
If it flew off one day
I'd drop down to the ground.

Bruce Berlind

THE SCENE

The blue. The green. The river-bed.
The shuffling of objects. As the scene
in my skull plasters the walls
like a circular movie-screen.

And they wake me even at night,
the wall has northern lights,
and gleaming knives: furniture –
and that fern yanks me to my feet,
its rotted intricate underleaf
including the spores,
like an intricate aerial photograph
of a large city –

Because they're sharp, they're sharp,
the images, because they're sharp,
it's blinding – this voiceless congestion –
as they come, go round in circles,
the tin, the sulphur, the birds,
the flights, the absence of expansion,
cosmic bodies stripped of electron-shells
jampacked into a crowd,
radices rolled in a ball,
revolving endlessly round
in a ceaselessly burning now,
where there are no intervals.

I live in a tree.
                    Its foliage knows no seasons,
it reaches to the sky, to stammering,
and I see it crowded with angio-spermous
fruits.

Bruce Berlind

TO A POET

My contemporary. He died, not I.
He fell near Tobruk, poor boy.
He was English. Other names, for us,
tell the places where, like ripe nuts,
heads fell and cracked in twos,
those portable radios,
their poise of parts and volume
finer than the Eiffel, lovely spinal column
as it crashed down to the earth.
That's how I think of your youth –
like a dotard who doesn't know
now from fifty years ago,
his heart in twilight, addlepated.

But love is complicated.

Bruce Berlind

TO FREEDOM

You cathedral, you! Pure astonishment!
All those lovely-eyed frilly angels!
From here below their soles are gigantic,
but their heads are narrow as needles.

The theatrical set high on the cupola
– large pillars, a painted fiery sky between them –:
what good is it if you exist and I don't believe in you?
If I believe in you and you don't exist, what then?

Leftover God! You drag me this way, that way.
I'm through chasing you like a fool, I'm sick of you.
A few friends starved to death the other day.
I say this because evidently you don't know.

What straw did they bite into finally?
What sort of mouths, what sort of skulls?
You could have provided perhaps a pot of peas,
you could have worked a few puny miracles.

I wish I could see their mouths again,
their tepid chins that came unhinged –
I'd like to be in Rome marvelling at the gardens,
and to gorge on rich food, go on an eating binge.

Give bananas! Meat! Be the world's udder!
Give Naples at night, Switzerland in the morning.
You, of all my wishes the faithless lover,
give air vibrating over the meadows!

Give airship! An image of paradise! Trust!
Crash through the law! Give yourself! Then
the speculators won't eat so much,
then the dead may rise again!

– One peony stands on the table,
its beauty compacted, like that of a gem.

Bruce Berlind

WINTER ANGEL

Thin Mary sits there
And in her lap the son

She hears faint airy noises
She shudders: the angel is here
And she knows: every angel is
Dreadful

Dreadful wind that March
There was a windy red sky clinkers
He landed before sunset
And he was enormous
His bristling, hawkshade wing
Couldn't fit in the cottage
Half his cloak stayed out
And the ring round his eye
Was a predator's
How the place shook
He pierced door and window
He perched on roof and wall
In the mortar between bricks
Wrapped in the windbreak
Boxing the compass

Now the angel stands in snow
Up to the knee comes snow
Stands alone at the door
Dumber than dumb and more
An old twig stuck in the snow
Hungry grass covered by snow.

Hugh Maxton

THE TRANSFORMATION OF A RAILWAY STATION

It is unlikely
there is earth underneath, though the cobblestones of the
road surface retain the outline of earlier intrusions. Yet it seems that
under the stones, the cables, the delicate lymph of the apparatus
there is still earth down there, in spite of all, earth.

Here a crater. Or a majestic operation. On a rare and large beast at
the zoo, with local anaesthetic, huge instruments. A pile for each of
the inner organs. Because this body is jointed, tissue by tissue. The
liver set aside, likewise the kidneys. Crudely exact movements be-
tween massacre and therapy.

The neighbourhood of the wound is sensitive. The tormented houses, plaster coming off like a second-degree symptom, tramcars lazily tumbling into the clipped veins, patched-up joints, the subsiding lack of stone, those swollen sutures the tracks. And the plants, utterly defenceless things, whose stems thrown in the dustbin are broken like (as it were) Jesus's legs coming off the cross, the plants in their dusty horror.

And at the centre the operation itself. Excavators with fixed platforms. The operator up there like a dangling pilot. In lemon-yellow rubber suits astronauts climbing down the holes. Among the unbearable barricades of noise the quiet of disasters, indifference which has panicked. Lunch-packs nesting on a knot of wires. (Food parcels of the world. Paper, plastic, slivers of linen. Textures, knots and fasteners. Yes, my brethren, even here and there.) And what strange caps! Perhaps the headgear of sharkhunters or skimpy ritual masks. And the huge gloves – hand-imitating, abstracted hands.

This will be the central administration. This will be the hall. Aspidistras and information. This will be ... do you see? Up there, where entire cubic metres of air are still vacant, up there is nonexistence. Transparent still, open to question. Too much wind blows through it. But nothing that a good lens couldn't fix. With an adequate intensity of light, of course. Because such a thin layer excludes it, such a thin layer preventing existence. The edges are almost visible up there in the space between certainty and doubt so that it almost becomes describable while this inverted diminution (a large dim body of a ship) floats into the picture with its pre-natal and impenetrable storeys.

You still remember, don't you, the railway turntable? At that time the station ended in a rubble ellipsis, and at the head of the ellipsis was the steel drum. The engine stood on it and turned with it like a dancing elephant. The old yellow station is still there with its outdated and operative nostalgias. The lamps behind the curling steam, dawn in the rain. And the rails and the sleepers at night (consider them from overhead, from the bridge) hovering, celestial ladders in a horizontal infinity.

But turn back. Look once again at the building site. (I mean, between the slabs of action try to find what may be called presence.) Then look at the Blood Garden. And the Castle above it. Quiet of the long-standing wounded. Watch them (even in their retroactive relations), then – more precisely – inspect that mound where the geological basin begins at the foot of the hill. Right. Now the picture's in focus, sharp.

Do you remember when it was completed? Were you present when it all came to a stop? Were you there at the opening? It became expansive. Combative. Though the escalator joints are not quite ... but never mind. Traffic control. Complex of buildings. Junction.

Do you remember the lemon-yellow rubber suits? The food parcels of the world? The space between certainty and doubt. Do you remember the Blood Garden? The geological basin under the hill? Retroactive relations? Transformation? Complex of buildings? Transformation again? Airport? Do you remember that city?

Were you there at the opening?

Hugh Maxton

Dan Pagis   ISRAEL

DAN PAGIS (1930–1986) was born in Bukovina, into a Germanized Jewish home. He spent the early part of his adolescence in a Nazi concentration camp. In 1946 he resettled in Israel, learned Hebrew and became a teacher in a kibbutz. Within three or four years he was publishing poetry. He settled in Jerusalem in 1956 and received a doctorate from the Hebrew University, later becoming a professor of medieval Hebrew literature there. His scholarly work included studies of the medieval poets Moses Ibn Ezra, Judah Halevi and Solomon Ibn Gabirol. Pagis also taught at Harvard, the Jewish Theological Seminary in New York and the University of California. His volumes of poetry include *The Shadow Dial* (1959), *Late Leisure* (1964), *Transformation* (1970), *Brain* (1975) and *Twelve Faces* (1981).

Dan Pagis, more than Yehuda Amichai and Natan Zach (also born in German-speaking Europe), was a poet of displacement. In his introduction to the selected poems in English translation, *Points of Departure* (1981), the critic Robert Alter says of Pagis that his 'rapid determination to become a poet in Hebrew was not only a young person's willed act of adaptation but also the manifestation of a psychological need to seek expression in a medium that was itself a radical displacement of his native language'. In stressing the role of Hebrew in the poet's linguistic 'medium of displacement', Alter adds, however: 'I do not mean to suggest that Pagis is estranged in any way from the language in which he writes. In fact, the revolution in Hebrew verse that he, Amichai, and Zach helped bring about was above all the perfection of a natural-sounding colloquial norm for Hebrew poetry.' Here one is reminded, by contrast, of Pagis's fellow Bukovinan, Paul Celan, like Pagis often regarded as primarily a poet of the Holocaust, who continued to write in German, though he might, one supposes, have adopted Romanian, or even French, and whose verse radically abandoned most norms of colloquial speech. What takes place in Pagis's work too, however, with all his ease of diction, is a striking defamiliarization, a refraction of the European cataclysm, a distortion of perspective (to use Alter's term). The imaginative freedom that he enjoys recalls Amichai's, but Pagis is more haunted, therefore more constrained, by the Holocaust. There is less unmediated personal biography in his work than in Amichai's. On the other hand, he identifies fully with those about to be annihilated, about to vanish without trace – one thinks too of Sachs and Pilinszky – and this, hardly surprisingly, sometimes puts his language under greater pressure than it can sustain. But he is a resourceful poet and more often than not is able to take the strain, or enough of it for the reader to do the rest. The risks of an impression of detachment, of mere fancifulness, are perhaps, under the circumstances and given a highly accessible idiom, inevitable, but the conversational diction generally renders Pagis's verse, despite his use of personae – often drawn from the Bible, especially from the story of Cain and Abel – entirely individual and compelling.

ROLL-CALL IN THE CONCENTRATION CAMP

He stands, cold in the morning wind,
stamping his feet, rubbing his hands,
death's diligent angel
who worked hard and rose in rank.
Suddenly he feels he has made a mistake. All eyes,
he checks again in his open book
the bodies waiting for him in formation,
a square within a square. Only I
am missing. I am a mistake.
I extinguish my eyes quickly; I erase my shadow.
Please God, let me not be missed, let the sum
add up without me.

Here, forever.

Robert Friend

END OF THE QUESTIONNAIRE

Home address: galaxy and star number.
Grave number.
Are you alone: Yes. No. Circle one.
What kind of grass grows above, and from what
(from, for example, eye, belly, throat, and so forth)?

You have the right to appeal.

In the blank space below, indicate
1) how long you have been awake, and
2) why you are surprised.

Robert Friend

THE LAST

I am already quite scarce. For years now,
and only here and there, I have been found
on the fringes of the jungle. My clumsy body
shelters in the reeds or clings
to the moist shade nearby.
Civilization would be the death of me.
I'm tired. It's only the huge fires
that keep driving me from hiding place to hiding place.
And now what? My whole reputation rests
only on the rumour
growing truer and truer
that from year to year,
from hour to hour even,
I grow fewer and fewer.
What is true is that at this very moment someone's
on my trail. Cautiously I prick
all my ears and wait. Already there are footsteps
in the dead leaves. Very near. Rustling. Is this it?
Is it me? Yes.
It's already too late to explain.

Robert Friend

IN THE LABORATORY

The data in the glass jar: some ten scorpions
of various species, a community
lazy, adjustable, moved by feelings of equality,

each treading, each trodden upon.
Now the experiment:
an inquisitive, private providence blows
poisonous fumes.
At once,
each is alone in the world,
erect on his tail, begging one moment more
from the glass wall.
The sting is superfluous now,
the pincers do not understand.
The dry straw body stiffens
against the last judgment.
Distant in the dust, the angels of doom
are terrified.
But it's only an experiment, an experiment,
not a verdict
of poison for poison.

Robert Friend

SCRAWLED IN PENCIL IN A SEALED CAR

Here in this transport
I Eve
and Abel my son
if you should see my older son
Cain Adam's son
tell him that I

Robert Friend

AUTOBIOGRAPHY

I died with the first blow and was buried
among the rocks of the field.
The raven taught my parents
what to do with me.

If my family is famous,
not a little of the credit goes to me.
My brother invented murder,
my parents invented grief,
I invented silence.

Afterwards the well-known events took place.
Our inventions were perfected. One thing led to another,
orders were given. There were those who murdered in their own
    way,
grieved in their own way.

I won't mention names
out of consideration for the reader,
since at first the details horrify
though finally they're a bore:

you can die once, twice, even seven times,
but you can't die a thousand times.
I can.
My underground cells reach everywhere.

When Cain began to multiply on the face of the earth,
I began to multiply in the belly of the earth,
and my strength has long been greater than his.
His legions desert him and go over to me,
and even this is only half a revenge.

Stephen Mitchell

TESTIMONY

No no: they definitely were
human beings: uniforms, boots.
How to explain? They were created
in the image.

I was a shade.
A different creator made me.

And he in his mercy left nothing of me that would die.
And I fled to him, floated up weightless, blue,
forgiving – I would even say: apologizing –
smoke to omnipotent smoke
that has no face or image.

Stephen Mitchell

INSTRUCTIONS FOR CROSSING THE BORDER

Imaginary man, go. Here is your passport.
You are not allowed to remember.
You have to match the description:
your eyes are already blue.
Don't escape with the sparks
inside the smokestack:
you are a man, you sit in the train.
Sit comfortably.
You've got a decent coat now,
a repaired body, a new name
ready in your throat.
Go. You are not allowed to forget.

Stephen Mitchell

DRAFT OF A REPARATIONS AGREEMENT

All right, gentlemen who cry blue murder as always,
nagging miracle-makers,
quiet!
Everything will be returned to its place,
paragraph after paragraph.
The scream back into the throat.
The gold teeth back to the gums.
The terror.
The smoke back to the tin chimney and further on and inside
back to the hollow of the bones,

and already you will be covered with skin and sinews and you will
   live,
look, you will have your lives back,
sit in the living room, read the evening paper.
Here you are. Nothing is too late.
As to the yellow star:
it will be torn from your chest
immediately
and will emigrate
to the sky.

Stephen Mitchell

THE STORY

Once I read a story
about a grasshopper one day old,
a green adventurer who at dusk
was swallowed up by a bat.

Right after this the wise old owl
gave a short consolation speech:
Bats also have the right to make a living,
and there are many grasshoppers still left.

Right after this came
the end: an empty page.

Forty years now have gone by.
Still leaning above that empty page,
I do not have the strength
to close the book.

Stephen Mitchell

János Pilinszky   HUNGARY

JÁNOS PILINSZKY (1921–1981) was born in Budapest, where he was also raised and educated. Besides poetry, he published plays, scripts, and prose. During World War Two he spent several months in prisoner-of-war camps. From 1946 to 1948 he co-edited *Újhold*, a modernist literary and critical journal. Pilinszky's first collection of poems, *Trapéz és korlát* (Trapeze and Parallel Bars, 1946) won him the prestigious Baumgarten Prize in 1947. But with the Communist takeover of Hungary *Újhold* was banned, and Pilinszky was silenced for over ten years. Other volumes of poetry include *Harmadnapon* (On the Third Day, 1959), *Nagyvárosi ikonok* (Metropolitan Icons, 1970), for which he won the Attila József Prize of 1971, *Szálkák* (Splinters, 1973) and *Végkifejlet* (Dénouement, 1974). His 1964 oratorio, *Sötét mennyország* (Dark Heaven), was set to music by Endre Szervánszky. He wrote several avant-garde film scripts reminiscent of Beckett. In 1977 he published *Conversations with Sheryl Sutton*, a fictional documentation of his relationship with the black American actress.

In her commemorative essay, 'János Pilinszky: A Very Different Poet' (*New Hungarian Quarterly*, Vol. XXII, No. 84, Budapest, 1981 and reprinted in *The Desert of Love*, 1989), Ágnes Nemes Nagy, Pilinszky's contemporary and friend, describes such poems as 'Harbach 1944', which appeared in Pilinszky's first volume, as already among the 'future basic poems of the new Hungarian literature'. Pilinszky himself writes: '... the war has ended and the gates of the concentration camps are shut, but I believe that it is precisely this final hush which signifies the supreme reality in our midst today' ('In Place of an Ars Poetica'). In fact, so total was his identification with the victims of the Holocaust that in his later years he turned increasingly to prose, especially to a kind of fiction. He explains this, in a 'Radio Conversation' (published in *New Hungarian Quarterly*, No. 77, as 'A Tormented Mystic Poet'): '... I've been very troubled lately by saying I think this or that, because I would much prefer to say *one* thinks that or the other ... in prose the self loses its rôle far more than it does in poetry.'

Ágnes Nemes Nagy aptly characterizes the unique force of Pilinszky's language: 'What was needed for his texts was the highly condensed load of his truck-sentences, the concrete sleepers of his poetic rail-system, and chiefly the ability to choose, the ongoing, ascetic renunciation of s ...'. It is this quality of 'renunciation', in particular a verbal poverty', which Pilinszky himself ascribes, somewhat apocryphally, to his having been brought up by an aunt whose own speech, due to a childhood accident, had never developed beyond a stammer, that paradoxically permits his poetry to transcend its own concentration on the particular. Thus the intensity and luminosity of the writing redeem a vision of suffering, deprivation and isolation.

Ted Hughes's introduction to his and János Csokits's selection from Pilinszky is as insightful a piece as any, but I think it is fitting to conclude by further quoting Ágnes Nemes Nagy. Describing Pilinszky's identification with the death camp experience, she writes:

> ... he recognized the death camp as his imaginings come true, the way a space-creature recognizes the cold of space.... He had so little to do with the everyday world, he was as much a stranger on the anthropomorphic earth as a man could be, or perhaps could not be, and it was precisely here, and through this, that his being reached and swam into the non-anthropomorphic final judgement of the camps, that which is beyond the comprehensible.... He had a single message, single and huge: suffering....
>
> It was this existential suffering, this figure descended to hell that met the wars and gas chambers of the twentieth century. And through this, through the wild metabolic decay of the meeting, the extreme, the other, the no-place figure turned into a paradigm and Pilinszky's poetry into a burning public question. It became apparent that the world resembled Pilinszky, his dimension, his prisons and his apocalypse....
>
> Pilinszky added a dimension to our lives ... he enriched us with want, with being lost, the dearth of existence pared down to the bone. The extraordinary catharsis of his poetic power arched over such dearth. It would be good to look now into those places to which he opened a breach, look in through the inner doors of the antechamber, to those places where destruction is spread out like the sky.

HARBACH 1944

To Gábor Thurzó

At all times I see them.
The moon brilliant. A black shaft looms up.

Beneath it, harnessed men
haul a huge cart.

Dragging that giant wagon
which grows bigger as the night grows
their bodies are divided among
the dust, their hunger and their trembling.

They are carrying the road, they are carrying the land,
the bleak potato fields,
and all they know is the weight of everything,
the burden of the skylines

and the falling bodies of their companions
which almost grow into their own
as they lurch, living layers,
treading each other's footsteps.

The villages stay clear of them,
the gateways withdraw.
The distance, that has come to meet them,
reels away back.

Staggering, they wade knee deep
in the low, darkly-muffled clatter
of their wooden clogs
as through invisible leaf litter.

Already their bodies belong to silence.
And they thrust their faces towards the height
as if they strained for a scent
of the far-off celestial troughs

because, prepared for their coming
like an opened stock-yard,
its gates flung savagely back,
death gapes to its hinges.

János Csokits and Ted Hughes

THE FRENCH PRISONER

If only I could forget that Frenchman.
I saw him, a little before dawn, creeping past our hut
into the dense growth of the back garden
so that he almost merged into the ground.
As I watched he looked back, he peered all round –
at last he had found a safe hideout.
Now his plunder can be all his!
Whatever happens, he'll go no further.

And already he is eating, biting into the turnip
which he must have smuggled out under his rags.
He was gulping raw cattle-turnip!
Yet he had hardly swallowed one mouthful
before it vomited back up.
Then the sweet pulp in his mouth mingled
with joy and revulsion the same
as the happy and unhappy are coupled
in their bodies' ravenous ecstasy.

Only to forget that body, those convulsed shoulder blades,
the hands shrunk to bone,
the bare palm that crammed at his mouth, and clung there
so that it ate, too.
And the shame, desperate, furious,
of the organs savaging each other,
forced to tear from each other
their last shreds of kinship.

The way his clumsy feet had been left out
of the gibbering, bestial elation –
and splayed there, squashed beneath
the torture and rapture of his body.
And his glance – if only I could forget that!
Though he was choking, he kept on
forcing more down his gullet – no matter what –
only to eat – anything – this – that – even himself!

Why go on. Guards came for him.
He had escaped from the nearby prison camp.
And just as I did then, in that garden,
I am strolling here, among garden shadows, at home.
I look into my notes and quote:
'If only I could forget that Frenchman. . . .'
And from my ears, from my eyes, my mouth
the scorching memory roars at me:

'I am hungry!' And suddenly I feel
the everlasting hunger
that poor creature has long since forgotten
and which no earthly nourishment can lessen.
He lives on me. And more and more hungrily!
And I am less and less sufficient for him.
And now he, who would have eaten anything,
is yelling for my heart.

János Csokits and Ted Hughes

ON THE WALL OF A KZ-LAGER

Where you have fallen, you stay.
In the whole universe, this is your place.
Just this single spot.
But you have made this yours utterly.

The countryside evades you.
House, mill, poplar,
each thing strives to be free of you
as if it were mutating in nothingness.

But now it is you who stay.
Did we blind you? You continue to watch us.
Did we rob you? You enriched yourself.
Speechless, speechless, you testify against us.

János Csokits and Ted Hughes

PASSION OF RAVENSBRÜCK

He steps out from the others.
He stands in the square silence.
The prison garb, the convict's skull
blink like a projection.

He is horribly alone.
His pores are visible.
Everything about him is so gigantic,
everything is so tiny.

And this is all.
        The rest —
the rest was simply
that he forgot to cry out
before he collapsed.

János Csokits and Ted Hughes

FRANKFURT

In the river bank, an empty sandpit —
all that summer we took the refuse there.
Gliding between villas and gardens
we came to a bridge. Then a dip of the road
and the wooden fence of the racetrack.
A few jolts, and the truck began to slow down.
But even before the brakes could tighten
the first surge of hunger overwhelmed us.

Among the spilling buckets and the bursting sacks —
horror of the spines, bent into position!
Then among those toppled crates began
the pitiless pre-censorship,
interrogating the gristles of the offal.
And there, on all fours, hunger
could not stomach its own fury,
but revolted and surrendered.

They were lost in the dust and filth.
The whole truck shook, howling.
The swill clogged their hearts.
It swamped their consciousness.
They burrowed into the depths of the filled bins
till mouths and eyes were caked.
They drowned in that living sludge
and there, upside down, they were resurrected.

And brought back, scrap by scrap,
what had been utterly lost with them,
wringing their salvation, drunkenly,
out of the gouged mush –
but before their joy could be consummated
the poison of understanding stirred.
First, only the bitterness in their mouths,
then their hearts tasted the full misery.

Abruptly, they backed from the crush. Almost sober
they watched how this drunkenness –
betraying their despair –
possessed their whole being.
But then again, reckless, they abandoned themselves,
now merely enduring, till their organs,
sating themselves, should have completed
the last mistakes of pleasure.

Only to get away – no matter where!
Only to get out, now!
The glowing pack drove us from them
without a flash! They did not even touch us.
All around – the blank walls of the pit.
Only to get home! Probably a steamer
went past quite close by on the river below
and its smoke and soot screened perfectly

the steep, crooked exit. Out across the field!
Bounding eagerly over the mounds
on to the flaming concrete. Then the villas!
The green world streaming back!

The wooden fence of the racecourse.
And after the volley of gaps between the palings
the hot scent, swooning from the gardens!
Then all at once – the shock of loneliness!

In a moment the splendour of the foliage burned out –
its flame hung darkly to the road.
And our faces, and our hands, darkened.
And with us, the paradise.
While behind us between the jouncing cans
and the tattered dusty trees
emerged the crepuscular city
of Frankfurt – 1945.

János Csokits and Ted Hughes

APOCRYPHA

I
Everything will be forsaken then

The silence of the heavens will be set apart
and forever apart
the broken-down fields of the finished world,
and apart
the silence of dog-kennels.
In the air a fleeing host of birds.
And we shall see the rising sun
dumb as a demented eye-pupil
and calm as a watching beast.

But keeping vigil in banishment
because that night
I cannot sleep I toss
as the tree with its thousand leaves
and at dead of night I speak as the tree.

Do you know the drifting of the years
the years over the crumpled fields?

Do you understand the wrinkle
of transience? Do you comprehend
my care-gnarled hands? Do you know
the name of orphanage? Do you know
what pain treads the unlifting darkness
with cleft hooves, with webbed feet?
The night, the cold, the pit. Do you know
the convict's head twisted askew?
Do you know the caked troughs, the tortures
of the abyss?

The sun rose. Sticks of trees blackening
in the infra-red of the wrathful sky.
So I depart. Facing devastation
a man is walking, without a word.
He has nothing. He has his shadow.
And his stick. And his prison garb.

2

And this is why I learned to walk! For these
belated bitter steps.

Evening will come, and night will petrify
above me with its mud. Beneath closed eyelids
I do not cease to guard this procession
these fevered shrubs, their tiny twigs.
Leaf by leaf, the glowing little wood.
Once Paradise stood here.
In half-sleep, the renewal of pain:
to hear its gigantic trees.

Home – I wanted finally to get home –
to arrive as he in the Bible arrived.
My ghastly shadow in the courtyard.
Crushed silence, aged parents in the house.
And already they are coming, they are calling me,
my poor ones, and already crying,
and embracing me, stumbling –
the ancient order opens to readmit me.
I lean out on the windy stars.

If only for this once I could speak with you
whom I loved so much. Year after year
yet I never tired of saying over
what a small child sobs
into the gap between the palings,
the almost choking hope
that I come back and find you.
Your nearness throbs in my throat.
I am agitated as a wild beast.

I do not speak your words,
the human speech. There are birds alive
who flee now heart-broken
under the sky, under the fiery sky.
Forlorn poles stuck in a glowing field,
and immovably burning cages.
I do not understand the human speech,
and I do not speak your language.
My voice is more homeless than the word!
I have no words.

        Its horrible burden
tumbles down through the air –
a tower's body emits sounds.

You are nowhere. How empty the world is.
A garden chair, and a deckchair left outside.
Among sharp stones my clangorous shadow.
I am tired. I jut out from the earth.

3
God sees that I stand in the sun.
He sees my shadow on stone and on fence.
He sees my shadow standing
without a breath in the airless press.

By then I am already like the stone;
a dead fold, a drawing of a thousand grooves,
a good handful of rubble
is by then the creature's face.

And instead of tears, the wrinkles on the faces
trickling, the empty ditch trickles down.

János Csokits and Ted Hughes

FABLE

(Detail from *KZ–Oratorio: Dark Heaven*)

Once upon a time
there was a lonely wolf
lonelier than the angels.

He happened to come to a village.
He fell in love with the first house he saw.

Already he loved its walls
the caresses of its bricklayers.
But the window stopped him.

In the room sat people.
Apart from God nobody ever
found them so beautiful
as this child-like beast.

So at night he went into the house.
He stopped in the middle of the room
and never moved from there any more.

He stood all through the night, with wide eyes
and on into the morning when he was beaten to death.

János Csokits and Ted Hughes

EXTRACT FROM A DIARY

What day is it today? The way I live,
I keep on confusing
time's timetable.

'Like thieves' – in Simone Weil's wonderful words –
'on the cross of space and time
we human beings are nailed.'
I drift off, and the splinters shock me awake.
At such times I see the world with piercing sharpness,
and try to turn my head in your direction.

Peter Jay

ONE FINE DAY

Always I have searched for the mislaid tin spoon,
the bric-à-brac landscapes of wretchedness,
hoping that one fine day
tears overcome me, and I'm gently taken back
by our home's old yard,
its ivy silence, whisper.

Always,
always I have longed for home.

Peter Jay

MONSTRANCE

I sink in the falling snow,
have disappeared, disappear
in the pious view
of the young reformatory girls,
groves, trees,
my first playmates,
the beautiful young prison-fodder.

Peter Jay

THREE-COLOURED BANNER

The first colour? Just like a captive
at the moment sentence is passed.
The second? Like lost
soldiers falling down
in huge, soft heaps.
And the third? The colour of the third –
it is you.

My beautiful three-coloured banner!

Peter Jay

THE HANGMAN'S ROOM

Bacon-smell. Geranium-smell.
The sea can never be seen
from the window of the hangman's room.
The sea is God's,
and the window is closed.

How different is the scent of the scaffold,
and the lamb, when they come for it.

Peter Jay

STONE WALL AND CELEBRATION

Hommage à Robert Wilson

After the act of stabbing and
the hand's unhappy stations?

Beyond the interrupted strains,
the bedraggled celebrations and the
light of the tangled chandelier?

Before the wall? After the wall?

What happens, what really happens
during the unhappy, hideous
time of all our actions?

Peter Jay

SCAFFOLD IN WINTER

The one being led?   I don't know.
The ones leading?   I don't know.
Slaughterhouse or scaffold?   I don't know.
Who's killing who? Man killing beast
or beast man?   I don't know.
And plunging, the unmistakable,
and the silence after?   I don't know.
And the snow, the winter snow? Perhaps
the exiled sea, God's muteness.

Scaffold in winter. There is nothing we know.

Peter Jay

ON THE BACK OF A PHOTOGRAPH

Hunched I make my way, uncertainly.
The other hand is only three years old.
An eighty-year-old hand and a three-year-old.
We hold each other. We hold each other tight.

Peter Jay

Vasko Popa   YUGOSLAVIA (Serbo-Croat)

VASKO POPA (1922–1991) was born in Grebenac, Banat, in northern
Yugoslavia. He studied at the universities of Belgrade, Vienna and
Bucharest and received his degree in French and Yugoslav literature in
Belgrade in 1949. Subsequently he worked as an editor for several
publishing houses, most recently Nolit, in Belgrade. He published
several collections of poems, including *Kora* (Bark, 1952), *Nepočin-polje*
(Unrest Field, 1956), *Pesme* (Poems, 1965), *Sporedno nebo* (Secondary
Heaven, 1968) and *Uspravna zemlja* (Earth Erect, 1972), and received
numerous awards, among them the Branko Radičević Prize (1953), the
Zmaj Prize (1956), the Lenau Prize (1967), and the National Austrian
Prize for European Literature. His work has been translated into nearly
every European language.

Vasko Popa's poetry shares many of the characteristics of that of other
poets from Eastern or Central Europe, of the first post-war generation.
In the preamble of his introduction to Anne Pennington's translations,
Ted Hughes says as much and, as a result, was accused by some
subsequent commentators of lumping all these writers together, of
blurring distinctions. But that the family resemblance is more than just
wishful thinking on our part is evidenced by the spareness and precision
of Popa's language, its objectivity, concreteness, lack of sentimentality,
its philosophical-ethical preoccupations. Hughes does, in any case,
begin to define what distinguishes Popa's work from that of his contem-
poraries when he talks about the 'primitive pre-creation atmosphere ...
as if he were present where all the dynamisms and formulae were ready
and charged, but nothing created – or only a few fragments.' He goes on
to contrast literary surrealism and 'the far older and deeper thing, the
surrealism of folklore'. The former has 'abandoned the struggle with
circumstances ... has ... lost morally and surrendered to the arbitrary
imagery of the dream flow', whereas the latter 'is always urgently
connected with the business of trying to manage practical difficulties so
great that they have forced the sufferer temporarily out of the dimension
of coherent reality into that depth of imagination where understanding
has its roots and stores its X-rays.' Charles Simic, in his introduction to
his own translations (1970), speaking of Popa's language as being
immersed in magic formulas, riddles, proverbs and even jokes, likewise
refers to his 'elemental surrealism'.

It is certainly possible to perceive a kind of tendentiousness, a grand scheme or overall conception, here. Many commentators, foreign as well as native, have concerned themselves with the poet's habit of writing in cycles and the way that these cycles echo or reflect one another. An epic quality is noted, underlined by the fact that Popa's universe embraces not only the 'primitive', the 'pre-creation' elements, but also history and the legends of his native Serbia, his personal history too finding its place within this larger context. Even before this became so generally apparent, the Yugoslav poet and critic Miodrag Pavlović was already talking of Popa's 'progress towards a new form of modern mythic-philosophical epic poetry' (1964). Ted Hughes, comparing Popa's cycles to 'Kekulé's whirling dream snake', described how the cycles seemed to 'smoulder along through years, criss-crossing each other, keeping the character of their own genes, working out their completeness'. 'As Popa penetrates deeper into his life, with book after book,' he concluded, 'it begins to look like a Universe passing through a Universe.' 'Each cycle', says Simic, 'is like a spoke of a wheel reaching from a different cycle towards a common centre in which the poet's entire conception of the world lies. The impulse is towards the epic. It is the drama of the universe where each particle contains the cosmic, or in the words of the hermetic proverb: "As above, so below".' What Simic, Hughes and others sense so strongly, Ronelle Alexander, in a detailed analysis of Popa's œuvre (*The Structure of Vasko Popa's Poetry*, 1985) tries to demonstrate, making a persuasive case for the comprehensive, symmetrical organization of his poetic material, from interconnected, thematically related books of cycles, down through individual cycles, to individual poems within each cycle.

It will be obvious from this how hard it is to excerpt from Popa's œuvre. I have taken poems from five of his books, selecting from a number of the cycles. Much as I admire it, I found it impossible to extract individual poems from the marvellous *Vučja so* (Wolf Salt), where historical or legendary material is synthesized in the form of a 'myth about the meaning of Serbianism' (Ronelle Alexander's words), embodied in the Serbian totem animal, the wolf. One cycle, 'The Quartz Pebble' (with its striking resemblance to Zbigniew Herbert's 'stone' [see 'Reconstruction of a Poet']), is, however, given in its entirety. It is hoped that something of the physiological, psychological, historical, mythical, cosmological, and personal density and development of Popa's writing can be gathered from this. That there was something profoundly healing in the impulse behind this work is clear. The scope of his poetry, with its reminder that the world is graspable as a whole, encourages us to take care of that world, for how can we preserve and cherish what is only partially glimpsed, or what is seen to lie in ruins? To that extent Popa, though, I think, methodologically unique among his European peers, joins with them in an essential enterprise of recovery.

From Besieged Serenity

ECHO

The empty room begins to growl
I withdraw into my skin

The ceiling begins to whine
I fling it a bone
The corners begin to whimper
To each I fling a bone
The floor begins to bay
I fling it a bone too

One wall begins to bark
To it I fling a bone
And the second and third and fourth walls
Begin to bark
I fling each one a bone

The empty room begins to howl
And I myself empty
Without a single bone
Turn into a hundredfold
Echo of the howling

And echo echo
Echo

JOURNEY

I journey
And the highway journeys too

The highway sighs
With a deep dark sigh

I have no time for sighing
I journey further

No longer stumbling
Over sleeping stones on the highway
I journey lighter

No longer does the workfree wind
Delay me with chatter
It's as if he couldn't see me
I journey faster

My thoughts tell me I have left
Some bloody some dull pain
At the bottom of the abyss behind me

I have no time for thinking
I journey

Anne Pennington

From Far Within Us

2

Look that is that uninvited
Stranger presence look it's here

Horror on the ocean of tea in the cup
Rust taking a hold
On the edges of our laughter
A snake coiled in the depths of the mirror

Shall I be able to hide you
Out of your face into mine

Look it's the third shadow
On our imagined walk
The unexpected gulf
Between our words

Hoofs that clatter
Under the arched vaults of our mouths

Shall I be able
On this unrest-field
To set up a tent of my hands for you

11
The streets of your glances
Have no ending

The swallows from your eyes
Do not migrate south

From the aspens in your breasts
The leaves do not fall

In the sky of your words
The sun does not set

15
These are your lips
That I return
To your neck

This is my moonlight
That I take down
From your shoulders

We have lost each other
In the boundless forests
Of our meeting

In my hands
Your adam's apples
Set and dawn

In your throat
Flame up and fade
My impetuous stars

We have found each other
On the golden plateau
Far within us

Anne Pennington

From Games

THE NAIL

One be the nail another the pincers
The others are workmen

The pincers grip the nail by the head
Grip him with their teeth with their hands
And tug him tug
To get him out of the floor
Usually they only pull his head off
It's hard to get a nail out of a floor

Then the workmen say
The pincers are no good
They smash their jaws and break their arms
And throw them out of the window

After that someone else be the pincers
Someone else the nail
The others are workmen

HE

Some bite off the others'
Arm or leg or whatever

Take it between their teeth
Run off as quick as they can
Bury it in the earth

The others run in all directions
Sniff search sniff search
Turn up all the earth

If any are lucky enough to find their arm
Or leg or whatever
It's their turn to bite

The game goes on briskly

As long as there are arms
As long as there are legs
As long as there is anything whatever

THE SEED

Someone sows someone
Sows him in his head
Stamps the earth down well

Waits for the seed to sprout

The seed hollows out his head
Turns it into a mouse hole
The mice eat the seed

They drop dead

The wind comes to live in the empty head
And gives birth to chequered breezes

Anne Pennington

The Quartz Pebble

THE QUARTZ PEBBLE

For Dušan Radić

Headless limbless
It appears
With the excitable pulse of chance
It moves
With the shameless march of time
It holds all
In its passionate
Internal embrace

A smooth white innocent corpse
It smiles with the eyebrow of the moon

THE HEART OF THE QUARTZ PEBBLE

They played with the pebble
The stone like any other stone
Played with them as if it had no heart

They got angry with the pebble
Smashed it in the grass
Puzzled they saw its heart

They opened the pebble's heart
In the heart a snake
A sleeping coil without dreams

They roused the snake
The snake shot up into the heights
They ran off far away

They looked from afar
The snake coiled round the horizon
Swallowed it like an egg

They came back to the place of their game
No trace of snake or grass or bits of pebble
Nothing anywhere far around

They looked at each other they smiled
And they winked at each other

THE DREAM OF THE QUARTZ PEBBLE

A hand appeared out of the earth
Flung the pebble into the air

Where is the pebble
It hasn't come back to earth
It hasn't climbed up to heaven

What's become of the pebble
Have the heights devoured it
Has it turned into a bird

Here is the pebble
Stubborn it has stayed in itself
Not in heaven nor in earth

It obeys itself
Among the worlds a world

THE LOVE OF THE QUARTZ PEBBLE

He fell for a beautiful
A rounded blue-eyed
A frivolous endlessness

He is quite transformed
Into the white of her eye

Only she understands him
Only her embrace has
The shape of his desire
Dumb and boundless

All her shadows
He has captured in himself

He is blind in his love
And he sees
No other beauty
But her he loves
Who will cost him his head

THE ADVENTURE OF THE QUARTZ PEBBLE

He's had enough of the circle
The perfect circle around him
He's stopped short

His load is heavy
His own load inside him
He's dropped it

His stone is hard
the stone he's made of
He's left it

He's cramped in himself
In his own body
He's come out

He's hidden from himself
Hidden in his own shadow

THE SECRET OF THE QUARTZ PEBBLE

He's filled himself with himself
Has he eaten too much of his own tough flesh
Does he feel ill

Ask him don't be afraid
He's not begging for bread

He's petrified in a blissful convulsion
Is he pregnant perhaps
Will he give birth to a stone
Or a wild beast or a streak of lightning

Ask him as much as you like
Don't expect an answer

Expect only a bump
Or a second nose or a third eye
Or who knows what

TWO QUARTZ PEBBLES

They look at each other dully
Two pebbles look at each other

Two sweets yesterday
On the tongue of eternity
Two stone tears today
On an eyelash of the unknown

Two flies of sand tomorrow
In the ears of deafness
Two merry dimples tomorrow
In the cheeks of day

Two victims of a little joke
A bad joke without a joker

They look at each other dully
With cold cruppers they look at each other
They talk without lips
They talk hot air

(1951–1954)

Anne Pennington

From The Yawn of Yawns

A WISE TRIANGLE

Once upon a time there was a triangle
It had three sides
The fourth it hid
In its glowing centre

By day it would climb to its three vertices
And admire its centre
By night it would rest
In one of its three angles

At dawn it would watch its three sides
Turned into three glowing wheels
Disappear into the blue of no return

It would take out its fourth side
Kiss it break it three times
And hide it once more in its former place

And again it had three sides

And again by day it would climb
To its three vertices
And admire its centre

And by night it would rest
In one of its three angles

PETRIFIED ECHOES

Once upon a time there was an infinity of echoes
They served one voice
Built it arcades

The arcades collapsed
They'd built them crooked
The dust covered them

They left the dangerous service
Became petrified from hunger

They flew off petrified
To find to tear to pieces the mouth
The voice had come out of

They flew who knows how long
And blind fools didn't see
They were flying round the very edge of the mouth
They were looking for

THE YAWN OF YAWNS

Once upon a time there was a yawn
Not under the palate not under the hat
Not in the mouth not in anything

It was bigger than everything
Bigger than its own bigness

From time to time
Its dull darkness desperate darkness
In desperation would flash here and there
You might think it was stars

Once upon a time there was a yawn
Boring like any yawn
And still it seems it lasts

Anne Pennington

From St Sava's Spring

THE LIFE OF ST SAVA*

Hungry and thirsty for holiness
He left the world
His own people and himself

He entered the service
Of the winged lords

He tended their golden-fleeced clouds
And groomed their thunder and lightning
Hobbled in the great tomes

He spent all his years
Earned a serpent-headed staff

He mounted the staff
Returned to the world
And found there his own people and himself

He lives without years without death
Surrounded by his wolves

ST SAVA'S FORGE

From the besieged hills
The wolves call him
Their backbones ablaze

---

* St Sava (1175–1235) is the patron saint of Serbia. He is portrayed here as the
wolf shepherd, wolves traditionally representing the Serbs.

He stretches out his serpent-headed staff
So they may crawl
Peacefully to his feet

He bathes them in the hot blood
Of the holy ancestral metal
And dries them with his red beard

He forges them new backbones
Of young iron
And sends them back to the hills

With endless howling
The wolves greet him
From the top of the liberated hills

ST SAVA'S JOURNEY

He journeys over the dark land

With his staff he cuts
The dark beyond him into four

He flings thick gloves
Changed into immense cats
At the grey army of mice

Amid the storm he releases his chains
And lashes the ancient oaken land
To the fixed stars

He lashes his wolves' paws
That no trace of the dark land
Should remain on them

He journeys without a path
And the path is born behind him

Anne Pennington

From The Blackbird's Field

THE BATTLE ON THE BLACKBIRD'S FIELD*

Singing we ride over the field
To encounter the armoured dragons

Our most lovely wolf-shepherd
His flowering staff in his hand
Flies through the air on his white steed

The crazed thirsty weapons
Savage each other alone in the field

From the mortally wounded iron
A river of our blood streams out
Flows upward and streams into the sun

The field stands up erect beneath us

We overtake the heavenly rider
And our betrothed stars
And together we fly through the blue

From below there follows
The blackbird's farewell song

Anne Pennington

---

* The Blackbird's Field (Kossovo Polye) was the scene of the battle of 1389 when the Serbs were finally routed by the Ottoman army.

From *Raw Flesh*

IN THE VILLAGE OF MY FOREFATHERS

One hugs me
One looks at me with wolf eyes
One takes off his hat
So I can see him better

Each one asks me
Do you know who I am

Unknown old men and women
Usurp the names
Of boys and girls of my memory

I ask one of them
Tell me old chap
Is George Kurya
Still alive

That's me he answers
In a voice from the other world

I stroke his cheek with my hand
And silently beg him to tell me
Whether I am alive still too

TIME SWEPT UP

The sweeper collects dry leaves with his broom
Under the chestnut trees
Along the Avenue

He stops under each tree
And shakes it with all his might

He'd like autumn to hurry up
If he had his way

Vershats would be left in a flash
Without autumn and the other seasons

He'd be left
With his broom to gnaw

I'd warn him
Only a chestnut
Got stuck in my throat

BE SEEING YOU

After the third evening round
In the yard of the concentration camp
We disperse to our quarters

We know that before dawn
Some of us will be taken out and shot

We smile like conspirators
And whisper to each other
Be seeing you

We don't say when or where

We've given up the old way
We know what we mean

Anne Pennington

Tadeusz Różewicz　　　　　POLAND

TADEUSZ RÓŻEWICZ (1921–) was born in Radomsko. Besides poetry he has written plays, short stories and novels. During the war he worked in the Polish underground. After the war he studied art history at the Jagiellonian University in Cracow. He has published nineteen volumes of poetry. His many theatrical pieces have been collected in *Sztuki teatralne* in 1972, and *Poezje zebrane* (Collected Poems) appeared in 1971. He received the highest Polish literary award, the State Prize for Literature, First Class, in 1966. Różewicz now lives in Wrocław and is closely associated with the monthly *Odra*. His work has been translated into many languages.

In a 1976 interview with Adam Czerniawski (Appendix 8), Różewicz said: 'I tend to find any old newspaper more absorbing than the finest edition of poems: that a dog is run over or a house got burnt down.' This anti-art stance, with its resolute down-to-earthness – 'I used to be a reader, a passionate reader over many years. I searched books and poems for practical help. I hoped they would help me overcome despair and doubt ... Because I myself have always searched, begged for help, I began to think that I too may be able to help, though of course I also have moments when I feel it's not worth anything' – seemed to many of us who encountered Różewicz for the first time in the sixties a particularly appropriate response to the catastrophic historical reality, at the centre of which he and his contemporaries had found themselves. Our convictions were further reinforced by the poet's frank acknowledgement of his ambivalence about the artistic legacy of the past. It seemed to us that he had discovered how to make objective use of himself and his experiences, and that this objectivity was realized in a language which had shed the burden of a (literally) exploded culture. This new realism, which attempted to identify the psycho-physiological conditions of survival, was a prerequisite for any further development. No other poet we encountered at the time undertook this essential task so uncompromisingly.

The contrast Różewicz draws, however, between his poetry, represented as 'thinking in images', and the 'philosophizing' (which he does not denigrate) of an Eliot, a Benn, or a Brecht, is perhaps debatable, particularly as regards the latter, even if Brecht was more explicit about what he was doing. And, of course, looking back over Różewicz's work, especially of the late fifties and sixties, it is easy to pick holes in such an assessment. Nor is it possible for Różewicz himself to disarm the sceptics simply by owning up to, even incorporating in his work, a certain admiration or affection for the cultural monuments of the past. The concept of anti-art, or anti-poetry, stubbornly remains a contradiction in terms, and as such renders him susceptible to charges of evasiveness, even disingenuousness. Indeed one is tempted to speculate that it may have been increasing discomfort with the logical inconsistencies implicit in this attitude that contributed to the decline, after the sixties, in Różewicz's hitherto prolific poetic output.

None of this, however, lessens his achievement. And even if, in our earlier assessment, we had allowed ourselves to be outflanked, I think that we were not so wrong after all. Różewicz's post-war world view was perhaps relatively less sophisticated, and perhaps his language was not so far in advance as it seemed to be at the time, but the posthumous life of poetry found a champion in him, even if a despairing, sometimes nihilistic, one. Czesław Miłosz in *The History of Polish Literature* (1969) calls Różewicz, with some justification, 'a poet of chaos with a nostalgia for order'; but perhaps 'nostalgia' is too dismissive a term to use of a writer who had the courage, hard for us now fully to grasp, to take the first steps in a post-apocalyptical world.

THE SURVIVOR

I am twenty-four
led to slaughter
I survived.

The following are empty synonyms:
man and beast
love and hate
friend and foe
darkness and light.

The way of killing men and beasts is the same
I've seen it:
truckfuls of chopped-up men
who will not be saved.

Ideas are mere words:
virtue and crime
truth and lies
beauty and ugliness
courage and cowardice.

Virtue and crime weigh the same
I've seen it:
in a man who was both
criminal and virtuous.

I seek a teacher and a master
may he restore my sight hearing and speech
may he again name objects and ideas
may he separate darkness from light.

I am twenty-four
led to slaughter
I survived.

Adam Czerniawski

LAMENT

I turn to you high priests
teachers judges artists
shoemakers physicians officials
and to you my father
Hear me out.

I am not young
let the slenderness of my body
not deceive you
nor the tender whiteness of my neck
nor the fairness of my open brow
nor the down on my sweet lip
nor my cherubic laughter
nor the spring in my step

I am not young
let my innocence
not move you
nor my purity
nor my weakness
fragility and simplicity

I am twenty years old
I am a murderer
I am an instrument
blind as the axe
in the hands of an executioner
I struck a man dead
and with red fingers
stroked the white breasts of women.

Maimed I saw
neither heaven nor rose
nor bird nest tree
St Francis
Achilles nor Hector
For six years
blood gushed steaming from my nostrils
I do not believe in the changing of water into wine
I do not believe in the remission of sins
I do not believe in the resurrection of the body.

Magnus J. Krynski

SHE LOOKED AT THE SUN

In the marketplace where St Florian
pours forth a wooden stream of water
on a red comb of fire
beneath a silvery cloud
in the bright of day
stands a girl
and smiles to herself
sweetly as an angel

no one has seen
she rejoices in sun and warmth
and hums a tune

suddenly in my eye

in the eye of a passing stranger
who has survived the war
darkness pierces
light and joy
through the sun I see
a black sewer
a pit dank fetid
at the bottom
a little Jewish girl
who on liberation day
came out of hiding
after many years
she looked at the sun
stretched her arms before her went blind

Magnus J. Krynski

I SEE MADMEN

I see madmen who
had walked on the sea
believing to the end
and went to the bottom

they still rock
my uncertain boat

cruelly alive I push away
those stiff hands

I push them away year after year.

Adam Czerniawski

PIGTAIL

When all the women in the transport
had their heads shaved
four workmen with brooms made of birch twigs
swept up `
and gathered up the hair

Behind clean glass
the stiff hair lies
of those suffocated in gas chambers
there are pins and side combs
in this hair

The hair is not shot through with light
is not parted by the breeze
is not touched by any hand
or rain or lips

In huge chests
clouds of dry hair
of those suffocated
and a faded plait
a pigtail with a ribbon
pulled at school
by naughty boys.

The Museum, Auschwitz, 1948

Adam Czerniawski

IN THE MIDST OF LIFE

After the end of the world
after death
I found myself in the midst of life
creating myself
building life
people animals landscapes

this is a table I said
this is a table
there is bread and a knife on the table
knife serves to cut bread
people are nourished by bread

man must be loved
I learnt by night by day
what must one love
I would reply man

this is a window I said
this is a window
there is a garden beyond the window
I see an apple-tree in the garden
the apple-tree blossoms
the blossom falls
fruit is formed
ripens

my father picks the apple
the man who picks the apple
is my father

I sat on the threshold
that old woman who
leads a goat on a string
is needed more
is worth more
than the seven wonders of the world
anyone who thinks or feels
she is not needed
is a mass murderer

this is a man
this is a tree this is bread
people eat to live
I kept saying to myself
human life is important
human life has great importance

the value of life
is greater than the value of all things
which man has created
man is a great treasure
I repeated stubbornly

this is water I said
I stroked the waves with my hand
and talked to the river
water I would say
nice water
this is me

man talked to water
talked to the moon
to the flowers and to rain
talked to the earth
to the birds
to the sky

the sky was silent
the earth was silent
and if a voice was heard
flowing
from earth water and sky
it was a voice of another man

Adam Czerniawski

WARNING

Look he trusts again It's good
he's embracing a woman's body
He will live and create life
Look he takes in his hands the tools of work
He recalls what people
used to build the future from
It's good He will build

He walks through a field
Distinguishes tastes and colours
Recalls laughter
You mustn't startle him

The tables are laid with
crystal and china
Each hand of the woman
holding the pink flower
has five fingers

All the hairs on the heads
of the banqueters are numbered
and not a single hair will fall
without authority's leave

The pink flower flares and dies

why do the women have
three black legs each
and not a single head
where is the finger
with the gold ring
carpets woven from smoke
self-consumed
animals trees sheeted in flame
the pink flower flares and dies

the living and the dead commune
float in the air
and vainly seek a place
on the earth.

Magnus J. Krynski

FIGHT WITH AN ANGEL

The shadow of wings grew
an angel crowed he hummed
his wet nostrils
touched my eyes my lips
we fought on earth
made of trampled newspapers
on a garbage dump where
blood spit and bile
lay mixed with
the dung of words

the shadow of wings grew
and lo
there were two wings
huge from ear to ear
rose-coloured
among the clouds
on both sides of the head
our excrement covered
the playing field
and at last
he overpowered me
bound me dazzled me
with the word
drooled
chatted optimistically
and ascended the heaven of poetry

I grabbed his legs
and he fell
by the wall
into my garbage
and here am I
the form of a man
with light in my eyes
like thumbs

Victor Contoski

TO THE HEART

I saw
a specialist a cook
place his hand in the mouth
push it down
through the sheep's throat
touch the beating heart
close his fist on it
and tear it out with
one jerk
yes sir
that was
a specialist

Victor Contoski

THE LARVA

I am dead
but never have I been
so attached to life
my jaws are firmly locked
on small warm throats
on wrists
on pulses on the source
my fingers
have crooked
tightened
in warm
in warmth

I am dead
but never before
have I talked so much
about the future
about the future that is coming
about the future without which life
they say is impossible

and yet I have adjusted
I who grow cold
have fallen in love with movement
I desire movement I shift
from place to place arms outstretched
between Paris and Peking
Rome and Moscow
Warsaw and Hamburg
I decompose
ever more rapidly grandly
deafened I listen
simultaneously to the music of all ages
to all sounds blinded I examine
simultaneously the paintings of all schools

dead I create
hurriedly
new forms
that collide
and crushed create a new shape
dead I
have no love for silence

I value food and drink
attach importance
to the schedule of activities
live a full life
I am so much alive
that I cannot imagine
the second death

dead I
am so very busy
I keep on writing
though I know one goes off
always
with a fragment
with a fragment of the whole

the whole
of what
am I the larva of the new

Magnus J. Krynski

DRAFT OF A MODERN LOVE POEM

And yet white
is best described by gray
bird by stone
sunflowers
in December

love poems of old
were descriptions of the flesh
described this and that
for instance eyelashes

and yet red
should be described
by gray the sun by rain
poppies in November
lips by night

the most tangible
description of bread
is a description of hunger
in it is
the damp porous core
the warm interior
sunflowers at night
the breasts belly thighs of Cybele

a spring-clear
transparent description
of water
is a description of thirst

ashes
desert
it produces a mirage
clouds and trees move into
the mirror

Lack hunger
absence
of flesh
is a description of love
is a modern love poem

Magnus J. Krynski

MEMORY OF A DREAM
FROM THE YEAR 1963

I dreamed of
Leo Tolstoy

he was lying in bed
huge as the sun
in a mane
of tangled hair

the lion

I saw his
head
the face of corrugating golden iron
down which flowed
unbroken light

suddenly he was snuffed out
he turned black
and the skin of his hands and face
was rough

cracked
as the bark of an oak

I put the question to him
'what is to be done'

'nothing'
he replied

through all the furrows
crevices
the light began streaming toward me
an immense radiant smile
kept kindling

Magnus J. Krynski

PROOFS

Death will not correct
a single line of verse
she is no proof-reader
she is no sympathetic
lady editor

a bad metaphor is immortal

a shoddy poet who has died
is a shoddy dead poet

a bore bores after death
a fool keeps up his foolish chatter
from beyond the grave

Adam Czerniawski

BUSY WITH MANY JOBS

Busy with very urgent jobs
I forgot
one also has
to die

irresponsible
I kept neglecting that duty
or performed it
perfunctorily

as from tomorrow
things will be different

I'll start dying meticulously
wisely optimistically
without wasting time

Adam Czerniawski

Wisława Szymborska   POLAND

WISŁAWA SZYMBORSKA (1923–) was born in Prowenta-Bnin. She studied Polish philology and sociology at the Jagiellonian University in Cracow. Her earliest volumes of poetry, *Dlatego żyjemy* (That's Why We're Alive, 1952) and *Pytania zadawane sobie* (Questions for Oneself, 1954), are highly political. Later volumes were more philosophical and feminist, including *Wołanie do Yeti* (Calling to the Yeti, 1957), *Sól* (Salt, 1962) and *Sto pociech* (A Barrel of Laughs, 1967). Szymborska has received a number of awards, including the Cracow Literary Prize (1954), the State Prize (1955) and the Prize of the Ministry of Culture and Art (1963).

Wisława Szymborska is a versatile poet, her range extending from discursive political fable, or social allegory, to the personal lyric. The natural power and inventiveness of her writing occasionally produce what on first sight seems to be an excess of detail. But appearances are deceptive. She is just as capable of an excess of simplicity where the meaning seems utterly plain, the tone almost naive. Something about this puts one on one's guard: suddenly all is not so simple, so plain. Suddenly even the identity of the narrator is unclear. Intimations of horror, of negativity, infuse more or less conventional, if colourful, affirmations; poems change direction without missing a beat, posing what, in terms of the preceding material, are unanswerable questions. Szymborska's poetry, by diverse means, is constantly opening up surprising perspectives, juxtaposing illusion and reality, time and timelessness, history and actuality, the individual self and the forces that mould it or are moulded by it.

A single voice is heard through the different themes and styles, the ambiguities and paradoxes that she so elegantly deploys. It is fluent and supple, conversational, yet it does not buttonhole you, nor is it confessional in the sense of inviting you into a private world without regard for what is happening on the outside (or whether you want to be invited in). On the contrary, her poems, even the most apparently personal, gesture quite unaffectedly towards more universal themes. What emerges repeatedly is Szymborska's commitment to human beings as opposed to ideology, scientific dogma, or mere fashion, all that paraphernalia that is so apt to confuse us. Like the other poets represented in this anthology, she engages in an unending struggle with the forces of dehumanization, against everything that is allowed to take precedence over human beings, for it is here, in Holub's words, that 'begins the massacre of the innocents'.

Exaggeration? Under the circumstances, hardly. Compromise is out of the question. In the final analysis, Szymborska's all-knowing Cassandra knows less than those who live on in the shadow of their imminent destruction. Life itself is the supreme value, even *in extremis*. This paradox must be insisted upon, or the worst can be deemed to have already happened.

THE MUSEUM

There have been plates but no appetite.
Wedding rings but no love returned
for at least three hundred years.

There is a fan – where are the rosy cheeks?
There are swords – where is the anger?
Nor does the lute twang at dusk.

For want of eternity ten thousand
old things have been assembled.
A mossy guard is having sweet dreams
his moustaches draped over a showcase.

Metals, earthenware, a bird's feather
quietly triumph in time.
Just the giggle of a sweet thing's pin from ancient Egypt.

The crown has outlasted the head.
The hand has lost out to the glove.
The right shoe has won out over the foot.

As for me, I'm alive, please believe me.
The race with my dress is still on.
You can't imagine my rival's will to win!
And how much it would like to outlast me!

Magnus J. Krynski

THE WOMEN OF RUBENS

Giantesses, female fauna,
naked as the rumbling of barrels.
They sprawl in trampled beds,
sleep with mouths agape for crowing.
Their eyes have fled into the depths
and penetrate to the very core of glands
from which yeast seeps into the blood.

Daughters of the Baroque. Dough rises in kneading-troughs,
baths are asteam, wines glow ruby,
piglets of cloud gallop across the sky,
trumpets neigh an alert of the flesh.

O meloned, O excessive ones,
doubled by the flinging off of shifts,
trebled by the violence of posture,
you lavish dishes of love!

Their slender sisters had risen earlier,
before dawn broke in the picture.
No one noticed how, single file, they
had moved to the canvas's unpainted side.

Exiles of style. Their ribs all showing,
their feet and hands of birdlike nature.
Trying to take wing on bony shoulder blades.

The thirteenth century would have given them a golden
    background,
the twentieth – a silver screen.
The seventeenth had nothing for the flat of chest.

For even the sky is convex,
convex the angels and convex the god-
mustachioed Phoebus who on a sweaty
mount rides into the seething alcove.

Magnus J. Krynski

MEMORY AT LAST

Memory at last has what it sought.
My mother has been found, my father glimpsed.
I dreamed up for them a table, two chairs. They sat down.
Once more they seemed close, and once more living for me.
With the lamps of their two faces, at twilight,
they suddenly gleamed as if for Rembrandt.

Only now can I relate
the many dreams in which they've wandered, the many throngs
in which I've pulled them out from under wheels,
the many death-throes where they have collapsed into my arms.
Cut off – they would grow back crooked.
Absurdity forced them into masquerade.
Small matter that this could not hurt them outside me
if it hurt them inside me.
The gawking rabble of my dreams heard me calling 'mamma'
to something that hopped squealing on a branch.
And they laughed because I had a father with a ribbon in his hair.
I would wake up in shame.

Well, at long last.
On a certain ordinary night,
between a humdrum Friday and Saturday,
they suddenly appeared exactly as I wished them.
Seen in a dream, they yet seemed freed from dreams,
obedient only to themselves and nothing else.
All possibilities vanished from the background of the image,
accidents lacked a finished form.
Only they shone with beauty, for they were like themselves.
They appeared to me a long, long time, and happily.

I woke up. I opened my eyes.
I touched the world as if it were a carved frame.

Magnus J. Krynski

LAUGHTER

The little girl I was –
I knew her, naturally.
I have a few photos
from her brief life.
I feel a mirthful pity
for several little verses.
I remember a few events.

Yet
to make the man who's now with me
laugh and put his arms around me,
I recall only one small story:
the puppy love
of that plain little thing.

I tell
of her love for a student,
that is, how she wanted
him to look at her.

I tell
how she ran to meet him,
a bandage around her unhurt head,
so he'd at least – oh! – ask
what had happened.

A funny little girl.
How could she have known
that even despair yields profit
if by some good fortune
one should live a little longer.

I would give her money for a sweet.
I would give her money for a movie.
Off with you now, I'm busy.

But can't you see
the light is out.
Can't you understand
the door is closed.
Don't pull at the knob –
the man who laughed,
who put his arms around me,
is not that student of yours.

You'd better go back
where you came from.
I owe you nothing,
I'm an average woman
who only knows
when
to betray another's secret.

Don't look at us like that
with those eyes of yours
open much too wide
like the eyes of the dead.

Magnus J. Krynski

VOICES

You scarcely move your foot when out of nowhere spring
the Aborigines, O Marcus Aemilius.

Your heel's mired in the very midst of Rutulians.
In Sabines and Latins you're sinking up to your knees.
You're up to your waist, your neck, your nostrils
in Aequians and Volscians, O Lucius Fabius.

These small peoples are thick as flies, to the point of irritation,
satiation and nausea, O Quintus Decius.

One town, another, the hundred seventieth.
The stubbornness of the Fidenates. The ill-will of the Faliscans.
The blindness of the Ecetrans. The vacillation of the Antemnates.
The studied animosity of the Lavicanians, the Pelignians.
That's what drives us benevolent men to harshness
beyond each new hill, O Gaius Cloelius.

If only they weren't in our way, but they are,
the Auruncians, the Marsians, O Spurius Manlius.

The Tarquinians from here and there, the Etruscans from
    everywhere.
The Volsinians besides. The Veientians to boot.
Beyond all reason the Aulercians. Ditto the Sapinians
beyond all human patience, O Sextus Oppius.

Small peoples have small understanding.
Stupidity surrounds us in an ever-widening circle.
Objectionable customs. Benighted laws.
Ineffectual gods, O Titus Vilius.

Mounds of Hernicians. Swarms of Marrucinians.
An insect-like multitude of Vestians, of Samnites.
. The farther you go the more there are, O Servius Follius.

Deplorable are small peoples.
Their irresponsibility bears close watching
beyond each new river, O Aulus Junius.

I feel threatened by every new horizon.
That's how I see the problem, O Hostius Melius.

To that I, Hostius Melius, reply to you,
O Appius Pappius: Forward. Somewhere out there the world must
    have an end.

Magnus J. Krynski

EXPERIMENT

As a short before the main feature,
where the actors did all they could
to move me and even make me laugh,
an interesting experiment was shown
involving the head.

The head
a moment before had still belonged to –
now it was cut off,
everyone could see it had no body.
Protruding from the neck were glass tubes
that enabled the blood to keep circulating.
The head
was doing well.

With no sign of pain or even surprise
its eyes followed the movement of a flashlight.
It pricked up its ears at the sound of a bell.
Its wet nose could tell
the smell of fatback from odourless nonexistence,
and licking its chops with obvious relish,
it salivated to the greater glory of physiology.

A dog's faithful head,
a dog's worthy head,
when stroked it half shut its eyes,
firmly convinced it still was part of a whole
that arched its back when patted
and wagged its tail.

I thought of happiness and suddenly was afraid.
For if that's all life is about,
the head
was happy.

Magnus J. Krynski

WORDS

'La Pologne? La Pologne? It's very cold over there, isn't it?' the lady asked and sighed with relief. So many new countries have cropped up recently that the weather is the only safe subject for conversation.

'Oh yes, dear,' I wanted to answer her, 'poets have to write in gloves in my country. I won't say they don't ever take them off; they do when the full moon warms them up. They extol the simple life of sealherds in thundering stanzas because nothing less sonorous could overcome the roaring blizzard. Our classics, icicles of frozen ink in hand, carve on snowdrifts stamped smooth. The rest, a bunch of decadents, weep over their bad fortune, their tears little stars of snow. Whoever wants to drown himself, must buy an axe and cut a hole in the ice. That's how it is, dear.'

I wanted to tell her all this. But I forgot the French word for seal. Neither was I sure about icicle and axe.

'La Pologne? La Pologne? It's very cold over there, isn't it?'

'Pas du tout,' I answered icily.

Krystof Zarzecki

INNOCENCE

Conceived on a mattress of human hair,
Gerda, Erica, perhaps Margarette.
She doesn't, really doesn't know anything about it.
That kind of knowledge is impossible
to accept or transmit.
The Greek Furies were simply too just.
We'd be put off today by their winged savagery.

Irma, Brigide, perhaps Frederike.
Twenty years old, scarcely more.
Fluent in the three languages useful for travel.

Her firm offers for export
only the best mattresses of synthetic fibre.
Export draws nations together.

Bertha, Ulrika, perhaps Hildegaard.
No beauty, but tall and slim.
Her cheeks, neck, breasts, thighs, belly
in full bloom just now and glorious sheen of novelty,
treads in barefooted joy on Europe's beaches,
shaking loose her blond knee-length hair.

Don't have it cut – said her hairdresser –
once cut, it never grows again so rich.
Please believe me – it's been tested
tausend – und tausendmal.

Jan Darowski

WRITING A CURRICULUM VITAE

What must you do?
You must submit an application
and enclose a Curriculum Vitae.

Regardless of how long your life is,
the Curriculum Vitae should be short.

Be concise, select facts.
Change landscapes into addresses
and vague memories into fixed dates.

Of all your loves, mention only the marital,
and of the children, only those who were born.

It's more important who knows you
than whom you know.
Travels – only if abroad.
Affiliations – to what, not why.
Awards – but not for what.

Write as if you never talked with yourself,
as if you looked at yourself from afar.

Omit dogs, cats, and birds,
mementos, friends, dreams.

State price rather than value,
title rather than content.
Shoe size, not where one is going,
the one you are supposed to be.

Enclose a photo with one ear showing.
What counts is its shape, not what it hears.

What does it hear?
The clatter of machinery that shreds paper.

Grazyna Drabik and Austin Flint

SEEN FROM ABOVE

A dead beetle lies on a country road.
On its belly, carefully folded, three pairs of legs.
Instead of the chaos of death – neatness and order.
The grimness of this sight is moderate,
the scope strictly local: from spear-grass to mint.
Sadness is not spreading.
The sky is deep blue.

For the sake of our peace,
as if their death were more shallow,
animals do not perish but simply die,
losing, we want to believe, less of feeling and the world,
coming, we imagine, off a less tragic scene.
Their meek souls do not haunt us at night,
they respect the distance,
keep their place.

And here on the road this dead beetle,
unlamented, shines in the sun.
We give it no more than a glance:
it looks as if nothing important happened to it.
The important is connected, it seems, only with us.
With our life only, only with our death,
the death that enjoys a forced priority.

Grazyna Drabik and Sharon Olds

MONOLOGUE FOR CASSANDRA

It's me, Cassandra.
And this is my city covered with ashes.
And this is my rod, and the ribbons of a prophet.
And this is my head full of doubts.

It's true, I won.
What I said would happen
hit the sky with a fiery glow.
Only prophets whom no one believes
witness such things,
only those who do their job badly.
And everything happens so quickly,
as if they had not spoken.

Now I remember clearly
how people, seeing me, broke off in mid-sentence.
Their laughter stopped.
They moved away from each other.
Children ran towards their mothers.
I didn't even know their vague names.
And that song about a green leaf –
nobody ever finished singing it in front of me.

I loved them.
But I loved them from a height.
From above life.
From the future. Where it's always empty

and where it's easy to see death.
I am sorry my voice was harsh.
Look at yourselves from a distance, I cried,
look at yourselves from a distance of stars.
They heard and lowered their eyes.

They just lived.
Not very brave.
Doomed.
In departing bodies, from the moment of birth.
But they had this watery hope,
a flame feeding on its own glittering.
They knew what a moment was.
How I wish for one moment, any,
before –
I was proved right.
So what. Nothing comes of it.
And this is my robe scorched by flames.
And these are the odds and ends of a prophet.
And this is my distorted face.
The face that did not know its own beauty.

Grazyna Drabik and Sharon Olds

ONION

It's really something, the onion.
It doesn't have entrails.
It is itself, through and through,
all of it just onion.
Onionlike on the outside,
oniony to the core,
the onion could look into itself
without any fear.

In us lurks the strange and the wild
barely covered by the skin.
In us, an inferno of guts,
violent anatomy.

In the onion, nothing but the onion,
no twisted intestines.
Undressed many times, it repeats itself
to its depths.

A consistent creature, the onion,
a well-made thing.
Inside one, simply another,
in a larger, a smaller,
and in the next, the next.
Centrifugal fugue.
Echo in unison.

The onion, I do appreciate it:
the prettiest belly in the world.
It wears halos
for its own glory.
In us, fat, nerves, veins,
valves, and secrets.
For us, it's unattainable,
the idiotism of perfection.

Grazyna Drabik and Sharon Olds

CLOTHES

You take off, he takes off, we take off
coats, jackets, blouses, shirts,
made of cotton, nylon, wool,
pants, skirts, underwear, socks,
folding them, hanging them, throwing them over
backs of chairs, screens, for the moment,
the doctor says, it's nothing serious,
please dress, take a vacation, don't worry,
use these in case of, before sleep, after meals,
come back in three months, a year, a year and a half,
you see? and you thought, and we suspected,
and he imagined, and they feared,

it's time to tie, to fasten, hands still trembling,
shoelaces, buckles, zippers, snaps,
buttons, collars, neckties, belts,
and to pull from your sleeve, your handbag, your pocket,
a crumpled scarf, dotted, flowered, striped,
suddenly useful again.

Grazyna Drabik and Sharon Olds

IN PRAISE OF MY SISTER

My sister doesn't write poems,
and I don't think she'll suddenly start writing poems.
She is like her mother who didn't write poems,
and like her father, who didn't write poems either.
Under my sister's roof I feel safe:
my sister's husband would rather die than write poems.
And – this begins to sound like a found poem –
none of my relations is engaged in writing poems.

There are no old poems in my sister's files
and there aren't any new ones in her handbag.
And when my sister invites me to lunch,
I know she has no plans to read me her poems.
Her soups are excellently improvised,
there is no coffee spilt on her manuscripts.

There are many families where no one writes poems,
but where they do – it's rarely just one person.
Sometimes poetry splashes down in cascades of generations,
creating terrible whirlpools in mutual feelings.

My sister cultivates a quite good spoken prose
and her writing's restricted to holiday postcards,
the text promising the same each year:
that when she returns
she'll tell us
all

all
all about it.

Adam Czerniawski

HOMECOMING

He was back. Said nothing.
But it was clear something had upset him.
He lay down in his suit.
Hid his head under the blanket.
Drew up his knees.
He's about forty, but not at this moment.
He exists – but only as much as in his mother's belly
behind seven skins, in protective darkness.
Tomorrow he is lecturing on homeostasis
in metagalactic space-travel.
But now he's curled up and fallen asleep.

Adam Czerniawski

THE TERRORIST, HE WATCHES

The bomb will explode in the bar at twenty past one.
Now it's only sixteen minutes past.
Some will still have time to enter,
some to leave.

The terrorist's already on the other side.
That distance protects him from all harm
and well it's like the pictures:

A woman in a yellow jacket, she enters.
A man in dark glasses, he leaves.
Boys in jeans, they're talking.
Sixteen minutes past and four seconds.
The smaller one he's lucky, mounts his scooter,
but that taller chap he walks in.

Seventeen minutes and forty seconds.
A girl, she walks by, a green ribbon in her hair.
But that bus suddenly hides her.
Eighteen minutes past.
The girl's disappeared.
Was she stupid enough to go in, or wasn't she.
We shall see when they bring out the bodies.

Nineteen minutes past.
No one else appears to be going in.
On the other hand, a fat bald man leaves.
But seems to search his pockets and
at ten seconds to twenty past one
he returns to look for his wretched gloves.

It's twenty past one.
Time, how it drags.
Surely, it's now.
No, not quite.
Yes, now.
The bomb, it explodes.

Adam Czerniawski

MIRACLE MART

Common miracle:
the happening of many common miracles.

Ordinary miracle:
invisible dogs barking
in the silence of the night.

A miracle among many:
a tiny ethereal cloud
able to cover a large heavy moon.

Several miracles in one:
an alder reflected in water

moreover turned from left to right
moreover growing crown downwards
yet not reaching the bottom
though the waters are shallow.

An everyday miracle:
soft gentle breezes
gusting during storms.

Any old miracle:
cows are cows.

And another like it:
just this particular orchard
from just this pip.

Miracle without frock coat or top hat:
a scattering of white doves.

Miracle – what else would you call it:
today the sun rose at 3.14
and will set at 20.01.

Miracle which doesn't sufficiently amaze:
though the hand has fewer than six fingers
yet it has more than four.

Miracle – just look around:
the world ever-present.

An extra miracle, just as everything is extra:
what is unthinkable
is thinkable.

Adam Czerniawski

π

π deserves our full admiration
three point one four one.
All its following digits are also non-recurring,
five nine two because it never ends.
It cannot be grasped *six five three five* at a glance,
eight nine in a calculus
seven nine in imagination,
or even *three two three eight* in a conceit, that is, a comparison
four six with anything else
two six four three in the world.
The longest snake on earth breaks off after several metres.
Likewise, though at greater length, do fabled snakes.
The series comprising π
doesn't stop at the edge of the sheet,
it can stretch across the table, through the air,
through the wall, leaf, bird's nest, clouds, straight to heaven,
through all the heavens' chasms and distensions.
How short, how mouse-like, is the comet's tail!
How frail a star's ray, that it bends in any bit of space!
Meanwhile, *two three fifteen three hundred nineteen*
my telephone number the size of your shirt
the year nineteen hundred and seventy three sixth floor
the number of inhabitants sixty five pennies
the waist measurement two fingers a charade a code,
in which *singing still dost soar, and soaring ever singest*
and *please stay calm*
and also *heaven and earth shall pass away,*
but not π, no, certainly not,
she's still on with her passable *five*
above-average *eight*
the not-final *seven*
urging, yes, urging a sluggish eternity
to persevere.

Adam Czerniawski

A CONTRIBUTION ON PORNOGRAPHY

There is no debauchery worse than thought.
This wantonness is rampant like a wind-blown weed
on a bed reserved for begonias!

For those who think, nothing is sacred.
Brazenly calling everything by name,
perverse analyses, meretricious syntheses,
wild and dissolute pursuit of naked facts,
lustful petting of sensitive subjects,
a spawning ground of opinions – that's just what they're after.

On a clear day, under cover of darkness,
they consort in pairs, triangles and rings.
No constraint on age or sex of partners.
Friends corrupt friends.
Degenerate daughters deprave their fathers.
Their eyes gleam, their cheeks glow.
A brother pimps for his younger sister.

They prefer the fruit,
of the forbidden tree of knowledge
to pink boobs in illustrated mags –
that essentially simple-minded pornography.
The books that divert them have no pictures,
their sole pleasure are special sentences
scored with thumbnail or crayon.

In what shocking positions
with what licentious simplicity
mind can impregnate mind!
Positions unknown even to the Kama Sutra.
During these trysts only tea is steaming.
People sit on chairs, move their lips.
Each crosses his own legs.
So one foot touches the floor,
the other swings free.

But occasionally someone gets up
goes to the window
and through a chink in the curtains
watches the street.

Adam Czerniawski

Natan Zach

NATAN ZACH (1930–) was born in Berlin, and came to Israel in 1935. He began to write as a student at the Hebrew University in Jerusalem, publishing his first collection of poems in 1955. He worked as repertory director and later as advisor to the Israeli theatre, from 1960 to 1967. Zach is also a translator and has rendered plays by Brecht, Dürrenmatt, Frisch, Strindberg and others into Hebrew. He co-translated a collection of Palestinian–Arab folk songs, *Dekalim U'temarim* (Palm and Dates, 1967), with the Palestinian poet Rashed Hussein. In 1968 Zach settled in England, receiving a doctorate from the University of Essex and working as the London news editor for the Jewish Telegraphic Agency. In 1979 he returned to Israel and began teaching at Haifa University. He received Israel's most prestigious literary award, the Bialik Prize, in 1981.

Natan Zach's linguistic origins, like those of his compatriots Dan Pagis and Yehuda Amichai, are German, but more than them, he seems to have become a new type of being in the new land of Israel. In some respects, he seems actually identifiable with that individual who appears so frequently in Pagis's allegorical poems – transported, astonished to find himself not yet extinct, re-made yet remembering everything. Peter Everwine (in his preface to *The Static Element*, 1982) has well described the unique quality of Zach's work: 'To follow the movement of a Zach poem is to follow a nervous and analytical intelligence that refuses to be taken in by conventions of sentiment or poetry. A tenacious ironist, deeply aware of human isolation and the elaborate illusions we construct as our refuge (the refuge of poetry included), his characteristic attitude is "be careful ... Don't expect." His reticence becomes a way of holding things in check, an integrity that is both a literary position and a personal response to experience.' Zach is cautious, level-headed, serious, in the most potent, least self-important way. There is not a hint of shrillness in the irony referred to above. In these respects and others, he strikes me as an exemplary poet.

BE CAREFUL

Be careful. Open your life
only to the wind that has touched distance.

Suffer the absent. Speak up
only in the nights of solitude. Know the day,
the fixed season, the moment,
and don't beg. Pay attention to what is still. Learn to bless
the shadow just beneath the skin. Don't
hide in words. Sit with the counsel of worms,
the wisdom of the maggot. Don't expect.

Peter Everwine and Shulamit Yasny-Starkman

GREATER COURAGE

The courage to wait
is greater than the courage to confess.
With pain it's easier to gain the sympathy
of others, which is not the case
with waiting.

You are alone here. You have a picture
on the wall, straighten the rug, listen to footsteps pass,
think that you're miserable but remind yourself
in this you are not unique. Yet carefully
you tear a letter into shreds.
Here you are wholly on your own: judge yourself,
if you must. But remember: this also
is not what matters.

Peter Everwine and Shulamit Yasny-Starkman

AGAINST PARTING

My tailor is against parting.
That's why, he
said, he's not going away;
he doesn't want to part
from his only daughter. He's definitely
against parting.

Once, he parted from his wife
and he never did see her
after this (Auschwitz).
Parted
from his three sisters and
these he never again
looked upon (Buchenwald).
He once parted from his mother (his father
died at a ripe old age). Now
he's against parting.

In Berlin he was
my father's close companion. They passed
a good time in
that Berlin. The time passed. Now
he'll never go away. He's
most definitely
(my father died meanwhile)
against parting.

Peter Everwine and Shulamit Yasny-Starkman

BE ATTENTIVE

Be attentive to this trembling shade.
Stretch out your hand to feel the wind, touch
carefully this tree. It's green, and greener still
at the crown, the trunk
a little bitten, though it still drinks deeply
from the earth which no one sees
in the city.
Be attentive, feel, touch carefully. Breathe in
the light, harder. Illuminate
each cloud. It's passing. And night
won't wait.

Peter Everwine and Shulamit Yasny-Starkman

KING SOLOMON'S CAMEL*

King Solomon's Camel is a hypocritical creature.
The encyclopaedia (always objective) attributes,
without scruple, to him the description of dangerous carnivore.
Dangerous, it is said, because of his
developed ability for camouflage.
In South America he devours even frogs and lizards.

Here in Israel, he is green; or white and green; less voracious;
satisfied with flies and other insects. And yet
here, too, he's not loath – just as abroad – to eat up
his own species: females, the males; larvae, their brothers.

And he can deceive: when he's in wait for his prey,
he can be seen sitting, calmly; only his head, nodding,
with his predatory legs, upright, like the hands of man
held in prayer together. This posture produced,

with ancient people, an illusion. The Greeks possessed
the finest, mistaking this dangerous predator
for a holy man, and seer. The Germans named him:
'He who prays to God'; whereas the Muslims believe
that Solomon's Camel prays with his face towards Mecca.

For us Jews, the direction matters less; although even
for us, the sight of a head nodding may excite
certain associations; not all of them zoological.

Strange then that creature, small, dangerous carnivore,
white and green, that was able enough to deceive
not only frogs and lizards, but such respectable hosts
of believers, religions; with just a few movements
executed in perfect mental calm.

Jon Silkin

---

* *Gemal Hamelekh Shlomo* (King Solomon's Camel) is the Hebrew for Praying Mantis.

Reiner Kunze

REINER KUNZE (1933–) was born in Oelsmitz. He studied philosophy and journalism at the University of Leipzig, where he stayed on, to teach, for four years. In 1959 he left the University, under political attack from the academic community. He worked as an industrial labourer, and then in 1962 turned to freelance writing. Kunze's work was first banned in East Germany in 1968, when he publicly protested against the invasion of Czechoslovakia. That same year the Czech Writers' Union honoured him with a prize for his adaptations from the Czech. In 1971 he received the German Youth Book Prize, and in 1973 the prize of the Second International Writers' Conference in Molle, Sweden. Kunze began to publish in West Germany, where his reputation grew steadily, although he continued to live in East Germany. In 1973 he received the literary award of the Bavarian Academy of Fine Arts. The East German government finally authorized the publication of a carefully selected volume of his poetry, which contained only poems previously published, after which the ban on his work was reimposed. In 1976, as a result of the publication in West Germany of the best-selling *Die wunderbaren Jahre* (The Wonderful Years), Kunze was expelled from the East German Writers' Union. He resettled in the West and now lives in Greiz.

Kunze has been placed last in the present anthology, not only because he is of a somewhat later generation than most of the other poets represented, but also because there is, it seems to me, a terminal quality about his work. Kunze's poetry contains almost too much bitterness to be called ironical, though he still manages to maintain a sufficient distance from his material to be able to keep it in focus. Even if his poetry has, perhaps, taken on an even heavier burden of despair than that of his immediate predecessors, it is still able to continue doing its work: exposing, warning, calling us back, either at, or after, the eleventh hour. Kunze's severe, deliberate, meticulously fashioned poem-splinters are strategically placed so as to alert us to the dangers of oppression, in whatever form, aesthetic, political, or physical. They tell us what we think we know already but with such a controlled venom or anger, such a probing perception of evil, that we are startled into a new awareness. This is a last-ditch poetry – resist *now*, or it will be too late; or, perhaps, that it already *is* too late, but all the writer can do is warn. Still implicit, of course, is hope, even if it is hope on the very edge of extinction.

THE BRINGERS OF BEETHOVEN

For Ludvik Kundera

They set out to bring Beethoven
to everyone.
And as they had a record with them
they played for speedier understanding
Symphony no. 5, in C minor, opus 67

But the man M. said
it was too loud for him, he
was getting old

In the night the bringers of Beethoven put
up poles in streets and squares
hooked up cables, connected
loudspeakers, and with the dawn
for more thorough acquaintance came the strains of
Symphony no. 5, in C minor, opus 67,
came loud enough to be heard
in the mute fields.

But the man M. said he had a headache,
went home about noon, closed
doors and windows and praised
the thickness of the walls

Thus provoked, the bringers of Beethoven strung
wire on to the walls and hung
loudspeakers over the windows, and in
through the panes came
Symphony no. 5, in C minor, opus 67

But the man M. stepped out of the house and denounced
the bringers of Beethoven;
they all asked him what he had
against Beethoven.

Thus attacked, the bringers of Beethoven knocked
on M.'s door and when they opened up they
forced a foot inside; praising the neatness of the place
they went in.

The conversation happened to turn
to Beethoven,
and to enliven the subject they happened
to have with them
Symphony no. 5, in C minor, opus 67

But the man M. hit the bringers of
Beethoven with an iron ladle.
He was arrested just in time.

M.'s act was called homicidal
by lawyers and judges of the bringers of Beethoven.
But they must not give up hoping.
He was sentenced
to Symphony no. 5, in C minor, opus 67,
by Ludwig van Beethoven

M. kicked and screamed,
until the loudspeakers stopped
beyond the mute fields

He was just too old, the bringers of Beethoven said.
But by M.'s coffin, they said,
are his children

And his children demanded
that over the coffin of
the man M. should be played
Symphony no. 5, in C minor, opus 67

Gordon and Gisela Brotherston

THE END OF ART

You must not, said the owl to the capercailzie,
you must not sing of the sun
The sun is not important

The capercailzie took
the sun out of its poem

You are an artist,
said the owl to the capercailzie

And all was dark

Michael Hamburger

BRIEF CURRICULUM

DIALECTICS

Ignorant people so that
you'll remain ignorant

we shall
school you

AESTHETICS

Until imperialism has
been defeated
regard as an ally

Picasso

ETHICS

In the centre stands
mankind

Not
this man or that man

Michael Hamburger

THE NEED FOR CENSORSHIP

Everything
can be retouched

except
the negative
inside us

Michael Hamburger

LOW VOLUME

Then for
twelve years
I was forbidden to publish
says the man on the radio

I think of X
and start counting

Michael Hamburger

REPLY

My father, you say,
my father down the pit
has gashes in his back,
scars,
        traces of fallen rock,

while I, yes I,
sing of love.

I say:
yes, that's why.

Ewald Osers

THE AERIAL

1
The street threatened
to saw it down

The aerial fled
to the roof-tree, here

the house pointed
its finger at it

The aerial fled
into the room, here

the walls pointed
their fingers at it

The aerial fled
into the head, it

offered safety

2
For the moment

Ewald Osers

HYMN TO A WOMAN UNDER INTERROGATION

Bad (she said) was
the moment of undressing

Then
exposed to their gaze she
discovered everything

about them

Ewald Osers

FIRST LETTER FROM TAMARA A.

You say you had a letter from
Tamara A., fourteen years old and soon
to join the Komsomol

In her town, she says, are
four monuments: Lenin
                    Chapayev
                    Kirov
                    Kuybyshev

A pity, you say, she doesn't write
about herself

She does write
about herself, daughter

Ewald Osers

Appendix 1

YEHUDA AMICHAI

In conversation with Daniel Weissbort

AMICHAI: What was your main question? What sums up all the rest?

WEISSBORT: *I expect, I hope, I'll come to it in due course! But let me start here. In the early sixties, Ted [Hughes], travelling around Europe – specifically, to certain poetry festivals in Europe, Spoleto, for example – came across the work, in anonymous translations which were done for the purpose of the festival, of various poets, about whom we knew nothing at all at the time, though they were already famous in their own countries. I'm speaking of poets like Różewicz, Popa, Holub ...*

AMICHAI: Voznesensky ...

WEISSBORT: *And I think he came across your work ...*

AMICHAI: I also was in Spoleto, but it was the second. Ted was in the first. No, I know exactly how it was. You wrote a letter to Dennis Silk and you wanted from him just Israeli poets, because he had translated some, so he sent you a bunch of them, mostly my poems.

WEISSBORT: *I think only your poems.*

AMICHAI: Even only my poems.

WEISSBORT: *I was starting a magazine,* Modern Poetry in Translation, *with Ted. The reason I started it was because Ted, as I said, had come across these poets and had given me some examples of their work, and these rough translations – they were really quite good translations, I think – impressed us both a good deal. So, it was really coming across this wealth of poetry, about which we knew nothing before, and particularly in view of the inertness of the English scene at the time, and the American scene too, as it seemed to us, that we felt the need to start a magazine. That was in the early sixties. And so when he suggested it to me, I wrote to people – just trying to find out.*

AMICHAI: People you knew?

WEISSBORT: *Yes, people I knew. For contacts. Max Hayward, at Oxford, for instance, put me on to a man called Aleksandr Stefanović, who was a critic in Yugoslavia, and this man sent me some poems by Vasko Popa. I had Dennis Silk's name from someone at the Israeli Embassy and he sent me poems by you, in various translations, but one or two by himself – very good. We published these in the first number of the magazine and it was through that that Ted got interested in your work and that he interested Assia Gutmann. So, really, this anthology is just a kind of – not exactly commemorative, because that sounds as if it's all over already! – but an anthology of...*

AMICHAI: ... the good old days!

WEISSBORT: *Yes, a good-old-days anthology! There seemed at the time to be something, which I couldn't define and I'm not sure whether I could define it even now, but there seemed to be something, nevertheless, linking these poets, more than just the fact that they belonged to roughly the same generation, born in the mid-to-late twenties. So the anthology focuses on this group. It springs from some sort of a conviction, an irrational conviction perhaps, of the existence of a connecting thread. Anyway, what does link them, at least in my mind, is that they are all terribly good, terribly interesting, and terribly bright! I mean bright, not just in the sense of intelligent, but that their poetry is bright.*

AMICHAI: It's also bright, I think, because of so much pressure and suffering, which clears, so to say.

WEISSBORT: *It's clairvoyant.*

AMICHAI: It's clairvoyant, but because all these lives, the historical lives and political lives, are so much involved in our world that this makes all the other stuff sink down ... Because people live in so much turmoil, so it's actually a real function of poetry to keep things clear, to be clear-minded. There is the other theory, that the earth is clear-minded and dull, and the poet should put some mystery and drunkenness into it ...

WEISSBORT: *The anthology really concentrates on what Milan Kundera calls Central Europe, Central rather than Eastern. And yet, somehow, I've always associated you with this, even though you weren't in Europe during the war. You've been in plenty of wars, but you weren't in Europe.*

AMICHAI: The Israeli wars are a sort of continuation of World War Two: the good guys against the bad guys! It was the underdogs against the big oil thieves and the wicked capitalists, so I think it was a kind of ... just the other day, we were talking about the Israeli War of Liberation and I told how our unit, which was a kind of partisan unit ... We had volunteers who came from nowhere; there was no registration, people just came, but one was an Englishman. And then there was a group of ex-French *maquis* people, even a French nobleman, the Marquis de something. He was one of the leaders of the *maquis* in the south. After the war he went to Israel and worked. So someone told me that he knew someone who said: "That was my only way to fight after the Spanish Civil War.'

WEISSBORT: *You were born in Germany, but in fact you're not ...*

AMICHAI: I'm not, because I grew up also in a very orthodox home. I knew Hebrew from childhood.

WEISSBORT: *So it was partly accident, I suppose, that we discovered your work at the same time as we discovered Holub's and Różewicz's, though, for me, it's part of a single experience in a way, and a very important one. It made me see that poetry was writeable! That sounds pretty simple-minded, to say the least. But, somehow, the British literary tradition put a wall around experience. It admitted certain parts and excluded the rest. When I read Holub, or Różewicz, or you, I realized that poetry could be everything, or anything. On the other hand, when we read, say, Popa, or Różewicz – Różewicz, in particular – another quality which impressed us was the spareness, the (now fashionable) minimalist quality; whereas your work, of course, is quite the opposite, tremendously rich in metaphor. And yet, somehow, this doesn't seem to be a contradiction.*

AMICHAI: No, no. Because the metaphors hold the poems, the images and metaphors. A metaphor is like a little poem. To me, the core of the poem is really the image. For me, the invention of the metaphor is the greatest human invention. Because it opened up the ways that you think of something, which is like something else, so it establishes some kind of dual existence and it opens up an endless richness. Poets actually still share the firstness of human invention, because poetry hasn't changed much in thousands of years. And you can read very great poems of the past with twentieth-century eyes. You don't have to switch over. The same goes for more ancient poetry, for the Bible, and more ancient texts still. Only the material has changed, the material of the images and metaphors. Instead of saying, as in the Bible, *The Song of Songs*, 'You are beautiful like the Tower of David', or 'You are beautiful like an Egyptian horse', so now they would say: 'You are beautiful like a cardinal' or something. But the difference is very little. And in a war poem, once they used to write about arrows and bows; now they say, 'I want to lay down my machine-gun.' So, still in our day, a lot of people seem to think that you can't use in a poem a word like 'machine-gun', or 'computer' or 'television'. Of course, there are a lot of poets who so much want to be *in* that immediately they fill their poems with computers and Star Wars and whatnot, which is also wrong. But on the other hand, to write war poems, like the great Israeli poet, Nathan Alterman, who during the '48 war wrote very good poetry, but never mentioned the words 'sub-machine-gun' or 'hand grenade', it was always 'sword' and 'arrow' ... I once asked him and he simply said, 'You can't write in a poem ...'

WEISSBORT: *So, he was inhibited by the convention ... What I like about your work is that somehow you're not exclusive. You just draw on whatever's going on around you, in your world, and everything enlivens everything else. Not only do you draw on the world around you, but you also draw on the past.*

AMICHAI: Yes, because it's a part of that world ... You know, there is an old Jewish saying, from the Bible, that there's nothing early and late, everything is constantly present. I have the feeling also, in my personal life, that I can still go back to my childhood. Not physically, but it all exists in one big space, totally timeless. So, I can reach out everywhere: to the times of King David or to the times of my childhood, because it's all known and it's one space. There's no past and future.

WEISSBORT: *In a way, this seems to distinguish your verse from some of the poets I've mentioned, in that they seem to be more focused ...*

AMICHAI: ... on things of culture, yes.

WEISSBORT: *And there's less personal involvement.*

AMICHAI: Herbert. I'm thinking of his Hamlet poem, which is his most famous poem ...

WEISSBORT: *The specific question, the main question, I had wanted to put to you, the same question I put to Holub when he was here was – I suppose in a way we've answered it! – Did you feel, or do you feel, that you belong to a distinct generation of poets, whose work crosses linguistic frontiers more readily than poetry appeared to do before? Of course, your poetry – I'm using the plural form! – is very much bound up with its respective languages, and yet it is more – I dislike the word! – more 'international' than some of the earlier poetry.*

AMICHAI: Also, than the later ... It's more biographical, because we were shaped by history much more, because those born in the mid-twenties, don't forget, were old enough to get the whole thing, most of us as soldiers, and, in my case, I was still young enough to get three wars in the Middle East. So, we are really at the core of the twentieth century, the whole existential experience of World War Two. It started with the Spanish Civil War and with a lot of people coming to freedom, and, I would say, even the disappointment from communism, which also plays its part – without turning us into cynics. I think the writing helped us not to turn into cynics.

WEISSBORT: *But there's certainly a lot of irony.*

AMICHAI: Okay, yes, but not cynicism.

WEISSBORT: *And there is a lot of sadness, of reflection on the horrors of our century. But the very fact of writing such concrete, such enjoyable poetry is already, it seems to me ...*

AMICHAI: ... a way out?

WEISSBORT: *A way out, however sad the message. Another question I put to Holub, although I don't know that this is really relevant to you ... Różewicz said something in an interview, which I found particularly striking at the time: 'I cannot understand that poetry should survive when the men who created that poetry are dead. What I revolted against is that it had survived the end of the world as though nothing had happened.' And he added 'I regard my own poems with acute mistrust. I fashion them out of the remnants of words from the great rubbish dump, the great cemetery.' I don't feel that about your poetry, and yet ...*

AMICHAI: It's like the bottom of a big kettle ... scraps of the whole mixture of things, remnants of history and everything.

WEISSBORT: *I'm not going to ask you about influences – or perhaps I shall! – but when did you get to know about the other poets of your generation, Celan, for example?*

AMICHAI: Celan, quite late. The first poets were Rilke and Else Lasker-Schüler. And then, when I was in the British army, I came by chance across ... It was a very funny chance, really, in the mobile library which the British had in World War Two ... This one turned over in the sand, somewhere in the Egyptian desert, and it had rained, so it was all muddy and no one cared about lifting the car up, so the whole box with the books was spilled out, and I came across an anthology, the Faber anthology – I think in 1938 it came out; it had a blue cover ...

WEISSBORT: *Yes. Edited by Michael Roberts.*

AMICHAI: Yes. I think it's one of the best anthologies. It's there I came upon Auden and Eliot, these two ... and Spender. This was in 1944, and I didn't write much poetry at the time, I didn't consider it.

WEISSBORT: *And when did you come across poets like Herbert, Różewicz?*

AMICHAI: Only through your magazine, and then through the international festivals.

WEISSBORT: *So, that was all in the sixties?*

AMICHAI: Yes, in the sixties.

WEISSBORT: *Were they translated into Hebrew?*

AMICHAI: Now they are. It started in the last five years. There is a translation of Miłosz and Herbert, and Else Lasker-Schüler.

WEISSBORT: *And then you met them ... Do you think there is a danger – this is on a somewhat different theme – because of English being a world language, and because of the publicity surrounding the arts, of writers writing in order to be translated? Writing something that is translatable, so to speak?*

AMICHAI: I am sure. The same way as I believe there are a lot of writers who write something because they think it could be made into a movie.

But that's more excusable, because, after all, a good movie is as good as a good novel. But I'm sure it becomes kind of wishy-washy, like ... There is this revolutionary-first poetry ... it produces the worst literature. The anti-Vietnam War movement was a good movement, but it corrupted a lot of very good poets! And then there is this other kind of poetry, like workshop poetry in America, which all looks alike. You know it? And then women's poetry, black poetry, Jewish poetry, and they all look alike in a way. That's a danger. It's so easy now to read things. Many things are translated and people go to each other's country. Which is okay, but immediately – it doesn't have time to be well digested – so, immediately it comes out.

[*Next day*]

WEISSBORT: *You said that you, in fact, got to know about poets like Popa, Holub and Różewicz partly through the magazine?*

AMICHAI: And later through those international meetings. But especially it was the first number of the magazine. It triggered off, really, a lot of international activity.

WEISSBORT: *I suppose that it's precisely the first issues of any magazine where the essence is to be found, because you want to make ...*

AMICHAI: It expresses a certain cultural tendency, not just a magazine.

WEISSBORT: *I suppose we had a somewhat more synoptic view, whereas individual writers, particularly writing in countries that did not have immediate access to such material, didn't so much ... Anyway, I'm harping on this a bit, but when you in fact finally got to know some of the poets I've mentioned, in the sixties and seventies, did you have much influence on one another? Or perhaps influence is the wrong word.*

AMICHAI: I'm not so sure, because each one of us came already with ... Influence, sure, because no one escapes it ... People growing up in the same area, experiencing the same events, are influenced in the same way, of course. In learning language, you're influenced by your parents and teachers. But, the main thing is to get *free*, to find your *own* way! The music of Mozart is all influences, Italian, etc. etc., and yet ... I know there's an avant-garde – probably has to be in all fields of life – but these are not always the best musicians or artists. The great ones are those who really sum up something. Every writer should express his age. People say, well, I'm not well known now, but in the twenty-first century I'll be known. The twenty-first century will look after itself, don't worry! Use yourself and your life as an indicator, like a thermometer, and put it in the world, to indicate your position, like in ships you have to find your position constantly. We do it all the time.

WEISSBORT: *Plotting a course.*

AMICHAI: Yes, where we are and where we're not. That's what art is. It's not an artificial thing which we learn to shoot into the next century.

WEISSBORT: *Or looking back, for that matter.*

AMICHAI: Or looking back, which is romantically going back and denying our time. Both go to denying our time.

WEISSBORT: *As we said yesterday, poets like Herbert or Różewicz seem to be more involved with social, with political issues. Of course, they are also plotting their position, but in a rather different way. You seem somehow to occupy a position between that and, say, the introspectiveness of the poets of an earlier American generation, like Lowell. That appeared to be a kind of dead-end. It didn't relate enough, perhaps, to the surroundings.*

AMICHAI: On the contrary, it was sometimes a means to close themselves away from them.

WEISSBORT: *Perhaps you were able to do what you did, because circumstances permitted it. In Central Europe there is the pressure of the State to contend with, whereas Israel is a democracy, although there is a tremendous pressure of history, and also the pressure from outside Israel. Nevertheless, you were able to involve yourself to a much greater extent . . .*

AMICHAI: When younger people come to me and ask me what to do, because they can't make a living, I always say: You should be in life, in real life, and forget about being a poet, and then you should write a poem and forget about life. When you write a poem, you have to detach yourself from life. But when you are out there, you can't see yourself as a huntsman or treasure-hunter, who uses the real life in order to come back with little metaphors and images to enrich his poetry. You have to live it full-heartedly, really *want* to live it. There's also another thing. You know there's – I was saying this to one of the young people in the café last night – there's this expression, 'being high', either by drugs or just being jubilant . . . anyway, you're high, which is a marvellous expression, which means you get high, you get out of this. Poets mostly – I think it's in the nature of poets – start so *low* that for them to be high means to reach the level of normal people. They start so low, in the abyss, that for them the high is to be a father to children, and to behave like all the bourgeois! So, for us a great bliss is to be like other people, just to go to work and go home to the children . . .

WEISSBORT: *Whereas one feels poetry should be about extraordinary things, not the ordinary?*

AMICHAI: No, I don't think there is that kind of division, either. I think there are two kinds of poetry. In the nineteenth century it was called Apollonian and Dionysian. The Dionysian was a clear-sighted thing, the other is drunkenness and hallucination.

WEISSBORT: *And that still happens.*

AMICHAI: Yes, there are always two kinds, I think. A poet, in a way, should be able to be both. That's the greatness of Shakespeare.

19–20 October 1986

Appendix 2

MIROSLAV HOLUB
In conversation with Daniel Weissbort

WEISSBORT: *Różewicz – who has always seemed to me justified in his claim to have created a new kind of language, out of what was left over of the old – is too literary for some of the more recent Polish poets, like Stanisław Barańczak or Adam Zagajewski. They believe that their poetry is – or was, in a certain phase – a more naked poetry, turning the clichés of communism, the language of propaganda, against itself. Yet for me, their work seems a kind of continuation, if more narrowly – some might say more sharply – focused than Różewicz's.*

HOLUB: Yes, the scope and aim of the poetry is now closer to concrete protest.

WEISSBORT: *Is the same phenomenon evident in Czechoslovakia?*

HOLUB: The social situation is quite different. The Polish Solidarity is some steps ahead. And the people, the young generation seems to be more reserved, much more frozen. With the exception of the really brave dissidents.

WEISSBORT: *As I've already mentioned, the purpose of the anthology is not to give a profile of Eastern Europe, or anything so ambitious as that, but to focus on your generation, because it seems to me the key generation, probably because of when you were born, though you say you have less direct experience of the war than someone like Różewicz ...*

HOLUB: I don't say *less* direct, because we were there, and we saw the bombs falling all the time, and we saw the prisoners-of-war of both sides, and the labour camps of both sides, and so on. But I was never in real-life danger, or a menacing, a shooting situation. Maybe the others were ... or, perhaps, I am less personal about it. I am much less personal. And sometimes – it's interesting – sometimes *you* perceive it – I've seen it in *MPT 1983* – you perceive it as a sort of moment in the post-war movement. And it may be, of course. My coming into poetry was to find out if it was poetry, if what I was doing was poetry at all! I didn't find any correspondences, I just discovered that I might be another kind. Which I was very doubtful about. So, I was always – I'm not joking – very reserved and very modest about any personal rôle I played in national or international poetry. There are many types of poets and many types of poetry, just as there are different types of dogs.

WEISSBORT: *Sure. I'm not really trying to suggest that these poets constitute a gang, a group! They* are *all very different. Różewicz and you, for instance . . .*

HOLUB: Or Popa and me. And yet, he is *so* interesting. Again it is very impersonal. What have surrealist games in common with any living message? And still it's there. And that's what I want to say, maybe it *is* a group, not intentional, but an unconscious part of a general world consciousness, which could be defined as having some extra-personal relationship with the general life. The more I learn about American poetry, which I have always admired because of its consistency and scholarly evolution, the more I feel, my God, they are so good and yet they are missing something, something from my household, something more concrete, beyond the personal . . .

WEISSBORT: *I feel that American poets – unfair to generalize in this way, of course! – and British poets, too, are very insecure when they move beyond what they themselves know personally. It's as though they don't feel it can be poetry. One of the things that struck me when I first came across your poetry – in the very first issue of MPT we had some of your poems – was that somehow this poetry was assimilating, talking about, things that we hadn't believed poetry could talk about. It was another revolution, like the Romantic revolution in its time, and then the counter-Romantic revolution of the early twentieth century. It seemed like a new movement, more radical perhaps than the Modernism of T.S. Eliot, because the mistrust of words, of language, went further, as it had to, of course, given the circumstances.*

HOLUB: It may be. We felt it as a counter-cultural movement, as a protest against the generalizing, solemn, official poetry. Against the poetic celebrations, all types of poetic celebrations. And we called it – our group, that is – the 'Poetry of Everyday Life'. But in more general terms – and not talking in terms of any literary group – there was the feeling that whatever you are doing represents the feeling of the guys in the street. All of them. Alvarez's title *Under Pressure* describes it best. You have a society which has only one stratum. There is no stratification. So, by definition, whatever one, who is just a single voice, says, is very much representative of the feelings of the others. And that's what is missing in the academic poetry as well. And it is giving some hope also to what I called the frozen generation.

WEISSBORT: *Yes, that sounds right . . . When you're writing, you don't have in mind an audience of literary people particularly, do you?*

HOLUB: Usually, I have no audience in mind at all, but for . . . I don't know . . . for biological reasons, I can't use any kind of expression – I don't mean ideas or metaphors or the structure of the poem – but in the wording process, there is a sort of inner bar against using too hermetic words, because my vocabulary is weighted with scientific terms and I could easily introduce all kinds of esoteric variations. I always go for something rather middling, which can still be understood in the context, doesn't have to be looked up in the *American Heritage Dictionary*! But I also feel, why should we understand every single word? We expect lots of ambiguities in words, and if I, perhaps, use a lot of scientific terms, allusions, I am just increasing the ambiguity. And still they can be understood. The Czech publisher objected even to the title *Interferon*, because it is less known there than it is here. Of course, nobody can define what Interferon really is, but you have the feeling that it is something anti-, anti-flu, or anti-cancer, maybe synthetic, maybe natural, and so on . . . I'm thinking of a title for a book: *Standard Error of the Mean*. Just SEM, which is a statistical expression. Or another, which is much more beautiful, which is the abbreviation for the words Mean Time Between the Failures, for a new tank or something. Perhaps it fails every second day! The Mean Time Between the Failures, twenty-four hours, MTBF! Nobody knows SEM or MTBF. But still the sound is intriguing. Interferon is simply intriguing. And that's enough for the poetic use of a word.

WEISSBORT: *Ewald Osers, in a Czech issue of MPT, makes the point that you have expanded the poetic language by introducing scientific terms. He relates this to Modernism, or the experimental side of your writing.*

HOLUB: I like the notion of experimental. What I basically like is novelty, knowing by experiment, trial and error maybe. But still it's too lofty a definition for what I am doing. A more concrete or realistic definition would be, I just write as a game. Yes! It's a game in the laboratory, with certain rules, and it is another game in a book, with other rules, and I just don't like – the experimental thing about it – I don't like to repeat any one game too many times . . .

WEISSBORT: *In your book* Although, *are you experimenting?*

HOLUB: Yes.

WEISSBORT: *There the setting is basically American, or at least much of it is.*

HOLUB: Yes, this was after two years in New York.

WEISSBORT: *Would you say it was influenced by American writing?*

HOLUB: Actually, I felt very dissatisfied with the result . . . I don't think I really got my New York into it. It just hovered about somewhere on the edge of the city. I now have a Los Angeles poem, and it's not the best poem I have written, but still I am more in Los Angeles than I was that time in New York!

WEISSBORT: *It takes a long time to get the hang of a city?*

HOLUB: No, I think, when I compare these poems, just thinking about this difficult task of writing on a foreign city, a foreign country, I may be really – which would be a good thing, of course! – changing, because I am now using much more – how should I say it? I never speculated about this – internal images, even more personal or private images of me and of us all, than I used before. I was always describing or trying to analyse the cool surface. Now, maybe, I am trying to penetrate more deeply into the common darkness.

WEISSBORT: *And yet one of the points Alvarez makes in his Introduction to the Penguin selection of your work – also in* Under Pressure, *I think – is that the primary impulse of Western – American, British – poetry has been inward, whereas the poets of Eastern Europe move in the opposite direction. And he quotes you as talking about 'putting your antennae out into the world of streptomycin.' Are you now saying that this is a period which is over?*

HOLUB: Maybe – this may be a personal development – it is difficult to say. But I know that I refer now more and more to real personal events. Actually – now I speculate on it – it's always something really new, or more typically, from the very old days. That means – not something I have seen, a street situation. Now I am turning to my own situation, which may be an internalization. Still, this should be extroverted into a sort of stylization of history, which is far from a personal diary. Yet it may be true ... This is a common experience in the East, compression, or experience of the general compression.

WEISSBORT: *It seems that the exploration of the psyche, of selfness, the poetry that came out of that kind of introspection and self-contemplation, was ultimately a kind of dead-end.*

HOLUB: That is what I felt at that time, and again now. I think this type of self-exploration is an illusion, which you can't really defend with any type of scientific approach. It has very little meaning and for me it has no interest. Because, in a way, I exist for myself as an intersection of other people. I always refer to somebody else. Maybe to a book, to a paper. I refer to my family, I refer to my parents, who died two years ago. I was always in an internal dialogue with them. With them I lost one of the intersecting lines. But, still, I see myself as an intersection, not as an entity.

WEISSBORT: *So, when you describe writing about more personal experience ...*

HOLUB: Yes, this is a personal experience of the intersection, of something about or beneath the intersection.

WEISSBORT: *Both seeing oneself and yet being detached?*

HOLUB: Yes, I felt this strongly, even physically, like when I did something very stupid, firing my gun, in February 1948, by accident. I had to hand it over and I pulled the trigger! People around ... an idiotic situation! And that moment I had the physical feeling I was about two metres above myself and looking down at this idiot. And I had the same feeling after the 1973 incident with my faked confession. For a couple of months I had the same feeling, the feeling I had lost my identity. At a soccer game, I have the feeling I am standing about three rows behind myself. This may be just one of my general approaches, being two or three steps away from myself ... But what I wanted to say about the Barańczak and Różewicz generations ... it's very hard to speak in personal terms, or in terms of personal development, or group development, or literary development, about changes, about intentions, because, of course, what basically changes is only the knowledge that something happened, somebody happened to exist ten years ago, five years ago. Even the knowledge that I wrote this book three years ago changes my present state of mind. So it's very hard to say what's based only on this awareness of the past, of the immediate or very distant past, and what is then a real ontogeny. In a way the new information changes the world around you. Of course, then, as a second feedback, you are changed yourself. It's just, with the new two million bits of information, the world is never the same. Just because there was a Różewicz, even if no one intends to change anything, there can be no other Różewicz. Or they have to be different. It's nothing to do with the will; it's just a biological fact.

WEISSBORT: *Yes, but I suppose what struck me about them was that, at least looked at from the outside, they seemed to be following in Różewicz's footsteps. Without Różewicz they could hardly have existed ... well, that's what you're saying, I suppose! ... Only, they themselves make such a point of their writing being closer to the bone than his, whereas for me Różewicz's seemed the barest, most stripped down kind of language. And yet in Poland, it didn't feel that way by the time they came along.*

HOLUB: This is a matter of definition and redefinition. And I think that one of the greatest problems in the general cultural life is self-interpretation. Since the artistic deed is already a self-interpretation, self-interpretation of the group, secondary self-interpretation, may be misleading, a double error, a compound error. The main problem for me, including the two-cultures problem, is not that of real creativity, the creative process, which is similar for scientists and poets, but that the self-image of the two is so different.

WEISSBORT: *Your training, it is true, is scientific, as a medical doctor. When you started writing, were you aware of writing in any tradition or was it just aimed ... what did you relate to?*

HOLUB: Well, I related strictly to literature, because I didn't believe I could be a writer, and so I just tried to imitate Nezval. And then I tried to imitate the French. And then I tried to imitate the Czech existentialists. My second poem was published in a journal, an anthology by Kamil Bednař, who was labelled an existentialist. Not believing in anything, in myself, I tried to make my version of them. Not to copy them, but to imitate. And only then the editors of my first book, especially Jan Grossman, assured me, 'Well, you are ... that's you.' I didn't know that's me! He told me that there was a common denominator in these attempts at imitation, and that that was me. So he made me! And from that moment on, I accepted the notion that this was my form of expression ...

WEISSBORT: *So he was your editor?*

HOLUB: Yes. He is now directing *Interferon* at the Viola Theatre. This is my only cultural manifestation in Prague right now, but I must tell you it's great, unbelievable, a production with Brzobohaty, with Malkova, Mareš, and with myself on a stage. Grossman is directing it. Of course, he tells me the way I read is just impossible, because it's the way I use here, due to my accent. I have slightly to overdo it, which contradicts the sense of my Czech. I have to be very reserved and matter-of-fact, with much less modulation, and much less romantic. I have to get it through to the people, through the language barrier ...

WEISSBORT: *When, actually, did you learn English?*

HOLUB: I never learnt English.

WEISSBORT: *You just picked it up when you came?*

HOLUB: I just picked it up. I learnt French and German. My mother was a teacher of German and French and she taught me. When I was four or five, she already gave me German lessons, then French lessons, and we read *Jean Christophe* together. Always before sleeping she would read in French *Jean Christophe*, which was – I must write a poem about this – never finished. Because I left home for Prague and then only came back for weekends.

WEISSBORT: *So, you came from a small town.*

HOLUB: From Pilsen! It's a big town. And I continued to commute there on weekends, to visit my parents, together with my adult son. They were still alive. My father died in '84. We had to bring my mother to my house in Prague, because she couldn't stay by herself. She was slightly disturbed, and she died the following October ... So it was my fate, never to really finish *Jean Christophe*!

WEISSBORT: *It is said there are religious links between England and Czechoslovakia. The only time I visited Czechoslovakia, Prague, it did feel oddly familiar ... The Czech temperament was certainly closer, it seemed to me, to the British temperament, than, say, the Russian, or Polish, or Hungarian.*

HOLUB: The Czech way of joking ... I think we have a Celtic component, but, of course, the Celtic element – because of routine historical genocide – has been exterminated, though it is partly incorporated in the Slavonic population. This is not a cultural tradition, a political tradition, but more a biological one, the Celtic component in the population. Because the Czechs are people from Bohemia which comes from the name of a Celtic tribe, taken over by the incoming Slavonic tribes. Actually, one of the dullest Slavonic tribes, because, in the migrations, it is always the greatest idiots who get the furthest! The more intelligent tribes, or populations, or types, stay closer, because greater intelligence enables you to adapt. And the greatest dullards have to migrate furthest, because they can't adapt. So we, the Czechs, got the furthest. Or else, we are a modest exception to the Matthews rule.

WEISSBORT: *The result of that is that you're, in a sense, the most Western of the Slavs.*

HOLUB: Yes, though of course in the wrong direction! The pilgrim father – the word Czech comes from the name of a man called Czech – saw the rich land from a hill in central Bohemia. This is a land flowing with milk and honey, he thought, here we can set our Gods upon the earth. I think it was the most stupid moment in our history, because why couldn't we have moved a little further on, to the sea!

WEISSBORT: *Yes, a landlocked country, like Hungary ...*

HOLUB: The Hungarians have been sort of squeezed in between. Basically an Avar, Aryan tribe, which has got squeezed in between the Slavonic ones. Of course, it will never be known who exactly stopped us, the Slavonic tribes, precisely in this location. Maybe it was some hostile German tribes, or Roman garrisons. Nobody even knows what century it was, the sixth, or the seventh, or the eighth. It's all very vague, the history.

WEISSBORT: *With whom do you feel most closely connected? The Poles?*

HOLUB: It's very hard to say I would say Slovenes and Poles. Of course, we have the Czech and Slovak nationalities. But that is a single state, single culture, almost one. But the Germans are very close too. Six or seven hundred years of interliving, so to speak.

WEISSBORT: *Your parents' generation was, of course, bilingual.*

HOLUB: I was bilingual too, meaning German as the second language.

WEISSBORT: *Does that distinguish the people of your parents' generation and yours, as writers say, from the following generation?*

HOLUB: Very sound point! This bilingualism was more important for my generation than for the second post-war generation.

WEISSBORT: *This must produce a certain ambivalence. On the one hand, the close relationship with Germany, which the Czechs have – the Poles don't have it, though the Hungarians do, I suppose – and then comes World War Two.*

HOLUB: Yes, besides there is another point, another national point, speaking of the Hungarians. Hungarians had a lower class and an aristocracy. Hungarian aristocrats. But we didn't have much of a Czech aristocracy; it was mostly German. And this was one of the reasons, even in the cities, among the rising bourgeoisie, that the Czechs adopted a sort of bilingualism or even just took up German, or for that matter changed back, because with the rise of national self-consciousness, there were even examples of Germanized aristocratic families, noblemen, changing back to the Czech ... The Sternbergs, Count Kaspar Sternberg, were one example. And they were one of the great families, recreating the Czech language, for example the educated and scientific language was artificially created at the beginning of the last century. This is one of the peculiarities of our language.

WEISSBORT: *As a writer, as a poet, are you still conscious of somehow creating a language? Languages are always changing, but some languages change more than others. Contemporary Hebrew, for instance, the language of the Bible, which had to be modernized. Yehuda Amichai talks about having to create words, to make new words. Does this apply in Czech as well?*

HOLUB: Yes. Actually, one of my peculiarities is that I am not too serious about anything, and not even about a personal language, which makes me sort of free. I play lots of games in my prose, which is quite provocative to some people, but makes my style in Czech very distinctive. So when I published, not using my full name, which I did actually for fifteen years – I published a weekly column in one of the magazines, but only under my initials – because of the style everybody knew. I have now collected these articles, and at least one of the books – they'll make two or three books – is likely to appear soon. This is very strange, but *Interferon*, my poetry, not so much on account of political content, but because it is about death, is pessimistic ... And I don't *like* to be pessimistic! It just comes! But at the same time as *Interferon*, I wrote these weekly columns, which are vigorous, optimistic, generally helpful. I don't know really why there's this division, why my prose writing, which is sort of prose-poem writing, represents more or less the sunny side, while in a real poem, it's ... I try to resist it!

WEISSBORT: *What you say about your language makes me feel that actually, contrary to what I originally thought, you are probably quite hard to translate! The games you refer to would be very hard to convey, and it seems to me now this is an important part of what you're doing ... That kind of play of language is almost impossible to translate, because the language situations are different.*

HOLUB: That is why I always speak about translation as transfer. When you translate, you can't transfer. I know, because I make the rough translations for David Young and I know what will be lost. But there is something else. I know it will appear in English some day, so, in a way, I already consider the English possibility.

WEISSBORT: *Because of your relationship with your translator, David Young?*

HOLUB: With him in the first place. There are others, English, German, Spanish, French translators, and I regard them as an integral part of my writing. They are an integral part of the *outward* direction of the writing, at times they are a means of survival – as in the seventies.

May 1985

Appendix 3

ZBIGNIEW HERBERT: A Poet of Exact Meaning

A conversation with Marek Oramus

ORAMUS: *Are you aware of the fact that in Poland you practically don't exist? I've been to a public library and haven't found any of your books. It's a long time since your works appeared in bookshops, and your plays are not being staged. You are frequently published abroad where you enjoy greater popularity than in your own country. I hear there are* Mr Cogito *clubs in America.*

HERBERT: There is a periodical in America called *Mr Cogito*, but I haven't heard of any clubs. You must have confused me with *Playboy*. I know I do not exist in Poland, but I cannot help it. I don't plead with publishers or cultural policy-makers. They know, or at least should know, what they are doing . . .

ORAMUS: *Once you were refused publication, you could have written for the drawer again, couldn't you? But you went abroad instead.*

HERBERT: . . . like a coward, you mean?

ORAMUS: *Were you bored with writing for the drawer?*

HERBERT: Writing for the drawer is a tiresome business. But let's not discuss it now. My principle is that under no circumstances should one be reduced to the rôle of a victim. Never. In some periods the authorities blamed me, I think, for signing open letters and appeals in cases which had nothing to do with literature. These were social problems, acts of injustice. Once I made the decision to act, I was bound to bear the consequences.

There is a monopoly of culture. I had made myself unpopular with the monopolist so he stopped publishing me. In the West, they did not.

I do not blame myself – or the touchy authorities. The languages of politics and literature are entirely different and so are the mentalities. Politicians are concerned with 'far-reaching' goals, personal games, gangster-style tricks. What interests me is human fate. What does me good is bad for politicians; what suits them I find indigestible. We use two separate styles. I have tried to use the conditional. I hesitate. I appeal to conscience . . . I don't like imperatives, exclamation marks, black-and-white divisions. I just don't.

ORAMUS: *In your poems you often refer to history and mythology, but what you*

do is transform and reshape. You pursue history and correct mythology. My hypothesis is that you dislike history because you are dissatisfied with reality.
HERBERT: A very pertinent question. But you see – all my life, and I am nearly sixty, I have virtually stayed in one place and yet my citizenship has changed four times. I was a citizen in pre-war Poland, the Second Commonwealth; then Lwów was annexed to the West Ukraine, there is still a note in my passport stating that I was born in the USSR; then I became a Kenn Karte citizen in the German Government General and eventually I came to live in People's Poland. I have lived through four distinct political systems. This specific condensation is responsible for my sense of history – some kind of empathy, an ability to understand people of distant epochs. [. . .]
ORAMUS: *In your poems you write about your native Lwów. You must have been greatly devoted to it. Would you like to see the old place again?*
HERBERT: No. I wouldn't. The things I used to love are no longer there. Besides, there is the idealizing power of our memory . . . The mansion in which I used to live may not be as beautiful as it seems to be in my thoughts. I try not to cherish sentiment for the town lest the nostalgic feelings should grow, and there have been too many of them already.

Lwów used to be a centre for humanists and scholars; father would recite the *Odyssey* to me when I was three. There was no need to look up the word *polis* in the dictionary. It was obvious. I was growing up in it.
ORAMUS: *By the way, here is the cover of an anthology of contemporary poetry which you compiled and your volume of selected poems. Although some time has elapsed between their publication, they have the same photograph of you. It resembles a Greek or Roman sculpture in profile. Was it deliberate stylization?*
HERBERT: Just to surprise you I will show you the whole photograph. It was taken on a state collective farm where I carried sacks. I happened to be sitting under a dilapidated wall, hens by my feet, exhausted. There is nothing Roman about it, is there?
ORAMUS: *Your nostalgic feelings seem to multiply. Surely there is more than one.*
HERBERT: I miss Greece very much – and Italy. And England I like very much, and America – for their way of living, completely different than in Europe. Since 1939, I have always been on the move. I happen to have dreams about walking through Vienna, for example.
ORAMUS: *It is impossible that they only refer to geographical places.*
HERBERT: That's right. It is the people I have lost in the first place. Now I can look more closely because I am sorting out papers, manuscripts, etc. My mother died recently. This is her room. I had to have it redecorated and to carry out the disposition of her relics. I somehow cannot bring

myself to the task. I am tidying the letters, prescriptions, electrocardio-gram slips. From the remains I try to mould something for myself. A precept, some wisdom, admonition. I have found a letter from Professor Elzenberg – he used to be my Master. Two pages covered in tiny handwriting – he found some fault with my *Barbarian*. I suppose I replied arrogantly.

ORAMUS: *Are you sensitive to criticism?*

HERBERT: No – because I'm conceited. I have seldom written with a deadline or for money. And if I have done my best, does it matter whether I am worse than, say, Chateaubriand? OK, I am. But what matters is my readers' voice. Once I had a poem published in *Tygodnik Powszechny* [the leading Polish Catholic weekly]. I listed all the grudges I had against God. A believer was hurt – I don't blame him.

ORAMUS: *Do you believe in God?*

HERBERT: I was asked the same question by Julian Przyboś [a prominent representative of the inter-war poetic *avant-garde* and member of the Communist Party, d. 1970]. I did not quite believe then. I had enormous doubts and yet I answered 'Yes, I do.' It was then that I started to believe. Przyboś was puzzled. 'You are so intellectual,' he said. 'Do you really believe in that crucified slave? You of all people, an aesthete, a lover of Greek gods.' The more he blasphemed and disparaged, the stronger my faith grew. I think Pascal was right when he said that by assuming the existence of God we have more possibilities than if we supposed that there was no God at all. One does not lose by believing, but one misses a lot if one does not …

ORAMUS: *Miłosz regards poetry as a mission, something sublime. For him a novel always comes second, especially when compared with poetry. Are you of the same opinion?*

HERBERT: I read very few novels. What Miłosz has in mind is probably the hypocrisy that a novel invokes. It is a fabrication, a make-believe kind of life, it results in mundane truths. Too many words. A poem, however, is a condensed experience. Miłosz is a twofold poet – romantic with a classical programme, highly sensual as well as intellectual. We happen to be walking in the forest. He keeps on naming all the birdies whereas I just look out for a stump to sit on and have some wine. He goes on hooting and calling birds, all exposed to nature.

ORAMUS: *In his attempt to define himself, Miłosz said that a poet lives on contradictions.*

HERBERT: That's very true. I am fond of the antique; but when it begins to bore me, I make naturalistic paintings. I need to move on two rockers, as it were. You may have noticed I am a chatterbox and yet, when writing, I strive for maximum brevity. Isn't this a contradiction?

ORAMUS: *As a poet you are concerned with polishing little knick-knacks, you play around with tiny rings. Haven't you ever felt compelled to rush out in a bulldozer, roll over heaps of soil, or simply make something large enough to be seen from an aeroplane? Briefly: Do your plans allow for writing a novel?*

HERBERT: I shall let you in on a secret I have never told anyone before. I started with prose writing. When the Nazi occupation was over, my experiences of the underground and partisan fighting materialized in a cycle of short stories which I called *The Life Shell*. It was a bitter act of settling accounts with the past. And then, when my friends were jailed [by the Polish post-war Communist Government], I thought I must not bring it out, as there were no conditions for a true, uninhibited literary discussion. Each pronouncement was treated as a political act.

ORAMUS: *The fabric of a poet's work is language. Language consists of words. 'Honour, loyalty, constancy' – what do these words mean nowadays? Can they make a poem?*

HERBERT: They can, but it requires great talent. It can be done indirectly, that is, without actually mentioning the word 'honour' whose concept, incidentally, matters greatly to me. Other words can be by-passed, too. They belong to a smashed table of values. In our time such concepts may be hinted at, discussed. One can point out what they mean in a given situation and prove that they are still binding and important. Great words should be spared. One must see the inter-relation of words.

ORAMUS: *Marek Grechuta has recently sung that our age no longer needs poets. The lyrics were written by a poet. Is poetry still needed?*

HERBERT: It has never been needed very badly. Why should it be now? Humanistic values are on the defensive, the absurdity of existence being the leading motif of contemporary literature. But a world with only technology and politics would be a horrid one. I would move out. You see what I mean, don't you?

ORAMUS: *You do not welcome changes in the world or in life. They merely upset you. Perhaps one should not cling so pathetically to the old principles. Perhaps one should follow the changes?*

HERBERT: A man who changes too often does not arouse my friendly feelings. The transformations are usually planned in advance. We may have many gifts but we ought to strive for continuity and consistency in our activities. Whatever we do – write, paint or compose – we each build up our own personality.

ORAMUS: *Does this apply to life, too?*

HERBERT: One is not always consistent in one's life, but it is not a disgrace. When it comes to such fundamental issues as one's beliefs or moral principles, one should not compromise. Each of us composes a part of the universe – an effort should be made to become a meaningful part of the whole. It is far from easy. I keep on asking myself what part of Polish society I compose. Is it a meaningful, accidental or dispensable one?

ORAMUS: *And what is the answer?*

HERBERT: The answer is that it is I who must or should try to bring meaning to my own life. I will try to prove that I constitute a meaningful part of the whole. One of Chesterton's novels deals with the problem of the existence of God. The sceptical voice says that perhaps God exists but we are merely playthings in his Chinese garden. He toys with us, laughs at our successes and failures, aspirations and goals. To him it is just play. The other voice says that perhaps this is so but it is through my suffering that I have given meaning, my very own meaning, to the game. I have established myself in this world as its meaningful part.

Perhaps the world is not really that important after all. We all know that life will not last forever, everything will come to an end – the *Iliad*, cathedrals, Picasso. Still I am capable of suffering. I can fight for a better moral order. By means of such a funny thing as writing poetry, I am trying to defend the matters that are significant to me. It is still possible to put words together and read them. There is a ghost of a chance in it. The sense of suffering clashing with reality – that's what it is all about. I know that I am unable to save my nation or the occupants in my block of flats, but I must act in such a way as though it were possible. Just try. There is no government on earth which could deprive me of that struggle. To extract meaning is our primary task.

ORAMUS: *Why is there so much bitterness in your poetry? The calm irony does not counterbalance the bitterness. You said in your poem 'Prologue':*

> The ditch where a muddy river flows
> I call the Vistula.
> It is hard to confess
> they have sentenced us to such love
> they have pierced us through with such a fatherland.

HERBERT: A bitter truth is better than a sweet lie. The poem you have quoted belongs to the so-called 'patriotic poems'. My image of patriotism is the following: if the Germans or the French act foolishly in their own country, I do not really care. The same foolishness or wickedness committed by Poles in Poland infuriates me. My nation is certainly not a chosen one but since it is closest to me, I have imagined that it ought to strive for perfection. That is why I feel much more strongly about its faults or acts of social injustice. The effectiveness of my social appeal or yours is limited. One should fully realize that. Moreover, when one intervenes in social matters, one becomes suspected of disagreeing with reality, being a natural malcontent or even an enemy. The task of a man of reason is never to accept reality, any reality under any circumstances. There is no perfect society, a society both wise and just. Our only duty is to revolt against each single act of personal injustice. A writer is obliged to do it – hence his conflict with government ...

ORAMUS: *You used to go in for funny jobs, didn't you? You were editor of a trade union paper, shop assistant, accountant, designer of sanitary devices and safety-wear, bank clerk. Your literary record, however, does not reflect these experiences. Do you think them unimportant, pointless and a waste of time?*

HERBERT: I don't think so. I just do not like autobiographies.

ORAMUS: *What were the advantages of having these jobs?*

HERBERT: I survived physiologically. That was the main advantage. I was at the bottom. I would not give in. The experiences made an imprint on what I wrote about – even Greek mythology. 'Atlas', which was written a year before the rising of the Gdańsk workers, expresses my solidarity with manual workers. I knew it from my own experience, not from books. I employed mythology because I thought it would have more universal appeal. I could have written a satire on the secretary who bullied me; but with the disappearance of the secretary, the satire would have lost its appeal.

We ought to seek general statements, messages that can be addressed to everybody instead of just digging into our own unique experience.

ORAMUS: *What is the secret of your popularity abroad? Miłosz says you are easy to translate.*

HERBERT: I have never written for translators or a selected circle of readers. People cannot be divided into black and white. What matters is why they laugh and what makes them weep. When I was being translated by an American, he wrote me enthusiastic letters but was amused by my quoting the Bible. He was anxious to find irony in work which was meant to be quite serious. He was trying to uncover the allegedly hidden comic undertones so that his students might laugh like mad.

ORAMUS: *Your work leaves you and you lose control over it.*

HERBERT: Absolutely, and I do not care. I sometimes get furious when others laugh at the moments that make my throat go dry. They, as

[Antoni] Słonimski [1895–1976, celebrated pamphleteer and humanist] put it, 'tick differently'. The Americans are pragmatic, but they lack our sense of history.

ORAMUS: *Maybe that is why they are more effectual in action than we are. They choose more straightforward ways whereas we are always going around the bend.*

HERBERT: Civilization must reckon with matter. We were on our way back to Poland. We had crossed the border glad to be amidst our own – up to the moment when we drove into a crack in the road and nearly smashed the car. In a provincial town our hotel window would not close. They nailed it shut. I have a civilized heart. It hurts me. Why, in this country, can't matter and spirit go together? My primary task now is to make language free of hypocrisy and restore the logic of objects – so things won't weep.

ORAMUS: *You seem to be treating objects with special consideration. You dedicate poems to chairs, pebbles, door-knockers. Do you believe in an inward world of things? Do you believe they lead a certain kind of life?*

HERBERT: I am fond of things. I am almost sensually attracted to them. Say I am walking down a street and I spot a stiletto in an ornate scabbard in an antique dealer's window. I go inside. I pretend I want to buy it. I look at the thing, examine it – just to feel the cold touch of the blade, experience the weight. You may want to know how it started. Well, when I was a boy I used to look out of the window at the street outside. I saw people passing by, a brick wall and the setting sun. And in my mind's eye, I was the people in the street and also the wall that was soaking up the sun.

Our lives pass amidst things, and that is why we ought to associate with them. I fight dust – the element that destroys objects. An unbound book, a loose page, make me suffer. A chair with a broken leg seems as crippled as a human being . . .

ORAMUS: *The last question. Why did you, in 1948, leave the Polish Writers' Union?*

HERBERT: Because of a lie. Social realism had sounded. I had no chance to publish what I was writing then, and by my withdrawal I think I anticipated a dismissal from the Union. It was like this: I was taken to observe an action to destroy *kulaks*. Armed bands of 'workers', who were not workers at all, would come and loot the property of the foes of the proletariat. They took away everything. Grain was loaded on horse carts; and the carts would stand outdoors in the rain and snow, the grain going to waste. It was the economic price of an historical experiment. I was a writer and could join a band to see for myself, in practice, not in the papers. I wanted to find out who was right, the spirit of the day or common sense. And conscience.

They took grain away from a woman, Malcowa, who worked for a *kulak*. She went wild with despair. What could one do? Give the woman a hundredweight of grain lest she and her son should die of starvation in the coming winter. I went to see the organizer of the action so that I could write a report and get them to give her a sack of grain. They explained that I did not understand the dialectic of history. Some time later I learned that Malcowa had hanged herself.

I unstuck my photo. I sent my membership card back to the Union. I went down to the bottom.

Translated by Michael March 1981

Appendix 4

ZBIGNIEW HERBERT: Why the Classics

WHY THE CLASSICS
for A.H.

1

in the fourth book of *The Peloponnesian War*
Thucydides describes his unsuccessful expedition

amid long speeches by generals
sieges battles disease
thick webs of intrigue
diplomatic demarches
that episode is like a needle
in a forest

the Athenian colony Amphipolis
fell to Brasidas
because Thucydides' relief was late

for this he paid with life-long exile
from his native city

exiles of all time
know that price

2

the generals in recent wars
in similar predicaments
yap on their knees before posterity
praise their own heroism
and innocence

they blame subordinates
envious colleagues

and hostile winds

Thucydides merely says
it was winter
he had seven ships
had sailed at speed

3
should the theme of art
be a broken jug
a tiny broken soul
full of self-pity

then what shall remain of us
will be like lovers' tears
in a dingy small hotel
when wallpapers dawn

Adam Czerniawski

I chose this poem with misgivings. You see I don't think it's my best, nor
do I think it can represent my poetic programme. But it has – at least in
my opinion – two advantages: it's simple and dry, and it speaks, without
ornament or stylization, of things that actually are close to my heart.

The poem is made up of three sections. The first section is about an
event described by an author writing centuries ago. In the second section
I translate this event into the present in order to create tension, to reveal
any differences in attitude and conduct. The third section, finally,
contains the conclusion and the moral, and at the same time transfers the
problem from the realm of history into the realm of art.

You don't have to be a great expert on contemporary literature to
notice its main characteristics – the eruption of despair and the lack of
faith. All basic values of European culture are called into question today.
Thousands of novels, plays, and poems discuss the approaching, inevi-
table destruction, the meaninglessness of life, the absurdity of human
existence.

I don't intend to simply ridicule pessimism when it is a reaction to the
existence of evil in the world. But I do think the black tone of contempor-
ary literature stems from an attitude of today's authors toward reality.

And it's precisely this attitude that I wish to attack in my poem.

The romantic notion of the poet who displays his wounds, who sings his own misfortune, still has many followers today, despite the changes in style and literary taste. People believe that this compelling interest in the self, this manifestation of a wounded ego, is the sacred right of any artist.

If there were a school that taught literature, we would have to practise there the description of objects and not of dreams. Beyond the ego of the artist, a heavy, dark, yet real world stretches forth. We cannot allow ourselves to stop believing that we can capture this world in words, that we can even be fair to it.

It became clear to me very early on, at the beginning of my literary work, that I had to search for my object beyond the realm of literature. I found writing as a mere stylistic exercise unfruitful. Lyric poetry as the art of words bored me. It also became clear that I could not find nourishment for very long in the poems of other people. I had to break away from myself as well as from literature, I had to take a look around in the world, to conquer other realities.

Philosophy gave me the courage to ask the first really essential questions, the fundamental questions: does the world exist, what is its nature, and is it recognizable. If we can establish any use that lyric poetry can derive from this discipline, then it certainly lies not in describing systems but in revealing how people think.

I don't turn to history to gain from it a facile lesson of hope, I do it to confront my experience with that of others, to win for myself something I would like to call universal pity, and also responsibility, a feeling of responsibility for the condition of people's consciences.

Old is the poet's dream that his work will become a concrete thing, like the pebble or the tree, that, though formed from the material of language, subject to constant flux, it will achieve everlasting life. I believe this is one of the possible ways of conquering one's self, of blurring the relation the poem has to the author. This is how I take Flaubert's advice: 'The artist should conceal himself within his creations, just as the Creator conceals Himself within nature.'

I shudder when I imagine myself walking down an Athenian street – at the time of Pericles, of course (every one of us has a favorite epoch) – and running into Socrates (who else?) who takes me by the elbow in that cunning way of his and says:

'Greetings! I'm so glad I ran into you. Yesterday we spoke with our friends about poetry, what its nature is and whether it tells the truth or lies. Yet none of us, neither Sophron nor Criton, nor even Plato, is a practising poet. But you create poems and are even praised for your creations, you can tell us what poetry is.'

And now I know for sure that I have already lost. We are surrounded by a wide circle of gaping people. I'll share the fate of General Laches who could not define courage and that of Polos, the Sophist who didn't understand rhetoric at all, and also that of the priest Euthyphron who was so pious he could say nothing wise.

And the conclusion will certainly be this: I will slink away in shame, followed by their laughter, the voice of the dialectician in my back:

'What? You are going away and leaving us in ignorance, you, the only one capable of making things clear? Are you carrying the secret off with you so you can continue to deceive us with your miraculous voice? And we – we still don't know whether we should succumb to your magic or whether we should resist it!'

With all my admiration for the great Athenian, it has always seemed to me that in his dialogues, in the way he conducted them, there was a certain element of intellectual blackmail; after all you can be courageous and yet not be able to define courage, you can even write pretty good poetry and be a miserable poetologist.

The language of lyric poetry alone – the non-discursive flow of thought, the method of making use of image, metaphor, parable, the oscillation between what is clear and what can barely be felt – provides enough counter-arguments. I think lyric poetry, in all its exactingness, constantly tries to touch reality. In different ways than science does, of course.

Technocrats prophesy the end of lyric poetry. Cyberneticians claim its contents are no more than 'noises', that is, lack of information. If this is true, who is going to write the lyric poetry of tomorrow? The shaman who wears amulets and the symbols of our lost creeds? The man who conjures up the ancient myths of man? Or the jester at the court of scholars?

I read the report of the Rand Corporation. It's an organization of American scholars, fashioned like a collective of minds, who among other things concern themselves with the possibilities of scientific advances. In this document, I read – among many other things – that within the next sixty years we shall begin to use animals (monkeys, mainly), whose intelligence will be greatly increased, to replace unskilled labourers; the life-span of human beings will grow by fifty years, thanks to new chemical controls over the ageing process; besides interplanetary travel, we will have time travel, because it will be possible to freeze the body and to place the organism in a state of suspended animation.

The report is characterized by its identification of the progress of mankind with the progress of science and by its exclusion of history. As though the dull march of barbarism had never before destroyed, never before extinguished our bright visions of the future.

Teachers in our high schools pound it into us that 'historia' is 'magistra vitae'. But when history crashed down on us in all its brutal glory, I understood, in the very real glow of flames above my home city, that she was a strange teacher. She gave to the people who consciously survived her, and to all who followed her, more material for thought than all the old chronicles put together. A dense and dark material. It will require the work of many consciences to shed light on it.

Nicholas Flamel, the medieval astrologer, had a dream. An angel appeared to him who held in its hand an open book. All knowledge about the universe, about mankind, and about the future was written down there. Nicholas Flamel's pilgrimage in search of that book lasted twenty-four years.

That longing for the magic word, for the sign, that formula which will explain the meaning of life, will never release mankind. The need for a canon, for criteria which teach how to distinguish good from evil, for an exact table of values, is as strong now as it ever was.

When our fathers and grandfathers demanded eternal values, they always had a dim image of antiquity in mind. The classics exuded human dignity, seriousness, and strict objectivity.

But for the earlier lovers of antiquity, Greece was something like a fortunate island where the sun of reason allowed virtue, harmony, and equilibrium to flourish. For a long time the formula of Winkelmann – 'noble simplicity and quiet grandeur' – dominated the Western mind. The Greek statues came to us washed clean by the rain, divested of the colours of life, flawless as Plato's ideas. Only by deepening our historical prescience did we free our gaze to see the darker epochs.

My philosophy professor, who taught us the wisdom of the Greeks, infected me with an enthusiasm for the Stoics. When this happened, 'amor fati' was our salvation from insanity. So we read Epictetus and Marcus Aurelius, and we practised the art of ataraxy, attempting to banish outrage and passion from our souls. Life in harmony with nature, which means with reason, was difficult to experience in the midst of a raging world and the cries of hatred surrounding us.

Certain critics who view the world too optimistically accuse me of pessimism. I've always interpreted this as a misunderstanding. If dark tones dominate in a poem, it does not always mean that its author is mocking the imperfections of the world and wishes to add his personal misery to all the actual misfortune, or that he wishes to heighten our despair.

Just as irony is not the same thing as cynicism, but may actually proceed from mortification, so that which seems pessimistic may be a muffled call for goodness, a call to open our consciences, to increase goodness.

This dialogue with the past, this careful listening for the voices of those that have left us, this touching of stones on which partially erased inscriptions of past fates are still discernible, this calling up of shades so they may feed on our compassion ... this lingering in the past can, but need not, represent a flight from the present, a kind of disappointment. For if we embark on a trip into time while not yet frozen, with all the baggage of our experience, if we inspect the myths, symbols, and legends, to extract from them what is valid, then no one can deny that this effort will be active and productive.

Paracelsus said the creation of the world by God had been left uncompleted. Mankind is called upon to complete this act of creation. I consider this a very beautiful, humanistic belief.

The feeling of fragility and of the futility of human life is less depressing if we weave it into the chain of history, which is nothing but the handing down of a belief in the meaning of our actions and volitions. This way even the shriek of terror is transformed into a cry of hope.

Translated by Margitt Lehbert   1967

Appendix 5

JÁNOS PILINSZKY: Imagined Interview

Before falling asleep or while sitting at a table sipping coffee I catch myself conversing. But with whom? The easy answer would be to say with myself. But this is not so sure. Someone questions and another answers. But who is it? To answer this, I shall try to render such a 'conversation'.

QUESTION: *What, by the way, is a poetic image?*

ANSWER: It is indefinable, since it doesn't differ in any way from every other image in the world. When Van Gogh, while strolling, comes upon a tree and paints it, this tree is not superior to the others. The force of the encounter has raised it, made it gripping. But what, then, does this mean? It appears to be the kind of phenomenon which in a religious context we would call grace. And it is just as difficult to discuss. Since, mysteriously, not only are all trees present in Van Gogh's single tree, but present in it is also the whole universe, with the painter's whole existence included.

QUESTION: *But how?*

ANSWER: A theoretical answer is impossible. Only a practical answer may be attempted. The poet has even less potential than the painter. For the naming of any tree in this world, there is only one noun at his disposal. And that is 'tree'. But, we could say, there are adjectives, the manifold combinative potential of different forms and turns of speech with which to describe and illuminate the object. But practice teaches us otherwise. The properly grasped object is capable of creating its own surroundings (I am referring to linguistic surroundings), while no manner of artifice is capable of showing a tree with the force of naming. However ambitious, a poem written this way would have the effect of a pale translation. Namely, literature is not description, not even expression, but the addressing of objects.

QUESTION: *Doesn't this sound almost mystical?*

ANSWER: Reality and mysticism are blood-brothers. Many people believe that facts are the end station to cognition. This is not true, however. We have to lead the facts to reality. The same fact may be perceived differently by Dostoyevsky than by a journalist. But let's get back to literature. Nowadays it is fashionable to regard the text as independent, and then to examine it, as if it were some complex object. I don't believe in this. I would go so far as to state that the same text may be either dreadful or wonderful. Let me give an example. Christ's 'Blessed are they that mourn' would be worth very little had it originated with Oscar Wilde. It would only be a questionable paradox, a fake, rather than a gem.

QUESTION: *But what are the criteria of reality?*

ANSWER: Not the same as those of facts. Reality is beyond the facts, and facts are on this side of reality. A detective's work is immeasurably more unreal than a writer's.

QUESTION: *But once a work is finished it has to bear the unmistakeable imprint of the found reality.*

ANSWER: This is true. But reality is simply indefinable. It is impossible to point a finger at it. Its strength lies in its freedom, it cannot be encompassed. It can name everything, but it, itself, is indefinable. It is more disembodied than Nothing, since Nothing can be more or less objectified by our imagination. Existence just exists. But reality is.

Translated by Judith Balogh   1982

Appendix 6

JÁNOS PILINSZKY: On the Edge of the World

A radio interview with Éva Toth

TOTH: *What has the publication of* Metropolitan Icons *[Nagyvárosi ikonok, 1970] meant to you? Especially since it might be regarded as your Collected Poems.*

PILINSZKY: Indeed, it is a volume of my collected works. Its appearance has already brought me much joy. Also, naturally, to be able to realize the ending of a long process – it helps to start again.

TOTH: *So it is not a closing but, rather, a new beginning?*

PILINSZKY: Well, yes, as far as this represents a sharp boundary in poetry or in one's inner life. I feel that the awkward categorization of past, present and future somehow dissolves in the writing and that all these interact with one another constantly. I really think of my earliest poems as, in a sense, both the furthest and closest, because they preserve the beginning in its purest form.

TOTH: *Reading the whole volume from beginning to end – at least for the uninitiated reader – one does not sense the interval between the first and last poem. So, not knowing how long it took to write them, it would presumably not occur to anyone that thirty years have passed. What does this mean? Could you elaborate?*

PILINSZKY: There are many possible answers. I will try to give you the straightest, offhand. What I am going to say may sound rather odd. From my earliest days I was particularly interested in what seemed to get left outside. For instance, a beautiful ocean at dawn hardly needs affirming. But a discarded piece of newspaper does. It was really these things that interested me, the beings, the objects, the things squeezed to the edge of the world, and I felt that if somehow I were able to move these things into the centre, I would have achieved something more important than if I had been celebrating or affirming proven things. And I was somewhat this way, myself; I felt that somehow I too lived on the edge of the world, that I was not like my companions. I wasn't proud of it. And it was like this with the poetry too. I never felt myself to be a poet and I still don't. What interested me most was how to bring this into the centre of poetry, into the accepted centre, or the confirmed centre. These abandoned things. I would almost go so far as to say that while a modern poet, a true poet, is expected to relate to certain formal aspects of poetry in a revolutionary way, I related to it in a childlike way – as when a child enters the adult world. My concern was to take along with me these things which are, or are thought to be, squeezed to the edge of the world. It is hard for me to assess the effect on my poetry, but if it contains anything inventive, then it is precisely this. A spontaneity. I will not call it conservative, because I never like conservatives, who feel at home in the centre of the universe, whereas I always feel I'm a guest there.

TOTH: *Translating what you just said into plainer language, I would say that formally your poetry contains almost nothing innovative; it adheres quite strongly to traditional forms. What, then, constitutes the modernness of this poetry, and – as a follow-up question – how did this poetry, at first glance so esoteric, become so popular?*

PILINSZKY: The popularity greatly surprised me ... Well, I may have introduced those few lonely objects, those edge-phenomena, so to speak. And, perhaps, today I too am considered a poet. Interestingly, now that I have come this far, I am longing to be back on the edge where these mislaid objects and squeezed-out beings were. I would like to live in this world without having to discriminate, as if it were absolutely unified. And it is not by accident that one finds the greatest ideas, or the phenomena of the highest order, expressed in the lowliest of forms. So it is not by chance, let's say, that for us, for example, for Christians, God is an executed criminal. And beauty also resides here, somewhere. Today I feel that societies are all rather too severe; for instance, I see criminals as dupes of crime. The real criminals remain hidden. It seems that real crime can always protect itself. This leads to a certain tension between society and writers, since society is compelled to function within set forms, while the writer attempts to express a whole world, to a certain extent honouring these dupes and abandoned things.

TOTH: *You mentioned that you would like to draw into your poetry those beings and things left out or excluded earlier. Although they put it differently, others have already done this, even if, perhaps, they have drawn another part of the previously excluded into their poetry. Attila József, for instance.*

PILINSZKY: Yes, this is undoubtedly true, but we are always fascinated by life, our own, only concrete life.

TOTH: *Your own?*

PILINSZKY: My own, one-time-only life. Today the abstract is certain, so that during its fleeting but very real duration it doesn't hurt to emphasize – I wouldn't call it real but concrete – the one-time-only, which is more mysterious (and also more unnameable) for me than the abstract. By turning the concrete into the abstract I am able to speak in concepts, but it is the concrete that has the great power of fascination. A French philosopher said that a face whose final meaning I cannot conceive is another face. Yet its message is capable of determining the rest of my life. Without being able to express it. By calling it good or kind I banalize it. The secret, the really inexplicable mystery that the concrete possesses. When one comes upon the concrete in one's own life it has almost no antecedent. It is like one's own mother. It is really unique, once only. I didn't give my antecedents much thought; when something affected me I allowed it to happen. It was this way with effects, too – I did not seek them out, but I did not defend myself against them either. I believe that by really paying attention to the concrete, even the least ability will receive that unique something which is its own, which is worth talking about. Then, it may be questionable whether it will play the same part in the lives of others. But this is a secondary question.

TOTH: *We started our talk with the thirty-year gap between the first and last pieces in* Metropolitan Icons, *and with the difficulty in sensing this interval. It would seem that the ground, or the atmosphere, of the poetry was already there from the beginning, and although the experiences on which your poetry draws occurred between the earlier and the later poems – namely the Second World War, with all its associated ideas and images – the direction of the poetry remained apparently unchanged; so, we are witnessing an organic development.*

PILINSZKY: It is very hard to reply to this. Even if I didn't believe in the change, inside me I felt changes occurring. I feel that the poems of my youth are completely individualistic. I found out later what history was, and later still came another phase. But I am not able to judge this. Still, I believe that in some ways my poems became more bare. In my youth what mattered was ... to reach the essence, even if it involved repeated idling. Now I seem to be groping, a little lost, in the labyrinth, but striving, step by step, to return to accurate signals about the few things I encounter.

TOTH: *'Accurate signals' – I believe this is a very precise formulation. I would even amplify it: many of your poems, perhaps all your poetry, affects us with the force of evidence. Thus, you talk about more or less common experience. This evidence, the force of this evidence, is an unquestionably valuable part of your work. This is a very great accomplishment, perhaps harder to achieve than mere formal innovation – and, what we mentioned earlier – as this poetry doesn't concentrate on form, it can allow itself, within the limits of traditional forms, the most daring space exploration – what should I call it?*

PILINSZKY: I am very pleased to hear this. Actually, the main hardship in my life has been that I have lived so much alone, that I have searched for others so hard. I did not want to be different. I wanted to be like others; I wanted to be with others. So I was looking for this in my poetry too, not for separateness, not for differences, but for immersion. Meeting others on a level last imagined in childhood.

TOTH: *I would like to ask you whom you feel close to, among your contemporaries or among the classics?*

PILINSZKY: Many, many, and yet – without wishing to sound immodest – no one. Everybody's uniqueness, 'onceness,' seems to declare itself in a certain sense of shame, which everyone bears with a certain modesty, throughout his life. At the same time, I wrote recently that a perfect poem would be one whose author could not be detected, but which made everybody feel that it was written about him, or that he too could have written it.

Translated by Judith Balogh 1971

Appendix 7

VASKO POPA: The Little Box

THE LITTLE BOX

The little box grows her first teeth
And her little length grows
Her little width her little emptiness
And everything she has

The little box grows and grows
And now inside her is the cupboard
That she was in before

And she grows and grows and grows
And now inside her is the room
And the house and town and land
And the world she was in before

The little box remembers her childhood
And by most great yearning
Becomes a little box again

Now inside the little box
Is the whole world tiny small
It's easy to put in your pocket
Easy to steal easy to lose

Take care of the little box

Translated by Anne Pennington

Someone asks you what something in one of your poems, what the little box means. The question has made you dream about this poem, and your dreams have answered with a string of questions:

What is the little box? Or to be more exact: who is the little box? Is it a little bastard, and a strange bastard at that, whose human father may be known, but not the mother (who springs from a wooden, an iron, a crystal lineage, or perhaps some other noble or common one)?

Is it a new kind of monster which does not, this time, represent the adultery of man with animal (it is not a siren, not a centaur), nor the adultery of animals with those of different species (it isn't a dragon, nor is it a unicorn)? Is it a *new* monster which represents the adultery of man with an object, with a machine (thus half woman, half machine), and which has appeared to replace the old starved, perhaps already extinct, monsters in the industrial meadows of our ugly dreams?

Or is it a demigoddess who, for the good of mankind, impregnated herself with the huge world as with a seed and who, afterwards, takes care of this world the way she might care for a child in her womb, not wishing to give birth to it?

Or is it, quite the contrary, a half-demon who, to destroy mankind, has stuffed the whole huge world down her gullet and who has smashed it to bits within herself, the better to torment it?

Is it perhaps guarding a treasure, is it its own treasure vault as well, hiding the entire world within itself and even making it smaller, the better to guard it?

Or is it, on the contrary, a jailer who is its own jail as well and who has locked up the whole world within itself, turning it into a dwarf to make it even more difficult for it to get away?

Or is it simply a human head, perhaps that slightly squarish head which has produced mainly boxes lately and which has now changed itself into a box, into a little box, plotting dubious miracles?

Or is it one of those openings in the cosmos that hide all around us – in your, in everyone's closet – which sometimes grow and sometimes shrink, like a mouth that is breathing with difficulty?

Or is it the emptiness of the world itself, which doesn't know what to *do* with the world or with itself, and *when* it begins something, *doesn't* know how it will *finish* it?

Or is it nothing but the objectified great temptation of man, this little box? The temptation which man admires and fears at the same time, but unfortunately cannot resist?

What is the little box? Who is the little box? Is it really *everything* your dream has enumerated here, or is it *none* of all this?

People ask you what your poem means. Why don't people ask the apple tree what its fruit, what the apple means? If the apple tree could speak, it would answer: Bite into one and you'll see what it means!

How are you going to drag a meaning out of your poem? How do you propose to squeeze out, pulverize or cook your poem to a pulp in order to offer the poem-juice or poem-powder or the poem in tablet form to *those* who ask you for it?

You could – just like that, for fun – write a poem about your poem. What a pathetic poem it would turn out to be! It would be something like an apple tree piecing together an apple from its stem, its branches and its leaves. Quite a few people would find that useful! But this proves precisely that you, just like the apple tree, have no business saying anything about your fruit! Doesn't it also prove, by the way, that you are nothing like your poems? Only your poems are anything like your poems, and they are given your name as their common denominator.

By the way, what does the apple mean? Why doesn't anyone give you an answer? Your poem means a secret which came into being somewhere inside you and ripened, and when it was ripe, you expressed it with the syllables of your language. If you had known what this secret meant, you wouldn't have made such an effort to let it be born, so it could live in the sun, among people and beneath the clouds. And it is up to others, not up to you, to find an answer to the question whether the secret can be figured out or only experienced, whether it can be conquered or whether you must finally submit to it, whether it can be opened, or whether one must agree to becoming its captive.

Your eyes follow your poem at it leaves; it has flown out of your hands; you remain silent, rest up a bit, or at least you believe that you are resting; you let go of your poem, so that it can become its own answer. You can speak about your poem only as a reader, for you are its first reader. But that does not mean in any way that you are the authoritative, the best reader. Among those who ask you for the meaning of your poem, there are certainly smarter, more experienced, and less biased readers than yourself.

You are asked how you make your poem. Why don't they ask the stone how it made the little stone, or the bird how it laid the egg, or the woman how she bore the child?

The stone (*we* say) cannot speak, no one understands the language of birds (or else we have *forgotten* it), and the woman will tell of her love, the path of her love, the circumstances of her love; and in the end she will be able to say *nothing* which would be an answer to the question. Or has anyone ever heard of a mother who had spoken of how she made her child's head, how she chose its mind and the colour of its eyes, how she breathed a soul into it? You know there is no such person. She could not do that, but she would not stop claiming, because of that, that *she* and no other had borne the child.

In the same way you too cannot answer how you wrote your poem. You stand before this question as if made of stone, your head hidden under your arm (for you have no wings), your gaze concerned like that of a mother, you stand so helpless, so quiet and silent, like (or almost like) a stone, a bird, a woman. And if this answer, which they demand from you, were the *price* you had to pay for every one of your poems, you would probably stop writing poems. Or you would, worst of all, doubt whether you even wrote your poems yourself. (And this doubt, just between ourselves, wouldn't even be so unfounded!)

You will recount the ceremony that brings you to the poem. Basically you are talking about the behaviour which precedes the birth of your poem, which means: the outer aspect of the poetic ceremony, the only one of which you are aware. If you are honest you will not be able to say anything to anyone about the *other*, mysterious aspect of the ceremony, which crowns itself with the creation of the poem and which completes itself in you. Because you know nothing about it, just as little as *those* people who ask you. Your rôle in creating the poem is the rôle of a middleman: you mediate so that the poem which is forming inside you can reach the light of day, so that it can survive in this light and can live and act without you or your help in the future. This is neither a small nor an easy task, but God knows what you can say about it: a task like any other, in *which* this main, decisive piece of work has already been completed in the worker himself, but without his knowledge.

You are often asked where you get the words for your poems. There are word-bones which can lodge in your throat. They can make you suffocate. There are word-embers that fall into your heart. They can burn you to death. There are word-snakes that coil in your head. Because of them you must learn to play the magic flute. There are many words that can do you harm. You should never treat words frivolously. And among others there are word-keys. These word-keys are the only living words from which you can make a poem. These words always come to you unexpectedly, but never accidentally. They appear like stars or entire constellations in the heavens of your skull. They shimmer among the other words and sentences that have nothing to do with the future poem. These words shimmer as omens of the poem. One must *recognize* only *these* words. They strike you with awe, as if they were not your words. And you remember them darkly, as though you had heard them somewhere before, only you can't remember where and when; and this memory will remain dark for you for ever and will not become clear even after you write the poem down.

The richer and more mature your experience is, the more it teaches you that the words of a poem come to you from their own source. And where else, do you think, are they going to come from? Where this source of living words (the key-words) exists, neither you nor anyone else can tell the people who ask this question. The only thing you know is that the path from this source leads through your heart, through your head, through your soul. And that gives you the opportunity to write a poem, to write *the way* you have earned to write. To be a poet means – more than anything else – to be human, to be a human being who releases the words for his poem from their source with his life. Without self-obliteration, there is no concentration, without concentration no inspiration, without inspiration no revelation, without revelation there is and can be no poem. Or at least there can't be a poem like the one you wanted.

And you are asked just as often: to whom do you address the words of your poem? You bring them back to the place you received them from, you return them to their source. This time too, neither you nor anyone else can say where this source is. The only thing you know is that the path back to the source of the living word leads through the heart, through the head, through the soul of all human beings. And this in turn gives every human being the chance that he, too, may stand connected – through the words of the poem – with this life-giving source. In this, and in *nothing* else, does the communality, the love for mankind, and the humanity of the poetic act, of writing poetry, lie. Because every human being, not only the poet, has the daily need to speak with the source of the living word, but often does not know how to.

And for every human being, for every reader, the law applies that he earns the words of the poem if he wants to, that these words become his own. Otherwise he can stand above the poem as high as he wishes to, but the poem will never reveal itself to him. The words in the poem form a closed circle. You can see that they are dancing a circle dance, but you cannot see what centre they dance around. The words of the poem make up an image of the source from which they sprang and towards which they will flow back again. The words, one could say, turn their backs on *those* human beings who bend over the poem. And a person can look them in the face only when he enters the circle-dance without those ulterior motives he is so proud of; only when he doesn't ask where the circle-dance of words will take him, and only if he doesn't turn around.

Only in *this way* will the poem reveal itself to him: it will open up to him from the inside. There are no other entrances, no side entrances into the poem.

You are asked again and again why you write poems. To find out why you are *alive – that is why* you write poems. The living words spend the night, or spend the day, inside you, from time to time, on their endless journey to their source. Only in *them* do you see why you're alive. If it were not for *them*, you would *never* see what is *behind* the mountains which surround you. *Never* would you see *where* your field is, *nothing* could be discovered on it. Your sentences would be nothing but mouthfuls of earth until you die, and *after* you die even more so. You would stagger across your field and bang your forehead on invisible walls with your eyes wide open.

You keep watch in the middle of this endless journey that leads right through you, and you wait for the living words. You go out to meet them and to bring them your gifts, the *only ones* you have: watchfulness and silence. With *these* you hope to give them food and drink. You prepare for them your naked breath so that they may feel at home in *it*, as under the tent of the heavens or in the subterranean depths, depending on which is appropriate for them.

You keep watch far from this source of living words; you've never seen the source, but it seems to you that you can hear something of its sound, feel something of its shape, see some part of its clarity in every one of your poems. You have no fear that this source could ever dry up. You have no fear that someone could poison it or plug it up. You know very well that this source cannot be muddied, for no curse, no evil enchantment, no stone could ever reach it and fall into its depths.

If you are keeping watch like this, in the middle of the path on which the living words come from their source, then it is for *this* reason: because you are afraid that this path might become deserted and overgrown, turn into a dense, impenetrable turmoil, or that it might sink under a thick, dusty layer of silence. Because then you would never write another poem again. Your forehead would change back into a gravestone, covering up an entire world. Under this stone would forever lie all you cannot see with the naked eye. And you would no longer know why you were alive, because no living word would exist to tell you.

You are asked, *you*, who have dedicated yourself to writing poems, where your place is. Your place is among people who have a daily need for the living word of your poem. And precisely *because* you know that, you cannot remain silent with this word inside you, even if someone declares that you are a smuggler of things which do not exist. You must not silence the living word, even if someone declares you are a criminal in regard to *things* that really *do* exist. Because the spoken poetic word gives life to all human beings. The unspoken word, the word buried in flesh and silence, this same word rots, dissolves, and becomes a poison in all human beings, and can bring death to them. And this is where your responsibility to the living word begins in this time, as in all times. Today, when the very existence of this tiny, fertile star – whose shine should be mankind itself – is in question, today more than ever before, it is necessary that the living poetic word be heard.

Your place is in the long procession of people of your language who, in the course of centuries, have occupied themselves with the same strange task as you: they transform a little earth and a lot of sky, which they carried in their hearts, into a poem. They did not write poems because they felt like it, but because they did not wish to die. They did not wish to die, and they did not wish to see the human beings around them die. They turned the world into a poem to rescue it in that poem. For *them*, to write poems meant to love.

And you flatter yourself for nothing except for this. You know where, in the end, you stand beside your poem when you are done writing it. Your place is certainly not within the poem: just imagine you were to find, inside the apple, a bit of the earth that nourished the apple tree?! Neither is your place *behind* the poem: your shadow would fall on the poem and cloud it. Underneath your poem, deep under it, that is where your place is: like *that* of all nourishing earth.

Translated by Margitt Lehbert   1967

Appendix 8

TADEUSZ RÓŻEWICZ

In conversation with Adam Czerniawski

CZERNIAWSKI: *The English reader already knows something about you. You are the poet who emerged from war-time occupied Poland. You are the poet who has recorded the time of terror, disaster and agony. To express this you have created a minimal poetry which has ranged itself against all poetry. For the last thirty years you have been running away from poetry. From the very beginning you were saying that poetry is finished, that one could not be a poet in 1945. And yet during these years you have written a vast amount of poetry. How do you explain this apparent paradox?*

RÓŻEWICZ: For me this situation is quite clear. I feel it almost physically. I can see this character with two heads. One head belongs to the writer, the poet: by 1938 I was already well acquainted with the main stream of Polish poetry and I had written a few poems myself. So this literary head was always interested in poetry and in its latest developments. Even during the occupation I managed to get hold of new volumes of verse, both Polish and foreign, even though it wasn't at all easy. I remember coming across an anthology of Italian poetry in German. As a schoolboy I was reading Shakespeare in various Polish translations. I discovered Eliot and Auden.

CZERNIAWSKI: *You had read Wacław Borowy's pioneering essay on Eliot.*

RÓŻEWICZ: I read it very early on in 1945. I found it in one of the pre-war publications. But my other head kept saying, Listen, don't take any notice of what people have been writing, don't bother writing yourself, this happens to be your present situation, you are living through a particular time, confronting certain events. Throw everything away. If you can't create a poetry which will be a new form of human existence, the whole effort is not worth a candle. You will find yourself turning over existing poetics, becoming a rebel in verse, your attention will be concentrated upon poetic language. In other words, you will become a *littérateur*. But here you are living through a time which has no parallel in history, and this calls for an utterly new poetry. I don't mean a poetry of new sounds, new idioms, poems let us say in the form of blank pages, a poetry of smells, plastic poetry or poems in colour. No, it has to be a poetry of words that I actually knew, even though my vocabulary wasn't by any means like that of the author* of *Story of Sin*. It was the vocabulary of someone who had finished secondary school and suddenly found himself in a situation for which he bore no responsibility. So this second head kept saying, Don't play at literature, nothing will come of it. But at the same time there was, say, a copy of Rilke lying on the table. German is the only foreign language I know. German poetry is therefore closer to me than either English or French. So there was this continuous dialogue between these two heads. And not just heads: two hearts. On the one hand the history of art, on the other, everything's shit.

CZERNIAWSKI: *Is that what you had in mind when you wrote that you don't create poetry, only facts?*

RÓŻEWICZ: Yes. And it seems that in some of my poems the word has become flesh. They are something more than texts. It is not just that they entered poetry anthologies and school text-books: they have entered the blood-stream of a whole generation. It seems to me, if one could talk of achievements in poetry, and I don't wish to talk about achievements, only facts, then it seems to me these are the facts. I can feel them, I can touch them. Someone from outside could say more clearly what I am claiming to be the case: perhaps a critic, a translator, a reader, less likely a fellow-poet.

CZERNIAWSKI: *Would you agree that in a sense you are the ideal social-realist poet, not in that vulgarized, negative sense in which the term is normally used, but in the sense that your poetry always rests on very simple and direct experiences. It crystallizes facts torn out of ordinary life, the ordinary of course including the tragic and the grotesque, as well as the serene and homely.*

RÓŻEWICZ: Yes, I have poems like 'A Dithyramb in Honour of Mother-in-Law', 'The Father's Visit' or 'Poems to a Young Son', poems which might be included in family anthologies and lyrical first-aid kits. But all the same, these poems are the result of elaborate formal experiments. The second head, that of the professional writer, was hard at work. They tell me that my poems are as spontaneous as the cry of a terrified man under Nazi occupation, that I have uttered a cry of despair on behalf of a whole generation. Yes, I have uttered a cry, but before that I had worked upon the form that cry was to take. If my cry had been like that of my uncle in Częstochowa who also wrote about the war and also suffered – I have his diaries – if I had cried in the same manner I would have become

---

*Stefan Żeromski (1864–1925), Polish novelist celebrated for his 'poetic', intense and luxuriant prose. [A. Cz.]

my own uncle in Częstochowa. I think I have done something for the young. In some sense I have freed them from form. I never advised anyone to be formally slip-shod. My first poems used to go through some twenty to twenty-five revisions. Emancipation from form was to come after those revisions, not before. Polish poetry has a long tradition of exacting formalism. I declared a freedom from all forms. I advised the young to write in any way they pleased. You may write sonnets, rhyming couplets, prose poems, triangular poems, circular poems – whatever you like. That is not important. The only thing that is important is the internal energy, the material of poetry. This task fell to me, but anyone else could have done it. Someone called Philip or Humphrey. Somebody had to do it.

CZERNIAWSKI: *That is why your poetry is commonly described as simple, naked. This deceived people into thinking that it is easy to write. That is why you have had so many imitators. It seems to me that only when one tries to translate it does one discover its tightly thought-out structure which has to be carried across into the other language with great care. I often see English translations of your poetry which reproduce it word for word. It doesn't work. Perhaps the experienced translator, more than the critic, is able to see that here is art masking art.*

RÓŻEWICZ: Earlier you referred to something that I had once said. I have said a lot of things at various times, but I often run away very far from things that I have said. If anyone wants to pick up one of my books and pin me down, I don't think that is binding on me because I may well be entering into a new situation.

CZERNIAWSKI: *Naturally, opinions change with time, but your love-hate relationship with poetry is quite remarkable. It is constant and appears both in your prose reflections upon poetry and in the poetry itself.*

RÓŻEWICZ: Not just love and hate. There is also irony, sarcasm, contempt and of course indifference. I tend to find any old newspaper more absorbing than the finest edition of poems: that a dog was run over or a house got burnt down. Hence my sudden revulsion against Rilke. I could read his very simple poems but not the elaborate stuff. It's clarity I was also looking for in Polish poets like Kochanowski, Mickiewicz, Norwid, Leśmian, Staff and Przyboś. My motto was Norwid's 'A proper word to name each thing'. I was aiming at a poetry of absolute transparency, so that the dramatic material might be seen through the poem, just as in clear water you can see what is moving on the bottom. And so the form had to vanish, had to become transparent, it had to become identified with the subject of the given poem.

CZERNIAWSKI: *Yes, 'transparent' is a very good description of your poetry.*

Looking at it superficially, it appears typically modernist, aggresively avant-garde, consciously new, but as one reads it more closely, this aspect melts away and one no longer feels one is reading poetry that is striving to be modern. It is a contemporary poetry but not modernist in any strictly literary sense. You are not interested in elaborating metaphors, which was such a notable feature of the Polish modernist inter-war poetry out of which your poetry emerged.

RÓŻEWICZ: Yes, I was always ready to move back to positions long ago abandoned and to poke around in old things, but not in the sense of being attached to old furniture and grandmother's oil lamp. As I said, I was looking for that kind of clarity which I found in Kochanowski and in Staff. In Staff there is a transparency of thought, while my poetry presents miniature dramatic scenes. These are not philosophical poems. They think with their poetic matter, they think with images. Of course I am well aware of the great poets in the philosophical tradition like Eliot or our own Słowacki and Norwid. But that is not my type of poetry. I don't philosophize. I let an image or a situation think for me.

CZERNIAWSKI: *Have you Eliot's* Four Quartets *in mind?*

RÓŻEWICZ: Most of his works, including the plays. One could also think of such metaphysicians as Gottfried Benn, or Bertolt Brecht in his own very specific way. They also theorized in poetry very frequently.

CZERNIAWSKI: *You too theorize in your poems, but you do it in terms of what it means to be able or to want to write a poem, what it means to you creatively, almost biologically.*

RÓŻEWICZ: Yes, I have poems like that, because I find theoretical essays difficult to write. Whenever I see that I am being misunderstood I try once more to say in a poem what my poetry stands for. [...]

CZERNIAWSKI: *You also have poems in this [socialist-realist] convention in which you explore Polish Catholicism. I say Polish Catholicism, because here you do not present as it were an intellectual's discussion of faith. You express an 'ordinary' individual's attitude to traditional Polish faith. Here too I detect a dramatic paradox. You were brought up in an environment of faith but you yourself are not a believer. Neither are you an atheist, someone who dispassionately presents a rational case against faith. You are rather an unbeliever, you struggle with belief in God in a brutal, rebellious manner.*

RÓŻEWICZ: The rôle of Catholicism in the Polish home and school is well defined and deeply rooted, but it is also normal to break with this tradition in adolescence. At sixteen one normally stops going to confession, at seventeen one stops believing Catholic dogma, later a political element would be added. The conservatism of the majority of the clergy, the black reaction which was characteristic of most of the church hierarchy would repel any intelligent young person who would then naturally gravitate towards socialism and find himself anathematized by the priest. I published my first poem in a periodical dedicated to the worship of the Virgin Mary and like most secondary school pupils I was a member of the Marian Brotherhood until I was thrown out of it because of my cynical attitude. But, as far as I remember, my first poem was called 'The Wooden Church' and it appeared in 1938. Later I was tearing myself away not only from customary beliefs and the liturgy but also from the whole metaphysical setting, from the umbilical cord which tied me to heaven and to mysticism. But of course the seeds of childhood remained: the devil, angels, the good Lord.

This is a very complicated issue and I find it difficult to talk about it. Of course I am an unbeliever. One could actually call me a vulgar materialist who has to hold everything in his hands. As far as I am concerned, it is no good unless I can smell it. Even the spirit has to be material. 'I don't believe / as patently deeply / as my mother / believed.' Mother believes deeply, she teaches you how to pray. Or take my poems about the father who believes he will go to heaven. He does believe and he will go to his heaven, but not me. The editor of one of our Catholic weeklies once met me in Kraków and I said to him, 'Well, I don't have much of a chance, have I?' And he says, 'Oh, well, we'll make some arrangements for poets, some sort of special Purgatory.' And another Catholic critic discerned the presence of mysticism and metaphysics in the volume *Forms*. I don't agree with that, but of course each man has his subterranean, subconscious rivers. [...]

CZERNIAWSKI: *In his* History of Polish Literature *Miłosz calls you 'a poet of chaos with a nostalgia for order'.*

RÓŻEWICZ: That is very nicely and effectively put and it is true. But it would also be correct if one were to reverse it and call me 'a poet of order with a nostalgia for chaos.'

CZERNIAWSKI: *Miłosz also alludes indirectly to the social-realist period in Polish literature in the fifties. We have discussed this a little. I of course understand your social-realism very differently from the normal meaning, but Miłosz specifically observed that your fears about nuclear armament coincided with the peace campaign of the Eastern bloc, and that this allowed you to say things which you would not otherwise have been allowed to say and, on the other hand, that your poetry of that period had its moments of sentimentality and oversimplification. Miłosz mentions this in passing. I want later on to discuss the rôle of the poet in society and the pressures society exerts upon him, but for the moment I'd like to concentrate on one single issue. During that period you wrote a long poem called 'The Plain' in which you allude bitterly to Ezra Pound. When I last saw you in Warsaw last autumn, you were walking around clutching a transcript of Pound's treason trial. You are clearly very interested in Pound as a human being. Does this mean that you now see his predicament differently?*

RÓŻEWICZ: The Paris publisher l'Herne has issued a series of volumes devoted to distinguished contemporary authors. There is a volume on Gombrowicz and a massive two-volume publication on Ezra Pound, and in it I am the only Polish poet represented. The editors were content to publish 'The Plain' in a volume dedicated, after all, to Pound's memory and in homage to him. And it was the only work there which, as you observe, had simplified Pound's case. A court of a different nature would also, I think, have passed similar judgment. I knew nothing of his writings, I had no clear picture of his biography. Of course, as far as American law was concerned he was a traitor. Someone who during a war describes the president as a criminal – and especially a president who at that time was revered by the whole world – is a traitor, even if you leave out his insane attacks on other targets. The editors of the l'Herne volume liked 'The Plain' because it was a poem about the Polish resistance. It was the voice of someone who had learnt that a poet, apparently a great and famous poet, was a Fascist, in other words, a criminal. And this I had expressed quite straightforwardly. Professor Wyka, when he read the poem – and he liked the rest of it very much – said to me, in God's name, why have you written all that about Pound at the end? I wrote it on the basis of press reports. I have since come to know his life, his poetry, his rôle as instigator of literary movements, as a friend of many poets whom he materially supported, that he was like a nurse to them. I discovered the other side of the coin. But I don't withdraw what I said in 'The Plain'. On the other hand, when later a Canadian poet wrote to me asking permission to reprint the poem, I refused it, explaining that I had no right to pass judgment, and that poem did contain a judgment. When you are in the middle of battle, that's quite different. Here you have the resistance fighter, on the other side there is the enemy, a Fascist or someone else. You shoot, a man dies. That's not literature. I told him: let's now leave the old poet in peace. I came to see that I am not a judge. The judges did issue a verdict: they placed him in a mental hospital. My task was to try to understand him right to the end. Someone might say: well, you were immature then. No, that wasn't so. It's the atmosphere of war which simplifies. Certain problems are deliberately oversimplified. You make your adversary appear more stupid, more primitive, than he really is. In battle you can't take notice of your enemy's best sides, for if you did, what would be the point of fighting him?

I once wrote a political poem about Greece and Spain, about Fascists and the civil wars there. Politically, that poem was correct, but how on earth, after that last war, could I have used the words 'one had to kill'? This expression haunted me for twenty years. Was that my business? One ought not to kill them, but, on the other hand, what is one to do with them? What happens when poetry enters the battlefield? Here you have moral dilemmas which are insoluble. [...]

CZERNIAWSKI: *Wallace Stevens, the American poet, who spent his life as an insurance executive, said that every poet should pursue an occupation. In England people engage in poetry as a side-line. In Poland it is quite different. You are a professional writer.*

RÓŻEWICZ: Yes, in Poland poetry is often the subject of public debate but at the same time you keep hearing that it is undergoing a crisis, that nobody is reading it. Some editions reach 10,000 copies and they sell out. In our country poetry plays many rôles. It may, for instance, be a substitute for religion.

CZERNIAWSKI: *This entails constant confrontations with the authorities. Here in England nobody takes any notice of what the poets say, whereas in Poland poetry plays a political rôle.*

RÓŻEWICZ: Yes.

CZERNIAWSKI: *You of course maintain that poetry should be present in a social setting, in the midst of life, and if society, perhaps through its government, reacts unfavourably, that is a necessary consequence.*

RÓŻEWICZ: I couldn't really expand on this now. It's a complex and wide issue covering sociology, politics and literary tradition, the nation's history no less. It rather demands the attention of sociologists and historians of literature.

CZERNIAWSKI: *We discussed Pound. I would like to ask you about Wittgenstein and Eliot. What's your opinion of Eliot's plays?*

RÓŻEWICZ: Of course I know them only in translation. It seems to me that the linguistic values of Eliot's plays are very important. I think *Murder in the Cathedral* is his best play. It's in the Shakespearean tradition because of its expansive theme, and in this it differs from *The Cocktail Party* or *The Family Reunion*. As regards Wittgenstein's philosophy, I came across it only as an amateur through Norman Malcolm's biographical sketch.

CZERNIAWSKI: *It is the biography that I want to ask you about. In Pound's case you stressed that he was helpful and generous to his literary friends.*

RÓŻEWICZ: Whereas Wittgenstein was a misanthrope, something like schizophrenia shaped his attitude to people. But he was, as far as I am concerned, a secular saint, while in Pound there were elements of fanatical fury bordering on criminality. I am very often initially drawn to a man's biography, and then suddenly I become interested in his work as well. I think this was the case with Simone Weil and one or two painters. Soon after the war I came across Van Gogh's letters to his brother. I am searching for, if I dare put it like that, saintliness in creative people. In practice I may well be far removed from this but I have always been extremely fascinated by this concept.

CZERNIAWSKI: *Was this why you were drawn to Kafka?*

RÓŻEWICZ: Yes.

CZERNIAWSKI: *After the war you exchanged a painting by Nowosielski for a battered copy of Kafka's* Trial, *which was proscribed by the authorities in those days.*

RÓŻEWICZ: Yes. This also accounts for my interest in Dostoyevsky, Thomas Mann, and also Mann's brother Henry, whose moral profile appears to me even more remarkable than that of Thomas. Hence also my sudden interest in Klaus Mann, precisely because of the life situation: the impossible situation of the son, his suicide. These are quite simple matters, but this is precisely the way I find my access to an author. I would like to know how good Conrad was as a sailor. I place his novels and stories on the highest shelf but I have always wanted to know whether he was any good as a skipper or whether he was completely hopeless. Similarly with Hemingway, though of course I don't rate his work as highly as that of Conrad. But I was always curious to know what sort of a soldier he was. Wounded in the leg, decorated, was he perhaps just simply a medical orderly? We disapprove of our readers for showing interest in such banal details but we ourselves are simply fascinated. Perhaps that's why diaries and memoirs are so popular today. Sometimes it's more interesting to know what a man was like than what he wrote.

CZERNIAWSKI: *In the Afterword to your poems in* The Third Face *you quote Tolstoy who said that it's better to write a child's ABC than a novel. Miłosz has observed that you write your poems like an ABC. I don't know whether he had* The Third Face *in mind or whether he reached this conclusion independently, but in any case you should accept this as . . .*

RÓŻEWICZ: A compliment . . .

CZERNIAWSKI: *That you have created an ABC, a didactic book. In your collection of sketches and notes, which includes items on Eliot and Wittgenstein, you also write about Truman Capote's* In Cold Blood *and draw a contrast between Raskolnikov and our own contemporary murderers. You write that*

Hitchcock and Smith have neither a soul nor a conscience, that they murdered for the fun of it. 'The unresolved problem for me – you say – is whether it's worth writing very simple, didactic tales and whether these tales are likely to cause at least one man to give up murdering old women. What is the true rôle of books and literature in our time? This didactic element which pervades all your work, which Miłosz has noted and which you yourself regard as essential, seems to me to be your great achievement.

RÓŻEWICZ: Earlier in this conversation I made a distinction between two heads, the human head and the writer's head. There is also the reader's head. I used to be a reader, a passionate reader over many years. I searched books and poems for practical help. I hoped they would help me overcome despair and doubt, and strangely enough, I sought this both in Dostoyevsky and in Conrad, even though Conrad scorned and was repelled by Dostoyevsky. I sought help both from Lord Jim and Raskolnikov. Similarly I sought help during the occupation, and even before, in poetry. And when this led to disappointment – after all, these were only books – I became angry and disillusioned with the greatest works. I felt I was muddling things up in some way and yet I couldn't face up to this. Because I myself have always searched, begged for help, I began to think that I too may be able to help, though of course I also have moments when I feel it's not worth anything. Occasionally someone writes to me in a way that strengthens my conviction about turning words into practice.

Translated by Adam Czerniawski 1976

Appendix 9

TADEUSZ RÓŻEWICZ: My Poetry

MY POETRY

explains nothing
clarifies nothing
makes no sacrifices
is not all-embracing
does not redeem any hopes

does not create new rules of the game
takes no part in play
has a defined place
which it has to fulfil

if it's not a cryptic language
if it speaks without originality
if it holds no surprises
evidently this is how things ought to be

obedient to its own necessity
its range and limitations
it loses even against itself

it does not usurp the space of another poetic
nor can it be replaced by any other
open to all
devoid of mystery

it has many tasks
to which it will never do justice

ONE CAN

I recollect that in the past
poets composed 'poetry'

one can still write verses
for many many years
one can also do
many other things

Adam Czerniawski

The composer Artur Honegger said a few years ago that music would die
in much the same way that lyric poetry has. Who would have the courage
today to name his or her profession 'poet'? In a letter to Bernard Gavot,
the same composer wrote (in the book *I Am a Composer*): '... So I must
announce: "I am a composer!" Please try to imagine the derisive
laughter of an audience to whom a man wanted to disclose: "I am a
poet" ...'

As we know, God died. This, Nietzsche discovered. Later (after
various metamorphoses) the devil died, and then man died too. Finally –
as Honegger points out – the poet died ... *but we are still alive.* We are
witnesses to the posthumous life of God, the devil, man ... and poets.
The poet died. This Honegger declares sharply, clearly, brutally. But if
the poet died, what am I – here and now – doing among you? Are you
speaking with a dead man? Who is this sitting in front of you, what is he
reading, what is he talking about? Shall I tell you what the life of a poet is
like after his death?

I am forced to speak of my concept of poetry in this situation, from the
'Great Beyond'. I am far from dismissing Honegger's remark as an
aphorism, as a verbal quip. Quite the contrary: I too believe that the poet
is dead. I also believe in God's death, in the death of the devil, in the
death of man. It seems to me that it is time to determine the new position
of the poet and of poetry. The problem is not 'the poet and the polis', the
problem is 'the poet and the necropolis'.

As I write these words, in this beautiful capital on the Danube,
preparations are being made for a poetry festival which carries the slogan
'Poezja nie jest martwa, poezja nie może umrzeć! Die Lyrik ist nicht tot,
die Lyrik kann nicht sterben! La poésie n'est pas morte, elle ne peut
périr!' Under this slogan, a hundred or even two hundred poets from
socialist and capitalist countries are convening. They are discussing,
arguing, reading their new poems, they are themselves proof of the
vitality of poetry and of its eternal life. 'Poetry is not dead, poetry cannot

die.' I see an authoritative body of poets who are living proof not only that poetry is immortal, but that poets too live on and create in the face of all hardship.

And yet this literary bustle is nothing but a kind of life after death. That's right, gentlemen, yes, dear colleagues of the pen, my friends, my fellow sufferers. Poetry is mortal, poetry can die and deliver poets up to ridicule. This isn't just a macabre notion, it's the ugly truth – which, by the way, I don't intend to prove. Why should I? God died and didn't die, the same goes for the devil; man too died and yet lives on: what else died and what lives on anyway? Culture, civilization, humanism, poetry? In other words, we shouldn't take this as too much of a tragedy. So I don't allow any 'black' and therefore a bit boring, perhaps even suspicious, moods and thoughts to come up; I call myself not a dead, but a *passé* poet. Alive but *passé*. In this way I establish contact. And avoid laughter. Although I must admit that it's hard for me to do without my idea of the 'Beyond'. I would really like to tell you how a poet lives after his death. That would be something! That would be an idea!

I confess that for a while I suffered because I had no idea and no lyric conception. The inventors of the 'happening' led me into temptation; I thought: 'What do I have to face my public with, my critics, my . . .' What do I have that I can perform in the year 1966 *anno domini*? Poems? Or what? Should I enter the hall walking on my hands, should I stand on my head, shoot my translator, or hack a promising woman poet up into little pieces and strew the parts of her body – wrapped in my sonnet (it would have to be a sonnet!) – around the hall? I was embarrassed because I had only one head and not two, like some sort of freak calf; it was my old I, the 'living' poet, who was sad about the way his poetry and his existence as a poet were regarded. We should create poetry as surprising as a calf with three heads, then skin it, cut it into four pieces and . . . sell it!

I imagined what people would say after our meeting: 'Guess what, guess what . . . just think, I saw a poet today with two heads. His name is Tadeusz Różewicz . . . his poetry is quite unique!' And I was led into temptation by the demon of arrogance . . . he advised me to write a poem with my left foot and with my eyes closed, to demolish the word, to invent the word, to cheat on the word. Finally he suggested I hang myself. A whole kingdom of the avant-garde and of experimentation lay at my beck and call. But let's forget that. We poets of today – the (seemingly) live ones and the dead – are sick and dying because of our exaggerated self-love. We yearn to be original, admired, unique. None of us wants to be boring, uninteresting, easily dismissed . . . and that's precisely the great sin and the secret of our whitewashed graves. But I'm catching myself becoming almost witty and almost 'unique.' Beware!

Besides the posthumous life of contemporary poets, another, worse thing distressed me, namely ridicule. Please try to imagine the derisive laughter of an audience to whom a man wanted to disclose: 'I am a poet ...' 'I am a poet.' What's so ridiculous about that? Does someone who admits to being a chaplain, minister, policeman, butcher, barber, physicist, logger ... become ridiculous? No! Of course it's worse with jobs like executioner, slave-driver, counterfeiter, thief ... it's not right to admit to that, you just don't say that ... similarly, no one introduces himself to an assembly as a sadist, sodomite, as impotent, as a philosopher ... but 'poet'? Would laughter really erupt in the hall?

Obviously, changes have occurred, so that we can no longer publicly declare ourselves. Yes, own up to this guilt. To this mutilation, to this intimate disease ... What happened? Why does a contemporary composer confront us with this question so openly and so clearly? This riddle bothered me for a long time and I never did solve it. OK, so we are ridiculous. We cannot own up to our profession because of the danger of ridicule.

My conception of poetry, of the art of poetry? What a relief, what liberation! I have no conception. Obviously in the course of twenty-five years I did have various conceptions. I defined and classified my poetics, my 'lyric' and 'anti-lyric' poetry, both in poems and theoretical reflections. Now I really don't care at all: rhyme or no rhyme, metaphor or no metaphor, image or no image, idea or no idea – none of this is relevant ... There is only one thing I pay any attention to: the word. I never give that up. People who play with words are, to me, stupid and unhappy creatures, or happy and immature ones. You can address someone who is interested in the situation of our so-called lyric poetry not by stuttering, smashing, or torturing words, syllables, sounds ... it requires the word and the 'perfectly normal' sentence ...

I tried to express this in a poem with the title 'Season 1966'.

> It has been long past
> the season in the 'Paradis du Langage'
> I have been saying this for twenty years
> to our wordmakers
> wordwarblers wordbags
>
> Only now
> the real problems

of writing poetry are beginning
you shall see
even in this season
that the egg the poem
will have to be
laid
not into the chaff of words half and quarter words
but directly
into the abyss the void
here is a problem worthy of a poet
how not to write poetry
how not to write
one more little poem

I imagine a poetry without qualities. A poetry which would be anonymous again, would be 'the voice of Anon' again. For this I struggled all those years.

for so long have I been forming
my self
in the image and likeness
of nothing
forming its face
in the likeness and image
of everything

that at last my features
have dissolved
my words
no longer surprise each other*

That which appears to the 'innovators' of all types as purgatory, even as hell, this anonymity, the lack of creative personality, the absence of any identifying characteristics – is my cleansing. They made poetry ridiculous by chasing after originality and uniqueness, they crafted it into a child's toy, an avant-garde calf with two heads. So we had to bury all of this and trample the earth down over it. No artificial respiration, no manipulation helped. Poetry, in order to resurrect itself, had to die.

In the particular and limited realm given to me by birth and life, this event can sink like a stone flung into water. But it's possible that my

* Translated by Paula Windisch and Jan Darowski

experience will not disappear without a trace, that my circle of experience will touch the experiences of other poets from countries near and far that I have visited or shall never see. And I accept this fate with the humility and joy I feel by knowing the situation of poets in the world today.

I'm thinking back to the year 1945. I was in Kraków then and had just begun to study art history at the Jagiellonian University. That fall they cleaned and organized the rooms of the Writers' Union and threw out a stack of old magazines. Among them were issues of the *Contemporary Times* (Przegląd Współczesny) from 1936 to 1939. A couple of contributions and treatises caught my attention. The essay by Borowy on Eliot, the one by Zawodziński on 'Polish Poetry in the Time of Crisis', the one by Tatarkiewicz on 'Art and Poetry' ...

I remember I was writing a poem back then which I never finished – it was a poem about the reconstruction of St Mary's Church in Kraków. The fact that monuments of old Kraków objectively existed in no way confirmed their reality for me.

And here is the plan for that poem: '... people passing by think St Mary's Church still stands there unhurt. They don't see that it's a great prism of brick and stone. The church lies in rubble. The church is demolished within me. This structure I gaze upon is not a church, not a monument of architecture, nor a work of art, but a devastated, demolished shack, a heap of rubble ...'

I had a reason for wanting to study art history. I wanted to study art history in order to resurrect the Gothic temple. To build up the church within me, stone by stone. To reconstruct man, element by element. Both were inseparably linked. I see the poem itself as if through a dense fog, but I recall its intention exactly.

It was as if two people were living inside me at that time. One was full of admiration and respect for the 'fine' arts, for music, literature, and poetry ... the other was full of mistrust for the arts. The battlefield these two forces clashed on was my poetry. I admired works of art religiously (aesthetic experience had replaced religious experience for me), but at the same time my contempt for 'aesthetic' values grew and grew. I felt that something was over and done with, for me and for mankind. Something that neither religion, nor science, nor art had rescued. I understood too soon the words of Mickiewicz, who said that it's 'harder to live well for a day than to write a book'. I understood too soon Tolstoy's remark that the design of a school textbook was more important than all the world's clever novels combined.

So then I turned away from aesthetic sources. Only ethics – I thought – could be the source for art. But the sources, both of them, had run dry: 'The murderer had washed his hands in them.'

So I tried to resurrect what seemed most important for my life and the life of poetry. Ethics. And because, since my youth, ethics for me was linked to politics, not to aesthetics, my art took on a political aspect. This applies especially to my first poems, written right after the war.

So for me poetry was a form of action and not the writing of beautiful poems. My objective was not poems, but facts. I created – so I thought and still think – certain facts and not (more or less successful) lyric constructions. I reacted to events with facts which I moulded into the shape of poems – and not with 'poetry'. For this reason I was never interested in so-called 'schools of poetry', their markets and their haggling over measure or metaphor, and this despite being an eager pupil of the masters of the word ... In order to explain my views more clearly and to classify my mental state, I will cite what François Mauriac said: 'In view of the political and military events, all else seems unimportant – it is these events which distract me from literary fiction. In waiting rooms, people read newspapers, at best ...'

But back to the issues of the *Contemporary Review*, to the treatise of Professor Tatarkiewicz. In the fourth section of 'The Concept of Beauty,' Tatarkiewicz says, 'the Greek concept of beauty ... had a different range from ours: it was much more comprehensive, including either ethics or mathematics.' 'Beautiful' usually meant 'worthy of admiration' and only a fine nuance separated it from what was considered 'good'. In Plato especially, the concept of beauty included 'moral beauty', the good qualities of character which we don't take into consideration today, which we actually separate, painstakingly, from aesthetic qualities.

At that time, in the year 1945, several months after World War Two, I thought expressions such as 'aesthetic experiences' or 'artistic experiences' were ridiculous and suspect. Afterwards, in August, the first atomic bomb was dropped. And today I still think so-called 'aesthetic experiences' are ridiculous, though I no longer consider them despicable. The conviction that the earlier 'aesthetic experience' is dead is the unchanging platform of my literary activity. Speaking 'directly' should lead to the source, to regaining a banal faith, banal hope, banal love. Love that conquers death and love that is conquered by death. I was concerned with such simple things as these. Poems in which I gambled on originality, uniqueness, surprise have secondary importance for me. Even if they were possibly better from the point of view of 'aesthetic experiences'.

The dogmatists of the avant-garde have caused such chaos among the 'detailists' and 'luminaries' that there remains only one cure: to replace so-called 'poetic sense' with normal sense, that is, with healthy common sense. I had to give 'banality' back its rights.

In 1948, during the Congress of Young Writers in Nieborów, I spoke a lot with Tadeusz Borowski. It was our second meeting. We spoke of various things, among them poetry. Borowski was wondering whether you could still use expressions like 'the moon shines' in a poem ... 'You can't very well make a poem from that any more, can you?' he asked. 'I don't know,' I answered, 'but I could try.' I recall sitting down and trying it after my return from Nieborów. I wrote the poem 'The Moon Shines'.

> The moon shines
> the street is bare
> the moon shines
> a man flees
>
> the moon shines
> a man falls
> a man dies
> the moon shines
>
> the moon shines
> the street is bare
> a dead man's face
> a puddle of water.

Producing 'beauty' to achieve an 'aesthetic experience' seems to me a harmless, though ridiculous and childish pastime ...

'Manifestoes' and definitions hem in our movements, stiffen our attitudes. Therefore I want to emphasize that these remarks do not exhaust the source of my poetics, or even throw much light on the problem. They remain fragments. Similar to the way in which my notes on sound and image in contemporary poetry, published in 1958, were only a contribution to a particular debate. And the poem 'My Poetry', which I began my talk with, is yet another attempt to illuminate this problem.

Translated by Margitt Lehbert   1966

BIBLIOGRAPHY

This bibliography, far from being comprehensive, lists only a selection of the secondary works that the editor of the present volume has found useful. An attempt has, however, been made to include most of the individual collections available in English translation up to the present (spring 1990) by the poets represented in the anthology, with the exception of Tymoteusz Karpowicz and Edvard Kocbek, whose poetry has not yet been published in book form in translation. Many if not most of these collections also contain useful introductions. It is to be noted that articles appearing in *Cross Currents* (Ann Arbor: University of Michigan) have not been listed, since so many are relevant. Interested readers are urged to consult all volumes of this indispensable publication. The magazine *Index on Censorship* (London: Writers and Scholars International) is an equally indispensable tool, regularly carrying articles and reports on, as well as contributions from, Central Europe. The magazine *World Literature Today*, formerly *Books Abroad* (Norman: University of Oklahoma Press) is also well worth scanning for articles and special features relating to Central European writing.

1. GENERAL

Alvarez, A., *Under Pressure. The Writer in Society: Eastern Europe and the USA*. Harmondsworth: Penguin Books, 1965.

Beradt, Charlotte, *The Third Reich of Dreams*. Chicago: Quadrangle Books, 1966.

Bialoszewski, Miron, *A Memoir of the Warsaw Uprising*. Ann Arbor: Ardis, 1977.

Bettelheim, Bruno, 'The Holocaust. Some Reflections, a Generation Later'. *Encounter* Vol. LI No. 6. London, December 1978.

Borowski, Tadeusz, *This Way for the Gas, Ladies and Gentlemen*. Harmondsworth and New York: Penguin Books, 1976.

Collins, R. G., and McRobbie, Kenneth (eds.), 'The Eastern European Imagination in Literature'. *Mosaic* Vol. VI No. 4. Winnipeg: University of Manitoba Press, 1973.

Delbo, Charlotte, *None of Us Will Return*. Boston: Beacon Press, 1968.

Des Pres, Terrence, *The Survivor. An Anatomy of Life in the Death Camps*. New York: Oxford University Press, 1976.

Enzensberger, Hans Magnus, 'In Search of the Lost Language'. *Encounter* Vol. XXI No. 3. London, September 1963. Essay.

Friedrich, Otto, 'The Kingdom of Auschwitz'. *The Atlantic*. Boston, September 1981.

Jong, Louis de, 'Sobibor'. *Encounter*. London, December 1978.

Keith-Smith, Brian, *Essays on Contemporary German Literature*. London: Oswald Wolff, 1969. Contains essays on Celan, Bachmann, Enzensberger etc.

Kundera, Milan, 'The Tragedy of Central Europe'. *The New York Review of Books*. New York, 26 April 1984.

Kundera, Milan, *The Art of the Novel*. New York: Grove Press, 1987.

Langer, Lawrence L., *The Age of Atrocity. Death in Modern Literature*. Boston: Beacon Press, 1978.

Langer, Lawrence L., *The Holocaust and the Literary Imagination*. New Haven and London: Yale University Press, 1975.

Lanzmann, Claude, *Shoah. An Oral History of the Holocaust*. New York: Pantheon Books, 1985.

Miłosz, Czesław, *The Captive Mind*. New York: Knopf, 1953.

Rosenfeld, Alvin H., *A Double Dying: Reflections on Holocaust Literature*. Bloomington and London: Indiana University Press, 1980.

Rousset, David, *The Other Kingdom*. New York: Reynal and Hitchcock, 1947.

Steiner, George, *In Bluebeard's Castle. Some Notes Towards the Redefinition of Culture*. Harmondsworth and New York: Penguin Books, 1969.

Steiner, George, *Language and Silence. Essays 1958–1966*. London: Faber and Faber, 1967.

Vladislav, Jan (ed.), *Vaclav Havel or Living in Truth*. Twenty-two essays published on the occasion of the award of the Erasmus Prize to Vaclav Havel. London: Faber and Faber, 1986.

Wiesel, Elie, *Night*. New York: Discus Books, 1969.

Wright, Iain (ed.), 'Eastern Europe'. *Cambridge Review* Vol. 92 No. 2203. Cambridge, 28 May 1971.

2. ANTHOLOGIES

Bassnett, Susan and Kuhiwczak, Piotr (eds.), *Ariadne's Thread. Polish Women Poets*. London: Forest Books, 1988.

Deletant, Andrea and Walker, Brenda (eds.), *Silent Voices. An Anthology of Romanian Women Poets*. London: Forest Books, 1986.

Duczynska, Ilona and Polanyi, Karl (eds.), *The Plough and the Pen. Writings from Hungary 1930–1956*. London: Peter Owen, 1963.

George, Emery (ed.), *Contemporary East European Poetry*. Ann Arbor: Ardis, 1977.

Gömöri, George and Newman, Charles (eds.), *New Writing of East Europe*. Chicago: Quadrangle Books, 1968.

Hamburger, Michael (ed.), *East German Poetry*. Oxford: Carcanet Press, 1972.

Johnson, Bernard (ed.), *New Writing in Yugoslavia*. Harmondsworth: Penguin Books, 1970.

MacGregor-Hastie, Roy (ed.), *Anthology of Contemporary Romanian Poetry*. London: Peter Owen, 1969.

Mayewski, Pawel (ed.), *The Broken Mirror. A Collection of Writings from Contemporary Poland*. New York: Random House, 1958.

Mihailovich, Vasa D. (ed.), *Contemporary Yugoslav Poetry*. Iowa City: University of Iowa Press, 1977.

Miłosz, Czesław (ed.), *Polish Post-War Poetry*, third expanded edition. Berkeley, Los Angeles and London: University of California Press, 1983.

Nyczek, Tadeusz (ed.), *Humps and Wings. A selection of Polish poetry since '68*. San Francisco and Los Angeles: Red Hill Press, 1982.

Tezla, Albert (ed.), *Ocean at the Window. Hungarian Prose and Poetry since 1945*. Minneapolis: University of Minnesota Press, 1980.

Theiner, George (ed.), *New Writing in Czechoslovakia*. Harmondsworth: Penguin Books, 1969.

Vajda, Miklós, (ed.) *Modern Hungarian Poetry*. New York: Columbia University Press, 1977.

Weissbort, Daniel and Hughes, Ted (eds.), *Modern Poetry in Translation* No. 5, a Czechoslovak issue. London: Cape Goliard, 1969.

– *Modern Poetry in Translation* No. 8, a Slovene (Yugoslavia) issue. London, 1970.

Weissbort, Daniel (ed.), *Modern Poetry in Translation* No. 22. London, 1974.

– Nos. 23–4, a Polish issue. London, 1975.

– No. 35. London, 1978.

Wieniewska, Celina (ed.), *Polish Writing Today*. Harmondsworth and Baltimore: Penguin Books, 1967.

3. AUTHORS

Yehuda Amichai

Selected Poems, trans. Assia Gutmann and Harold Schimmel with the collaboration of Ted Hughes. Harmondsworth: Penguin Books, 1971.

Songs of Jerusalem and Myself, trans. Harold Schimmel. New York: Harper and Row, 1973.

Amen, trans. Yehuda Amichai and Ted Hughes. New York: Harper and Row, 1973 and Oxford: Oxford University Press, 1978.

Travels of a Latter-Day Benjamin of Tudela, trans. Ruth Nevo. *Webster Review* Vol. III No. 3. Webster Groves, Missouri, 1977. Joint publication with The Cauldron Press, St. Louis and The Menard Press, London.

Time, trans. Yehuda Amichai. New York: Harper and Row, and Oxford: Oxford University Press, 1979.

Love Poems. A bilingual edition, trans. Glenda Abramson and Tudor Parfitt. New York: Harper and Row, 1983.

Great Tranquillity: Questions and Answers, trans. Glenda Abramson and Tudor Parfitt. New York: Harper and Row, 1983.

The Selected Poetry of Yehuda Amichai, trans. Chana Bloch and Stephen Mitchell. New York: Harper and Row, 1986 and London: Viking, 1987. As *Selected Poems*, London: Penguin Books, 1988.

Travels, trans. Ruth Nevo. New York: The Sheep Meadow Press, 1986.

Rudolf, Anthony, 'Mediterranean East: an interview with Yehuda Amichai'. *London Magazine* Vol. XIX No. 11. London, February 1980.

Ingeborg Bachmann

In the Storm of Roses, trans. Mark Anderson. Princeton: Princeton University Press, 1986.

Johannes Bobrowski

Selected Poems. Johannes Bobrowski and Horst Bienek, trans. Ruth and Matthew Mead. Harmondsworth: Penguin Books, 1971.

From the Rivers, trans. Ruth and Matthew Mead. London: Anvil Press Poetry, 1975.

Shadow Lands. Selected Poems, trans. Ruth and Matthew Mead. London: Anvil Press Poetry, 1984.

Keith-Smith, Brian, *Johannes Bobrowski*. London: Oswald Wolff, 1970.

Bertolt Brecht

Poems 1913–1956, ed. John Willett and Ralph Manheim. London: Methuen, 1976.

Nina Cassian

Blue Apple, trans. Eva Feiler. Merrick: Cross Cultural Communications, 1982.

Lady of Miracles, trans. Laura Schiff. Berkeley: Cloud Marauder Press, 1983.

Call Yourself Alive. The Love Poems of Nina Cassian, trans. Andrea Deletant and Brenda Walker. London: Forest Books, 1988.

Life Sentence. Selected Poems, ed. William Jay Smith. New York: W. W. Norton and London: Anvil Press Poetry, 1990.

Paul Celan

Speech-Grille and Selected Poems, trans. Joachim Neugroschel. New York: Dutton, 1971.

Nineteen Poems, trans. Michael Hamburger. Oxford: Carcanet Press, 1972.

Selected Poems, trans. Michael Hamburger and Christopher Middleton. Harmondsworth: Penguin Books, 1972.

Poems, trans. Michael Hamburger. Manchester: Carcanet Press, 1980.

Collected Prose, trans. Rosmarie Waldrop. Manchester: Carcanet Press, 1986.

Last Poems, trans. Katherine Washburn and Margaret Guillemin. Berkeley: North Point Press, 1986.

Poems of Paul Celan, trans. Michael Hamburger. London: Anvil Press Poetry and New York: Persea Books, 1989.

Lyon, James K., 'Paul Celan and Martin Buber: Poetry as Dialogue'. *PMLA* Vol. 86 No. 1. New York, January 1971.

Glenn, Jerry, *Paul Celan*. New York: Twayne, 1973.

Terras, Victor and Weimar, Kar S., 'Mandelstamm and Celan: Affinities and Echoes'. *Germano-Slavica* No. 3. Waterloo, Ont., 1974.

Cameron, Beatrice, 'Paul Celan: His Speech "The Meridian" (Der Meridian) in acceptance of the Georg Buchner Prize of the Deutsche Akademie für Sprache und Dichtung (in 1960) with an Introductory Note'. *Chicago Review* Vol. 29 No. 3. Chicago, 1978.

Washburn, Katherine and Guillemin, Margaret, 'Threads of Vision, Threads of Meaning'. *Parnassus* Vol. 9 No. 1. New York, 1981.

Felstiner, John, 'Translating Paul Celan's "Du sei wie du"'. *Modern Poetry in Translation: 1983*. Manchester: Carcanet Press and New York: Persea Books, 1983.

Felstiner, John, 'Reconsideration: Paul Celan, The Biography of a Poem'. *The New Republic*, Washington, D.C., 2 April 1984.

Felstiner, John, 'Translating Paul Celan's "Jerusalem" Poems'. *Religion and Literature* Vol. 16 No. 1. Notre Dame, Indiana, 1984.

Hollander, Benjamin (ed.), 'Translating Tradition: Paul Celan in France'. *Acts: A Journal of New Writing* Nos. 8–9. A special Celan issue. San Francisco, 1988.

Hans Magnus Enzensberger

poems for people who don't read poems, trans. Michael Hamburger, Jerome Rothenberg and the author. New York: Atheneum, 1967 and London: Secker and Warburg, 1968.

Selected Poems, trans. Michael Hamburger, Jerome Rothenberg and the author. Harmondsworth: Penguin Books, 1968. Same as above, without the German text.

Mausoleum: Thirty-Seven Ballads from the History of Progress, trans. Jerome Rothenberg. New York: Urizen Books, 1976.

The Sinking of the Titanic, trans. Hans Magnus Enzensberger. Manchester: Carcanet Press, 1981.

'In Search of the Lost Language'. *Encounter* Vol. XXI No. 3. London, September 1963. Essay.

Jerzy Ficowski

A Reading of Ashes, trans. Keith Bosley with Krystyna Wandycz. Foreword by Zbigniew Herbert. London: The Menard Press, 1981.

Zbigniew Herbert

Selected Poems, trans. Czesław Miłosz and Peter Dale Scott. Harmondsworth: Penguin Books, 1968.

Selected Poems, trans. John and Bogdana Carpenter. Oxford: Oxford University Press, 1977.

Report from the Besieged City and Other Poems, trans. John Carpenter and Bogdana Carpenter. New York: Ecco Press, 1985 and Oxford: Oxford University Press, 1987.

Barbarian in the Garden, trans. Michael March and Jarosław Anders. Manchester: Carcanet Press, 1985. Essays.

Czestochowski, Debra N., 'Herbert's "Study of the Object": A Reading'. *The Polish Review* Vol. XX No. 4. New York, 1975.

Czerniawski, Adam, 'The Power of Taste in a Beleaguered City (On the Poetry of Zbigniew Herbert)'. *Poetry Wales* Vol. 20 No. 2. Dyfed, 1983.

Alvarez, A., 'Noble Poet'. *The New York Review of Books*. New York, 18 July 1985.

Heaney, Seamus, 'Atlas of Civilization'. *Parnassus* Vol. 14 No. 1. New York, 1986.

Vladimír Holan

Selected Poems, trans. Jarmila and Ian Milner. Harmondsworth: Penguin Books, 1971.

A Night with Hamlet, trans. Jarmila and Ian Milner. London: Oasis Books, 1980.

Miroslav Holub

Selected Poems, trans. Ian Milner and George Theiner. Harmondsworth: Penguin Books, 1967.

Although, trans. Jarmila and Ian Milner. London: Jonathan Cape, 1971.

Notes of a Clay Pigeon, trans. Jarmila and Ian Milner. London: Secker and Warburg, 1977.

Sagittal Section, trans. Stuart Friebert and Dana Hábová. Oberlin: Oberlin College Press, 1980.

Interferon, or On the Theater, trans. David Young and Dana Hábová. Oberlin: Oberlin College Press, 1982.

On the Contrary and other poems, trans. Ewald Osers. Newcastle: Bloodaxe Books, 1984.

Poems Before and After. Collected English Translations, trans. Ian and Jarmila Milner, Ewald Osers and George Theiner. Newcastle: Bloodaxe Books, 1990.

Vanishing Lung Syndrome, trans. David Young and Dana Hábová. London: Faber and Faber, 1990.

The Dimension of the Present Moment and other essays, ed. David Young. London: Faber and Faber, 1990.

Heaney, Seamus, 'The Fully Exposed Poem'. *Parnassus* Vol. 11 No. 1. New York, 1983.

Peter Huchel

Selected Poems, trans. Michael Hamburger. Manchester: Carcanet Press, 1974.

The Garden of Theophrastus, trans. Michael Hamburger. Manchester: Carcanet Press, 1983.

Reiner Kunze

With the Volume Turned Down and Other Poems, trans. Ewald Osers. London: London Magazine Editions, 1973.

The Lovely Years, trans. Ewald Osers. London: Sidgwick and Jackson, 1978. Prose.

Artur Miedzyrzecki

14 Poems, trans. by the author, with the assistance of John Bakti. Iowa City: The Windhover Press, 1972.

Slavko Mihalić

Atlantis. Selected Poems 1953–1983, trans. Charles Simic and Peter Kastmiler. Greenfield Centre: The Greenfield Review Press, 1984.

Czesław Miłosz

Selected Poems, intro. Kenneth Rexroth. New York: Seabury, 1973.
Selected Poems. New York: Ecco Press, 1980.
Bells in Winter, trans. Czesław Miłosz and Lillian Vallee. New York: Ecco Press, 1978 and Manchester: Carcanet Press, 1980.
The Separate Notebooks, trans. Robert Hass and Robert Pinsky. New York: Ecco Press, 1986.

Cuddihy, Michael (ed.), 'Czesław Miłosz: A Special Issue'. *Ironwood* Vol. 9 No. 2. Tucson: Ironwood Press, 1981.

Ágnes Nemes Nagy

Selected Poems, trans. Bruce Berlind. Iowa City: International Writing Program, 1980.
Between. Selected Poems, trans. Hugh Maxton. Budapest: Corvina and Dublin: Dedalus Press, 1988.

Dan Pagis

Poems by Dan Pagis, trans. Stephen Mitchell. Oxford: Carcanet Press, 1972.
Selected Poems. T. Carmi and Dan Pagis, trans. Stephen Mitchell. Harmondsworth: Penguin Books, 1976.
Points of Departure, trans. Stephen Mitchell. Philadelphia: The Jewish Publication Society of America, 1981.
Variable Directions, trans. Stephen Mitchell. Berkeley: North Point Press, 1989.

János Pilinszky

Selected Poems, trans. Ted Hughes and János Csokits. Manchester: Carcanet Press, 1977.
Crater. Poems 1974–5, trans. Peter Jay. London: Anvil Press Poetry, 1978.
The Desert of Love, trans. János Csokits and Ted Hughes. London: Anvil Press Poetry, 1989. Revised edition of *Selected Poems*.

Szilágyi, János, 'János Pilinszky – A Tormented Mystic Poet'. A Radio Conversation with János Szilágyi. *New Hungarian Quarterly* No. 77. Budapest, 1980.

Polgar, Steven, 'In Memory of the Hungarian Poet János Pilinszky'. *American Poetry Review* Vol. 13 No. 6. Philadelphia, November/December 1984.

Nagy, Ágnes Nemes, 'János Pilinszky: A Very Different Poet (1921–1981)'. *New Hungarian Quarterly* No. 84. Budapest, 1981. Reprinted in *The Desert of Love*.

Forgács, Rezső, 'I Write to Find My Way Home'. The last interview with János Pilinszky. *New Hungarian Quarterly* No. 87. Budapest, 1982.

Kéry, László, 'Farewell to János Pilinszky 1921–1981'. *The Hungarian P.E.N.* No. 22. Budapest, 1981.

Vasko Popa

Selected Poems, trans. Anne Pennington. Harmondsworth: Penguin Books, 1969.

The Little Box, trans. Charles Simic. Washington: Charioteer Press, 1970.

Earth Erect, trans. Anne Pennington. London: Anvil Press Poetry, 1972.

Collected Poems 1943–1976, trans. Anne Pennington. Manchester: Carcanet Press, 1978.

Homage to the Lame Wolf. Selected Poems 1956–1975, trans. Charles Simic. Oberlin: Field Translation Series 2, 1979.

The Golden Apple. A Round of stories, songs, spells, proverbs and riddles, trans. Andrew Harvey and Anne Pennington. London: Anvil Press Poetry, 1980. From *Od Zlata Jabuka* compiled by Vasko Popa, Belgrade: Prosveta, 1966.

The Cut, trans. Anne Pennington and Francis R. Jones. *Poetry World 1*. London: Anvil Press Poetry, 1986.

Alexander, Ronelle, *The Structure of Vasko Popa's Poetry*. UCLA Slavic Studies Vol. XIV. Columbus, Ohio: Slavica, 1985.

Tadeusz Różewicz

Faces of Anxiety, trans. Adam Czerniawski. London: Rapp and Whiting, 1969.

Selected Poems, trans. Adam Czerniawski. Harmondsworth: Penguin Books, 1976.

The Survivor and Other Poems, trans. Magnus J. Krynski and Robert A. Maguire. Princeton: Princeton University Press, 1976.

Unease, trans. Victor Contoski. St Paul: New Rivers Press, 1980.

Conversation with the Prince, trans. Adam Czerniawski. London: Anvil Press Poetry, 1982.

Lourie, Richard, 'A Context for Tadeusz Różewicz'. *The Polish Review* Vol. XII No. 2. New York, 1967.

Czerwinski, Edward J., 'Tadeusz Różewicz and the Jester-Priest Metaphor'. *Slavic and East European Journal* Vol. XIII No. 2. Madison, Wisconsin, 1969.

Nelly Sachs

O the Chimneys. Selected poems including the verse play Eli. London: Jonathan Cape, 1968 and New York: Farrar, Straus and Giroux, 1970.

Selected Poems. Abba Kovner and Nelly Sachs, trans. Michael Hamburger, Ruth and Matthew Mead and Michael Roloff. Harmondsworth: Penguin Books, 1971.

Leopold Staff

An Empty Room, trans. Adam Czerniawski. Newcastle: Bloodaxe Books, 1983.

Anna Świrszczyńska

Building the Barricade, trans. Magnus J. Krynski and Robert A. Maguire. Kraków: Wydawnictwo Literackie, 1979.

Happy as a Dog's Tail, trans. Czesław Miłosz and Leonard Nathan. San Diego: Harcourt Brace Jovanovich, 1985.

Fat Like the Sun, trans. Grazyna Baran and Margaret Marshment. London: The Women's Press, 1986.

Wisława Szymborska

Sounds, Feelings, Thoughts. Seventy Poems, trans. Magnus J. Krynski and Robert A. Maguire. Princeton: Princeton University Press, 1981.

Selected Poems, trans. by Grazyna Drabik, Austin Flint and Sharon Olds. *Quarterly Review of Literature* Vol. XXIII: Poetry Series IV. Princeton, 1982.

Natan Zach

Against Parting, trans. Jon Silkin. Newcastle: Northern House, 1967.

The Static Element, trans. Peter Everwine and Shulamit Yasny-Starkman. New York: Atheneum, 1982.

ACKNOWLEDGEMENTS

The editor and publisher wish to thank the poets, their translators, representatives, and publishers as follows for permission to include copyright material.

YEHUDA AMICHAI: for poems translated by Harold Schimmel from *Songs of Jerusalem and Myself*, © Yehuda Amichai 1973: reprinted by permission of Harper & Row, Publishers, Inc. For 'The diameter of the bomb was thirty centimeters...' from *Time* by Yehuda Amichai translated by the author with Ted Hughes, © Yehuda Amichai 1979: reprinted by permission of Oxford University Press and Harper & Row, Publishers, Inc. All other poems translated by the author and Ted Hughes from *Amen*, © Yehuda Amichai 1978: reprinted by permission of Oxford University Press and Harper & Row, Publishers, Inc. For poems translated by Chana Bloch and Stephen Mitchell from *The Selected Poetry*, English translation copyright © 1986 by Chana Bloch and Stephen Mitchell: reprinted by permission of Harper & Row, Publishers, Inc. For the poems translated by Dennis Silk, to the author and translator. For the poems translated by Assia Gutmann from *Selected Poems* (Penguin Books, 1971): to the author and Olwyn Hughes. For the translations by Ruth Nevo from *Travels* (The Sheep Meadow Press, New York, 1986), to the author and translator.

INGEBORG BACHMANN: for poems translated by Mark Anderson from *In the Storm of Roses: Selected Poems of Ingeborg Bachmann*, copyright © 1986 by Princeton University Press: reprinted with permission of Princeton University Press. For poems translated by Daniel Huws: reprinted with permission of the translator.

JOHANNES BOBROWSKI: for the poems translated by Ruth and Matthew Mead from *Shadow Lands* (1984), to Anvil Press Poetry Ltd.

BERTOLT BRECHT: for the translations from *Poems 1913–1956* (Eyre Methuen, London, 1976) edited by John Willett and Ralph Manheim, to the translators and to Methuen London.

NINA CASSIAN: for 'I Left Those Walls' to Nina Cassian and Naomi Lazard. For 'The Other Life' to Daniel Weissbort. For the poems translated by Christopher Hewitt, to the translator. For poems translated by Andrea Deletant and Brenda Walker, to the translators and Forest Books. For all other poems from *Life Sentence* (1990) to W. W. Norton & Company Inc., New York and Anvil Press Poetry Ltd, London.

PAUL CELAN: for the poems translated by Michael Hamburger from *Poems of Paul Celan* (1988), to Anvil Press Poetry Ltd, London and Persea Books, New York. For poems translated by John Felstiner, to the translator and Suhrkamp Verlag: 'Todesfuge', 'Psalm' and 'Das Nichts' copyright © Suhrkamp Verlag 1983.

HANS MAGNUS ENZENSBERGER: for poems translated by Michael Hamburger from *Selected Poems* (Penguin Books, 1968), to the translator. For the extracts from *The Sinking of the Titanic*, to the author, Suhrkamp Verlag, Houghton Mifflin Company and Carcanet Press Ltd; copyright © Suhrkamp Verlag 1978. Translation copyright © 1980 by Hans Magnus Enzensberger. For the poem translated by Eva Hesse, to Suhrkamp Verlag and the translator. For the poems translated by Michael Hamburger, to the translator. For the poem translated by Jerome Rothenberg, to the translator.

JERZY FICOWSKI: for poems translated by Frank J. Corliss Jr and Grazyna Sandel from *Cross Currents no. 3*, 1984, to the University of Michigan. For poems translated by Keith Bosley with Krystyna Wandycz from *A Reading of Ashes* (1981), to the translators and The Menard Press, London.

ZBIGNIEW HERBERT: for poems translated by John and Bogdana Carpenter from *Selected Poems*, translation © John and Bogdana Carpenter 1977: reprinted by permission of Oxford University Press. For poems translated by Czesław Miłosz from *Selected Poems* (1968), to Penguin Books Ltd and The Ecco Press. For the excerpt from 'Reconstruction of a Poet' translated by Magdalena Czajkowska, *Modern Poetry in Translation* 1 (1965), to the translator. For 'At the Gate of the Valley' and 'Our Fear' to Doubleday Inc, New York. For 'The Abandoned' to Michael March and Jarosław Anders. For 'The Return of the Proconsul' and 'From Mythology' to *The Observer*. For 'Elegy of Fortinbras' to *Encounter*.

VLADIMÍR HOLAN: for poems translated by Jarmila and Ian Milner from *Selected Poems* (1971), to the translators and Penguin Books Ltd. For the poems translated by George Theiner from *New Writing in Czechoslovakia* (1969), to Penguin Books Ltd.

MIROSLAV HOLUB: for the translation by Stuart Friebert and Dana Hábová from *Sagittal Section* (1980), Field Translation Series no. 3, to Oberlin College Press. For 'The Corporal who Killed Archimedes' from *Although* (1971) translated by Ian and Jarmila Milner (1971), reprinted with permission of Jonathan Cape Ltd. For 'Brief Thoughts on Cats Growing on Trees', 'Brief Thoughts on Cracks' and 'Brief Thoughts on Floods' from *Notes of a Clay Pigeon* translated by Jarmina and Ian Milner (1977), reprinted by permission of Martin Secker & Warburg Ltd. For the translation by Káča Poláčková, from *Modern Poetry in Translation* 5, to the translator. For the translations by Ian Milner and George Theiner from *Selected Poems* (1967) to Penguin Books Ltd.

PETER HUCHEL: for the poems translated by Michael Hamburger from *The Garden of Theophrastus* (Carcanet Press, 1983), to Michael Hamburger.

TYMOTEUSZ KARPOWICZ: for the poems translated by Bogdan Czaykowski and Andrzej Busza, and those translated by Jan Darowski, from *Modern Poetry in Translation* 23–24 (1975), to the translators. For the poem translated by Czesław Miłosz, to the author and translator.

EDWARD KOCBEK: for the poems translated by Veno Taufer and Michael

Scammell from *Modern Poetry in Translation* 8, to the translators.

REINER KUNZE: for poems translated by Michael Hamburger, to the translator. For poems translated by Gordon and Gisela Brotherston, to the translators. For the poems translated by Ewald Osers from *With the Volume Turned Down* (1973), to London Magazine Editions and the translator.

ARTUR MIEDZYRZECKI: for poems translated by the author with John Batki from *14 Poems*, copyright by the Windhover Press of the University of Iowa, 1972, to the translators. For the versions by Stanisław Barańczak and Clare Cavanagh, to the translators.

SLAVKO MIHALIĆ: for poems from Slavko Mihalić, *Atlantis* (1984) translated by Charles Simic and Peter Kastmiler: reprinted by permission of the author, translators and The Greenfield Review Press.

CZESLAW MILOSZ: for 'A Felicitous Life', 'A Poor Christian Looks at the Ghetto', and 'Café ', 'On the Other Side' copyright © 1988 by Czesław Miłosz Royalties, Inc., from *The Collected Poems 1931–1987* first published by The Ecco Press in 1988, to The Ecco Press, New York, and Penguin Books Ltd. For 'A Felicitous Life' from *Bells in Winter* published in England in 1980, to Carcanet Press Ltd.

ÁGNES NEMES NAGY: for the translations by Frederic Will, to the translator. For the translations by Hugh Maxton from *Between*, copyright © Corvina Kiadó 1988, to the translator. For the translations by Bruce Berlind from *Selected Poems* (1980), to the translator and the International Writing Program of the University of Iowa.

DAN PAGIS: for the poems translated by Robert Friend, to the translator. For the poems translated by Stephen Mitchell from *Variable Directions: The Selected Poetry of Dan Pagis* (North Point Press, 1989), to the translator and North Point Press.

JÁNOS PILINSZKY: for the poems translated by János Csokits and Ted Hughes from *The Desert of Love* (1989), to Anvil Press Poetry Ltd. For the poems translated by Peter Jay, to Peter Kovács and the translator.

VASKO POPA: for the poems translated by Anne Pennington from *Collected Poems 1943–1976* (Carcanet Press, 1976), to Lady Margaret Hall, Oxford, Peter Jay and Anvil Press Poetry Ltd.

TADEUSZ RÓŻEWICZ: for the poems translated by Robert A. Maguire and Magnus J. Krynski from *The Survivor and Other Poems* by Tadeusz Różewicz, copyright © 1976 by Princeton University Press: reprinted with permission of Princeton University Press. For the poems translated by Victor Contoski from *Unease* (1980), to New Rivers Press and the translator. For the poems translated by Adam Czerniawski from *They Came to See a Poet* (1991), to Anvil Press Poetry Ltd.

NELLY SACHS: for the poems from *O the Chimneys* (1968), to Suhrkamp Verlag, Jonathan Cape Ltd and Farrar, Straus & Giroux, Inc. Copyright © 1967 by Farrar, Straus & Giroux, Inc.

LEOPOLD STAFF: the poems translated by Adam Czerniawski are reprinted by permission of Bloodaxe Books Ltd from *An Empty Room* by Leopold Staff, translated by Adam Czerniawski, Bloodaxe Books, 1983.

ANNA ŚWIRSZCZYŃSKA: for poems translated by Czesław Miłosz and Leonard Nathan, from *Happy as a Dog's Tail* by Anna Świrszczyńska, copyright © 1985 by Czesław Miłosz and Leonard Nathan, reprinted by permission of Harcourt Brace Jovanovich, Inc. For poems translated by Magnus J. Krynski and Robert A. Maguire, from *Building the Barricade* (1979), to Princeton University Press and the translators. English translation copyright © Magnus J. Krynski and Robert Maguire.

WISLAWA SZYMBORSKA: for 'Writing a Curriculum Vitae', 'Clothes', 'Onion', 'Monologue for Cassandra' and 'Seen from Above' copyright by *Quarterly Review of Literature Poetry Series*, Vol XXIII, 1982, Princeton, N.J. Reprinted with permission. For the poems from *Sounds, Feelings, Thoughts: Seventy Poems by Wisława Szymborska* translated by Magnus J. Krynski and Robert A. Maguire, copyright © 1981 by Princeton University Press: reprinted with permission of Princeton University Press. For poems translated by Adam Czerniawski, to the translator. For the poem translated by Krystof Zarzecki from *Poems from XV Languages*, The Stone Wall Press, Iowa City, to the translator. For the poem translated by Jan Darowski, to the translator.

NATAN ZACH: for poems from *The Static Element: Selected Poems of Natan Zach* translated by Peter Everwine and Shulamit Yasny-Starkman, copyright © 1977, 1982 by Peter Everwine: reprinted with permission of Atheneum Publishers, an imprint of Macmillan Publishing Company. For the poem translated by Jon Silkin, to the translator.

APPENDICES: we thank Daniel Weissbort for permission to include his unpublished interview with Yehuda Amichai (Appendix 1), and the interview with Miroslav Holub of which an abbreviated version appeared in *Poetry East* 29, DePaul University, Chicago, 1990 (Appendix 2); Michael March for his translation of Marek Oramus's interview with Zbigniew Herbert, which first appeared in *Antaeus* 53, New York, 1984 (Appendix 3); Margitt Lehbert for her translations, and Prof. Dr Walter Höllerer and the Literarisches Colloquium, Berlin for the German versions of talks by Zbigniew Herbert, Vasko Popa and Tadeusz Różewicz which appeared in *Ein gedicht und sein Autor, Lyrik und Essay*, Berlin, 1967 (Appendices 4, 7, 9); Peter Kovács for the estate of János Pilinszky and Judith Balogh for her translation of the article by János Pilinszky from *Vigilia*, Budapest, June 1982 (Appendix 5); Peter Kovács and Éva Toth for her radio interview with János Pilinszky, recorded in Budapest on 10 March 1971, broadcast 6 April 1971 (Appendix 6); and Adam Czerniawski for his interview with Tadeusz Różewicz, which first appeared in English in *The New Review* 25, London, 1976 (Appendix 8). The Polish version appeared in *Oficyna Poetów* no. 2, London, May 1976.

We would be grateful to be informed of any errors or omissions, for which we apologize.

INDEX OF TITLES